Jane Beaton lives in Lond...

Praise for Jane Beaton

'I love this book! It's funny, page-turning and addictive . . . just like Malory Towers for grown-ups'
Sophie Kinsella

'I have been waiting twenty-five years for someone to write a bloody brilliant boarding school book, stuffed full of unforgettable characters, thrilling adventures and angst – and here it is. Hurrah for Jane Beaton!'
Lisa Jewell

'A wonderful first novel that had me in tears and fits of laughter. Definitely an A★!'
Chris Manby

'If you were a fan of Malory Towers or St Clare's books in your – ahem – youth, you'll love this modern boarding school-based tale . . . Top of the class! ★★★★'
Closer

'This brilliant boarding school book, with its eccentric cast of characters and witty one-liners, should prove an unmissable dose of nostalgia. Whether you've recently left school, have rose-tinted memories of it or are a teacher looking for some escapism from classroom dreariness, this book will certainly score A★'
Glamour

JANE BEATON OMNIBUS

Class

Rules

SPHERE

This omnibus edition first published in Great Britain in 2011 by Sphere

Copyright © Jane Beaton 2011

Previously published separately:
Class first published in Great Britain in 2008 by Sphere
Reissued by Sphere in 2010
Copyright © Jane Beaton 2008
Rules first published in Great Britain in 2009 by Sphere
Copyright © Jane Beaton 2009

A CIP catalogue record for this book
is available from the British Library.

ISBN 978-0-7515-4721-4

Printed and bound in Great Britain by
Clays Ltd, St Ives plc

Sphere
An imprint of
Little, Brown Book Group
100 Victoria Embankment
London EC4Y 0DY

An Hachette UK Company
www.hachette.co.uk

www.littlebrown.co.uk

CLASS

First Year at
Downey House

For my mother

Acknowledgements

Thanks to Jo Dickinson, Emma Stonex and all at Little, Brown; The British Poetry Library; W. Hickham; Kathleen Jamie; and Gunn Media Inc.

Characters

Staff

Headteacher: Dr Veronica Deveral
Administrator: Miss Evelyn Prenderghast
Deputy Headteacher: Miss June Starling

Cook: Mrs Joan Rhys
Caretaker: Mr Harold Carruthers

Physics: Mr John Bart
Music: Mrs Theodora Offili
French: Mademoiselle Claire Crozier
English: Miss Margaret Adair
Maths: Miss Ella Beresford
PE: Miss Janie James
Drama: Miss Fleur Parsley

Governors

Dame Lydia Johnson
Majabeen Gupta
Digory Gill

Pupils

Middle School Year One

Sylvie Brown
Imogen Fairlie
Simone Kardashian
Andrea McCann
Felicity Prosser
Zazie Saurisse
Alice Trebizon-Woods
Astrid Ulverton
Ursula Wendell

Chapter One

Purple skirt *no*. Grey suit *yes* but it was in a crumpled ball from an unfortunate attack of dry cleaner phobia. Black, definitely *not*. Ditto that Gaviscon-pink frilly coat jacket thing she'd panic bought for a wedding and couldn't throw away because it had cost too much, but every time she came across it in her wardrobe it made her shiver and question the kind of person she was.

Job interviews. Torture from the pits of hell. Especially job interviews four hundred miles away which require clothing which will both look fantastic and stand up to seven hours in Stan's Fiat Panda, with its light coating of crisps. Oh, and that would do the job both for chilly Scotland and the warm English riviera. God, it sucked not being able to take time off sometimes.

Maggie Adair looked at herself critically in the mirror and decided to drive to Cornwall in her pyjamas.

Fliss was having a lie in – among the last, she thought, of her entire life.

I can't believe they're making me do this, she thought. I can't believe they're sending me away. And if they think they're fooling me with their jolly hockey-sticks utter bloody bollocks they can think again. Of course Hattie loves it, she

1

bloody loves anything that requires the brain of a flea, a tennis racket, a boys' school on the hill and eyelash curlers.

Well I'm not going to bloody love it. I'll sit it out till they realise how shit it is and they'll let me go to Guildford Academy like everyone else, not some nobs' bloody hole two hundred miles away. Why should I care about being sent so far from London just as everyone else is getting to go to Wembley concerts and on the tube on their own? I'm nearly fourteen, for God's sake. I'm a teenager. And now I'm going to be buried alive in bloody Cornwall. Nobody ever thinks about me.

I'll show them. I'll be home after a month.

Breakfast the next morning was even worse. Fliss pushed her All-Bran round her plate. No way was she eating this muck. She'd pass it on to Ranald (the beagle) but she didn't think he would eat it either. She patted his wet nose, and felt comforted.

'And I don't know for sure,' Hattie was saying, 'but I think they're going to make me prefect! One of the youngest ever!'

'That's wonderful, sweetie,' their mother was saying. 'And you can keep an eye out for Fliss.'

Fliss rolled her eyes. 'Great. Let everyone know the big swotty prefect is my sister. NO thank you.'

Hattie bit her lip. Even though she was eighteen months older, Fliss could still hurt her. And she wasn't *that* big.

'Behave yourself,' said their father. 'I don't want to hear you speaking like that.'

'Fine,' said Fliss, slipping down from the table. 'You don't have to hear me speaking *at all*. That's why you're sending me away, remember?' And she made sure the conservatory doors banged properly behind her as she mounted the stairs.

2

'Is she really only thirteen?' said her mother. 'Do we really have to put up with this for another six years?'

'Hmm?' said her father, buried under the *FT*. Selective hearing, he reckoned. That's all you needed. Though he couldn't help contrasting his sweet placid elder daughter with this little firecracker. Boarding school was going to be just what she needed, sort her out.

Dr Veronica Deveral couldn't believe they were still interviewing for staff three weeks before the beginning of term. It showed a lack of professionalism she just couldn't bear. She glanced in the mirror, then reached out a finger to smooth the deep furrow between her eyes. Normally she was without a hint of vanity, but the start of the new school year brought anxieties all of its own, even after thirty years, and Mrs Ferrers waiting for the very last minute to jump ship to Godolphin was one of them.

So now she was short of an English teacher; and with eighty new girls soon turning up – some scared, some weepy, some excited, some defiant, and all of them needing a good confident hand. She put on her reading glasses and turned back to the pile of CVs. She missed the days when she didn't need CVs, with their gussied up management language, and fancy euphemisms about child-centred learning, instead of simple common sense. A nicely typed letter without spelling mistakes and a quick once-over to see if they were the right stuff – that used to be all she needed.

Still, she mused, gazing out of the high window of her office, over the smooth lawns – quiet and empty, at least for a few more weeks – and up to the rocky promontory above the sea, which started just beyond the bounds of the school. It wasn't all bad. These ghastly 'inclusiveness' courses the board had suggested she attend – no one would ever instruct

3

Veronica to do anything – had been quite interesting in terms of expanding the range of people the girls could work with.

They had such hermetic upbringings, so many of them. Country house, London house, nannies and the best schools. Oh, there was divorce and absent parenting, and all the rest, but they still existed in a world in which everyone had help; no one had to worry about money or even getting a job. Now, wasn't there an application somewhere from a woman teaching in a Glasgow housing estate? Perhaps she should have another glass of mint tea and look at it again.

'La dee dah.'

'Shut it,' Simone said.

'La dee dah.'

'Mum! He's doing it again!'

'Joel!'

'I'm not doing *anyfink*.'

Simone tried to ignore him and concentrate on an early spell of packing, which was hard when he wouldn't get out of her tiny bedroom. And, even more irritating, she could kind of see his point. Even she'd winced at the straw boater, and the winter gloves on the uniform list, though at first she'd been so excited. Such a change from the ugly burgundy sweatshirt and optional (i.e., everyone wore them if you didn't want to get called a 'slut') grey trousers and black shoes at St Cats.

She tried to ignore her annoying younger brother, and bask once again in the memory of the day they'd got the letter. Not the months and months of long study that had gone on before it. Not the remarks from her classmates, which had got even more unpleasant the more she'd stayed behind and begged the teachers for extra work and more coaching – most of the third years were of the firm conviction

4

that she'd had sex with every single teacher in the school, male and female, in return for the highest predicted GCSE grades the school had ever seen, not that there'd been much to beat.

She'd tried her best to keep her head high, even when she was being tripped in the corridor; when she couldn't open any door without glances and whispers in her direction; when she'd spent every break-time and lunchtime hiding in a corner of the library (normally forbidden, but she'd got special permission).

No, she was going back to the day the letter came. In a heavy, thick, white envelope. *'Dear Mr & Mrs Kardashian . . . we are pleased to inform you that your daughter Simone . . . full scholarship . . . enclosed, clothing suppliers . . .'*

Her father hadn't said very much, he'd had to go out of the room for a minute. Half delighted – he'd never dreamed when he'd arrived in Britain that one day his daughter would be attending a private school – he was also annoyed that, even though it was a great opportunity for Simone, he wasn't paying for it himself. And he worried too for his sensitive daughter. She'd nearly worked herself ill for the entrance exams. Would she be able to keep up?

Simone's mum however had no such reservations. She flung her arms around Simone, screaming in excitement.

'She just wants to tell everyone,' said Joel. But Simone hadn't cared. She'd been too busy taking it all in. No more St Cats. No more burgundy sweatshirts. No more Joel! No more being paraded in front of Mamma's friends ('no, not pretty, no. But *so* clever! You wouldn't believe how clever!'). Her life started now.

It had to be around here somewhere. Just as she was ferreting with one hand for the last of the Maltesers in the bottom of her bag, Maggie crested the hill in the car. And there it was.

The school most resembled a castle, perched by the sea. It had four towers – four houses, Maggie firmly told herself, trying to remember. Named after English royal houses, that was right. Wessex; Plantagenet; York and Tudor. No Stuart, she noted ruefully. Maggie mentally contrasted the imposing buildings with the wet, grey single-storey seventies build she'd left behind her up in Scotland.

Uh oh, she thought. What was it Stan had said? 'The second you get in there you'll get a chip on your shoulder the size of Govan. All those spoilt mimsies running about. You'll hate it.'

Mind you, it wasn't like Stan was exactly keen for her to broaden her horizons. He'd been in the same distribution job since he left school. Spreading his wings wasn't really in his vocabulary. But maybe it would be different for her. Let's face it, there had to be more out there than teaching in the same school she grew up in and having Sunday lunch round her mum's? She had to at least see.

Veronica Deveral rubbed her eyes. Only her third candidate, and she felt weary already.

'So,' she asked the wide-eyed young woman sitting in front of her. 'How would you cope with a difficult child . . . say, for example, one who doesn't think she should be here?'

The woman, who was wearing pale blue eyeliner that matched both her suit and her tights, and didn't blink as often as she should, leaned forward to show enthusiasm.

'Well,' she said, in refined tones that didn't quite ring true – junior acting classes thought Veronica – 'I'd try and establish a paradigm matrix of acceptable integral behaviours, and follow that up with universal quality monitoring and touch/face time. I think non-goal orientated seeking should be minimised wherever appropriate.'

There was a silence.

'Well, er, thank you very much for coming in Miss . . .'

'Oh, I just like the kids to call me Candice. Promotes teacher–pupil sensitivity awareness,' said Candice sincerely.

Veronica smiled without using her lips and decided against pouring them both another cup of tea.

Getting changed in a Fiat Panda isn't as much fun as it looks. Maggie tried to imagine doing this in the car park of Holy Cross without getting a penknife in the bahookie, and couldn't manage it. But here, hidden out of sight on the grey gravel drive, it was at least possible, if lacking in the elegance stakes.

She put her make-up on using the car mirror. Pink cheeks, windswept from having the windows open for the last hundred miles, air-con not quite having reached Stan's mighty machine. Her dark, thickly waving hair – which, when properly brushed out by a hairdresser was really rather lovely but the rest of the time required lion taming – was a bit frizzed, but she might be able to get away with it by pulling it into a tight bun. In fact, frizzy hair in tight buns was exactly what she'd expect a boarding-school teacher to wear, so she might be right at home. She smoothed down her skirt, took a deep breath and left the car. Straight ahead of her, the sun glistened off the choppy sea. She could probably swim here in the mornings, lose the half stone caused by huddling in the staffroom ever since she'd left college two years before, mainlining caramel wafers in an attempt to forget the horror that was year 3.

Maggie stepped out onto the gravel drive. Up close, the building was even more impressive; an elaborate Victorian confection, built in 1880 as an adjunct to the much older boy's school at the other end of the cove, the imposing building giving off an air of seriousness and calm.

She wondered what it would be like full of pupils. Or perhaps they were serious and calm too. At the very least they were unlikely to have ASBOs. Already she'd been impressed by the amount of graffiti on the old walls of the school: none. Nothing about who was going to get screwed, about who was going to get knifed . . . nothing at all.

No. She wasn't going to think about what it would be like to work here. This was just an experiment, just to see what else was out there before she went back to her mum and dad's, and Stan, in Govan. Where she belonged. She thought of Stan from weeks earlier, when she'd talked about applying.

'"Teacher required for single sex boarding school",' she read out. '"Beautiful location. On-site living provided. English, with some sports".'

Stan sniffed.

'Well, that's you out then. What sports are you going to teach? Running to the newsagents to get an Aero?'

'I'm trained in PT, thank you!' said Maggie sniffily.

'It'll be funny posh sports anyway, like polo, and lacrosse.' He snorted to himself.

'What?'

'Just picturing you playing polo.'

Maggie breathed heavily through her nose.

'Why?'

'You're frightened of horses, for one. And you'd probably crush one if you keep on eating bacon sandwiches like that.'

'Shut up!' said Maggie. 'Do you think being Scottish counts as being an ethnic minority? It says they're trying to encourage entries from everywhere. Apply in writing in the first instance to Miss Prenderghast . . .'

'A girls' school with free accommodation?' said Stan. 'Where do I sign up?' He thought she was only doing this to annoy him, even when the interview invitation arrived.

'Dear Ms Adair,' he'd read out in an absurdly over-exaggerated accent. 'Please do us the most gracious honour of joining us for tea and crumpet with myself, the queen and . . .'

'Give that back,' she'd said, swiping the letter, which had come on heavy cream vellum paper, with a little sketch of the Downey school printed on it in raised blue ink. It simply requested her presence for a meeting with the headmistress, but reading it had made her heart pound a bit. It did feel a bit like being summonsed.

'I don't know why you're wasting your time,' Stan had said, as she'd worried over whether or not to take the purple skirt. 'A bunch of bloody poncey southern snobs, they're never going to look at you anyway.'

'I know,' said Maggie, crossly folding up her good bra.

'And even if they did, you're not going to move to Cornwall, are you?'

'I'm sure I'm not. It's good interview experience, that's all.'

'There you go then. Stop messing about.'

But as they lay in bed in the evening, Stan snoring happily away, pizza crumbs still round his mouth, Maggie lay there imagining. Imagining a world of beautiful halls; of brand new computers for the kids that didn't get broken immediately. Books that didn't have to be shared. Bright, healthy, eager faces, eager to learn; to have their minds opened.

It wasn't that she didn't like her kids. She just found them so wearing. She just wanted a change, that was all. So why, when she mentioned it, did everyone look at her like she'd just gone crazy?

*

9

The main entrance to the school was two large wooden doors with huge circular wrought-iron door knockers, set under a carved stone lintel on which faded cut letters read *multa ex hoc ludo accipies; multa quidem fac ut reddas.* Maggie hoped she wouldn't be asked to translate them as one of the interview questions. The whole entrance-way, from the sweep of the gravel drive to the grand view out to sea, seemed designed to impress, and did so. In fact it hardly even smelled of school – that heady scent of formaldehyde, trainers, uneaten vegetables and cheap deodorant Maggie had got to know so well. Maybe it was because of the long holiday, or maybe girls just didn't smell so bad, but at Holy Cross it oozed from the walls.

The doors entered on to a long black and white tiled corridor, lined with portraits and photographs – of distinguished teachers and former pupils, Maggie supposed. Suddenly she felt herself getting very nervous. She thought back to her interview with James Gregor at Holy Cross. 'Good at animal taming are you?' he'd said. 'Good. Our staff turnover is 20 per cent a year, so you will forgive me if I don't take the trouble to get to know you too well just yet.'

And she'd been in. And he'd been right. No wonder Stan was bored with her looking at other options. After all, college had been great fun. Late nights out with the girls, skipping lectures, going to see all the new bands at King Tut's and any other sweaty dive where students got in free. Even her teaching experience had been all right – a little farm school in Sutherland where the kids didn't turn up in autumn (harvest) or winter (snowed in), and had looked at her completely bemused when she'd asked the first year to write an essay about their pets.

'What's a pet, miss?'

'My dad's got three snakes. Are they pets, miss? But he just keeps them for the rats.'

Then she'd come back to Glasgow, all geared up and ready for her new career, only to find that, with recruitment in teachers at an all-time high, the only job she could find was at her old school, Holy Cross. Her old school where the boys had pulled her hair, and the girls had pulled the boys' hair and it was rough as guts, right up till that moment in fifth year when big lanky Stanley Mackintosh had loped over in his huge white baseball boots and shyly asked her if she wanted to go and see some band some mate of his was in.

The band sucked; or they might have been brilliant, Maggie wasn't paying attention and no one heard of them ever again. No, she was too busy snogging a tall, lanky, big-eared bloke called Stan up at the back near the toilet and full of excited happiness.

Of course, that was six years ago. Now, Stan was working down the newspaper distributors – he'd started as a paper boy and never really gone away, although it did mean he was surprisingly well informed for someone who played as much Championship Manager as he did – and she was back at Holy Cross. They never even went to gigs any more, since she left college and didn't get cheap entry to things, and she was always knackered when she got home anyway, and there was always marking.

Back in Govan. And it didn't matter that she was still young, just out of college – to the students, she was 'miss', she was ancient, and she was to be taken advantage of by any means necessary. She'd ditched the trendy jeans and tops she'd worn to lectures, and replaced them with plain skirts and tops that gave the children as little chance to pick on her as possible – she saw her dull tweedy wardrobe as armour. They still watched out to see if she wore a new lipstick or different earrings, whereupon they would try and turn it into a conversation as prolonged and insulting as possible.

Once she'd dreamed of filling young hearts and minds with wonderful books and poetry; inspiring them, like Robin Williams, to think beyond their small communities and into the big world. Now she just dreamed of crowd control, and keeping them quiet for ten bloody minutes without someone whacking somebody else or answering their hidden mobiles. They'd caught a kid in fourth year with a knife again the other day. It was only a matter of time before one got brandished in class. She just hoped to God it wasn't her class. She needed to learn another way.

The elegant tiled corridor leading off the grand entrance hall at Downey House towards the administrative offices was so quiet Maggie found she was holding her breath. She looked at the portrait right in front of her: a stern looking woman, who'd been headmistress during the Second World War. Her hair looked like it was made of wrought iron. She wondered how she'd looked after the girls then, girls who were worried about brothers and fathers; about German boats coming ashore, even down here. She shivered and nearly jumped when a little voice piped, 'Miss Adair?'

A tiny woman, no taller than Maggie's shoulder, had suddenly materialised in front of her. She had grey hair, was wearing a bright fuchsia turtleneck with her glasses on a chain round her neck and, though obviously old, had eyes as bright as a little bird's.

'Mrs Beltan,' she said, indicating the portrait. 'Wonderful woman. Just wonderful.'

'She looks it,' said Maggie. 'Hello.'

'I'm Miss Prenderghast. School proctor. Follow me.'

Maggie wasn't sure what a proctor was but it sounded important. She followed carefully, as Miss Prenderghast's tiny heels clicked importantly on the spotless floor.

Veronica glanced up from the CV she was reading. Art, music, English . . . all useful. But, more importantly, Maggie Adair was from an inner-city comprehensive school. One with economic problems, social problems, academic problems – you name it. So many of the girls here were spoiled, only interested in getting into colleges with good social scenes and parties, en route to a good marriage and a house in the country . . . sometimes she wondered how much had changed in fifty years. A little exposure to the more difficult side of life might be just what they needed – provided they could understand the accent . . . she put on her warmest smile as Evelyn Prenderghast knocked on the door.

Oh, but the young people were so *scruffy* nowadays. That dreadful suit looked as if it had been used for lining a dog's basket. And would it be too much to ask an interviewee to drag a comb through her hair? Veronica was disappointed, and it showed.

Maggie felt the headmistress's gaze on her the second she entered the room. It was like a laser. She felt as if it was taking in everything about her and it made her feel about ten years old. You wouldn't be able to tell a lie to Dr Deveral, she'd see through you instantly. Why hadn't she bought a new suit for the interview? Why? Was her mascara on straight? Why did she waste time mooning at all those portraits? She knew she should have gone to the loos and fixed herself up.

'Hello,' she said, as confidently as she could manage, and suddenly decided to pretend to herself that this *was* her

13

school, that she already worked here, that this was her life. She gazed around at the headmistress's office, which was panelled in dark wood, with more portraits on the wall – including one of the queen – and a variety of different and beautiful objects, that looked as if they had been collected from around the world, set on different surfaces, carefully placed to catch the eye and look beautiful. Just imagine. Maggie looked at a lovely sculpture of the hunting goddess Diana with her dogs, and her face broke into a grin.

Veronica was quite taken aback by how much the girl's face changed when she smiled – it was a lovely, open smile that made her look nearly the same age as some of her students. Quite an improvement. But that suit . . .

Veronica was frustrated. This girl was very nice and everything – even the Glaswegian accent wasn't too strong, which was a relief. She hadn't been looking forward to an entire interview of asking the girl to repeat herself. But so far it had all been chat about college and so on – nothing useful at all. Nothing particularly worthwhile, just lots of the usual interview platitudes about bringing out children's strengths and independence of thought and whatever the latest buzzwords were out there. She sighed, then decided to ask one question she'd always wondered about.

'Miss Adair, tell me something . . . this school you work at. It has dreadfully poor exam results, doesn't it?'

'Yes,' said Maggie, hoping she wasn't being personally blamed for all of them. She could tell this interview wasn't going well – not at all, in fact – and was resigning herself to the long trip back, along with a fair bit of humble pie dished up by Stan in the Bear & Bees later.

Dr Deveral hadn't seemed in the least bit interested in her new language initiatives or her dissertation. Probably a bit much to hope for, that someone from a lovely school like this would be interested in someone like her from a rough school. Suddenly the thought made her indignant – just because her kids weren't posh didn't mean they weren't all right, most of them. In fact, the ones that did do well were doing it against incredible odds, much harder than the pony-riding spoon-feeding they probably did here. She suddenly felt herself flush hot with indignation.

'Yes, it does have poor results. But they're improving all the—'

Veronica cut her off with a wave of the hand. 'What I wonder is, why do you make these children stay on at school? They don't want to go, they're not going to get any qualifications . . . I mean, really, what's the point?'

If anything was likely to make Maggie really furious it was this. Stan said it all the time. It just showed he had absolutely no idea, and neither did this stupid woman, who'd only ever sat in her posh study, drinking tea and wondering how many swimming pools to build next year. Bugger this stupid job. Stan had been right, it was a waste of her time. Some people would just never understand.

'I'll tell you the point,' said Maggie, her accent subconsciously getting stronger. 'School is all some of these children have got. School is the only order in their lives. They hate getting expelled, believe it or not. Their homes are chaotic and their families are chaotic, and any steadiness and guidance we can give them, any order and praise, and timekeeping and support, anything the school can give them at all, even just a hot meal once a day, that's what's worth it. So I suppose they don't get *quite* as many pupils into Oxford and Cambridge as you do, Dr Deveral. But I don't think they're automatically less valuable just because their parents can't pay.'

Maggie felt very hot suddenly, realising she'd been quite rude, and that an outburst hadn't exactly been called for, especially not one that sounded as if it was calling for a socialist revolution. 'So . . . erhm. I guess I'm probably best back there,' she finished weakly, in a quiet voice.

Veronica sat back and, for the first time that day, let a genuine smile cross her lips.

'Oh, I wouldn't be so sure about that,' she said.

Simone held her arms out like a traffic warden's, feeling acutely self-conscious.

'We'll have to send away for these,' the three-hundred-year-old woman in the uniform shop had said, as all her fellow crones had nodded in agreement. 'Downey House! That's rather famous, isn't it?'

'Yes it is,' said her mother, self-importantly. Her mum was all dressed up, just to come to a uniform shop. She looked totally stupid, like she was on her way to a wedding or something. Why did her mother have to be so embarrassing all the time? 'And our Simone's going there!'

Well, obviously she was going there, seeing as she was in getting measured up for the uniform. Simone let out a sigh.

'Now she's quite big around the chest for her age,' said the woman loudly.

'Yes, she's going to be just like me,' said her mum, who was shaped like a barrel. 'Look – big titties.'

There was another mother in there – much more subtly dressed – with a girl around Simone's age, who was getting measured for a different school. As soon as they heard 'big titties', however, they glanced at each other. Simone wished the floor would open and swallow her up.

As the saleslady put the tape measure around her hips, Simone risked a glance out of the window. At exactly the

16

wrong time: Estelle Grant, the nastiest girl in year seven, was walking past with two of her cronies.

Immediately a look of glee spread over Estelle's face, as she pummelled her friends to look. Simone's mum and the lady were completely oblivious to her discomfort, standing up on a stool in full view of the high street.

'Can I get down?' she said desperately, as Estelle started posing with her chest out, as if struggling to contain her massive bosoms. It wasn't Simone's fault that she was so well developed. Now the other girls had puffed out their cheeks and were staggering around like elephants. Simone felt tears prick the back of her eyes. She wasn't going to cry, she *wasn't*. She was never going back to that school. Nobody would ever make her feel like Estelle Grant did, ever again.

'Now, your school requires a boater, so let's check for hat size,' the lady was saying, plonking a straw bonnet on her head. This was too much for the girls outside; they collapsed in half-fake hysterics.

Simone closed her eyes and dug her nails into her hands, as her mother twittered to the sales lady about how fast her daughter was growing up – and out! And she got her periods at ten, can you imagine?! The saleslady shook her head in amazement through a mouthful of pins, till Estelle and her cronies finally tired of the sport and, in an orgy of rude hand signals, went on their way.

Never again. Never again.

Chapter Two

Maggie Adair was making the long trip a second time, but now she was a little more organised, and didn't mind at all. She kept glancing at the heavy card envelope on the seat beside her, as if it were about to disappear if she didn't keep it under constant attention.

When it had arrived, just two days after she'd returned from Cornwall ('Did you make friends with any sheep while you were there?' Stan had said, and that was all he'd asked her about it), she'd got a huge shock. Then she'd assumed that anything arriving this quickly could only be a rejection, which was belied by the size of the envelope. Sure enough:

'. . . we would be pleased to offer you the post of junior English mistress . . .'

And that was all she read before dropping it on the floor. 'Oh,' she said.

'What is it?' said Stan, lumbering down the stairs with his polo shirt buttoned up wrong and sleep still in his eyes.

'Uhm . . . uh . . .' she looked up at him, realising she was about to drop a bombshell. 'I got that job.'

'What job?' said Stan. He wasn't quite himself before two

cups of builders' tea in the morning. Then, as he reached the kettle, he stopped suddenly and turned round. 'The posh job?'

Maggie nodded. Her hands were shaking, she just couldn't believe it. Dr Deveral had given nothing away at all and she'd driven the whole evening back convinced she'd wasted her time – the woman next in line for the interview looked like Gwyneth Paltrow in a netball shirt, for goodness' sake.

Stan stared at her. She wondered how long it had been since she'd really looked at him – really taken in the person she'd been with since the last night of school. He'd put on weight, of course, they both had, and they'd never again be as skinny as they were then, at seventeen. But his spiky hair still stuck up in all directions, and he still looked a mess whether in his work clothes, his pyjamas or his kilt. Even now she could feel toast crumbs compelling themselves towards him from all corners of the kitchen. Her daft Stan.

'But you can't take it,' he said, doggedly, staring at her.

Maggie stared back at him and realised that, up until that moment, she hadn't been quite sure what she was going to do.

'But I want to,' she said, slowly.

Simone watched as her mother piled the car high with silver foil packets.

'Mum, you know, they feed us there.'

'Yes, but what kind of food, huh? Bread and jam! Cup o' tea!'

'I like bread and jam.'

'Too much,' said Joel. 'You look like a jam roly-poly.'

'Shut up! Mum, tell Joel to shut up.'

Her mum raised her heavily painted eyebrows, sighed, and continued packing the car. It was a five-hour drive, but her mother had enough stashed away for a full scale siege. There were cottage cheese doughnuts, meatball soup, pickled cabbage in jars . . . It looked like a toss-up for her mother: was she going to starve to death at school, or were they all going to succumb on the drive?

'Jam roly-poly! Jam roly-poly!'

Simone concentrated very hard on her Marie Curie biography. Perhaps she'd had a small very annoying brother whose constant torments had strengthened her resolve to become a great heroine of science.

Dad was already sitting in the driver's seat. He'd been ready to leave since seven a.m., even though they didn't have to be at the school until teatime. He was wearing a suit and tie, even though he normally went to work in overalls. The tie had teddy bears all over it. She and Joel had bought it for him for Father's Day years ago. It didn't look very good, but she wasn't going to say anything. He was in a right mood. He should be happy for her, she thought. It wasn't like he would miss seeing her – most days he was out the house to work before they'd got up for breakfast, then he got back after eight o'clock, ate his dinner and fell asleep on the sofa.

Simone glanced at her suitcase. She wished it wasn't so tatty. It had been her grandfather's, and her dad had brought it over from the old country. It had been made to look like leather but here and there where the fabric was torn you could tell it wasn't really, there was cardboard poking through. Bogdan Kardashian was stencilled on the top of it, and it smelled musty – like it had been put in the attic with someone leaving some old socks in it.

Still, inside were her new clothes – she couldn't think of

them without being pleased. She knew the 'Michaelmas term' list by heart:

Navy blazer with school crest
Bedford check winter-weight skirt
Navy V-necked jumper with school crest
4 x white short-sleeved blouse
2 x T–shirt with school design for Drama lessons
2 x white polo shirt with school crest
Navy games skirt
Navy felt hat with school crest
Navy cycle shorts
Navy sweatshirt with school crest
Navy tracksuit trousers with school crest
Royal blue hockey socks
Navy swimming costume with gold stripe
Navy swimming cap

She'd tried everything on, but only once, so she didn't get it crushed. Her mother had invited lots of her aunties round (they weren't all her real aunties, but she'd called them aunty for so long sometimes she couldn't even remember who she was actually related to) and they'd made her do a fashion show for them in the living room, as they ummed and ahhed and talked about the quality of the cloth and the weight of the material and Simone had done the occasional slightly clumsy turn, as her mother warned people eating the *mamaliga* not to get their fingers on any-thing and Joel played up like a maniac, running around being a very noisy Dalek, desperately trying to regain some of the attention.

Now, ironed a second time, it was all tightly packed up in the suitcase, with underwear, tights and socks squeezed in the gaps in between. Simone had wanted to ask whether or not she'd be getting a new bra; just one wasn't really enough, but her mother hadn't mentioned it and it hadn't come up, so she kept quiet. Her father had looked at her, navy blue from top to toe and smiled, a little sadly.

'You look quite the little English lady,' he'd said. Simone supposed it was meant to be a nice thing to say, but she wasn't 100 per cent sure.

'What's the matter with everyone?' Maggie had said to her sister as she was preparing to leave. 'It's just a job.'

'I don't know,' said Anna. 'I suppose I just always thought you'd be teaching Cody and Dylan, you know? That they'd always grow up with their auntie in the school.'

But Cody, the eldest, was only three, Maggie thought, even if, with his shaved head and Celtic football club shirt, he looked like her year 2 troublemakers already. But that meant in nine years' time everyone thought she'd still be exactly where she was. She didn't want that to happen. She wasn't going for ever. She was going to get some experience, somewhere excellent, then come back to Glasgow and apply it where it was needed, that was all.

Anna had passed over a glass of warm white wine; it was after hours in the salon, and she was putting navy blue streaks in Maggie's hair. She'd been experimenting on Maggie for so long Maggie hardly noticed any more – in fact it had helped at school, made her a bit more trendy having a hairdresser for a sister who used her as a free guinea pig, despite the occasional results that made her actually resemble a real guinea pig.

'I'd better be able to wash this out before I go,' she warned. Anna ignored her.

'And the thing is, Maggie, kids round here, they need

good teachers. They need people like you who are dedicated, who care about things. What do you want to go wasting your time with a posh bunch of nobs who already have everything and are only going to leave school and sit around on their arses waiting for a rich man for the next fifty years?'

Maggie looked at her glass. 'Well I want to . . .' she said. Then she tried again. 'If I stay here . . .' That didn't sound right either. 'The thing is, Anna, I just want to get out a bit. If I keep on here . . . it's not that it's bad or anything . . .'

'But it's good enough for all of us,' said Anna.

'That's not what I mean. But I think I'll just get jaded and a bit bitter . . . I won't be a good teacher. I won't be good for the kids, I'll just turn into one of those rancid old harridans, like Fatty Puff. Mrs McGinty. Just shouting all the time. I think it'll be good for me to work in a different place for a while, just get some more experience. Then come home.'

'And Stan agrees with that, does he?' Anna slapped on some colour with what felt like malice. Maggie wondered if it was time for a chop. What did southern teachers look like?

Veronica smoothed down her soft grey cashmere cardigan. She supposed pearls weren't exactly fashionable any more, but then what was fashionable was just so horrific she could hardly bear to think about it – in fact, if she could stop the upper sixths coming back from holiday with tattoos she'd be delighted. Didn't their parents even mind? Half of them were so busy working or having affairs they probably didn't notice. All those little butterflies and fairies on their shoulders or down their backs. Surely they'd live to regret them. Veronica tried to imagine having a tattoo when she was at school, but she couldn't. It wouldn't even have crossed her mind; she might as well have been told not to fly upside down. She'd forbidden them time and time again, but it didn't seem to make any difference; they got to the Glastonbury Festival and every sensible thought flew right out of their heads.

So, her pearls might not be fashionable, but they had been her mother's best. She remembered so vividly her mother getting ready for a night out. She'd wear stiff petticoats under her skirt – satin was a favourite. She liked ice cream colours: pistachio, pale pink. And she wore 'Joy' by Yves St Laurent. You didn't get that much these days either; for years Veronica hadn't been able to smell it without being taken straight back to her childhood. She'd crouch down by the dressing table (her mother wouldn't let her on the bed in case she creased the counterpane) and watch in awe as her mother deftly applied powder, lipstick, and a block mascara. She'd thought she was the most beautiful woman in the world.

All of that was before, of course. In fact, those were the only happy memories she had of her mother, painted and pretty, heading out with her father, with his hair scraped down with oil.

Later on, it had been snatched meetings in Lyons Corner Houses, her mother having told some lie to her father to get out of the house, as Veronica's belly got bigger and bigger. On one of these wet and rainy occasions, as they sat over scones and tea with damp coats and dripping umbrellas, both trying to avoid looking at the empty third finger of Veronica's left hand, her mother had handed her the small box, wrapped in cloth.

'Just,' she muttered, 'something to pass on. If it's a girl I mean. Your father won't notice.'

That night, back at the convent – the grim home for

unmarried mothers she'd been despatched to – sitting stoically as she always did after the nine p.m. curfew, whilst other girls sobbed their hearts out on the cold, greasy-blanketed cot beds that lined the walls, or talked defiantly about how their men would come for them, she had let the pearls run over her hands like water, feeling their perfect smoothness and cool beauty.

Veronica shook her head briskly to clear her brain, and focused on what she'd say to the new parents this afternoon. In fact, the pearls would help there. They normally did. They said, this is what our school is about: class, family, traditional values. That was what the school was about. The pearls were from somewhere else altogether.

It had not been a girl.

Fliss was in her favourite spot, underneath the cherry tree in a far corner of the old orchard. No one could see you there from the house, unless they stood on the roof. She had the new Jacqueline Wilson, Ranald, and a bag of cherries she'd filched from the kitchen, but it wasn't doing the trick. All she could think of was that they were sending her away. OK, so she hadn't exactly covered herself in glory at Queen's middle; she winced as she thought back to her report cards. 'Felicity has plenty of ability but tends towards laziness'. 'If she focused, she'd do as well as her big sister'. 'Felicity's conduct does occasionally give cause for concern'. And so on and so on, blah blah blah. She didn't care. School was stupid, and now they were sending her somewhere even stupider. Great. She obviously didn't come up to her parents' high standards, so they were just chucking her out like rubbish. She cuddled Ranald.

'It's easy for you,' she whispered into his panting neck. 'You don't have to go to bloody school. I wish I were a dog.'

Ranald whimpered his agreement, as the grass ruffled gently in the breeze.

And she wondered what would be the best way out of there. Not expelled – too much trouble. Just a way of showing them that the local school, with her real actual friends and not some of Hattie's horrid swotty cast-offs, would be best. At the local school in Guildford they were allowed to go into London when they were fifteen, *and* they didn't have to wear uniform. So completely the opposite of Downey bloody House then.

'Hurry up!' she could hear her mother shouting. 'We have to go or we'll get stuck on that bloody A303 again, and I'm quite old enough as it is.'

Finally ensconced in the car, Fliss flicked through *Cosmo Girl* and sighed loudly for the nine hundredth time.

'I *told* you,' said her dad. 'We're nearly there.'

'I don't give a . . . crap . . .' said Fliss, wondering how strong a word she could get away with when they were on the motorway with nowhere to stop, and she was leaving for ever anyway, '. . . how far it is to go. You can just keep driving as far as I'm concerned. Why couldn't we bring Ranald anyway?'

'Because I didn't want the window open the entire way,' said her mother, looking crossly out of the window. Hattie had her head well and truly down and was supposedly reading one of her swanky upper-fourth books but Fliss could tell she hadn't turned over a page in nearly twenty minutes. She'd considered instituting back-of-the-car territory wars, but that really did make the parents stop so it probably wasn't worth it. It didn't look like they'd had any last-minute changes of heart.

'So last night,' she said airily, staring at the pylons flicking past, 'you didn't, say, have some kind of psychic dream that said how awful it was to lose a child when they were very very young?'

Her parents both ignored her, only glancing at each other. After the sulks and the door slamming had had no effect, she was doing what the *Sugar* magazine problem page suggested and presenting logical sides to her problem.

'You know, studies show that marriages are at very great risk from empty nest syndrome when the children leave home. Of course, for *most* families this doesn't happen for years yet. Think what a higher risk you must have trying to do it so early.'

Fliss's mother turned round awkwardly in the front seat of the Freelander.

'Darling,' she said. She'd had her roots done, Fliss thought. She used to be really proud that her mother looked after herself – she was more in shape than Hattie was, that was obvious. But now she wasn't sure; her mother spent half the blooming day at the hair salon or getting her nails done, and Fliss wondered if she didn't have to bother with all that crap, maybe she'd have more time for not having to send her away to school. She thought of her friend Millie's mum, who had long grey hair. Millie always said it was a huge embarrassment and that her mum made her feel absolutely brassic whenever she turned up anywhere because she looked a million years old, but Fliss liked going round there. Millie's mum was always cooking something for dinner and taking lovely bread out of the Aga or playing with the dog in their big messy kitchen. Fliss sometimes thought this was how mummies were meant to be. Mind you, when Millie came round to her house she liked to go upstairs and secretly try on some of Fliss's mum's make-up.

Fliss's mum didn't cook much. She heated stuff up for them, with a big sigh, as if it were a terrible chore to take the wrapping off a Waitrose packet. She let them have a lot of ketchup with their veg, though. She was always dashing out and complaining about being tired, though she still found plenty of time to go out in the evenings or have dinner with their dad or do a million things that seemed a bit more important than making soup or something.

It wasn't that she wasn't fun, though. Sometimes they'd all go to London and hit Selfridges and Harvey Nicks and their mum would buy them cool clothes and say, 'Oh, this is too naughty' when she got her credit card out and then take them for smoothies – Hattie and Fliss would rather have gone to McDonald's, but if they mentioned it their mother would say, 'Got to watch those hips girls!' so they didn't mention it any more.

They'd also do their best not to fall out on those trips. Falling out meant fewer goodies. So they'd go to Oxford Street, and Hattie would get posh face cream for her spots, and Fliss would get lip gloss, and they'd try on loads of things in Top Shop which was miles better than the one in Guildford and when they got home their dad would cover his eyes and go 'Oh my God, how have my girls been trying to bankrupt me today' but he didn't mean it really, he was actually quite pleased. Then they'd do a fashion show with all their new kit unless they'd got anything too short, when their dad would call them a Geldof girl and make them hide it away.

Fliss sniffed hard. There wouldn't be much more of that. She bet there wouldn't be a Top Shop in the whole of Cornwall, not even a tiny concession one. She thought back over her hideous school uniform, all heavy navy blue which didn't really work with her blonde hair, and the stupid hats and elasticated gym knickers. She hated it! She hated it. She hated it.

She let out another long sigh. So did her mother.

'It's only Cornwall,' Maggie had said, for what felt like the millionth time. 'It's not the moon! There's not even a time difference! It's only for ten weeks at a time, they get loads of holidays.'

The only person who'd been completely sanguine about the whole thing had been her headmaster, funnily enough. 'Jumping from the sinking ship?' he'd said on the phone, as she nervously steeled herself to say she was leaving not long before the start of term. 'Don't blame you. Don't worry about notice, there's enough wee lasses kicking around at the moment who'll jump at your job.'

'Right then.' Maggie had felt quite insulted. OK, she hadn't exactly thought that everyone would be standing on their chairs like in *Dead Poets Society*, but it would have been nice to think that her headmaster would remember her name.

On the home front, though, she thought as she travelled through Birmingham and down towards the west, the Fiat Panda making its displeasure known with suspicious little grunty noises, it hadn't been like that at all. Although no one would say it out loud, it seemed to be the general consensus that she'd gone all snobby on Govan and thought she was too good for them all, especially Stan.

'You know I'm not leaving you,' she'd whispered, late at night, after another evening of Stan studiously ignoring her whilst eating a fish finger sandwich in front of *A Question of Sport*.

'So, just moving out of the house to the other end of the country. I'm so glad that's not leaving me,' Stan had said.

29

'It's only for a few weeks at a time! You can fly down to Exeter for weekends!'

'Well, I'll have to, won't I? You're taking the car.'

'I need the car.'

'You need, you want, your job, your things,' said Stan, turning over. 'Yes, Maggie. I know it's all about you.'

They hadn't even made love since she'd got the job offer. Maggie was worried. Why wasn't she more upset?

Chapter Three

Veronica stood up at the lectern and surveyed the hundreds of girls and their parents, crowding out the long hall. Part of the original cathedral structure, the long hall retained its original features – two rows of stern looking carved stone angels, punctuating the tall arched windows that lined both sides. They seemed to be gazing down on the girls, kindly, but with a look in their eyes that suggested they'd not be amused by any mischief. That's what Simone had thought anyway. Her own mouth had been permanently open since their old car had drawn up on the sweeping gravel drive. She'd seen the pictures – *pored* over the pictures, of course – but nothing had really prepared her for the scale of the great grey towers, silhouetted against the blue sea and sky. She simply couldn't believe this was her new home; her place. Even Joel had been temporarily stunned into silence.

'Zoiks,' he'd said finally. 'It looks like Hogwarts.'

It didn't really. It looked like a castle from long ago, set against the wind and the waves. Simone, whose tastes in reading were running quite quickly in advance of her age, was lost in a Daphne du Maurier dream, looking at the oriel windows set in the towers, and the ivy clambering up the north side.

She came back to earth with a bump as her dad, who'd

been quiet the whole journey, followed the temporary signs pointing towards the 'parents' car park'. Simone's heart started to pound even harder. This was it! She was here! She looked at the other cars entering the car park. There wasn't a single other ancient, creaky old beige Mercedes Benz there, and there certainly wasn't one with a gold-encrusted tissue box holder in the back seat. The car park was full of 4x4s, new shiny Audis and BMWs, huge creamy Volvos and even a couple of Bentleys, which she only recognised when Joel went, 'Fffooo! Bentleys! They cost, like a million squillion pounds!!! And the insides are made out of gold and diamonds and stuff.' And when their mother told him to be quiet, in an uncharacteristically nervous sounding voice, he was for once.

The car rolled to a stop.

'Let's get on with it then,' growled her father.

Oh God, what the hell was that? Fliss squinted at the big ugly car blocking their way to the entrance.

'Great,' she said. 'I see they run a minicab service.'

'Felicity,' said her father, in his 'trying to tell her off' tone of voice, which never worked. Hattie had already jumped out of the car, spying several thousand of her very closest friends and screaming at them at the top of her voice. Fliss rolled her eyes. She'd met Hattie's friends before, when they came up to visit, and she thought they were all pants. As slowly as she dared she drew her hockey stick out of the boot, and turned round to see a dumpy girl emerging from the hideous brown car.

The girl was plump, with rather sallow skin and hair tightly pulled back in a ponytail. She was already wearing her full school uniform; didn't she know you got to wear your home clothes on your first day?

She looked over at Fliss with a brave, friendly smile on her face. Oh great, new girls time. Better luck next time, podge, thought Fliss viciously. She didn't want friends here. She had her friends. In Guildford. Where she was going back to, just as soon as she'd figured this place out. As she turned round to pick up her suitcase, a large woman, obviously the girl's mother, and dressed in what looked like evening wear – a lot of black and sequins – clambered out of the front of the car.

'Simone! Simone!' she screeched at the top of her voice. The entire car park turned round. 'We've got a present for you!'

Simone, as the plump girl must be called, gave an embarrassed looking half smile and turned round as her mother handed over a small package and then looked directly at Fliss's mum.

'It's an extra bra,' she announced proudly, out of the blue, just like that, as if it was the kind of thing you would just say in normal conversation to everyone in the world. 'They grow up so fast, no?'

'Yes they do,' said Fliss's mum, with the smile she got on her face whenever she wanted to get moving somewhere down the street and they got stopped by someone who wanted them to sign up for charity.

'I am Mrs Kardashian, Simone's mother. This is Simone's first day.'

No kidding, thought Fliss, looking at Simone's skirt, which hung way below her knees. Fliss was already planning on rolling hers up as far as she could get away with. And then a bit further.

'Caroline Prosser. Hello.'

Her mother gave a rather limp handshake. Mrs Kardashian raised her eyebrows looking at Fliss and Hattie.

'I think maybe our girls will be friends, yes?'

Not in a million years, thought Fliss, digging her hockey stick into the gravel.

Not in a million years, thought Simone, catching the look of disgust on Fliss's face. And on her mother's, come to that.

'Welcome,' Veronica said. It was nice to have the whole school quiet; that wouldn't happen again for another year. 'We're very pleased to welcome you here to Downey House; for our returning girls, and our new ones.'

She addressed the little ones – she knew they were thirteen, not exactly babies, but they looked so young, with their scrubbed faces and long hair. Not like the older girls, who were affecting to slouch against the back of the hall, as if assembly was just too unutterably dull for words. The school – a middle and upper school – started at year three when the girls were going on fourteen, and ran up to an upper sixth. There were just over three hundred and fifty students.

Of course they were just as nervous, she knew – they had their new haircuts; their new experiences of whatever the summer had brought them, ready to be shared and picked over with the other girls. Would they still be friends? Would someone have a boyfriend when they didn't? Would they pass their exams? The jutting lips, cutting-edge outfits, careful hairstyles and overuse of make-up (the rules about that didn't kick in till the next morning) betrayed just as many nerves as the little plump sallow-skinned girl just in front of the lectern, whose right knee was jiggling so hard she wanted to put her hand on it.

Maggie spied the little girl jiggling too. Her heart went out to her. She didn't mind sitting up at the front of the room with

34

all the other teachers – she was used to that. She was just a little unnerved by the level of scrutiny going on. At Holy Cross you got a quick once-over whilst the pupils worked out the best nicknames they could for you, so if you had a big nose, or big breasts, or anything else about you whatsoever, so much the better. Then they went back to either ignoring you or working out persecution tactics.

Here, it felt oddly like being judged by a group of your peers. You didn't need to glance too long at the girls here to realise just how big the poverty gap in Britain was. Very few of these girls were overweight – there were a few plump with puppy fat, but it was a healthy, pink-cheeked big-bummed horse riding look, thought Maggie; not the gloopy rolls that accumulated on so many of the girls at her old school through endless processed meat and pastry and no fruit and veg. And regardless of the cover of the school's prospectus – which looked like those old Benetton ads – there was a lot of homogeneity; blonde hair, pale skin. One or two staggeringly beautiful black girls who looked like (and probably were) African princesses of some kind; some Middle Eastern girls too, but nothing like the ragtag mix of Polish, Hindi and patois she'd been used to.

Her mind jumped to the surprisingly comfortable suite of rooms in the East Tower that Miss Prenderghast had shown her to. There was a pretty sitting room with a lovely view out to sea (currently rather grey and imposing), a floral sofa and a round dining table. She also had a small bedroom at the back with a single bed covered by a toile counterpane. Maybe when Stan came down they could book a bed and breakfast somewhere. Nobody had asked about her marital status, but there'd been a few glances at her empty ring finger, which was quite funny. She was also to share a small office, though with whom she didn't yet know, where she was expected to meet the girls and take seminars for the older ones preparing for university.

Bringing herself back to the assembly, she glanced round at her fellow teachers; she'd only had ten minutes to try and meet as many of them as possible. The deputy head, and head of English – in effect her immediate boss – was a pinched woman, far too thin for her age, called Miss Starling. Not Ms. The Miss was unmistakeable. She'd obviously been at Downey House for about nine thousand years and wasn't intending to look on Maggie as anything else but an interloper till she'd been there three generations, probably. From first glance (or rather, the first time Miss Starling had said, 'Now, I know that modern com-pre-HEN-sive teaching doesn't emphasise discipline, but here, Ms Adair, we like SIlence in the classroom', over-emphasising odd syllables and making, not for the last time, Maggie figured, reference to her more humble beginnings), Maggie had guessed that Miss Starling might be a teacher the pupils respected, but not one they liked or enjoyed. Which felt like such a shame; if you couldn't have a bit of fun and interest in English, you were unlikely to get it anywhere in the curriculum.

Then there was Mam'selle Crozier, the French mistress. Maggie had liked her immediately. Tall and slender – *mais bien sûr* – she looked like she too might be quite stern but in fact had immediately let out an infectious giggle and said in a low voice how *'superrr'* it was to have someone around her own age, and that they must go out for a drink, which cheered Maggie immensely; she'd had images of lots of long dark evenings in her room on her own, correcting papers and worrying about whether Stan had eaten any vegetables.

'Do not worry,' the French teacher had said. 'Some of them are leetle sheets, but that is simply teaching, *non*? And the rest are superrr.'

Maggie was sitting in the front row on the stage, waiting to be introduced to the school. She felt a shot of adrenalin run through her and a distinct shiver of nerves.

Veronica hoped she'd done the right thing employing Margaret Adair. She looked so nervous sitting there, and quite out of place in the same old suit – she'd really need to have a word. She knew students had debts and so on these days, but this was quite ridiculous, there was no excuse for not grooming yourself. She hoped the girls would understand her and not start laughing the moment she opened her mouth (this hadn't occurred to Maggie) – the accent really was very Glaswegian. However. Nothing ventured, nothing gained.

'I'd like to introduce our new English teacher, replacing Mrs Ferrers,' she said. 'Ms Adair has come to us all the way from Glasgow. She's worked in different types of schools that have given her a real view of life at the sharp edge, which I think is going to make her a huge asset here at Downey, so please give her your warmest welcome, girls.'

'Sink,' said a voice next to Fliss. They were sitting cross legged on the floor. Fliss didn't think she could keep it up for much longer – what was it, some kind of prison camp torture? Nobody else seemed to mind, but her calves were killing her.

'What?' she whispered. She was sitting next to a beautiful black-haired girl, with dark blue eyes and a slightly supercilious expression.

'She's a sink teacher, isn't she? Obvious. "Life at the sharp edge". They must be getting desperate.'

Fliss glanced sideways with some admiration, not only for the girl's obvious prettiness. She was obviously annoyed to be here too.

'Do you know lots about the school?' she whispered, as Maggie stood up on stage, thanked everyone nicely and said how much she was looking forward to . . . blah blah blah. She sounded like that politician who made her dad swear whenever he came on the radio. Oh God, if the teachers were going to be crap too, that was all she needed. She looked about Hattie's age.

'Enough to know I don't want to be here,' said the girl. 'Hello. I'm Alice.'

'Fliss. I don't want to be here either.'

'Excuse me,' came a voice. 'Are you two chatting?'

It was Miss Starling. She was their head of year so they'd met her already. Fliss felt a thrill of fear.

'No, miss,' said Alice contritely, looking innocent.

'A teacher is talking,' said Miss Starling. 'Not a peep out of you two please. On your first day too!'

Maggie felt her face burn up. She was furious. How dare another teacher impose discipline when she was talking? She'd immediately been shown up as an amateur in front of the whole school. She shot a quick glance at Miss Starling, a glance not missed by Veronica. Interesting, thought Veronica. Quite the little spark of temper in there. But she was quite right; June Starling had absolutely no business telling off girls in front of other teachers; it was sheer showing off. Perhaps it was time for the school song, the rousing 'Downey Hall', named after the original building. She nodded to Mrs Offili, the hearty, beefy and universally adored head of music, who banged down on the piano with a rousing hand.

We are the girls
The Girls of Downey Hall
We stand up proud

And we hold our heads up tall
We serve the Queen
Our country, God and home
We dare to dream
Of wider plains to roam
We are the girls
The Girls of Downey Hall.

Simone, having learnt the song off by heart before she arrived, had jumped up with pride when she heard the piano start up. Quickly, she'd realised she was first up, and that her enthusiasm was being met with sniggers from some of the surrounding girls. She felt her face flame pink, before the teachers all stood up too and there was a general shuffling of chairs being pushed back and feet clomping up on the dusty wooden floor.

To Simone, used to a *laissez-faire* comprehensive environment, everything so far had passed in a whirr of queues and laundry bags and a blur of girls running all around. Quite a lot of the girls, it seemed, already knew each other from their 'prep' schools. Simone didn't know what a prep school was, exactly. And they were all so ... they were so small, and petite, and pretty. Or, the ones who weren't small were tall and willowy, like reeds, with long limbs lightly tanned by the sun. One or two were even wearing sandals showing painted toenails.

Miss Starling, the head of Plantagenet House, to which she'd been assigned, had terrified her – simply glancing up briskly, saying, 'You're the scholarship girl, are you? Well done. Well, we hope to see a lot of work out of you. Not just for yourself, but to inspire the other girls. In fact, I don't expect to have to pay you much attention at all. You know what will happen if you don't pull the finger out, don't you?

There's a lot of girls from backgrounds like yours that would kill for the opportunity. Don't mess it up.'

'No, miss,' Simone had said, her head pointed directly towards the floor.

'No, Miss Starling,' Miss Starling had said.

'No, Miss Starling.'

They were called in to meet the headmistress too before her parents left. Simone just wanted them to go. She could see they didn't belong, and they felt it too. The other mothers were all chic and sleek looking; they had short blonde hair and wore gently draping things in soft colours, or smartly tailored suits, or even slim-cut trousers. Nobody was wearing a large black dress with sequins at the neck, nobody, even if Simone's mum had announced that she thought everyone would dress like the Princess Diana so she was going to too.

Simone was in awe of the headmistress's office immediately. It was so beautiful. The far wall was a heavy old-fashioned print wallpaper, but nearly obscured by paintings which, although different in styles – some abstract, some figures, a large oil painting of a horse that Simone adored immediately – all seemed to blend together well. The other wall was filled with floor-length windows that looked straight out over the cliffs and out to sea. Many had been the badly behaved girl who'd sat there, staring and wishing herself on a boat, far, far away!

Veronica looked up from her desk. She was aware – more than any of the other teachers or students knew, or ever would – of the difficulties of coming from one world into the next. Many of the scholarship girls they got were what she thought of as the 'genteel poor': middle-class girls whose parents had fallen on hard times, but still knew the value of an excellent education. Some of them went through the school quite happily with no one even knowing; the school

40

gave a grant for uniforms, and families scraped together for the rest, so it was only the lack of Easter suntans and talk of new cars at seventeen that would give the game away, and then only to a close observer.

From her first glance at Mrs Kardashian's hair, however, she realised that this was something else – a genuine girl from a difficult background. Her heart softened as soon as she looked at Simone, whose body was pasty from too much time in with her books, and fat from too many sweets and biscuits, no doubt given as well-intentioned treats. She needed lots of fresh air, exercise, good food and encouragement of the right sort; she sensed the problem might be prising Simone away from her books, rather than the other way around.

'Welcome,' she said. Over the years Veronica's voice had become incredibly genteel. Simone might have felt more at home if she'd known how it started out. 'Welcome to Downey House.'

'Thank you,' said Simone. Her mother nudged her. 'I mean, thank you for the opportunity to attend your, ehm, august seat of learning, and I hope that I'll be a credit to you and this institution for many years to come.'

Veronica stifled a smile. Actually she could do with more girls coming in with that attitude, even if they were forced to learn a rote speech.

'Well, good. Thank you. That's nice to hear.'

'We're just so proud of her,' said the mother. 'You know, she's such a good girl, and so obedient and never stops studying . . .'

Veronica ignored her, but in a positive way.

'Simone,' she said. 'We're very pleased to welcome you here. Many girls aim for a scholarship to Downey, and very, very few succeed. It's a great achievement.'

Simone went bright pink and stared at her lap.

41

'But, now you're here, I want you to take advantage of everything we can offer you. Downey House isn't just about books and exams, although those are part of it. It's about becoming a confident, rounded young woman. It's about being able to take on the world. So I don't want you to chain yourself to the library. I want you to get out there; to enjoy the fresh air; to make good friendships with the other girls; to participate in as many sports and societies as you can and to throw yourself into everything with as much enthusiasm as you've thrown yourself into getting in here.'

Simone nodded mutely. The idea of her becoming a confident young woman like the ones she'd seen standing around the assembly hall, so terrifyingly beautiful and self-assured – well, she'd never be like that in a million years, about as long as it would take her to . . . get on a pony. But she knew she always had to agree with what the teacher said.

'You'll get a lot out of Downey House – as long as you give a lot back.'

Simone looked up through her glasses. What an unprepossessing child, thought Veronica. Just one big bundle of nerves. She really did hope the school would knock some of it out of her, and not drive her more into herself.

'Yes, miss,' said Simone.

Simone's mother had finally been persuaded to get back into the car, howling and wailing, just as the very last of the parents were setting off. Simone watched her, her insides clenching with embarrassment. Not one of the other mothers had clung to their daughters, weeping huge tears, and certainly none of the other fathers had had to pull off the mothers and practically fold them into the car.

From above, though, through one of the dormitory windows, the girls were watching.

Each spacious dorm took four girls and had its own bathroom, comfortable single beds that the girls brought their own duvet covers for, and a cupboard, desk and bedside cabinet for each one. Fliss Prosser looked down from her assigned room into the car park below (sea views were reserved for older students).

'Look at this,' she scoffed to Alice, who was in the same dorm. 'God, if my mother did that I'd be so embarrassed.'

'So's she,' pointed out Alice. 'But still – eww.'

They both looked over to the still empty bed in their room. The third was taken by a quiet student called Imogen, who'd unpacked her belongings immaculately and immediately sat down at her desk with her back to the room and started to swot up on their maths course. But the fourth was ominously empty.

'Oh God,' said Alice. 'That means . . . she's ours! The hippopotamus!'

'Ssh!' said Fliss. It wasn't nice, really it wasn't. But Alice was so pretty and funny and lively, it was impossible not to want to be her friend.

'What if she makes big snuffling heffalump noises at night? And cries all the time? And leaves hairs all down the sink? It'd be *terrible*.'

Fliss couldn't help herself. She snuffled up her nose and did a pretty good imitation of grunting.

'Snorty . . . I'll just sleep here . . . SNORT.'

'Got any turnips I can eat?' said Alice. 'That's what we have back in my country.'

'Yes,' said Fliss. 'My mum had some decorating her hat!'

The girls collapsed into fits of giggles that suddenly went silent. There, framed in the doorway, pale and scared looking, was Simone.

Fliss's first instinct was to apologise. Simone looked like a wounded animal; like Ranald with a thorn in his paw, and her instinct was for kindness, and to look after the weaker person. But she felt Alice's eyes upon her, sizing her up to see what she would do. And Fliss remembered how cross she was to be there, and how she certainly wasn't going to worry about anyone else.

'Oh, hi,' she said, in a disdainful tone of voice. 'I suppose that's your bed then.'

Maggie sat on her bed with her hands clasped. It was odd; she felt like she didn't know what to do. She tried ringing Stan again, and this time she got him. She had the weird feeling that he wasn't picking up his mobile before. It was odd, that sense that she felt he was there, but deliberately not answering the phone. It wasn't like him; normally he was thrilled to hear from her in the day.

'Hiya,' he said, in a neutral tone.

'Hi sweetie,' she said, trying to sound as normal as possible. 'How are you? How are you doing?'

'I'm not in hospital,' said Stan irritably. 'I'm just having my life as normal, remember? It's you who's disappeared.'

'I haven't disappeared,' said Maggie, rolling her eyes. She didn't want an argument, just a friendly voice when she was hundreds of miles away, in a tower of a castle filled with four hundred people she didn't know.

'Hmm,' said Stan. He was eating.

'Are you having chips?' she asked him. Dinner had been perfectly serviceable, but undeniably plain, lamb chops, green beans and mash. Some chips from the Golden Fry down the road suddenly felt like a fabulous idea.

'Uh huh,' said Stan.

'Are they good?'

'Why, are youse somewhere too poncey for chips now?'

'I am actually,' said Maggie. 'There must be some at the seaside. But I think the school is a chip-free zone. That's what you pay for.'

'People paying to be deprived of chips,' scoffed Stan. 'Sounds a pretty stupid set-up to me.'

Maggie found herself agreeing with him – anything to hear his voice soften.

'So, how is it then?' he asked grudgingly. 'Do you live in a castle now?'

'It is a bit like a castle actually,' Maggie admitted. 'It's very formal, much more than I thought. All the girls have to stand up when the head passes, that kind of thing.'

'Bloody hell. Do they still get caned and stuff?'

'No, not here. Apparently the boys' school over the hill still does, but only for real transgressions. And even that's only because the parents like it, apparently – they never do it really, they just put it in the prospectus.'

'Sick,' whistled Stan.

Maggie wanted to tell him about all the new teachers she'd met, and the grand hall, and her neat little suite of rooms, and how excited and trepidatious she was about the next morning and taking her first class. But she knew deep down that he wouldn't – couldn't – share her enthusiasm and that it wasn't really fair to try and make him.

'So, how was your day?' she asked, timidly.

Stan paused. 'It was the same as every day,' he said, as if surprised she'd asked. 'Same old jerks, same old distribution problems. Oh, no, hang on, I came home to an empty house with no dinner. That was a bit different.'

Maggie didn't take the bait. She was so tired anyway, it had been such a long day. 'I'll be back soon,' she said soothingly. 'And you must come down. We'll find chips, I promise.'

Stan made a non-committal grunt, then there was a silence.

'Well, I'd better get to bed,' Maggie said. 'Big day tomorrow and everything.'

'Yeah,' said Stan. 'Well, you have a big day tomorrow. Mine is pretty small, I expect.'

'Hmm,' said Maggie, feeling tired of his whingy tone, and then guilty for being annoyed. 'Well, goodnight then . . .'

Stan either didn't hear the appeal in her voice – for him to say something nice, to say he loved her or he missed her; anything at all. He either didn't hear it, or he ignored it.

Veronica couldn't believe it had taken her all day to get round to opening the post. Yes, she was terribly busy, but even so . . . Miss Prenderghast would have taken care of much of it this morning, but would still have left out the pieces she felt Veronica should see – invoices to initial; letters from concerned parents or applicants; and government circulars trying to interfere with things, which she generally binned immediately.

This was different, however. It was from the charities commission – many private schools were registered charities and, as such, didn't pay tax – talking about an assessment.

Veronica's school was exempt from Ofsted inspections, belonging as it did to the private sector. However, there were 'voluntary' assessments that could be carried out which worked in roughly the same way. They were becoming less and less voluntary as parents became more and more savvy about standards and league tables, and Veronica knew, deep down, that she wasn't going to be able to refuse – she'd put them off in the past, and if she put them off again, it would start to ring warning bells.

Sitting up in bed, she smoothed her neat grey hair behind her ears. If she hadn't ruthlessly trained it out of herself, she would have sworn. The last thing she needed was people picking over the school, nosing their beaks into her affairs. This was a wonderful school and she ran it very well. And beyond that was nobody's business.

Chapter Four

Maggie woke up blinking at the unfamiliar sunlight glancing off the rough white painted ceiling of her small bedroom. At first she had no idea where she was. Then she remembered, and a sharp bolt of excitement ran through her. She, Maggie Adair, was assistant head of English at one of the smartest girls' schools in the country! She was going to take fine young minds and fill them with words, and creativity and learning and . . .

A loud bell roared and Maggie jumped out of her skin. It sounded like a fire alarm, but didn't last. She looked at her phone. Seven o'clock! Did the bells really start ringing at seven o'clock in the morning? Every morning? This she was not going to like.

Still, she was up now. She went to the window and opened it wide, inhaling the lovely, ozoney air off the sea. Why had she never lived by the sea before? Why had she always looked out on housing estates and not the little white hulls of trawlers bobbing off in the distance? Because she couldn't afford it, she supposed. Well, she was coming up in the world now. As she gazed out in a reverie, she heard a frantic cursing next to her in what sounded like French. She leaned over and looked to her left. Sure enough, there was Mademoiselle Crozier and, tumbling from her fingers, a lit cigarette.

'Hello,' she said. Mademoiselle Crozier was wearing a black satin robe that looked incredibly luxurious for a teacher. Maggie instantly swore to finally get rid of her old towelling dressing gown that Stan had repeatedly pointed out made her look like the Gruffalo.

'*Merde*,' said Mam'selle. 'Oh, it's you. I 'ave dropped my cigarette.'

'Won't they think it's one of the girls?'

'*Mais oui*, and then there will be a grand inquisition, *non*?' She stared gloomily at the grass below. 'Perhaps it will all catch on fire and the evidence will be gone.'

'We could sneak down and pick it up,' offered Maggie. 'I won't tell anyone.'

'Sank you,' said Mam'selle. 'It is strictly *non* here, *non*?'

'*Oui*,' said Maggie smiling. 'Shall we go for breakfast?'

Mademoiselle rolled her eyes. 'You have not tried the coffee. No breakfast for me. But please, call me Claire.'

Maggie felt pleased. She thought she was going to like Mam'selle. Then she thought about her first class, and her chest tightened uncomfortably. It was one of the first forms, or what she thought of as year three – there were four forms, one from each house, so hopefully they'd be as nervous as she was and not inclined to try and trip her up. She *hoped*.

She had her lesson plan set out, based on what had worked well with her smarter pupils at Holy Cross, and had chosen for her first years a book she'd found the most terrifying thing she'd ever read when she was a teenager, *Brother in the Land*, about a young male survivor of a nuclear holocaust in England. She found it worked perfectly by being so scary that, if you got it as your first book, you also assumed that the teacher was very scary and might well bring down Armageddon on your head at any time. Almost as effective as displaying lots of strong discipline, and vastly easier. Obviously there was the odd complaint from parents when their thirteen-year-olds started wetting their beds again, but surely they were made of sterner stuff at boarding school.

Pulling on a jumper over her pyjama bottoms, she decided it was too beautiful a morning to waste; and that there wasn't much point in not living on a housing estate any more if she didn't get out and enjoy it.

The main hall, with its plaster angels, was eerily quiet – the girls were all in their towers, she assumed, brushing teeth and getting ready for the day. She padded across the hall in her Birkenstocks – ugly, but incredibly useful – and out into the dewy morning.

Goodness, but it was beautiful. The crests of the distant waves were whipped white, the morning with its last streaks of pink in the air. A fresh pure salty wind was blowing that felt as though she was getting her brain washed.

First, Maggie rounded the East Tower and peered at the grass. Sure enough, there was a handful of butts, some with lipstick around them. Surely Claire didn't wear lipstick to bed? Well, maybe the French did that kind of thing – Maggie had never had a friend from another country before. She took a bag out of her pocket and started lifting them up.

'Ah,' came a voice. Maggie looked up. It was Miss Starling, immaculate in a purple tweed suit. Maggie smiled nervously, conscious of her old University of Strathclyde sweatshirt and pulled-back hair.

'Good morning,' she said. She had to get it into her head that this woman was a colleague, not her teacher. Her boss, yes, but not her housemistress.

'Miss Adair. Good morning!'

She stared at Maggie with the cigarette butts in her hand. 'I don't know if it was made clear at the interview, and I know things are different in . . . our more *deprived* parts of the country, but we don't tolerate smoking at this school. At all. It's against the law and it's a bad example for the girls. When you're in town, I suppose, if you must, but it's *completely* forbidden on school property . . .'

'I don't . . .' stuttered Maggie, looking at the butts in her hand. Miss Starling raised an eyebrow. Maggie considered dropping Claire in it, but realised she couldn't. 'Uh, all right.'

'Well, let us say no more about it. Off for an early morning walk?'

Maggie nodded, not knowing the right answer.

'Very good. Helps the constitution. Good day!'

Maggie watched her stalk off, feeling a little weak and trembly. This was ridiculous. She couldn't be frightened of her boss. She thought of her old head of English, Mr Frower, invariably known as Percy, even though the children weren't old enough to remember how he'd got his nickname. He'd nipped out for fags in the middle of lessons and was regularly to be found sticking on videos of shows only roughly connected with the topic and wandering off for a sit down. The time two of his children fluked their way to 'B's, they practically had to have a party for him. Oh yes, things had changed.

Maggie struck out for the clifftops, feeling, despite her telling off, that the world belonged to her. The only soul she could see was a gardener, down in the far end of the grounds. There was a whole team of gardeners. 'I have a whole team of gardeners,' Maggie thought to herself with a grin, and almost broke into a skip as she headed towards the garden gate.

'Look at that,' said Alice scornfully, looking out of their dormitory window as the small figure of Maggie could be seen, wandering over the grounds. 'What on earth is she wearing? What does she think she looks like? Are those *pyjamas*?'

Fliss had never seen a teacher in pyjamas before. She couldn't resist taking a peek.

'God,' Alice said. 'Look at the arse she's displaying to the world! That is rude, man.'

Fliss looked at herself in the mirror. Then she looked at Alice, who was combing out her long dark hair and looked beautiful and extremely confident. She needed a bit of that. She'd love to be so sure of herself. So she nodded and joined in.

'Isn't it true they all eat deep fried Mars Bars in Scotland?' she said.

'I don't know,' said Alice. 'It's impossible to understand a *word* they say. I think they all have heart attacks, though. Which should get us out of double English.'

Quietly, as if trying to make herself as small and unnoticeable as possible, Simone shuffled past into the bathroom. She was wearing huge pink pyjamas covered in little pictures of dogs. She'd noticed that the other girls wore slinky Calvin Klein bottoms and tiny little vest tops to bed, which showed off their little Keira Knightley tummies and high round breasts. How did they know what to wear to bed? Was there some sort of a memo sent round? Her mum had bought her these pyjamas because they'd both thought they were cute, and they were cheap in Primark, and nice cosy flannel, because Mrs Rishkian down at the laundrette had heard that these boarding schools weren't heated and she'd need to be nice and warm.

Alice regarded her steadily in the mirror.

'Nice pyjamas,' she said in a neutral tone.

'Thanks,' said Simone, colouring and looking for her toothbrush.

'Primark?' Alice asked.

'Yes!' said Simone, amazed that this gorgeous girl seemed to be making reasonable conversation with her.

Alice looked at Fliss. 'I'd never have guessed.'

Fliss felt bad. 'I'm going to go and get dressed,' she said. 'Your pyjamas are cute, Simone.'

Alice rolled her eyes.

The blowing blustery clifftops brought some of Maggie's confidence back. She felt exhilarated by the whipping waves and the clouds racing over the sky, as the sun steadily warmed her back.

'*I wandered lonely as a cloud!*' she shouted into the head of the wind. '*That floats on high o'er vales and hills . . .*'

Getting into it now she started to declaim louder and louder, enjoying the sensation of roaring into the wind and being so very far away from everything she found familiar.

'*. . . And then my chest with pleasure fills,*' she concluded, throwing out an arm to a hovering audience of gulls and cormorants, and imagining her new class applauding and being inspired and moved by poetry. '*And dances with the daffodils!*'

'Oh, very good,' came a voice, and, from almost directly beneath her feet, a man emerged from the undergrowth, clapping.

'Shit!' shouted Maggie and jumped back, almost losing her footing.

'Sorry, sorry!' said the man, putting up his hands to make it clear he wasn't a threat. As well he might, thought Maggie, hiding in the undergrowth next to a girls' school. She fumbled in her pyjama pockets for her mobile phone. Maybe she'd have to call the police. She hadn't brought it. Shit. Shit. She felt her face flush.

'It's OK' he said. 'I was on the path, see? It goes just below here. I was walking my dog.'

As if to prove this to her he whistled and a lovely mongrel bounded up, hopping joyously.

'Oh what a nice dog,' said Maggie, unable to help herself. She was fairly sure that paedophile perverts didn't have nice dogs. 'What is it?'

'A bitter,' said the man. 'Bit o' this, bit o' that, you know?'

She smiled, despite herself. 'I was just . . .'

'Yes, what *were* you doing? I can see you're questioning my motives, but I'm afraid you are *much* more suspicious. Out shouting loudly in your underwear?'

Oh God. Maggie felt her face get even redder. 'I was just practising some poetry. And these are perfectly decent pyjamas, thank you.'

'Well, you obviously haven't seen the hole in the back. And a bit of Wordsworth. Very nice. Although I think you'll find it's "my *heart* with pleasure fills".'

'I'm the new English teacher at Downey House.'

'*Are* you?' His face split into a wide, slightly manic grin. 'Well, very nice to meet you, New English Teacher at Downey House. I'm your opposite number.'

He stuck out his hand. Maggie stuck hers out to meet it before realising it was covered in cigarette ash from picking up Claire's butts. She quickly pulled it back and scratched the dog's neck instead. The man didn't seem to mind.

'What do you mean?'

'I'm David McDonald. Head of English at Downey Boys.'

Maggie still didn't know what he was talking about.

'The boys' school? Over the headland? Downers? That's what the boys call it. Or Downey's Syndrome, if they're in the mood to be really horrid, which as we know all boys are. You'd think they'd use a bit of imagination . . .'

Maggie wasn't entirely sure how to get him to stop talking.

'Oh,' she said, just pitching herself in in the middle. 'Wow. Hello then!'

'We'll be seeing a bit of each other then,' said David. Maggie realised to her horror that she was meeting a new professional colleague (and possible ally – though his grin was a bit loopy she liked his dog) whilst still in her damn pyjamas. She was going to bin these things asap. 'Inter-school debates, that kind of thing. Are you interested in drama?'

'Uh, yes, definitely.'

'I think I could tell by your excellent presentation. Well, good. We should talk about that sometime.'

'Uh huh,' said Maggie, embarrassed now by her wild hair bushing around her face and her nicotine-stained fingers.

'Well, I'd best get going. The brutes will be going feral. And as for the boys . . .'

'OK then,' said Maggie, smiling. 'OK. Bye.'

'Come on, Stephen Daedalus!' It took a minute for Maggie to realise he was shouting on his dog. 'See you around!'

'Uh, yeah OK!'

But her voice was swept away on the wind as she watched him descend back along the cliff path.

Back at the school, things were much, much busier, even though Maggie hadn't been away twenty minutes. She realised immediately one of her worst fears – who on earth had she thought she was, dashing out onto the moors without a second thought? Catherine from *Wuthering Heights*? Yes, probably. Impetuous behaviour; always a fault in her, she knew, particularly unsuited to being a teacher.

The front courtyard was teeming with girls looking for

their classes. Oh no, Maggie thought crossly. She was going to have to go through the whole courtyard, full of girls, in her pyjamas. Which possibly had a hole in the back – she wasn't 100 per cent sure she believed the rather mischievous looking Mr McDonald. On her very first morning. This kind of thing, she knew, could ruin a teacher's rep for ever. At her old school a new recruit, Mr Samson, had turned up on his first day with a stain on his tie. He'd spent the rest of his career as Bird-shit Samson, and never knew why. She had such a short time to make a good impression – she was already going to seem so strange and foreign to most of them, at least if it worked the other way as to how strange and foreign they felt to her.

Stupidly, she found herself hiding behind her parked car. What was she going to do? What? Wait until they all went into lessons? But then she'd be late! That wasn't much better, Miss Starling would doubtless have a thing or two to say about it. Who was she less afraid of, the girls or Miss Starling? She wasn't sure.

Veronica replaced her teacup thoughtfully as she considered drawing down the blinds. Was that her new teacher hiding out in the car park? *Surely* not. Obviously she'd gone out on a limb with the appointment, but it was rare that her judgement was quite as poor as that. Oh, that would be all she needed, a new headache to add to the other things they were going to have to go through this year. She returned her gaze to the pile of paperwork on her desk. Examiners were suggesting commencing over a three-week period during which they would sit in on classes, talk to selected pupils (selected by whom, Veronica wondered drily), look at the school accounts and generally poke their big noses into everything. Including, Veronica worried, herself.

Goodness me, what *was* that ridiculous Scottish girl doing? The whole point of this school was to teach young ladies calm and order, not how to run about in their smalls, something half the sixth form needed almost no practice in anyway. She would definitely have to have a word.

'Pssst,' came a voice. On the verge of panic, Maggie cut her eyes to the side. There, sidling through the car park and squeezing through the very small spaces between the cars with an elegant swing of her hips, was Claire.

'What are you doing? *Qu'est-ce que vous faites?*' she demanded, obviously so used to teaching in two languages she didn't really let it go at any other time. As she got close Maggie could smell the cigarettes on her breath.

'I can get out but I can't get back in,' whispered Maggie frantically. 'I've never taught at a school where there were people *all the time* before.'

'That ees no problem,' said Claire. 'Follow me.'

And she sidled off (Maggie found it difficult to get through some of the smaller spaces between the parked cars) all the way round the building, via the hedges, to a small door round the back of their turret that Maggie hadn't even noticed.

'Fire exit,' explained Claire. 'It should not be open from the outside, huh, it will encourage the girls to misbehave. But for one morning only . . .'

'I think,' said Maggie, 'you behave worse than any of the girls here.'

Claire smiled. 'You cannot get a reasonable loaf of bread from here to Le Touquet,' she said. 'One must do sometheeng for fun, *non?*'

Maggie made it upstairs, showered, changed and into assembly with mere moments to spare. She was ready.

Chapter Five

Fliss looked at the card as she stood by the old-fashioned wooden pigeon holes, trying to ignore all the older girls shouting and gossiping to one another. Alice had disappeared and she felt entirely on her own. Half of it made her want to sneer and rip it up. Half of it made her want to cry.

Our darling Felicity, the card said. *We know this is the first day of a great adventure for you. You may not think we are doing the right thing, but we think you will thrive and grow up into the wonderful young woman we know you can be.*

Fliss's throat had got a lump in it just then. She was glad no one else was around to see.

So do what you can to make us proud and we know you'll be happy too.

All of a sudden she felt a whirl in her stomach as someone picked her up and spun her round.

'All right baby sis?'

It was Hattie. She was wearing her prefect's badge proudly on her blazer and her navy jumper tied loosely over her shoulders in a way Fliss couldn't help finding extremely irritating.

'Hey,' said Hattie, grabbing the card out of Fliss's hands. 'Is that from home?'

'Give it back!' said Fliss. 'It's private mail! It's MINE!'

'Don't be silly,' said Hattie, who'd never had the faintest

problem with bursting into Fliss's room at odd times of day, or flicking through her diary (which Fliss kept out in the stables now). 'What could they possibly be writing to you that they wouldn't want me to see?' She scanned the note quickly. 'Oh yeah. They sent one just like this to me.' She sniffed.

'Did they?' Fliss felt immediately crestfallen. She'd thought she'd detected Daddy's hand in the card; that he had wanted to send her some reassurance, try and suggest that he hadn't really wanted her to go at all, that they loved her too much.

'Yeah, yeah. It's just meant to make you work hard. Mind you, did the job for me.'

'What do you mean?' said Fliss, red-faced and upset.

'Oh yeah, I didn't want to come here either. Thought you'd get to stay behind having all the fun. But I did what they said, and it's been the making of me,' said Hattie. 'I might even make captain of netball this year. So. Listen to them. They know what's best for you.' She gave a patronising smile. 'And so do I. Even if you don't think so at the moment.' She bustled off importantly.

Fliss's fists clenched by her sides and she felt fury burn up inside her. So everyone knew what was best, did they? Well, they'd see about that! She wasn't going to turn into a useless pi busybody suckbutt like Hattie, no way.

'Hello Fliss,' said Alice, wandering up, looking pristine in an oddly impertinent way – her uniform was a little too tidy; her shirt a little too white. It looked as though she was challenging you to say something about it. 'Want to pretend we got lost and be late for class?'

Fliss realised one of her fists was clenched, and slowly let it unfurl.

'Sure,' she said.

*

Simone looked round the empty classroom. Where was everyone? Was she in the right place? Her skirt button was rubbing. She shouldn't have had that extra slice of bacon this morning. But the breakfast had been brilliant; fried bread and sausage and yoghurt and fresh fruit. No coffee, like she got at home, except for sixth formers, but she'd had tea with four sugars and there was no one to tut like her mum did. Plus she'd heard the girls say they only got a top-up feed on the first morning so she should make the most of it.

The refectory was a high-ceilinged panelled room, with high-set windows, long wooden tables and benches that sat eight or ten; the room's bad acoustics meant that whilst the clanging of knives and forks was always loud, it was some-times difficult to hear even your neighbour. Hence everyone shouted.

From where she'd been sitting on the end of the row by herself, Simone couldn't believe all the other girls seemed to have coupled up already. How was that possible? It wasn't that she wasn't used to eating by herself; God, at St Cats it had happened all the time. But how had all these girls man-aged to fit in so quickly? Even their haircuts were similar. Was there some memo that went round that said you had to have long silky straight-cut hair without a fringe, as well as the PE kit and a boater? Had she missed it? She'd stroked her fuzzy plaits nervously. Simone didn't realise that a lot of these girls came from the same small number of 'feeder' schools that educated them to take the exam. Half of them had already met at pony club; or their mothers were friends, having been to the same school twenty years before.

Sitting at the end of the row she'd watched them enviously as she stuffed two sausages inside a sandwich and covered it liberally in ketchup.

'Oh, this food is great,' one girl was saying.

'Heavenly.' But, oddly, neither of them was actually eating. Carefully, one of the girls had fished a piece of kiwi fruit out of the fruit salad and popped it in her mouth.

'I'm stuffed,' she said. 'Huge supper last night.'

'Ya, me too,' said another.

'And my tuck is just to die for,' said a third. 'My mother sent me an entire bloody fruit cake. I think I ate the whole thing.'

Simone had stuffed down the rest of her sandwich and sidled away as quickly as she could, to puzzled glances from the others. As soon as she was nearly out of earshot, naughty Alice had said, 'I just can't make up my mind – transfer from Roedean or, perhaps . . . *scholarship*?' And the whole table had dissolved in laughter.

Now Simone sat alone in the English classroom, trying to figure it all out.

Assembly and roll call over – a lengthy and tedious allocation of classrooms, timetables, groupings and house leaders – Maggie was at last ready to teach her first lesson. All her classes were Plantagenets, and she had a pastoral role towards Middle School 1. So, thought Maggie, running it through her head. Pregnancy, skag, fighting and usually the first time they got thrown out of the house and temporarily rendered homeless. Oh, no, hang on. It wouldn't be like that here. With any luck it would only be periods and missing tennis racquets.

She looked through it all nervously in the staffroom. Some modern poetry, nothing too frightening, plus the novel. She was looking forward to *Wuthering Heights* and *Tess* for the older ones; she'd never been able to teach those before, as the boy halves of her classes, even the small senior ones, groaned and rolled their eyes laboriously whenever they

61

came out, whereas the girls could just float away on a cloud of doomed romance. Although, she wondered, maybe all the girls here would have read those books already? They were going to be way ahead of what she was used to. What if this was the equivalent for them of Noddy stories?

Well, it was on the curriculum, so that was what they would have. The A-level students, who came in in the afternoon, were doing Chaucer. She cursed. She hated Chaucer, always had done. So hard to interpret and not that funny when you finally managed it. Still, Miss Starling had just told her, before dashing out to get over to Tudor, that the A-level students were quiet, studious girls in this house, expected to do extremely well and good self-starters. They way she'd said it left Maggie in no doubt that the reason they were such paragons of virtue was because of Miss Starling's immaculate regime, that she had no wish of changing.

Well, we'll see, thought Maggie, smoothing down her checked jacket in the ladies and checking she didn't have any grass in her hair, just as the bell tolled again loud and clear. Maggie took a deep breath and headed out to her classroom.

'Hello,' she said cheerily to the lone girl, a chubby lass who seemed to be eating. 'I'm Miss Adair. The new English teacher.'

'Hello, miss,' mumbled Simone, embarrassed that she'd been caught out. Her mother had sent her some *mamaliga* cakes in the post – she must have posted them before they'd even left yesterday. The grease had stained through the wrapper, but they tasted of home; so good she didn't care. Even the smell made her think of them all sitting on the big brown settee, watching *X Factor* and bugging their dad to let them phone in again. She even missed Joel kicking her in the ankle when he thought she was taking up more than her fair share of the cushions. She had a lump in her throat. What was she doing here?

'Are you eating?' asked Maggie, thinking as she always did, how much saying this made her sound like a teacher.

'Yes miss,' said Simone, turning a deep shade of purple. In trouble! On her first day.

'Well, are you allowed to eat with your other teachers?'

'No, miss.'

'So why do you think I'm going to be any different? Give me that please.'

Snivelling, Simone handed up the parcel of home. Maggie debated throwing it in the bin – it looked like soggy bread and smelled very peculiar – but she could sense with this girl she probably wasn't going to have to be too tough.

'You can pick it up after school,' she said. Simone nodded numbly.

Great, thought Maggie. Been here ten seconds and have already reduced my first pupil to a dumbstruck sodden mess.

'What's your name?' she asked kindly.

'Simone.'

'Do you need a tissue, Simone?'

Simone nodded quietly, whilst Maggie retrieved one from the packet no sensible teacher did without in her handbag. She was about to ask if the girl was all right, when suddenly, with a noisy chatter, the main river of schoolgirls burst into the room.

Chatting, yelling, giggling, they were making a lot of noise, Maggie knew, to cover up their essential nerves at this, the start of a new school, with new girls and new ways of doing things. Although the way this lot threw themselves about, it was as if they'd known one another for years. She was used to first years being a little more cowed than this, if only because the ones at Holy Cross weren't sure whether they were going to get mugged at break time for their mobile phones.

Maggie gave them a couple of minutes to choose their seats and settle down. The desks were the old-fashioned kind she hadn't seen in years – wooden, with proper lids and inkwells, scored and scratched with years of discussion about who loved whom and which pop group was the best, etched by compasses.

Then she wrote her name up on the board and turned round to face them all.

'Hello,' she said. 'I'm Miss Adair. For those of you who are new here, I'm also new here, and very happy to be. Here. Now, who can tell where my accent is from?'

Maggie had expected to be able to start some friendly banter, but no one said a word. She looked around the class until a few people tentatively raised their hands. She picked a dark-haired girl at random.

'Scotland?' said the girl, as if slightly puzzled that she'd asked such a stupid question.

'That's right,' said Maggie. 'Have you been there?'

'Well, my family own an estate there,' said the girl, looking bored.

'OK, well done,' said Maggie trying not to show that she was flustered. 'Who else has been to Scotland?'

Pretty much the entire class raised their hands. Maggie wondered if she'd have got the same response if she'd said the Caribbean, or America, or France. Probably. Thirteen years old and they'd done it all. She noticed her little muncher hadn't raised her hand yet. She'd have to keep an eye on her.

'Well,' she said. 'I thought, just for us to get acquainted, we could start with a Scottish poem, from the land of my birth. A great poet, called Liz Lochhead. Then we can discuss it, see what you think, and open up the floor.'

The girls opened their jotters obediently, with only one low groan from the back. Maggie's heart sank a little. Maybe she'd just ignore this one. She knew she needed to flaunt her authority at an early stage, but maybe not just yet.

'It's called "The Choosing",' she said. And she read the beautiful verse, of two girls growing up, one to go on to study and do well for herself, one forbidden by her father to continue her schooling, the first spending all her time in the library, running in to her pregnant friend upstairs on the bus, 'her arms around the full-shaped vase that is her body'. Maggie remembered so well the first time she'd heard it; how clearly she had identified herself with the two girls on the estates. That she would be the one in the library, with the prizes there for the taking. Was it having the same effect? She cast half an eye in their direction. Perhaps this was wrong. There wasn't a choice for these girls. Of course they would succeed. Effortlessly. Failure wasn't an option when you could pay thousands of pounds a year to buy your girls the best education possible.

But they listened politely enough, and she tried to elongate her vowels and not roll her r's too much to give them a fair shot.

'So . . .' she said, leaning back, trying to look cool and collected and utterly unfazed by the new world she found herself in. 'Any thoughts?'

There was a long moment when nobody moved a muscle in the class and Maggie had that thought she sometimes got that she should have done primary teaching after all and they could have just pulled out some colouring-in books at this point.

Fliss sat at the back, and glanced at Alice, whose eyes were dancing, full of mischief. Alice nodded. 'Go on,' she whispered. Fliss rolled her eyes. Alice giggled.

'You two,' came Maggie's voice firmly. 'Do you have something to say?'

'Well, the thing is,' drawled Fliss, quite amazed at where on earth she'd found the courage. 'I'm afraid I didn't really understand what you were saying.'

Maggie felt the class stiffen.

'Was it English?' Fliss went on, scarcely believing her own daring.

Maggie stared at her. 'Well you'll find out,' she said. She rifled through her file, scarcely able to believe she was doing it, and pulled out another poem.

'Why don't you read this to the class, if your diction is so much better.'

She stared at Fliss who stared back. She couldn't mean it, could she? She couldn't possibly be expecting her to read something out loud?

Maggie was doing her best inside to look steely. That was the only way, she kept telling herself. Be tough, and you only had to do it once. And never, ever let them get to you.

She held up the paper. 'Out at the front please. What's your name?'

'Felicity Prosser,' Fliss mumbled, her cheeks going scarlet. Maggie was surprised to see her blushing. Obviously not quite as shameless as she liked to pretend. Still, she wasn't going to back down now.

'Out you get then.'

For a short period nobody moved a muscle. Then, gradually and as sulkily as she could manage, Fliss pushed herself out to the front of the class.

'What's this?' she asked.

'Some foreign poetry,' said Maggie. 'Read it to the class, please.'

The class stared at Fliss, looking awed and amazed. She felt her face burn but didn't feel she had any choice.

Gradually, haltingly she began:

'Go fetch to me a pint o' wine,
An' fill it in a silver tassie,'

Felicity kept her head down and muttered into the paper.

'That's a cup,' said Maggie. 'Speak louder, please.'

'That I may drink, before I go,
A service to my bonnie lassie.'

'That means girl,' said Maggie.

'I know,' said Fliss.

'OK. Sorry, it's just you said you didn't understand foreign.'

'I'm sorry, miss.'

'Keep reading, please.'

As Fliss stumblingly reached the second verse, even she could see it was quite exciting, and the class was looking interested as she intoned,

'The trumpets sound, the banners fly,
The glittering spears are rankèd ready;
The shouts o' war are heard afar,
The battle closes deep and bloody;'

And when she reached the end, Maggie checked and saw the class were listening intently. Good. It had worked.

'That's Robert Burns,' said Maggie. 'One of the greatest

poets that ever lived. Do you think you're still going to have trouble understanding Scots? I have lots more poems here that we can move on to if you don't.'

'I'm sure I'll be fine, miss,' said Fliss, still feeling sick with the humiliation.

'All right. Sit down please.'

Maggie turned back to her class.

'Right. Now where were we? On Liz Lochhead. Does anyone have any trouble with translation?'

Everyone else fervently shook their heads.

'All right. Comments, please. The sheets are on your desks.'

There was a long, long wait whilst it seemed as though no one was going to speak. Until, finally, a small girl tentatively raised her hand.

'Yes. You,' said Maggie, in a much friendlier voice, pointing her out. 'Can you say your names too, when you answer? Makes my job easier.'

'I'm Isabel,' said the girl, and Maggie jotted it down on her seating chart.

'What did you think, Isabel?'

'Well, she kind of feels sorry for the other girl, but a bit jealous too, doesn't she?'

After that the class relaxed and went much better. Except for one girl, sitting at the back. I will never forgive her, thought Fliss. Never.

'Simone?' asked Maggie. 'Who do you empathise with in the poem?'

Simone had loved the poem. That was her. All those other girls at school could just go out and get pregnant and she was going to go and do something else. She had to articulate it. She had to get it out. Flushing horribly in front of everyone she stuttered.

'The poet,' she said. 'I mean, she was going to the library and getting on with her life and . . .'

'Not the vase?' came a voice from behind her. The whole class sniggered. Simone was by far the heaviest one there. Immediately her face turned bright pink and she stared down at her desk.

'Who said that?' said Maggie, annoyed. Fliss was delighted. It wasn't just going to be her who hated this teacher.

As always happens in schoolrooms, the girls imperceptibly moved away from the culprit, leaving her encircled. Maggie glanced at her chart.

'Alice Trebizon-Woods?'

Alice was a pretty blank-faced girl with long dark hair and an innocent looking expression Maggie didn't trust for an instant.

'Yes, miss.'

'Did you interject?'

'Did I what, miss?'

Maggie waited a couple of seconds.

'Did you want to say something to Simone?'

'I was just adding to the debate, miss. About whether she felt like the other woman. I thought we were opening up the floor.'

There wasn't much Maggie could say to that.

'Well, keep things out of the realm of the personal, please.'

Alice opened her eyes wide and blinked them.

'I wasn't, miss.'

'Continue, Simone,' said Maggie, but Simone couldn't, and stared hard at her desk. Maggie stared hard at Alice and made a mental note to mark her card. The other girls too, all new, stared at the bold girls in the back desk, impressed.

*

'Hi, Stan.'

There was a long pause.

'Yeah, hi, Maggie.'

There was another long pause.

'It was my first day in the classroom today.'

'Oh yeah?' he said. 'Sorry, I haven't been keeping an eye on my academic calendar, you know.'

'That's OK,' said Maggie. 'It went . . . fine. Not great. Not bad.'

'So they haven't immediately twigged you're just a schemie girl frae Govan and chucked you out on your bahookie.'

Maggie stiffened. 'Was that supposed to be funny?'

Stan wasn't sure. 'Uh, yes.'

'Well, it wasn't. There's no earthly reason I can't be a teacher here.' She thought back to Clarissa Rhodes. The tall, beautiful, elegant sixth former, who looked like a young Gwyneth Paltrow, with her clear blue eyes and shiny mass of hair, had flawlessly recited six stanzas of the Chaucer, then deconstructed them with a skill and elegance that left Maggie gasping her admiration.

'I'm not sure,' Clarissa had said afterwards when she had taken the time to meet the girls individually. 'I was thinking of discussing it at my Oxford entrance. But I've also got an offer from the Royal College of Music for the cello and Mr Bart – that's the physics teacher – he thinks I should really take this offer from Cambridge seriously.' She'd blinked her large blue eyes. 'It's hard being a teenager, Mrs Adair.'

'It's "Miss", actually,' Maggie had said, feeling about two feet tall.

'I deserve to be here,' she said now to Stan, but it was as much to convince herself as anything.

'Course you do, love,' said Stan then. 'We just miss you, that's all.'

'I miss you too,' said Maggie. 'Tell me the gossip.'

Stan thought for a while. Gossip wasn't really his thing. He thought of it as a totally female thing. Football for blokes, gossip for girls, and he wasn't about to feign an interest now. 'Your dog got sick,' he said suddenly.

'Muffin? What happened?' Suddenly Maggie felt a homesick wrench.

'Oh, Dylan and Cody were feeding him turkey twizzlers. And he took up and spewed all over the carpet. It was hilarious.'

'Is he all right?'

'Well, he ate the sick,' said Stan.

A bell rang loudly.

'I have to go,' said Maggie. 'We've a dinner meeting.'

'Whenever I bring up spew, you always have to go,' said Stan.

Maggie paused. 'I do,' she said.

'Yeah yeah yeah,' said Stan. 'Right, I'm off to find the bleach.'

And he hung up. Maggie had been hoping for a bit more interest and support on her first day. But she supposed other people's lives were still going on.

She made her way to the headmistress's office where they were having a small reception so all the teachers could meet, along with the staff of their brother school over the hill. She wondered if the crazy man from that morning would be there. Well, be nice to see a familiar face. She felt as nervous as . . . who was that terribly awkward girl in the first form? Simone. Yes. She dipped into the staff toilets to rub a piece of lipstick on, and smelled smoke as she got in there.

'Claire? *C'est vous*?' she said.

71

The French mistress appeared from the cubicle she'd been hiding in.

'Ah, no. Well, of course. Yes. We must go to a boring cocktail party and still they say, no, you must not smoke. But for sure, teachers always smoke. It is unusual and cruel punishment.'

'It's horrid, Claire. And it's bad for the girls.'

'Ah, *oui oui*, OK. She threw her butt down the toilet and came over and inspected her perfectly made-up face in the mirror.

'*Mon dieu*, I shall rot in this place.'

'You look beautiful,' said Maggie, truthfully.

'And what about you, you have a boyfriend?'

Suddenly Maggie wasn't desperately keen, for some reason, to talk about spew-obsessed Stan and his grumpy ways. She couldn't see him coming here and making small-talk with Claire, who was wearing a beautiful white blouse under a grey cashmere sweater which somehow didn't look boring at all, but perfectly chosen and fitting. What would they talk about? Would Stan sneer as they went through the courtyard? What would he eat? She felt disloyal, even as she said, 'Oh, kind of, you know?'

Claire nodded her head fervently. '*Bien sûr*, I understand.'

Maggie smiled.

'He is married, yes?'

'No!'

'Very old and very rich?'

'Don't you think we should go?'

Maggie was glad she was with Claire as she walked into the office. The place was full of teachers and the noise level was high. Sixth form girls were helping the staff handing round canapés and drinks. Maggie wasn't sure this was a good idea.

Giving the girls access to alcohol and the potential to over-hear teachers' gossip. There was loud chatter and several animated conversations were going on. Maggie saw Miss Starling bending the ear of an elderly looking chap with whiskers who was either half-deaf or just politely nodding at random intervals. Dr Deveral was deep in conversation with a rather charming older man, dressed tweedily in the Oxford style, with a waistcoat and patches on the elbows of his jacket. On seeing Maggie, she beckoned her over.

'Yes, Margaret. Let me introduce you to some of the staff from across the way. This is Dr Robert Fitzroy, head-teacher of Downey Boys, just over the hill. It's a stunning Georgian building, you must make an effort to visit as soon as possible.'

'Nice to meet you,' said Maggie, unsure about what to do, but gratefully accepting the outstretched hand. She was a little wary of the English tradition of kissing strangers.

'Of course, you're Veronica's social experiment,' said Robert, smiling kindly.

'Of course she isn't, Robert,' said Veronica, a little pink spot appearing on her cheeks. 'She's a much valued new member of staff.'

'So, do you speak any of your beautiful languages from up there?' said Robert. '*Ciamar a thathu?*'

Maggie decided his face wasn't that kind after all. 'No,' she said.

'What about lallans?'

'I know some Burns,' she said.

'Some Burns! Well, that's a relief.'

'Robert,' said Veronica, reprovingly.

'I'm sorry, my dear,' said Robert to Maggie. 'I'm just making a comment on the state of comprehensive schooling, that's all. I'm so pleased you're here.'

'There are plenty of good comprehensive schools,' said Maggie, angry and prepared to be outspoken.

'My school,' said Robert, 'has two computers per boy, and fifteen acres of football pitch. Don't you think every child deserves access to those kinds of facilities?'

'I think one computer is probably enough for anybody,' said Maggie.

Robert raised his eyebrows. 'A socialist on our hands.'

'Robert, stop being annoying,' said Dr Deveral, with more charm than Maggie had seen before. 'Maggie, do ignore him, he's teasing you.'

'All right,' said Maggie. But it hadn't particularly felt like teasing. She looked around to see if there was anyone else she could talk to. Her gaze fell suddenly on David McDonald, who was standing on the periphery of some sports masters and mistresses who appeared to be demonstrating rounders pitching. He looked bored. But as soon as he saw her his face broke into a wide, slightly manic grin and he raised his glass. Then, seeing she didn't have one, he strode over.

'Hello! Where's your wine?'

'Of course,' said Veronica, looking round for one of the sixth formers, who stepped forward immediately. Maggie took a glass of white and hoped she wouldn't be asked to comment on the vintage.

'Margaret, this is David . . .'

'We've met,' said David, grinning broadly. 'Both fans of early morning walks.'

'Oh, good,' said Veronica.

'I think we should introduce compulsory cold early-morning walks for the pupils,' said Robert. 'What do you think? Blow the cobwebs away before classes.'

'Well,' said Veronica. 'One, they're hard enough to shift as

74

it is. Two, they'd probably take us to the European court of human rights. And three . . .'

'Boys and girls out together in the early morning is just asking for baby-shaped trouble,' said David, draining his glass. 'What about those cold showers, Robert?'

'Well, yes, that too . . .' started Robert, as David guided Maggie away.

'He's a dinosaur,' said Maggie.

'Oh, he's all right. Just old-fashioned. Bit set in his ways. Thinks school was better when there was a lot more whacking in it. The parents love him.'

'I'm not surprised – he looks like he walked out of the pages of the *Daily Mail*.'

'The boys love him too. He's all right. Anyway, if you're that dead set against the *Daily Mail*, what are you doing teaching in a private school in the south of England?'

'I wanted to learn some good techniques to take back to Govan.'

'Is that all?' asked David.

Maggie looked at her wine glass for a moment.

'And well, I just . . . I wanted a change. To see a bit more of the world, I think. I mean, I was teaching at the same school I went to, having to make small talk with my old teachers, can you imagine?'

David made an appropriate face.

'It just seemed a good opportunity. Robert's right in a way. The school I was in was kind of getting me down.' She looked up. 'Why are you here?'

'Holding the line against the philistines,' said David, gesticulating rather wildly with his wine glass. 'Against a world full of texters and magazine addicts and people who think punctuation is for pussies and only care about trainers and would beat you up if you liked poetry. Hearts and minds.'

'Hear hear,' said Claire, who was standing nearby.

'And also, I'm on the run from the French Foreign Legion.'

Maggie smiled. 'Really?'

'We had a misunderstanding.' He whirled off to get some more drinks.

'What a very peculiar man,' said Maggie to Claire.

'The boys they love him,' said Claire.

'I bet they do.'

'I can't believe the teachers are downstairs getting pissed,' said Alice to Fliss, as they mounted the stairs of their tower to prep. It was still light outside. Fliss was used to going to bed when she liked, pretty much. Her parents would try and pick their battles, and bedtime was no longer one of them. This was inhumane. Prep till seven-thirty, then television till nine, lights out at ten! Surely they could sue someone over it.

'This is why they send us to bed so bloody early,' said Alice. 'So we don't stumble on them completely half-arsed, throwing up on the lawn.'

Fliss laughed. 'And copping off with each other.'

Alice looked at her thoughtfully. 'Have you ever been pissed?'

'Course,' scoffed Fliss, although in fact, apart from the champagne they were allowed at Christmas and a few slugs of an alcopop Hattie had once lowered herself to letting her try, she hadn't at all. Hat was so bloody perfect all the time, far too busy with her sports clubs and guiding to get caught up in any kind of 'nonsense' as her father called it. So there wasn't any illicit vodka swilling all round the house, like Fliss had heard other girls talk about. Some even claimed to be going to nightclubs already, though she wasn't sure if this were true.

'What about . . .'

'What?'

But Fliss knew what was coming next, and wasn't looking forward to the question. She thought she'd better lie.

'Have you ever . . . snogged a boy?'

'Of course,' said Fliss, fiercely jumping in.

She thought back over the last summer. She'd had the biggest crush on Will Hampton, the eldest son of their near neighbours. He was tall and slim with floppy brown hair, was going up to Oxford in the autumn and went out with one of the local girls who was emo and gorgeous, really skinny with her huge eyes outlined in black liner. Fliss used to hang around the village shop just in the hopes that she'd catch him going in to buy *The Times* (she'd vowed to take *The Times* when she was older, even if boring old Mummy got the *Mail* and Dad liked the *FT*) and he'd grin and say hello to her and that would be enough to last her the whole day. Once, he'd patted Ranald.

Her hopes were high when her parents had his round at Christmas for a couple of glasses of wine, but he showed up for five minutes then scooted off to a party in town. How she'd wished he'd turn round to her, in this totally stupid dress her dad had wanted her to wear, and ask her to come with him. Of course he hadn't. Still, at least he hadn't asked Hattie, that would have been too mortifying. Hattie pretended she didn't care that she wasn't asked. Everyone would like to be asked somewhere by Will Hampton. But *this* Christmas . . . surely she'd be out of this dump by then.

Apart from that, opportunities for snogging were pretty limited, although Fliss was absolutely riven with curiosity. She'd read *Cosmo* and so on, but they were terribly graphic. And everyone had chattered at school when Faith Garnett had reportedly tongue-smashed one of the jockeys up at the pony club and Faith had briefly been the most interesting and popular girl at school as they'd all queued up for details (sloppy and a bit wet was the consensus), then some of the girls had started saying nasty things and it had ended up with Faith in floods in the toilets surrounded by concerned onlookers and Miss Mathieson giving them all a strict talking to on the perils of gossip, most of which had gone completely over Fliss's head.

'Oh,' said Alice. 'Have you got a boyfriend?'

Fliss would have given anything to be able to answer 'yes' to that question: 'Yes . . . he's going up to Oxford . . . his name is Will Hampton.'

'No,' she said. 'I'm too young.'

'I've been asked out a lot,' said Alice. 'Most people think I look older than thirteen. When I'm not wearing stupid effing knee socks.'

'I know, it's harsh,' agreed Fliss vehemently. 'You do, you look loads older.'

'Thanks,' said Alice. 'I think I have a mature face. Though it's ugly.'

'No, you're beautiful!' said Fliss. 'I'm disgusting.'

'You're beautiful,' said Alice immmediately. 'I'm so disgusting.'

'You're not, you're gorgeous,' said Fliss.

Alice started getting undressed for bed with a sigh. 'We're never going to meet boys here. What do you think, Imogen?'

Imogen was still studying, her face towards the wall, her back towards the room. She just shrugged. Alice turned to Fliss with a merry look.

'God, Imogen, do you have to be so noisy all the time?'

Simone trooped in from the bathroom in her big pyjamas and slippers.

'What about you, Simone?' said Alice, sitting on the bed.

'What?' said Simone, colouring again. Fliss thought what a shame it was she was carrying so much weight; there was a very pretty face in there. If only she wasn't so heavy.

'Got a boyfriend?'

'No,' said Simone shortly, taking her book and climbing into bed.

'Well I was only *asking*,' said Alice. 'You don't need to be so touchy.'

'Sorry,' said Simone, in a miserable voice.

'Maybe she likes women,' whispered Alice to Fliss quietly. 'Better watch out for yourself.'

'Stop it, Alice,' said Fliss. And the bell came, ringing for lights out.

Back at the drinks party Veronica eyed two women sidling in, both wearing wildly unflattering trouser suits. One was carrying a clipboard. Not, thought Veronica to herself, the most elegant of accompaniments to a drinks party. Neither of them was smiling. Veronica checked her hair (perfect, as ever – not a strand would dare defy her kirby grips) and glided over towards them.

'Liz, Pat,' she said. 'Thanks so much for coming to join us.'

'We just found our way,' said the older of the two women. She had very short hair, unflatteringly layered along the side of her head, clear glasses, pale lipstick and a couple of chins too many. Veronica didn't want to see what the stretched seat of her trousers must look like. 'It's not easy to get here.' She said this in an accusatory tone.

'No,' said Veronica. 'I think when it was built it wasn't particularly easy to get anywhere, so it didn't really matter. And I've always thought our location and views are so worth it, don't you think?'

'All right for some,' said the other woman, who had grey hair that looked like it was standing as a rebuke to other, lesser women who dyed theirs.

Veronica's heart sank. She knew the school had to be inspected, she'd just hoped she'd get some people sympathetic to what they were doing here, not ex-local government class warriors. She gave the second lady, Pat, a cool stare. 'You are here to examine the school's facilities? So of course you're hoping everything will be as good as possible?'

'Yes, good for the kids whose parents can afford it.'

'I realise that,' said Veronica, bristling. 'But that's the world as it is. And you're here to see that we're doing as well as we can for the girls here, isn't that right?'

The first woman grunted, and looked around to see where the girls were with their canapés. She beckoned them back and took a handful, cramming them into her mouth. Veronica privately thought that if one of her girls ate like that in company she'd have taken them outside and had a quiet word. Then she started considering her strategy. What a shame that scholarship girl was so timid this year. That's what they needed to be pushing; how Downey House could be a force for good in poorer communities and bring out potential that would get squashed elsewhere. She must keep an eye on that girl.

And that outspoken Scottish teacher should impress them too. They could share the chips on their shoulders.

Veronica smiled at Pat and Liz and asked them if they'd like more wine. They would, of course.

'Betjeman,' said David disconcertingly.

'What?'

'We should add some Betjeman for the Christmas concert. He's fallen so far out of fashion; we could remind people just how good he is. It's a great poem. Got bells, vicars.'

'I know the poem,' said Maggie, impatiently. 'I come from Scotland, you know. Not classical Mesopotamia.'

'But you've heard of classical Mesopotamia,' said David, with an engaging grin. 'Everyone in Scotland is a genius anyway, it's a well-known fact. So. Your predecessor, incidentally, was a ninny, who never wanted to get herself involved in cross-school work. Or work of any kind in fact. Are you like that?'

'I'd have to check with Miss Starling,' said Maggie, thinking that being involved in the Christmas concert would be such a huge treat for the girls and really fire their enthusiasm. At Holy Cross they'd had talent shows at Christmas, which had usually become sexy dancing and rap competitions. They were good fun, rowdy affairs but not the same thing at all. And it would have to be with the younger girls; the older ones had mock exams coming up and wouldn't have time for rehearsals.

'Ah, the fire-breathing Miss Starling,' said David. 'Moral guardian of our humble state. Although you know she's all right really.'

'Miss Starling? Are you serious? She's terrifying.'

'She's a poppet.'

'A *poppet*?'

'A poppet,' said David decisively.

Maggie glanced at June Starling, who appeared to be giving short shrift to some messy looking women with sour faces. Their trouser suits looked shabby and cheap next to Veronica's immaculate twinset. With sinking heart Maggie knew she probably looked more like the women than the head. She really must reconsider her wardrobe. The girls had all looked like off-duty models in their home clothes from the first day, so there was no point trying to compete on the casual end of things. Could she look classic without looking like a gran? It would be nice to stand out a bit for . . . for any men that might be around, not that she was looking.

'What are you thinking?'

Maggie spluttered a little into her drink. 'Nothing. I just . . . she doesn't seem like a poppet at all.'

'I would have thought you were quite hot on not judging a book by its cover.'

Maggie smiled. 'I know. Just settling in I suppose.'

'Well, watch this.'

David left Maggie hovering by the punch and sidled up to the group.

Oh, thank goodness, thought Veronica to herself. That young English teacher from over the hill was something of a maverick, but a good example. There weren't anything like enough smart men going into teaching these days. Too many nebulous accusations from a Childline-savvy generation. She'd have liked to poach him, actually, but there were too few male teachers these days to risk a tall skinny one with quick dark eyes and a wide grin – she didn't want anyone flunking their A-levels because they'd gone puppy lovesick for a master, and, equally, she knew how beautiful and eloquent her eighteen-year-olds were, because she'd worked incredibly hard to make them that way. Best not tempt fate.

'David,' she said, graciously. 'Would you like to meet Patricia and Elizabeth? They've agreed to survey the school for Centrum Standards.'

'Oh, that's great!' said David.

Pat and Liz smiled a little.

'Where are you from?'

'Reading,' said Pat.

'I live in Hackney,' said Liz. 'Everyone else has moved

out, you know, like "white flight", but I believe it's important to stay in local communities.'

'I couldn't agree more,' said David. 'In fact, maybe you could come over to the boys' school one day and talk to them a bit about where you live? Share a bit of experience about your environment?'

'Reading is very mixed too,' said Pat, eagerly. Liz shot her a dirty look. 'We might be too busy,' she said. 'We have a lot to do. We're always really incredibly busy.'

Pat took the opportunity to refill her glass for the fourth time.

'Well, if you can,' said David. 'It's been a real pleasure to meet you.'

'Thank you David, that's a very interesting offer,' said Veronica, slightly irritated that it took a man to get a smile out of these two self-professed feminists.

'Anytime,' he said. 'June, I was just talking to your very nice new English teacher Margaret, and we were thinking of putting some of her girls up for the Christmas show.'

Dear me, thought Veronica. I hope that one doesn't run away with itself. But it certainly was time they had a good turn-out again. Mrs Ferrers had always had lots of excuses as to why she couldn't quite put her girls up this year.

Miss Starling sniffed. 'Maybe,' she said. 'What were you thinking of?'

'Christmas poetry and prose set to music,' said David. 'Lots of Dickens and Eliot and so on. Huge fun.'

'I think Eliot is terribly elitist,' said Pat.

'Good,' said David.

'That sounds suitable,' said June Starling, ignoring Pat completely. 'I expect you'll be wanting our auditorium.'

'You do have the proscenium arch.'

'We do,' said Veronica, smiling at him, and wondering

how many good kudos points they'd get for doing it. 'Well, the third formers don't often get a chance to join in . . . that sounds wonderful. As long as you don't distract our Miss Adair too much.'

'I promise,' said David.

'You know, many of our schools now prefer to use "ms",' said Pat.

'Or first names only, to foster a sense of equality,' said Liz.

'Good God,' said David, beating a hasty retreat.

'See?' he said on his return. 'It's all arranged. She's lovely.'

'You did that on purpose,' said Maggie.

'What?'

'Pretended to ask those two boots over to your school.'

David's face turned serious. 'No I didn't. Why would I do that? I think it's good for the boys to be exposed to all sorts of people.'

Maggie bit her tongue so she didn't say anything sharp.

'Not to worry,' she said, as Claire came up to them and started to moan about being trapped by the agony of the non-French French master from Downey Boys.

'His accent, it ees *atrocious*. Like un tiny petit horse who can't stop being sick.'

Maggie and David looked at each other and grinned. Great, thought Maggie. An ally.

Simone lay awake, listening to the waves outside crashing against the rocks below. She couldn't sleep, her heart pounding. The day had been confusing from start to finish. She didn't know what she was supposed to eat here. She didn't know what on earth the girls were talking about; St Barts, and the South of France and eventing and dressage and how many dogs they had. She'd understood completely, though, the looks they'd given her as she'd entered each new class. English had been followed by maths, at which she shone, even though the class moved at a much faster pace here.

She liked that and the skinny, slightly odd Miss Beresford who taught it in a quick, humourless clipped style, as if the laws of mathematics were the only important thing in the universe and everything else was ephemeral. Simone would have loved to agree with her. But she couldn't. Everything else *was* important. Having a friend. That was so important. Fliss and Alice were horrible, but she was so envious of how quickly they'd turned up and decided they liked each other. Both pretty – one dark, one blonde – and both so *thin*. Why did it work like that? Why did you only get to have friends if you were thin? She'd thought maybe Imogen, the other girl in the dorm, might be easier, with her thick glasses, but she didn't want to chat at all, just get back to her books. Based on what she had on her desk – molecular biology, introduction to canine anatomy, and the hundreds of postcards of animals pinned up – Simone had asked her shyly if she wanted to be a vet. Imogen had nodded vehemently. And that had been the end of the conversation.

Another nightmare had been the afternoon. Simone had been shocked to see on her timetable that there were four periods of PE a week. Back at her old school they'd been slashed down to one, and she'd always got her mother to give her a note. Her and Krystal Fogerty who was nearly sixteen stone and boasted about how when she left school she was going to get to go straight onto disability because she had obesity syndrome. They'd sit it out in the changing rooms and normally Simone would go to the vending machine for them – until they took the vending machine away.

Here, it was PE nearly every day. And half days on Saturdays girls were expected to take part in organised events of one kind or another – either sport *again*, or drama or music. Simone usually liked staying in and watching television all day on Saturdays.

So she'd got changed into the school PE kit; short skirts of the kind that had been outlawed at her school for years, as they made all the boys howl like dogs. They'd had to get the age sixteen size to fit her, so it came nearly to her knees at the front but stuck out over her bum at the back, displaying, she was sure, all the cellulite on the backs of her legs. The polo shirt made her breasts look absolutely massive, and her mother hadn't thought to buy her a sports bra, so she was terrified of having to do any painful running.

All the other girls looked so neat and fresh with their skinny legs bare under the skirts, their small breasts perky under the fresh white shirts as they tied numbers on their backs. Simone started to sweat with nerves. This was bound to show up on her shirt. Now she felt even more anxious. Everyone thought fat girls sweated a lot, and now this would prove it. She wiped her damp hands nervously on her skirt. Oh God, please, please let them not pick teams. She couldn't bear that.

Miss James, the games mistress, walked in, stern and muscular looking.

'Hello,' she said to everyone. 'Sit down.' The girls perched around the changing rooms in twos and threes. Simone sat on the edge, folding her arms over her stomach to stop other people looking at it. Fliss and Alice were sitting together with their hair tied up in identical high ponytails.

'Now,' she said. 'Downey House has a sports tradition to be proud of. We fight hard and we fight fair. Those are the rules of the school, and I want you to work just as hard here as you do for your university entrance or anything else you do. Fulfil your potential.'

She peered round fiercely for a moment.

'Because I don't like it when we get our arses kicked.'

For a second there was a stunned silence at a teacher swearing. Then a murmuring at the release of tension. Miss James was obviously all right.

'OK' she said. 'I've no idea whether you're a bunch of tigers or pussies. So . . .' Then she went round the room and numbered them one, two, one, two. 'The ones are playing the twos,' she said. 'Have you all got that or do I have to run through it again for the mathematically challenged?'

Sylvie, an inordinately pretty girl with golden curly hair and round blue eyes, blinked and looked as if she was about to raise her hand, then put it down again.

'OK then. If you don't have your own stick, grab one on your way out.'

Simone was a one. She made her way out as slowly as possible so nobody could walk behind her and look at her rear. The other girls had glanced at her but so far there'd been no remarks or unpleasantness. At least, not so she could hear. If there'd been boys here, they'd have already been doing whale imitations all over the floor.

'You,' said Miss James. Simone was looking out on the huge playing fields. It was quite a sight. There was a running track, several netball courts, hockey fields, a lacrosse pitch and equipment for track and field events. The grass ran on for what seemed like miles, down towards the cliff edge, where there was a wooden fence. And beyond the cliffs was just the sea, choppy waters all the way to France. It was beautiful. Simone was struck by the skyline, absolutely nothing like the single grey asphalt multi-purpose pitch with weeds growing up under the stones that graced St Cats.

'You!' said Miss James again. Simone realised she was being spoken to.

'Good morning! Glad to have you with us!'

Some of the girls giggled. 'Sorry, miss,' said Simone, staring at the grass. She couldn't believe she was getting into trouble with the teachers. The one thing that never happened to her was getting into trouble with the teachers.

'I want you in goal,' said Miss James. 'Think you could be useful there?'

It wasn't really a question. Simone opened her mouth to say that she'd never played hockey before, then thought better of it, donned the blue vest she'd been given and marched off to the far end of the pitch.

'OK,' Miss James was saying. 'Any volunteers for centre-forwards?'

It was pretty obvious how to play, Simone realised, watching the girls attack the small solid puck-like ball. You pretended you were going in to whack the ball, then you whacked the others' legs instead. It was clearly vicious. Simone shivered in the freshening wind coming off the sea. Fortunately most of it was taking place up the other end of the pitch for now, but she was dreading it coming her way. She had no idea what she was doing.

Miss James was right amongst the throng, sizing people up, seeing who could play and had serious potential, who hated pulling their weight and who slacked. She'd felt sorry for the bigger girl, who obviously felt horribly self-conscious. Trying not to be cruel she'd put her as far out of the way as possible, where she might even manage to get over her nerves. But really. What were parents thinking of, letting their children get so heavy? Didn't they know it was cruel?

Simone realised the play was hotting up as the girls in the green vests were coming her way, amongst them Alice, but not Fliss, as of course they'd been sitting next to one another. She stiffened with nerves.

'Goal! Goal!' some of the girls down the end were shouting, as the action moved closer and closer to Simone's end. She felt her heart in her throat. Suddenly, there was Alice, right in front of her, whacking the ball towards her with all her might. Without thinking, Simone launched herself and her stick at it – and the ball bounced off the end of her stick and back out into the field. A huge cheer went up from the girls in the blue vests as Miss James blew her whistle. Simone went pink, entirely taken by surprise, even as Alice said, 'Well, of course she's going to block the goal', in a nasty tone of voice, especially as the teacher said 'Well done'. Simone swallowed. She was so used to steering clear of sport. It must have been a fluke.

But, as the game progressed it became obvious that her goal-keeping skills weren't a fluke. That, ungainly and lumbering as she could be, she was good at anticipating when the ball was going to come thudding towards her, and from what angle. The blue team won by some considerable margin, largely due to her efforts. All the way back to the changing rooms the girls talked to her, asked her where she'd played before, and were friendly. Simone couldn't believe it, it felt like a totally new sensation. When she told them she'd never played before they were even more flatteringly surprised and one, a big sporty girl called Andrea whose parents lived in New Zealand, and who had scored all the goals for the blue team, announced that if they let her pick a team, Simone would be on it. Simone felt herself almost bursting with pride.

Back in the changing room, though, her heart sank as she

followed the girls into the showers. They weren't communal, but the girls sashayed up to them with only small white towels and, it seemed to Simone, so much confidence. Even though they kept squeezing non-existent bulges in the mirrors over the sinks and saying loudly, 'God, I am *so* fat' whereupon the rest of the girls would chorus, 'No you're not, you're *soo skinny*', and another one would take up the mantra. Simone wondered if she could take two towels in, and waited till everyone had dived off to break before she started to get dressed. There was no one to wait behind for her, even if she was not a bad goalie.

Chapter Six

The first few weeks of the new term passed in a blur. Maggie found every day her nerves at facing her classes grew less and less. It was such a refreshing change having classes filled with conscientious students, anxious to learn – often she discovered lesson plans were too short, as she had factored in her traditional disciplinary time.

In a funny way, though, she missed the boys. She missed their smart-alec remarks, their easy laughter; the way they bounded in like mischievous puppies, clouting one another with their schoolbags. She didn't miss their aftershavey, sweaty boy smell, but she did even miss the way they teased the girls. The lairy, shouty nature of it had always offended her at the time, and of course she'd had her fair share of girls in floods of tears; with late periods or worse. But now it was so much harder to get a sense for the emotional temperature of the forms. Girls' whispering was harder to monitor than boys' fighting, and whether they were sharing confidences that would make them intimate friends for ever, or planning to completely exclude someone else from the lunch table could be hard to ascertain.

And that was what was difficult. She could hear it in the elaborately elongated vowels the girls used when they were talking to her. The little remarks when she tried to introduce a contemporary poet, particularly a Scottish one. Obviously her strictness with Felicity Prosser hadn't had quite the desired effect. She was finding these girls intimidating, she couldn't help it. And on one level that was obviously showing, and they were taking advantage. Odd, how a rowdy class of forty kids shouting didn't bother her, but a silent one of fourteen was so unsettling. Plus their horrible assumptions. When reading about a character buying a lottery ticket, they'd all fixed her with large eyes.

'Have you ever bought one of those?' Sylvie Brown, her blue eyes wide and her golden hair cascading down her back, had asked her innocently.

'No,' lied Maggie. She bought one every week; she and Stan used their birthdays.

'My father says they're a stupidity tax,' announced Ursula confidently. Alice was watching Maggie closely.

'Would you say they're a stupidity tax, miss?' she asked slyly.

Maggie found herself slightly stuttering for words, and was sure the girls had noticed. And Stan wasn't best pleased to hear that he would have to buy the weekly lottery ticket from now on. Maggie didn't want to get caught out by someone from the school at the village store.

The weather grew colder. Now, some mornings, Maggie was waking with frost on the outside of the window pane. She'd thought it would be milder here, but out exposed at the edge of the country there was a real chill to the wind whistling through the eaves. Also, the central heating was on as low as was possible. She wondered if this was a money saving exercise, but Claire had assured her Veronica believed it was good for the girls not to get too stuffy, and good for the complexion too, and she'd had a cashmere throw for her bed sent over from a friend in Bruges, would Maggie like one too?

Maggie pushed her younger form on through more contemporary poetry that she thought they might like, and the compulsory Shakespeare, where she had to take the expanse of daunting-seeming blank verse and shape it; mould it into something digestible, alive and relevant to younger minds – to all minds she remembered a lecturer saying once. It could be a slog, but it was a highly satisfying one, as the girls finally caught the rhythm and intent behind the beautiful words. The work wasn't a problem; the girls were smart, and diligent. But their attitude to her was ... she sighed. Her problem.

Three weeks in, Veronica summoned her to her office. Maggie swore to herself, wishing she didn't feel so nervous. Veronica had spoken to her casually a few times, of course, but Maggie usually sat at meals with Claire, who was great fun and by some distance the youngest member of the staff, or took her lunch upstairs.

A couple of times when it had been sunny enough she'd taken her lunch out to the moor – the girls weren't allowed to leave the premises unsupervised until the fifth form, by which time they never wanted to go outside, just hang around the common room complaining about the curfew and pretending they were desperate for a cigarette. So Maggie would take a sandwich and stroll across the lavender-scented moors and find a sheltered spot overlooking the sea where she could gaze out and try and forget her petty frustrations; her overwhelming sense of not fitting in. Sometimes great freighters rolled past on their way to Ireland, but she never saw David out walking Stephen Daedalus again. She could have gone out early in the morning, but now with lesson plans and catching up on the marking she should have done instead of watching *Lost* the night before, mornings were too fussed. Plus, she was a bit embarrassed. She didn't want it to seem as if she was out looking for him.

She was, though, she admitted to herself one day, staring out across the white-crested heads of the waves at a long vessel loaded with Maersk crates, a little lonely. She missed Stan. Their nightly phone calls were degenerating into short recountings of their days, with a lot, she felt, being left unsaid. The silences were growing longer, the calls shorter. She had promised to go and see him at half-term but wasn't really looking forward to it and was half considering, if the situation didn't improve a little, accompanying the girls staying behind to London for an outing.

And her sister's emails, whilst friendly, were a little short. She still hadn't been forgiven for giving up on aunt duty. 'Cody and Dylan are fine,' Anna would write, and Maggie could almost feel the tightness behind the words. 'Dylan has been excluded from nursery and Cody has nits again.' Then she would relent a little and tell her about a zoo they'd visited, or how Stan had come round and played football with them and they'd pretended to be Celtic winning the European Cup and then all gone out for KFC then gone home and watched *Dr Who*, which had had Dylan up all night fretting, and Maggie would feel a huge tug of longing for home; a desire to say sod it all, you stupid posh girls.

She didn't mean to tell any of this to Dr Deveral, however, and sat rather nervously outside her office, as Miss Prenderghast smiled at her sweetly. Miss Prenderghast smiled at everyone sweetly, though, whether you were there for an award or there to get kicked out for ever. Maggie was aware, somewhat uneasily, that there was a probationary period in her contract, and she was still in it. Surely Veronica couldn't be about to tell her to go home? That she wasn't suited to this school? Maybe there'd been complaints. Suddenly she felt her heart beginning to race. OK, Miss Starling didn't seem to like her, but she hadn't really given her a fair chance from the start – she thought back to the previous week when Miss Starling had stopped her in the corridor and called her into her classroom.

'I hear you and Mr McDonald are doing a *performance*,' she'd said in the same tone of voice she might have used to announce, 'are planning to bring in poisonous *snakes*.'

'Yes, Miss Starling,' Maggie had said. 'I was just coming to discuss it with you, see which classes would be best. I thought Middle School 1 . . .'

'That class,' Miss Starling had said, whilst methodically arranging the exercise books on her desk. Miss Starling always seemed to be tidying something. '. . . is best suited to total disruption, mild hysteria, and attempting to destroy the confidence of whichever mite is unlucky enough to get the leading role. I don't approve. However, as it seems you got someone else to ask me in public . . .'

'That wasn't my idea,' said Maggie, instantly regretting it. Now she sounded like she was trying to weasel out of responsibility. Also, she really ought to have talked it over anyway, days ago. 'I'm sorry,' she'd added. 'I should have . . .'

'Well, it's done now,' Miss Starling had said, with a glance that made it clear that Maggie could leave. 'At least don't turn it into one of those dreadful PC Winterval shows you see at other schools,' she'd added disdainfully.

'No,' Maggie had said, and was then cross with herself for not standing up for her background. Although the semi-stripper dancing the fourth years had done last year at Holy Cross to the tune of *Santa Baby* and the howls and stamping of the boys probably wouldn't have done the trick.

95

She worried whether Miss Starling had complained to Veronica. Talked about trampling on her toes, or getting in the way? Maybe Miss Starling didn't think she was up to it. Maybe the girls had slagged her off to their parents and they'd made a complaint? Maggie steeled herself as Veronica came to the door.

'Maggie. Hello,' she said, with a small smile. Maggie followed her into the room with some trepidation. Veronica sat down on the red velvet upholstered couch and indicated that Maggie should do the same. Miss Prenderghast brought in the teapot on a tray, biscuits nicely arranged. Maggie tried to ignore them; she knew Veronica would no more eat a biscuit than perm her hair.

'So, Maggie,' said Veronica, leaning forward. 'How are you finding things?'

Maggie swallowed. 'Well . . . I mean, I really like it,' she said. 'I think it's a really good school. It's so nice to work with some great materials.'

This was true. For example, Maggie had always had a weakness for stationery. At Holy Cross she'd always had to sign in and out of the stationery cupboard and keep to a strictly rationed budget to make sure she didn't steal any staplers from the workplace. Here, although Miss Starling had eyed her beadily, seeing her face light up with the brand new equipment and wide range of teaching aids, pens, computers and AV, no one tried to intimate that she was about to pillage the place and set up a secondary concern. Here, nobody had to share a book (at Holy Cross it had been one between three, sometimes) or complain about their pens running out. Oddly this had the effect of making Maggie feel guilty.

'And what about our girls?' asked Veronica. 'Are they great materials too?'

Maggie felt herself colour. 'They're good. Most of them.'

'But? I sense a but.'

'Oh, nothing. I just wonder if they're perhaps a little complacent.'

Veronica twisted her pearl earrings. 'How so?'

Maggie thought of Felicity and Alice. Right from day one – when she had, she knew, shown a heavy hand with punishment – they had taken against her; chatted and made remarks whenever they felt themselves unobserved and in general showed a thorough lack of respect; turning up late, and usually sniggering. Felicity's work was poor too, which was strange as, according to her old school report, she was an extremely able pupil. From which Maggie could only conclude that she was doing it on purpose. To annoy her.

'I mean, they've just got such a sense of entitlement,' finished Maggie crossly. 'Sorry. That probably sounds really chippy.'

Veronica smiled to herself. 'A little.' Maggie glanced down.

'Felicity Prosser probably thinks she's the unhappiest girl in this whole school,' said Veronica.

'You're joking.'

'No. I could tell straight away. Her sister has done very well here. A little intense for my taste, if you know what I mean, but very much a success. I don't think Prosser minor wanted to come here at all.'

'Well, that's clear enough.'

'I'd keep her away from that little minx Alice Trebizon-Woods. I've had her two sisters through as well and they're all attention seekers of the highest order. Parents in the diplomatic corps, hardly notice them. But you might do all right then with Felicity – and all of your Middle School 1.'

So, she had heard. Maggie felt her ears burn.

'I know you can do it,' said Veronica gently. Maggie bit

her lip, in case she started to cry. Veronica spotted this immediately and swiftly changed the subject. 'Well, I wanted to mention two other things,' she said. 'Firstly, there's another girl in MS1 I want you to keep an eye on.'

'Simone Kardashian,' said Maggie without hesitation, glad for the change of subject.

'Yes. She's one of our scholarship girls. Very smart, but needs dragging out of herself. Miss James is doing wonders with her in sport, but it's not enough. She could do with a friend. I know you can't work miracles, but she's very bright and I'd hate for her to waste her potential.'

'I'll try.' Maggie was incredibly relieved. Veronica had referenced the situation, but didn't seem to think there was anything to worry about.

In fact, Veronica had expected this to happen. Downey's girls often hadn't met people from other backgrounds who weren't staff of some sort. Maggie needed to learn to cope. But she shouldn't be doing it alone.

Feeling slightly better, Maggie waited to hear what the other thing was. It must be the show. She and David had emailed a couple of times about it. She got a little surge of excitement whenever one of his emails pinged up. They were always chatty and beautifully written, and they'd narrowed the choice of extracts for the show down to four, which Mrs Offili, the music teacher, was now looking at how to stage.

'Secondly, you, Maggie. You know this isn't prison. You are quite welcome to get out and explore a bit, meet friends and so on. Go and visit your family.'

Maggie was surprised Dr Deveral had been so observant.

'Thank you,' she said, 'but they're so far away. And I have seen something of Claire and . . .' she felt a little embarrassed saying his name out loud, '. . . David.'

Veronica arched an eyebrow. She'd thought as much. 'Do you have . . . and forgive me for stepping outside the professional arena for a moment, but do you have a boyfriend?'

Maggie nodded, feeling obscurely embarrassed at Veronica even having to use such an adolescent word.

'Why don't you invite him down at half-term? He can't stay here, of course, but I can recommend a good B&B in the village. Teaching is a demanding job, Margaret, as you are currently finding. We all need to relax sometimes.'

Maggie had returned to her rooms with conflicting thoughts. After all, getting Stan down here was the right thing to do. He could see she hadn't run away from him for a life of champagne and fun and whatever else he seemed to think she was doing down here.

On the other hand, she thought suddenly, would Stan fit in around here? Could she trust him not to make inappropriate remarks all the time and, well, *embarrass* her? She imagined Claire, with her immaculate outfits, listening to Stan discuss his latest triumphs in Championship Manager, but it was difficult to picture.

Veronica watched her walk across the forecourt. Actually, Maggie was settling in much better than she had expected. Miss Starling had reported that although a little 'trendy' for her tastes (Veronica suspected anything that wasn't simply memorising lines would be a little trendy for June Starling, particularly given they were studying poetry that didn't rhyme), but committed and hard-working, which was the most important thing in a young teacher. Finesse could come later; they were all there to help. Oh. She remembered what she'd forgotten to mention. Maggie was wearing a blue and white striped shirt that looked like it was half of a pair of pyjamas, and a grey skirt that wasn't quite the right length for her. She *must* have a word with her about her dress.

'I can't believe they take away your phones.'

Fliss was raging, and Alice was agreeing with her.

'I mean, it's completely fascist. One hour a day? That's just, like evil and against your rights and things.'

'Yeah,' said Alice, whose mother could never remember the time difference and thus rarely rang.

'You know in Guildford, I'm allowed to go shopping on my own. Here you're not even blooming allowed out unless there's six of you and a teacher! Until upper fourth! It's prison.'

Alice was trying to do her prep, but Fliss was deliberately ignoring hers, so Alice pushed it to one side. Egging on Fliss was more fun anyway.

'And then they fob us off with stupid common teachers.' Fliss stuck out her bottom lip.

'We need to do a trick,' said Alice.

'A trick?' said Fliss, as they drank Orangina in the dorm. Imogen was working quietly. Simone was nowhere to be seen.

'Yeah, you know. A good practical joke that everyone will piss themselves about.'

'I know some good ones,' said Fliss. 'What about putting cellophane over the teachers' toilets?'

Alice sniffed. 'Old hat,' she said. 'We need something amazing.'

'Flour bombs?' ventured Fliss.

'You've got to think big,' said Alice. 'I shall put my brain to work. And who should be the victim?'

'Well, not Miss Beresford,' said Fliss, thinking uncomfortably back to a conversation they'd had earlier that week, when the stern maths mistress had unfavourably compared the marks she was getting here with how she'd done at her old school. It was hard to make a protest about how much you hated somewhere when you actually had to get in trouble and endure the consequences. Miss Beresford had exhorted her not to let herself down. Fliss wanted to burst into tears and claim it wasn't fair, her parents were letting her down, but she thought she was unlikely to meet with much sympathy, and she'd have been right. Miss Beresford came from a poor background and, although she enjoyed teaching maths here, thought some of these little madams didn't know they were born.

'No, she has no sense of humour at all,' agreed Alice. 'Why else would you be a maths teacher?'

Fliss couldn't think. She'd seen Alice's maths books though. She'd scored 94.

'What about that horrid old bitch Miss Adair?' Fliss was still stinging from Maggie's putting her down.

'Ah, Miss What Not To Wear,' said Alice thoughtfully. 'You know, I think she might be just right. She's so keen for everyone to like her, she'll probably laugh it off and not get us into trouble at all. Plus she's totally green.'

'Yeah,' said Fliss. 'Great. What shall we do?'

Alice smiled. 'Leave it to me,' she said.

They turned their attention to a parcel sitting on Simone's bed.

'Can you believe how much stuff she gets?' said Alice.

Fliss couldn't, especially when she was lucky to get the odd postcard. There was barely a couple of days went by without a large box arriving, with tinfoil-covered packages and cake boxes.

'Does she think that you have to pay for the food here?' said Alice. 'Honestly, there's so many empty cartons in the bin. It's really starting to smell. We'll get mice. You're not even supposed to have food here.' She went to her bed by the window. 'God, it smells. I hate it. I'm going to tell her.'

'No, Alice, don't.'

'I'm serious!' Alice looked crossly out the window. 'We all watch what we eat and I'm on like a total diet, and the place is a rats' nest of cakes. It's not fair. And she eats too much anyway.'

'Alice, don't be mean, please.' Fliss didn't mind being horrible to teachers and grown-ups, and whoever else it would take to get her out of here. But picking on another girl she didn't like.

But Alice had that glint in her eye as Simone came in. She'd been trying to use the old payphone down the hall and couldn't get it to work. She couldn't believe that her mum had used the guideline 'we discourage the middle school girls from having mobile phones' as an actual gospel law of the school. She was the only girl without one, not even for emergencies. As usual her mum's phone was engaged. She always had a million people to talk to. Just not her.

'Hi Simone,' said Alice. Simone looked up. Alice didn't usually do much more than grunt at her. Fliss was a bit better, but not much.

'Look, Simone,' said Alice, getting down from the window. 'Can we have a word?'

Fliss didn't like being dragged into this like it was a communal decision.

'Now, we know, you're like, a compulsive eater or whatever, and that it's like a disease and stuff and we want you to know that we're not prejudiced and we really care about you and your illness.'

Alice widened her eyes in fake concern. Simone stared at her, confused and cornered.

'But we were wondering if it might be possible . . . I mean, not if it's too much trouble . . . we don't want to make things worse or anything, but if you could keep your, like, totally disgusting food out of the dorm?'

She indicated the parcel Mrs Kardashian had stickily wound a whole rope of Sellotape around.

'Is that OK?'

Simone picked up the parcel, turned around and fled.

Maggie was heading for bed. It was her turn to do rounds, just to check all the girls were in bed and tucked up. It was a cold dark night outside, with rain throwing itself at the windows, and everyone seemed quite happy to be tucked up. Maggie picked up a couple of stray towels. She quite liked saying good night to everyone; it made her feel pastoral.

In Fliss and Alice's dorm room there was much whispering going on and no Simone. Maggie switched the overhead light on.

'Where is she?' she demanded. Fliss and Alice were both in bed, looking as though butter wouldn't melt in their mouths. Alice gave her most innocent look.

'I don't know, Miss Adair. She got a food parcel and went off . . . maybe to eat it?'

Maggie gave her a hard look. 'Did she seem in a strange mood?'

It wasn't like Simone to be late for anything.

Alice propped herself up on her elbows. 'You know, we're a bit worried about her. Like, she might have a problem with food or something?'

Maggie hated to admit it, but the dark haired little minxy girl might have a point. Even in the few weeks they'd been there, she'd noticed Simone taking extra rolls at breakfast, queueing at the little tuckshop. She'd put weight on, for sure. Although there was plenty of exercise prescribed on the curriculum, Simone did no extra sporting activities on offer at the weekends or after school hours; she didn't take any walks on the moors like the other girls did on their Sunday free time after church. And there was certainly plenty of hearty good fare – Mrs Rhys, head of the catering service, was of the old school. Traditional stodge, and lots of it; toast, steamed puddings, custard, stews and roly-poly. Maggie adored the food and was having to be very strict with herself. Simone, it appeared, was not.

'Lights out,' she said sharply to the girls. 'I'll bring her back myself.'

Fliss lay awake in the dark. It had sounded like Alice was being interested in Simone and worried about her problem. But she knew she wasn't.

Maggie didn't have to go far. Just around the corner was an alcove, the underside of a spiral staircase. It was covered from plain view by a curtain, and the girls normally used it for confidences, or phone calls. Tonight, though, Maggie could tell by the movement of the curtain that there was someone there.

'Simone?' she said, quietly. There was no answer. 'Simone?' she tried again.

A voice clearly trying to disguise its sobbing said, 'I'm fine. Go away.'

Maggie pulled across the curtain. Simone had obviously thought she was another pupil, as she genuinely flinched when she saw her.

'Miss Adair.'

'That's right,' said Maggie. 'And sorry, but I'm not going away.'

There was a bench in the corner of the alcove. Maggie sat

down and beckoned Simone to do the same. Her face was smeared with tears and what looked like jam.

Maggie sat in silence for a couple of minutes until Simone's hiccupy sobs had slowed. 'Now,' she said. 'What's up?'

'I don't fit in here,' said Simone.

'Oh, neither do I,' said Maggie, remembering Miss Starling, who that morning had mentioned that Maggie seemed to be 'rushing' in the corridor, and that if she was better prepared in the mornings, perhaps she wouldn't have to. 'I wouldn't worry about that.'

'The other girls,' sniffed Simone. 'They're so confident and pretty. None of them is fat and their mothers don't send them stuff to eat and they all got to be friends really quickly and . . .'

'Ssssh,' said Maggie, looking around for a handkerchief and making do with a paper napkin, presumably packed by the ever-prepared Mrs Kardashian.

'Now look,' she said. 'Of course you're not going to feel right here immediately. These girls all went to primary school together. Their mothers all came here. That's just how it was.'

Simone nodded.

'But that's not important, is it? Do you know how many of them could have got a scholarship like you did?'

Simone shook her head.

'None of them, that's how many.'

In fact, Maggie had been very impressed with Simone's work, particularly her poems which, whilst full of terrible angst and some horrible spelling, also had a good use of language and structure for her age.

'You're just as good as them, Simone. Better, in some instances. So you have no reason to do yourself down. And are you sure these . . .' She tilted her head towards the large pile of polenta cakes that had disgorged from the bag. 'Do you think these are helping, Simone?'

Simone shook her head miserably. 'But my mum sends them, and I'm just so fed up and I don't know what to do.'

'Would you like me to have a word with your mum, tell her she's not allowed to send you food for, I don't know, say environmental reasons or something. Would that help?'

Simone shrugged. 'I'm so fat though. It wouldn't make any difference.'

'You might be amazed,' said Maggie. 'And I hear you're doing brilliantly at sport.'

Simone twisted the corner of her pyjamas and didn't say anything.

'Fewer cakes, bit more sport, you'd look better in no time, with your lovely teenage metabolism,' said Maggie, adding quickly, 'only if you want to change, of course.'

'Of course I want to change,' said Simone. 'Nobody talks to me.'

'Well, I'm sure once everyone settles down that will change. It's very early in the year.'

'These things never change,' said Simone. Maggie didn't want to tell a lie and contradict her. Sometimes they did, sometimes they didn't.

'Well, listen,' she said. 'How about, when you feel like you need someone to talk to, you can come over and visit me.'

Simone gave a sidelong glance which indicated she didn't really believe her.

'Just pop in. I have lots of books. And not just set books either. I've got the new Sophie Kinsella *and* the new Lisa Jewell.'

Maggie could tell Simone's ears were pricking up. She wasn't the first girl to take solace in reading. And it would be better for her than hiding away stuffing cake in her face, that was for sure.

'The new new one?' said Simone, sniffing. 'In hardback?'

'I was saving it,' said Maggie. 'But I'll let you have first dibs.'

Simone got down from the bench. 'Thanks.'

'No problem. Will I take this away?' Maggie indicated the cake. Simone nodded.

'Right. Get to bed then before I have to report you and Miss Starling will have to see you.'

This had the desired effect. Simone scampered away.

'And brush your teeth!' said Maggie.

'I'm really going to get that sarky Miss Adair now,' Alice hissed to Fliss the next morning as they were brushing their teeth. 'Thinks she's bloody Mother McTeresa.'

'This school sucks,' agreed Fliss. 'We need out.'

Chapter Seven

The school was busy. First were auditions for the Christmas readings. The Christmas concert was a big point in the calendar. The school orchestra, jazz band and dance troupe were all expected to perform for the parents, but as the middle school girls were so new, they were given readings to punctuate the performances. Traditionally there were lots of girls interested in this, as they were joined by the choristers from the boys' school, which meant they got a chance to meet the boys – the first two years weren't allowed to attend the mixed Christmas party; neither the parents nor Veronica liked the idea. They had a party afternoon of their own in class and there was a special Christmas dinner and that was quite enough.

'I'm sure they'll just be babies,' Alice was saying, mugging heartily over 'Journey of the Magi'. 'No use to us.'

'Deffo,' said Fliss. 'I don't want to do it anyway.'

Stand up in front of her parents and the whole school? Not bloody likely. If anything was going to prove that she'd given in and was now sucking it up it would be that, and she'd never get the chance to get back before all her friends had formed a new clique without her and started treating her like she was stuck up and horsey, the way they'd always talked about boarding-school girls. That, and the fact that their parents hated them, of course.

There was a drama teacher at the school – the rather suspiciously named Fleur Parsley – who had long hair, long skirts and floated around the place (she also taught at Downey Boys). Lots of the girls had a crush on her. Maggie found her a tad emetic. As far as Maggie could tell, she spent a lot of time getting the girls to roll around the ground pretending to be animals. No wonder they loved drama and couldn't get their prep in on time.

Liz and Pat had loved Fleur's class, as Maggie discovered when the four found themselves sitting together at lunch.

'Then you took on the characteristics of multicultural animals from around the globe,' Pat was enthusing.

Fleur smiled modestly. She was very beautiful, with long pre-Raphaelite hair and an extremely slim figure, and Pat and Liz were obviously enjoying being around her.

'Well, I believe . . .' she said. She had a very affected voice clear as a bell, and liked to intimate that she'd given up a highly successful career as an actress because she was so dedicated to teaching. '. . . that the girls here should experience influences from all over the world. They can't help being so privileged, but it's no excuse for ignorance.'

Pat and Liz nodded emphatically. 'Exactly,' said Pat.

'It's a bit like doing the *Lion King*, isn't it?' said Maggie to make conversation.

'It's actually nothing like the *Lion King*?' said Fleur. Her voice tended to go up at the end of sentences. 'It's like an opportunity for the girls to experience the consciousness of different groups of animals that exist . . . and are often persecuted . . . throughout the world?'

'Oh,' said Maggie, tucking into her macaroni cheese. 'I see.'

'I feel it's important to bring a spiritual dimension to my work,' said Fleur. Pat, and Liz, who was on her second helping of macaroni, nodded vigorously.

'Well, I suppose I have the Christmas readings coming up,' said Maggie. 'I could do with your help, Fleur.'

'Oh, I'm *so* busy,' said Fleur, smoothing back her hair.

'What methodology are you using to action that?' asked Pat.

Maggie hesitated as she unravelled the question. 'Well, I thought I'd get them all to do a reading in class, then choose two girls from that.'

Pat and Liz recoiled in horror.

'You're planning to . . . humiliate the girls in front of their peers?' said Liz in horror.

'No,' said Maggie. 'But I think it's important that they can speak in front of other people, and I need to get an idea as to who can handle it and who will crumple in front of the audience.'

'I don't really, like believe in competition in art?' said Fleur, pushing her macaroni around her plate.

'I thought acting was very competitive,' said Maggie. Fleur didn't bother replying, but let a smile play around her lips.

'I'm not sure making the children *audition* . . .'

'I'm not necessarily looking for the best,' said Maggie.

'That's good, because I don't think terminology like "best" is very helpful in an educational scenario,' said Pat.

'I'm looking to see who would benefit the most.'

Pat and Liz looked at each other.

'With your permission, we'd like to sit in on that class,' said Pat.

'Of course,' said Maggie, trying to hide her disgruntlement. Actually, two complete strangers in the class would make it much harder for the girls, surely they could see that. But she didn't want to rock the boat or make things any more difficult than they were already.

The fifteen girls in Middle School Year One all felt nervous that Thursday, and resentful towards their teacher, no matter how cool they professed to be, or how much they pretended that the school concert was a complete waste of time for morons. In fact, secretly, most of them really did want the chance to stand in front of the school and get riotously applauded in front of their parents, especially if they weren't, like Astrid, so musical they'd already made it in to the orchestra.

Astrid Ulverton was such a beautiful clarinet player Mrs Offili was completely torn between wanting to keep her for school music, and urging her parents to march her off to the nearest conservatoire. Astrid's parents believed a career in music was a waste of time and kept trying to get her to work hard at sciences in preparation for medical school. Poor Astrid was a dunce in other subjects, however, and couldn't look at a textbook without making a tune of the words and rapping her fingers on the spine.

Fliss had hurriedly grabbed one of the set pieces the night before, in a thorough temper that Miss Adair was going to get the chance to make her stand up again in front of all her classmates. It was the opening of *Little Women*, which started, '"Christmas won't be Christmas without presents," grumbled Jo, lying on the rug.'

She was going to perform it in the most off-hand way possible, so that she wouldn't get chosen and could stand at the back of the choir and look sulky. Alice was doing 'Journey of the Magi', by T. S. Eliot, so she could be very dramatic and act out being an old man. She'd done it already for Fliss in the alcove and Fliss had been very impressed. The other option was a big long extract from *A Christmas Carol* which was far too boring and hard to memorise, so only the complete dweebs would pick that.

Maggie was nervous. She wasn't sure if this was a good idea, and talking to Pat and Liz hadn't helped matters. But no. It said in the prospectus that Downey House was about turning out confident, well-rounded young women. Jobs were all about talking to groups and it wasn't as if she was getting them to read out their own stuff, which she was thinking of doing with the year nines. It hadn't worked terribly well at Holy Cross. The boys tended to write stories about how their gang had beaten up another gang, and the class would bang on the desks and shout out at apposite moments and sometimes real fights would come out of it. She'd quickly abandoned the concept.

'OK, class,' she said. It was a bright and chilly late November day. She'd noticed in the mirror that morning that her cheeks were pinker than usual, probably as a result of spending more time out of doors. Her eyes were clearer too. A lot less alcohol and some decent food were really working on her looks.

'All right, class. We're going to go for it. Nobody has to memorise anything yet, we're just going to concentrate on projection and focus.'

'Miss Fleur says focus has to come from within,' said blonde wide-eyed Sylvie earnestly. 'She says it has to come from the heart.'

Pat and Liz, who were perched on their chunky bottoms on desks at the back of the class, nodded gravely.

'Well, Miss *Fleur* is right,' said Maggie, biting back a touch of irritation. 'Speak from the heart. These are lovely pieces, famous for a long time. So, do your best. I'm not looking for the loudest, or the most "acted". I'm looking for you to try hard and show the school what an engaged class we are.'

Sylvie went first, reciting from *Little Women* in a breathless chirp with slightly odd intonation. Maggie led the mandatory clapping. Next up was Astrid, who read the poem in a rhythmic monotone which rendered the scansion almost indecipherable. Third was poor shy Imogen, who was so quiet and mousy Maggie felt terrible asking her to speak up again and again. It didn't help when Pat and Liz started whispering to one another. Maggie was so furious at this rudeness she was tempted to tell them to shut up, before reminding herself that they were judging her, not Imogen, and that she really had to learn to keep her temper in check.

Just as the whole session looked like it was going to be a complete disaster, Alice, next to be called, stood up.

'A cold coming we had of it'

She started with a tragicomically grave, dramatic expression on her face. A few lines later she pointed downwards to some imaginary camels.

'And the camels galled, sore-footed, refractory,
    Lying down in the melting snow.'

She stared out of the window, allowing her pretty face to suddenly look very sad.

'There were times we regretted
    The summer palaces on slopes, the terraces,'

Now she shook her head wildly as if disturbed by the memories.

'And the silken girls bringing sherbet.'

Maggie had to bite her lip to stifle a giggle. She was a monkey, Alice, but she had spirit. Her overacting was ludicrous, but goodness, she was putting in the effort. She put a mark next to her name; if they didn't get any better, she might have to go in.

Alice came to:

'were we led all that way for . . .'

Then she let a dramatic pause linger . . . and linger . . .

'BIRTH? OR DEATH?' she shouted, suddenly, making Pat jump, as she hadn't been paying attention. Could work on lazy parents, Maggie mused.

'Thank you, thank you,' she said, as Alice finished the poem with '*I should be glad of another death*' before throwing herself into a great bow. The applause in the classroom was genuine and loud, and Maggie could see Alice had to work hard to stop a huge grin cracking across her face.

Next it was Simone. Maggie gave her her most encouraging look as the girl slowly got up. Alice smirked at her as she passed on her way back to her seat at the back of the class. Maggie hoped it wasn't going to be a massacre; the girls had enjoyed Alice's performance but wouldn't take too kindly to Simone stuttering along.

Suddenly, as Simone reached the front of the stage and turned to face the audience, Maggie glimpsed Pat and Liz swapping a very obvious look, Liz with an eyebrow raised like she thought she was Simon Cowell, Pat rolling her eyes to heaven. Simone could hardly not have seen it. If anyone ought to be sensitive to the girl, it should be them, with their belief in the virtues of the working classes and their supposed sensitivity to the underdog. Maggie felt the bile rising in her throat, and it was a few moments before she actually tuned in to what Simone was saying.

Simone had decided just to treat it as she did when she got called up every week by her mother to 'do something clever' in front of the aunties, something which had happened on a weekly basis since the moment she could talk. She simply steeled herself and did the best she could.

Years of being forced to perform, however, had rubbed off on her, and as she launched into the Dickens extract, she couldn't help but imbue it with some feeling. It was a book she'd always loved – her parents had bought an entire set of Dickens from a book club and she'd started working her way through them at the age of eleven.

Add to this her naturally gentle, very London-sounding voice, and by the time she reached the phrase, 'I have always thought of Christmas time . . . as a good time: a kind, forgiving, charitable, pleasant time . . . when men and women seem by one consent to open their shut-up hearts freely, and to think of people below them as if they really were fellow-passengers to the grave', Maggie was completely engrossed and marked her up for it immediately. The applause at the end was distinct and heartfelt and Simone looked surprised to hear it, as she'd tried only to focus on the meaning of the words she was saying, and not how she looked. If she stopped to think about how she looked to everyone, she'd just want to curl up in a ball. The applause was a pleasant bonus.

'Well done,' said Maggie, trying to keep her tone from sounding too surprised and patronising.

The next few girls were passable, if unremarkable, and everyone was getting bored with hearing the same three pieces regurgitated again and again. Fliss sighed with the tedium and stared out of the window. A storm looked to be coming in over the sea; the grass and scrub on the clifftops was bending over. There was so much *weather* here, thought Fliss, missing the gentler environs of Surrey. Apparently in London you hardly got weather at all, all the buildings protected you from it. It would be the Christmas party in the village soon. Will Hampton would probably be in town for it. She wondered if she'd see him over Christmas. God, if only her tits would grow. Then at least she might have a tiny chance of him noticing she wasn't a baby any more. She tried to imagine herself out of this bloody itchy navy wool skirt and navy bloody ribbed tights, and into something slinky and, well, maybe even a bit sexy. Or at least that showed a shoulder or something. She would just turn up at the party and it would be like that bit in *Enchanted* when the princess enters the ballroom and everything would go a bit slow and Will would just stop whatever he was doing to stare at her, then advance towards her, with his hands out, completely amazed that he'd never recognised her before . . .'

'Felicity? Felicity Prosser?'

Maggie hated daydreaming, even while she was a chronic sufferer herself. You never knew how much they'd missed and it wasted everyone's time.

'Yes, miss?' said Fliss, as cheekily as she could manage. She was embarrassed to get picked out and even more embarrassed about what she'd been thinking. If her bad marks didn't convince her parents to take her out . . .

'It's your turn,' said Maggie. 'If you could grant us a moment or two of attention.'

A couple of girls tittered, and Fliss felt her face flush.

'Do I really have to, miss?' she asked. 'I don't want to read out at the stupid concert.'

Silence fell immediately. *Nobody* questioned the concert.

Maggie weighed up what was the best way to handle it. If she let her off, she might have full-scale rebellion on her hands. Plus, all the parents were hoping their own daughters would have parts. Plus, this exercise was about reading in public anyway. And she was sick and tired of this girl, whatever Dr Deveral said.

'Don't talk about school events that way, please,' she said briskly. 'I won't have rudeness in my classroom. You can discuss it with Miss Starling if you like, but whilst you're in my class you will try out for the concert.'

Fliss pushed out her lower lip, but wasn't brave enough to continue her rebellion.

'This is like prison or something,' she said, mooching to the front.

'Yes, Felicity, it's exactly like prison,' said Maggie, folding her arms and waiting for Fliss to start reading.

'"Christmas isn't Christmas without presents,"' began Fliss sulkily.

Oddly, her sullen tones enlivened the reading, and Maggie could easily see the petulant Amy, and the stubborn Jo, in the set of Fliss's jaw. By the time she got to Jo examining the heels of her shoes in a gentlemanly manner, Maggie was wondering whether it might be a combination of a good punishment and a good concert to actually put Fliss up for it.

'Can we have a word?' said Pat, as Maggie left the classroom to go and have tea, and the girls dashed off outside.

'Of course,' said Maggie. She was still irritated by their distracting behaviour in her classroom, but wasn't about to mention it.

'You know, when Felicity Prosser said she didn't want to be included in the concert auditioning process . . . we're a little confused as to why you still made her do it.'

Maggie looked at them. 'Because that was the objective of the class – to perform a piece to the rest. Whether you get picked or not isn't really the point.'

'But,' said Liz, 'don't you think Felicity clearly demonstrated articulacy and reasoning skills when she said she didn't want to participate?'

'No,' said Maggie, feeling the heat rise in her face. 'She said it was stupid!'

'In the comprehensive system,' said Pat, adjusting her unflattering glasses, 'we don't believe in humiliating children like that.'

Maggie bit back a retort about how that explained a lot.

'I didn't humiliate her. It was part of the lesson plan, and she actually did very well. How did that humiliate her?'

'Forcing children to do things against their will can destroy their self-esteem,' said Pat, making a mark on a clipboard.

'Young adults,' reproved Liz.

'Young adults,' amended Pat immediately. 'They are individuals too, with their own desires and fears.'

'You don't think children should have to do what they don't want to do?' asked Maggie in amazement.

'We believe in child-centred learning,' said Pat. 'You should look it up sometime.'

Later, Maggie wished with all her heart that she had just let it go and left then. She could have forgotten all about it. But something inside her saw red.

'I *know* about child-centred learning, thank you,' she said, her voice louder than she'd intended. 'I did get a first. And I also think that being pushed outside your comfort zone on occasion is what education is actually about. If you asked some of these girls to direct their own learning we'd spend the entire day kissing ponies. And whilst we're talking about humiliating children – sorry, *young adults* – I could have done without you two whispering, muttering and rolling your eyes all through some of the readings. What do you think that was doing for the girls' self-esteem? You lot thinking you're Simon bloody Cowell! It was disgusting!'

Pat looked taken aback at Maggie's outburst. Liz looked rather jubilant and made some notes on her clipboard. Nobody said anything, as, just then, June Starling walked past.

June Starling had heard a raised voice from two class-rooms over and had headed towards it as quickly as she could. Now she saw Maggie, in some disarray, red in the face, squaring up to the women from the commission. Oh, this was all she needed. Some street fighting from the outsiders.

'What's this?' she asked.

'Did you know you had a lot of dissension in the ranks?' asked Liz in an unpleasant tone. June Starling raised her eyebrows.

'Really?'

Maggie coloured up immediately. 'They're trying to interfere with the way I run my classes,' she spat out, before Liz could get any further.

'That's why we're examiners,' went on Liz in the same patronising way. 'We're trying to help you make things better.'

'But it *doesn't* . . .'

June Starling clasped Maggie firmly by the arm, as she recoiled.

'Oh, you remember when we were young teachers,' she said in as blithe a tone as she could manage to Pat and Liz. 'So full of passion and fire. Keep it up, you two. I can't wait to see you for the girls' cooking afternoon tea. It's entirely vegetarian, and grown on our own grounds.'

'I can't believe your grounds are big enough to have orchards,' sneered Pat, but June was already on the move again, Maggie clamped to her side. She didn't say a word to her until they got to her office.

Maggie sat down on the hard chair there, sure when she explained her side of things, Miss Starling would understand immediately. But then she turned round.

'What on earth were you thinking?' she said, her sharp tone not hiding the anger behind the words. 'Hollering at our school examiners like a fishwife.'

Maggie opened her mouth. 'But . . . but they were being really unfair. Liz said . . .'

'I'm not interested in who said what,' said June. 'I'm interested in passing an assessment that means that parents will be interested in sending children to this school where we can teach them well. And that means, ideally, the young English teacher, who should be setting an absolute shining example of the comprehensive system, and showing that different worlds can exist and integrate side by side, not screeching her head off in full view of the girls. And I know Veronica would agree with me.'

Maggie's heart felt sick. She'd been so sure that when she told her about what the women had said she'd see her side straight away. But obviously this was not to be the case.

'I'm sorry,' she said, feeling her face burn up and not feeling sorry at all.

'Let's say no more about it,' said June. That girl had a very hot-tempered streak that she needed to learn to contain.

'You'll apologise to Patricia and Elizabeth.'

'I *can't*,' said Maggie. 'I don't agree with them.'

'Margaret, you're not one of my pupils. I can't order you to do anything. But you have responsibilities in being a teacher here, and one of them is handling disputes in an appropriate fashion. I don't believe you handled the assessment today in an appropriate fashion, do you?'

Maggie shook her head. 'No.'

'Very well then.'

Miss Starling indicated that she could leave. Maggie wondered whether she'd offer a consoling word on her exit. But she didn't.

'What, no poetry today?'

Stephen Daedalus had found her first, sitting sobbing on a mossy outcrop that led far out to sea. He'd come padding up gently and licked her hand, which only made her cry more. David wasn't far behind.

'Hey, what's the matter?' he'd said gently, as Maggie had desperately scrubbed at her face with one of the tissues she carried in her handbag.

'Nothing,' she'd said fiercely.

David crouched down beside her.

'It's OK, you know. To find everything a bit overwhelming sometimes. You've come a long way.'

'It's not that,' said Maggie, and found herself pouring out the whole story.

'She didn't even want to hear my side! She didn't care, just sided with them straight away.'

David stared out to sea. 'Didn't you ever get inspected at your last school?'

'Yes,' said Maggie, defiantly. 'They thought I was very good.'

121

David smiled. 'I'm sure they did. And did your school pass?'

Maggie wrinkled her nose. 'Well, we didn't get put on special measures. But it was a pretty close thing.'

'And did it affect the roll for the next year?'

Maggie saw what he was getting at. 'I suppose not. But. I was right and they were wrong. I thought June would back me up – or at least hear me out.'

David patted Stephen Daedalus and threw him his stick of the day.

'What you have to realise about June Starling—'

'The poppet,' said Maggie.

'The poppet,' said David. 'Now, don't get prickly. Is that she really, really, cares about the school. Above everything. It's her life's work. She isn't married, she's never had children. The school is all that matters.'

Maggie stuck out her bottom lip, unwilling to admit that he might have a point.

'Did you really shout at them in the corridor?' His face split into its characteristically manic grin.

'A bit. Maybe,' said Maggie. She felt a smile creep on her face. 'Well, they were totally asking for it.'

'Were they?'

'Yes. A bit. OK, OK OK.'

'What?'

'You are *very* irritating. Yes, I shouldn't have shouted at them in the corridor.'

'What did I say?'

'So now I have to go and apologise, do I?'

'Would it really be the hardest thing you've ever had to do?'

'Yes,' said Maggie.

'Really? Goodness, you *have* had an easy life.'

Maggie's lips twitched. 'You are so annoying.'

'That's not me,' said David, 'that's your conscience.'

'Well, I was right actually, so it's not.'

'OK,' said David. 'It's the school's conscience then.'

He stood up and Maggie, wiping her dirty cheek, accepted his hand to her as he pulled her up. When their fingers touched – his hand was warm and dry – she felt herself quiver, and told herself not to be so ridiculous.

'Come on, I'll walk you back.'

Maggie peeked a glance at him as they headed back to the school. 'You really believe all this, don't you?' she said.

'All what?'

'About loyalty to your school and all that.'

David shrugged. 'Why? Do you think I'm an old-fashioned weirdo?'

'No,' said Maggie, though she realised as she did so that yes, she did think he was old-fashioned, and he was perhaps a little bit weird.

'You do!' said David, sounding scandalised. 'You did a big pause! That means you do!'

'Well . . .'

'I'll get you for that,' he said. 'I'll set my very fearsome dog on you.'

'If you can catch me,' said Maggie suddenly, dancing away from him in the crisp autumn air.

'Oh, I can catch you.'

Maggie took off with the wind at her heels, and Stephen Daedalus not far behind. David, taken by surprise, took a moment to set off after her, but when he did he caught up with her with ease. Maggie, feeling his touch on her cardigan, let the baggy garment fall off her shoulders, as she reached the gate for the girls' school.

'I'm safe, you can't come in, unless I invite you across the threshold,' she panted.

'Isn't that vampires?'

'Oh, yeah.' Maggie was pink-faced and giggling, and David thought how young and fresh she looked. Then he banished the thought from his head immediately.

'So, do you have your Plantagenet readers for me?' he said.

'I do,' said Maggie, feeling a little foolish for teasing him as he immediately turned the conversation back to work. Her hand was still on the gate post.

'And I have mine,' he said. 'We're doing the Betjeman. *And is it true . . . and is it true.*'

'I love that,' said Maggie.

'I'll try and do it well, then,' he said, smiling.

'Thanks,' she said, and she didn't mean for the poem.

David gave her his grin, then summoned Stephen Daedalus with a whistle. From a high turret window, Miss Starling watched them, grimly.

In the end, it wasn't as hard to apologise as she'd feared. Pat and Liz had been delighted to take the young teacher under their wing and give her the benefit of their wisdom, acquired through about two years in the classroom and twenty in administration, as far as Maggie could work out. Two long lectures later and they were all friends. But Maggie made a vow to herself to steer well clear of Miss Starling.

Chapter Eight

Simone was absolutely delighted to be chosen to read at the Christmas concert, although she hoped it wasn't just because Miss Adair was taking pity on her. Fliss, on the other hand, was livid. As was Alice, although for the opposite reason.

'For goodness sake,' Fliss had said when she saw her name on the list. Hattie bounced downstairs. 'Well *done*, Felicity,' she said in that mock-parental tone Fliss hated above all others. 'Mops and Pops will be *so* proud.'

'Well, I'm not doing it,' said Felicity, fiercely. 'I know those women said it wasn't compulsory. So there.'

Hattie stopped and laughed. 'You funny thing! You have to do it now! You can't let the Plantagenets down! The Tudors will think it's hysterical.'

Fliss rolled her eyes. 'I'll get over that.'

'It's serious, Felicity.'

'*It's serious, Felicity*,' mimicked Fliss.

Hattie produced a mobile phone from her blazer pocket.

'You aren't allowed those,' said Fliss immediately.

'Prefects are,' said Hattie, 'for emergencies.' She tapped some buttons and let it ring. 'Daddy? Daddy? Guess what!'

Fliss started to move away, but Hattie grabbed her.

'Fliss is leading the Christmas concert!' She paused. 'I

know! Non-prefects can't use their phones so she couldn't tell you straight away but she's right here.'

Hattie held out the mobile to Fliss with a fearsome look, even as Fliss was backing away, shaking her hands at it. Hattie made a face and held it out further and with a resigned sigh, Fliss had to take it.

'Yes?' she said, nonchalantly. She couldn't deny it, though, hearing her dad's voice on the phone outside the normal Sunday hours, when her mother usually took over anyway and asked her whether she was eating too much jam roly-poly, was lovely.

'Is that my Flick-flack?'

'Hi Daddy,' she said, unable to keep the smile out of her voice.

'What's this I hear about you leading the concert?' He sounded puffed up with pride and his voice was louder than usual. She wondered if he was in a room full of people he worked with.

'I'm not *leading* the concert, Daddy,' she said. 'There's like, a million people doing it. The teacher only picked me to annoy the assessment people anyway.'

She could feel her dad's smile, all those miles away.

'Well, well done for being so modest,' he said. 'You know we'll be there with bells on.'

Fliss's heart sank.

'We're so, so pleased you're doing so well. Your emails are always so negative . . . we do worry about you, you know. We don't want you to be unhappy.'

Fliss felt a lump grow in her throat. She wanted to shout out that yes, she was unhappy, and they had to take her home, that she wanted to go Christmas shopping on Oxford Street with her friends and go ice-skating and she couldn't do all that because she was trapped in a horrible place with horrible food and freezing cold dorms and stupid teachers out in the middle of bloody nowhere. But right at this moment she didn't know how to tell her dad that; it sounded so petty when he was so happy.

'I miss you,' she choked out eventually.

'I know, sweetheart,' he said. 'We miss you too.'

'So why—'

But her dad knew better than to get involved in this argument again.

'That's why we can't wait to see you at the concert. And we're so pleased that you're getting on. Your marks are a bit disappointing . . . more than a bit.'

Fliss gritted her teeth. At least that was working.

'But we know you're going to buck up and do just fine.'

'Yes, Daddy,' finished Fliss quietly, handing the phone back to Hattie, who took it triumphantly.

'See. I told you so,' she said with a smug look on her face. Inwardly, Fliss decided: this was it. She was going to have to be a lot, lot worse if she had the slightest chance of ever getting home again. It wasn't fair on Ranald.

Maggie had thought about Veronica's advice, and had had a long chat with her mother, who had revealed that Stan was indeed missing her more than he'd said on the telephone; that he was still going round there for his Sunday lunch, even on his own, and that he'd been out a lot with his mates.

'Just because he misses you, of course,' her mum had said. 'We do too, darling. How are things?'

Maggie didn't want to mention that she'd had a very public dressing down from her boss and that her class had all turned against her – particularly after what was seen as vindictiveness in leaving Alice out of the school concert in favour of that fat girl, as Fliss had been saying loudly as she'd walked in the other day. 'Schemie types stick together,' someone else had offered and everyone had nodded loudly before pretending they'd just noticed her. She decided she would definitely invite Stan down, but hadn't been able to get him on the phone that Saturday, as she and Claire had gone out for tea and discussed their love lives. Or rather, she'd told Claire the whole story of Stan; Claire hadn't seemed to want to talk about her own situation too much. Romantically, Maggie wondered if she'd been involved in some terribly passionate French love affair that had gone horribly wrong and made her hide away here in the country, rather like the modern equivalent of going into a nunnery.

But all thoughts of Claire left her head when, still unable to raise Stan on his mobile, she'd gone to bed and later, much later, about two a.m., she'd received a text. The beeping woke her up.

'TX FR GRET NIGHT' it said. From Stan. She'd stared at it for a long time, her heart pounding, and a horrible sinking feeling in her stomach. This wasn't meant for her. Would it be for his mates Rugga and Dugga? But why would he text them in the middle of the night when he saw them every day at work?

With a trembling hand she called the number back, still groggy from sleep.

'Uh, yeah?' Stan sounded drunk, and a little nervous.

'Stan?'

'Wha? What time is it?'

'Did you just text me?'

There was a long pause.

'Uh, did I?' said Stan. 'Must have been a mistake.'

Maggie felt her stomach plummet into her shoes.

'What kind of mistake?' Maggie heard the steel in her own voice.

'A daft one, knowing me,' said Stan. 'Uh, it was . . . I must have meant Rugga.'

'Yeah?'

'Yeah. I saw Rugga. Call him tomorrow if you don't believe me.' He said this in a very defensive tone.

'It's all right,' said Maggie. But it wasn't, and they both knew it.

Maggie spent the next week in a blur. What was Stan doing? Was he telling the truth? He was daft as a brush when he'd had a few, that was for sure. But he wouldn't even look at another girl, would he? I mean, surely fidelity was just taken for granted, wasn't it? That they didn't even have to discuss it. After all, if it wasn't . . . but she quickly shook away any thoughts of David from her brain. No. This was nothing to do with anyone else. It was her and Stan. Is this what being apart meant?

Anna wasn't much help.

'I haven't heard anything,' she said. Normally in the hair salon Anna missed nothing that happened for miles around. 'But really, Mags, if you will move so far away . . . I mean, he's a young bloke.'

'Yeah, *my* young bloke,' Maggie said.

'Have you asked him about it?'

'Yes. He just says it's his mates, and would I stop going on about it.'

'Can you get up?'

Maggie thought about the heavy schedule of rehearsals and marking she had on. Plus she didn't think shooting back to Glasgow at the first sign of trouble was exactly what Veronica had had in mind when she'd said she should keep in touch with her family more.

'Maybe he'll come down,' she said.

'You can ask,' said Anna. She hadn't been at all as sympathetic as Maggie had hoped. In fact, she'd as much as implied that if she, Maggie, was going to head off and be hoity toity at the other end of the country, she basically deserved a boyfriend who'd cheat on her. Maggie didn't know what to think.

Feeling lonely and, for the first time since she'd arrived, really questioning whether she'd done the right thing in moving, Maggie threw herself into work. Sometimes it seemed the more she prepared her lessons for the girls, the less bothered they were. But what was the alternative?

Maggie was shocked to realise she'd been at Downey House for three months as December rolled around. Three months of bells, of teaching girls who sat in rows and (usually) paid attention; of almost no male company whatsoever. Half term had come and gone in a blur of lie-ins, marking and wandering around the local town, where the shopping amounted to an unbelievably dated department store that sold a lot of haberdashery, bras the size of barrage balloons, and day gloves; and an outlet of Country Casuals.

Maybe she should have gone home after all. Her parents were worried about her too, no matter how much she assured them she was getting plenty of fresh air and cream teas, and she missed her sister and her little nephews, terrors though they were.

Now the school was readying itself for Christmas. Even amongst the older girls, who had mocks in January, there was a palpable air of excitement running through the pupils, as great swathes of mistletoe and ivy wound their way around the banisters and the great hall. Veronica hated starting the whole Christmas folderol too early, but she did enjoy the school looking its very best.

Pat and Liz had gone away for a little while – their inspection would continue throughout the year at different points. However, Liz had gone off sick for an unspecified length of time apparently suffering from stress – Veronica had wondered whether it wasn't the set of Liz's trousers that had been suffering from all the stress, and whether the amount of chocolate biscuits Liz ate had anything to do with it – but Pat would be back at Christmas with another of her protégés. Veronica hoped they would be an improvement. The inspection was definitely not going well. It wasn't just Maggie's outburst that had had to be dealt with; Miss James in PE had insisted that if they wanted to understand her class they had to experience it, which hadn't pleased either of them – they were both very anti competitive sports; Mlle Crozier had the sixth form reading 'that disgusting old sexist', Jean-Paul Sartre, and they had been overheard discussing how to ask for condoms in Paris, something of which Veronica had thought the inspectors would have entirely approved. She tried to put them out of her head for now as she OK'd Miss Starling's request for a shorter Seniors' Christmas party this year and nothing the Downey Boys could pour booze into, e.g. punch.

Veronica wandered through the hallways. Really, this year Harold the caretaker and his ground staff had excelled themselves. The greenery gathered in from the grounds gave everything a beautiful scent, and she had ordered the large wood-burning fire in the entrance hall to be lit every morning. It was comforting for the girls, coming down from their chilly dormitories, to be confronted with the fire, the Christmas cards steadily arriving in pigeonholes every day, and warm porridge with cream, honey, maple syrup and occasionally all three, to set them up for the day ahead.

She liked hearing the laughter in the air as the girls fussed about the concert and the party to follow; to see their flushed faces as they dashed in from hockey for tea and scones by the fire. They hadn't had much trouble with the St Thinians craze – anorexia – which was endemic in some schools. Perhaps because Downey House was known for its devotion to outdoor life and health; perhaps sensitive and prone girls just avoided it. Or maybe they'd just been lucky so far, thought Veronica, who ate like a bird herself.

'Not running are you?' she enquired gently to one galumphing middle schooler, who immediately turned puce and slowed down. The gentle approach did seem to work the best.

Christmas was hard for her. Of course she could go to her brother's, but he was a nice simple chap, worked in a warehouse in Oldham, and his wife thought she was uppity because she didn't bring their spoilt children the latest trainers and PS3 games they wanted, even when she was told what they absolutely must have. It wasn't a prospect to relish. No, she was going to take that Greek islands tour with her friend Jane, who taught classics at a wonderful school near Oakham. A Swan Hellenic, lectures every day, walks in the winter sun and a little learning – it would do her a world of good. Christmas was a terrible time for . . . for people like her. Veronica tried to keep her thoughts in order. After all, who knew what her son would be doing now, and where? Veronica just hoped and prayed, as she did every year, that he was happy – he would be a grown-up man now, maybe with children of his own. Best she never knew. Best nobody knew.

'I do hope you're not chewing gum, Ursula,' she muttered gently to the dark-haired girl who passed her on her way to the post boxes. The girl swallowed audibly.

'No, miss,' she said, eyes wide.

'Good,' said Veronica. 'Good.'

*

Fliss headed to Bebo to catch up on her messages. The first one that struck her eye was from Callie, her worst behaved friend from back home.

FLISS!!! I kno you are locked to death in that school, but you have to have to have to come home for this – Will is in a band at his school and they're playing in the pub! And anyone over fourteen can get in and I think we will definitely count! It's on the 12th December!

Fliss's heart immediately started to race. The twelfth! Two days after the bloody concert, but also two days before they broke up. Would her parents let her go? Definitely not. But if Will saw her there, supporting his band – being a fan right at the beginning, before he became, like a famous singer and everything – he'd definitely definitely talk to her. And there wouldn't be Hattie or any of the other girls around because everyone would still be at school so she'd have him all to herself, practically.

She had to be there. She had to.

'What are you thinking about?' said Alice, who'd come to find her in the computer room.

'I need to get suspended,' said Fliss. 'I've had enough. I really really really have to do something so awful that I get sent home.'

Alice's eyes widened. 'A challenge, eh?'

'Don't you want to get sent home too?'

'Don't care,' said Alice. 'It would only be some diplomatic nanny. I can't even remember where they are. Cairo, I think. Cairo is *so tedious*.'

Fliss nodded as if she'd found Cairo very tedious every time she'd been there.

'But you really want to get chucked out?'

Fliss glanced at the frosty moors outside the window, and nodded enthusiastically. 'I want to go home,' she said. 'I'll miss you, though.'

'I'll come stay for the holidays,' said Alice, philosophically. 'See if this bloke you like has any mates.'

Fliss wasn't sure she wanted to introduce dark gorgeous Alice to Will, but having her to stay would be great. She'd probably be grounded and stuff for a little while – for ages, after they caught her sneaking out to the gig – but then it would be Christmas and everyone would soften up and forget; Christmas was great at their house, they all got loads and loads of pressies and got to watch telly and her mum just heated up some turkey stuff from M&S but then let them eat chocolates all day and gave them a taste of champagne – and by the new year everything would be back to normal and she'd be with her friends and at a normal school again.

'OK,' said Fliss. 'Well, I need your help.'

Maggie felt nearly as nervous at her first rehearsal with the boys' school as her girls did. She'd drilled them after school – having to get them to learn all the pieces off by heart was the first challenge, but they were making good progress. Fliss had suddenly become surprisingly good about it considering she hadn't wanted to be chosen in the first place. And Simone was stolidly professional, doing it the same way every time.

Simone had taken to coming over to Maggie's office occasionally, once or twice a week, to exchange a book from Maggie's large collection. They rarely spoke much, but it was a companionable silence as Maggie did her marking, or occasionally chatted with Claire, generally in Maggie's halting French so as to keep it from Simone's tender ears. When they did speak, Maggie saw further flashes of the sensitivities and humour that came through in her essays. Crippling shyness was such a terrible thing. Yet on stage she was perfectly fine. Most peculiar.

Maggie noticed that even though the girls shared a room, Felicity never included Simone in their conversations or little whispered private jokes; even when heading back to the dorm together they somehow contrived to leave Simone out. Maggie hated to see it and wished she could do something about it, but didn't know how.

All the girls involved in the performance were there for the readings, plus the orchestra, and they met in the great hall that doubled as a theatre. There was seating for six hundred; it was rather daunting, Maggie mused, standing on the stage and looking out. Downey House meant what it said about creating confident young ladies. She imagined the rows of parents watching her girls and applauding . . . perhaps she would be asked on to take a bow . . .

'Hello hello!' shouted a voice, startling her from her reverie. David strode into the hall on his long skinny legs, a Pied Piper leading a long line of young boys behind him. The boys looked around – they looked more confident and certainly had better skin and posture than the boys Maggie had taught, but they seemed to lack that jokey nonchalance her boys used to put on in new situations, where they would kick each other and pretend that they were twenty-five and could all drive cars. This lot probably had drivers and would be aiming for parliament by the time they were twenty-five. The girls behind her quietened down noticeably and stopped messing about.

'Right, first years all together!' said David. 'We're only going to do this twice, so no messing about. Girl readers stage right, boys stage left, orchestra in the middle, dancers do your thing, and it will all be fabulous.'

He stood looking up at Maggie on the stage and she was seized with a huge impulse to put out her hand and let him help her jump down. But she knew any hint of physical contact would be leapt on by the pupils and gossiped over obsessively, so she hopped down by herself. Nonetheless she could feel her heart beating, and checked again to see if the lipstick she'd surreptitiously applied earlier was still there.

'So, are your girls all ready then?' said David, giving her his grin. She felt her insides fizz.

'They're great,' said Maggie, loud enough for them to hear. 'It's the orchestra I'm looking forward to.'

'I wish I could conduct, don't you?' said David. 'It always looks like such fun. Just waving your arms about in a good coat and getting rounds of applause.'

'I'm not sure that's all there is,' said Maggie, laughing at his daftness.

'Yeah, course it is. Bet they earn tons of money too.'

Mrs Offili came out and shot David an affectionate look.

'Showing off your impeccable musical pedigree as ever, Mr McDonald.'

'Certainly am, Mrs O. You've seen me dance.'

Mrs Offili shook her head, although there was a smile playing on her lips, and started on the tuning up.

Watching everyone run through their parts, Maggie was impressed. But even as one of the boys, a tall, thin lad called Peregrine, was doing a spine-tingling rendition of the Carol of the Bells, she found herself glancing at David. He was totally rapt, mouthing the verse along with him and, although she was sure he'd be incredibly embarrassed if it was pointed out, actually conducting the verse. Maggie looked at his long fingers and wondered . . . No. This was nonsense. She shook her head. And wildly inappropriate. She'd clearly been holed up here for too long, and was getting frustrated. It wasn't

David's fault he was the only semi nice-looking man for twenty miles. She could see the girls eyeing him up too.

Both girls did well. Fliss really would be quite beautiful when she grew up, with her pale skin and even features, thought Maggie, however overshadowed she was at the moment by the glamorous, knowing Alice.

Everything went smoothly and well until after rehearsals had finished and David and his troupe were getting ready to leave – Maggie had slightly hoped he would linger and ask if she wanted to go for coffee, or even a drink in town, but he wouldn't – and the girls went into the changing rooms at the back of the auditorium to pick up their bags. Fliss came out looking slightly upset.

'Miss? Miss?'

'Yes, Felicity?'

'I've lost my watch. I took it off to put it on the side while I was timing myself, then I definitely left it in my pocket – definitely – but it's not there now.'

'What do you mean?'

'It was in my pocket before I came on stage,' said Fliss, looking miserable and staring at the floor. That watch had been her grandmother's. It had been left to her, and her parents had had severe misgivings about letting her take it away to school. She'd promised to look after it. Even though this would help her case to leave the school, she was still utterly devastated. Her grandmother had loved her to bits and she'd loved her too, and her little house, full of knick-knacks, and Malinkey, her gran's little Scottie, who always tried to fight Ranald. Of course Ranald would never fight back, he was far too much of a softie. Thinking about her gran, and her dog, made the tears prick Fliss's eyes.

'It was my gran's,' she said, lip starting to wobble.

'Let's go look,' said Maggie. 'It couldn't have fallen out?'

Fliss shook her head. 'I've looked everywhere.'

Simone, and Alice, who'd turned up to meet Fliss after class, were standing outside the locker room, looking dismayed. Maggie looked closely at their faces. Stealing at school was one of the most disagreeable things to deal with. It was time-consuming, unpleasant and caused a lot of talking behind pupils' backs. With a stab of guilt she wondered if, with the amount of time she'd spent out the front talking to David, she might have been able to prevent it.

The changing room backstage was quiet, as various girls from various houses sat around, looking worried. There was a passageway to a corridor exit on the side, noted Maggie, which meant it was accessible to almost anyone in the school. Alice and Simone both looked nervous. Maggie glanced at Simone. It couldn't be denied that she didn't own nice things like the other girls did. And that Felicity and Alice had basically ostracised her since she arrived. Could she do something like this to teach them a lesson?

And what about Alice? She didn't think Alice had been too thrilled about Felicity getting the part, and sharing in the glory that should have been Alice's alone. Could she be trying to get her own back? Surely she wasn't that sly?

'Hello everyone,' she announced to the silent room. All the excitement and good cheer of the rehearsals had gone; she'd also fetched in the boys from their locker room, and David stood behind her.

'We've had a report of a lost watch,' she said, firmly. It wasn't time to search the children or their belongings. She wasn't sure that was the best way to go about it anyway; stolen goods could be easily hidden, and searching promoted mistrust and implied the children had no sense of moral values at all and might as well steal. And the watch probably was just lost; the kids were so careless.

'Now, I'm sure it will turn up.' Behind her she could feel Felicity bristle. 'However. If anyone knows anything – anything at all – about this, can I urge them to come forward to Mr McDonald or myself, in strictest confidence, at the first opportunity, do you understand? Thanks!'

She glanced round the faces looking up at her, trying to catch a glimpse of embarrassment or guilt. Immediately she couldn't help noticing that Simone had gone brick red, and was doing her best not to catch her eye. Maggie's heart sank. The punishment for stealing could be suspension, or even worse. She really hoped Simone hadn't jeopardised her future for something as petty as this. It would be a tragedy if so.

'If for any reason this watch isn't just "lost" you can come and see me or Mr McDonald in our respective offices, or leave us a note. I'm sure we can clear this up without any unpleasantness being necessary. Do I make myself clear?'

There was a mumble of awkward consent.

'All right,' she said. 'Good rehearsal everyone. Your parents are going to be proud. Off you go.'

The children scrambled off to get a late tea the kitchen had made specially for them as Maggie and David looked at each other sadly.

'Say it isn't lost . . .' said David.

'I don't know,' said Maggie. 'What do you think we should do, cancel their concert?'

'They've worked so hard,' groaned David. 'And I hate this "punish the many" thing. It's so concentration camp. Kids never rat anyway.'

'I know. Bugger.'

They stood in silence for a moment.

'Do you think it was stolen?' asked David.

Maggie nodded. 'One of the girls went very red.'

'Oh no,' said David.

'I think it's my scholarship girl. Fliss isn't nice to her at all. Not bullying, but just excludes her. She just looked so horribly guilty.'

'You can't jump to any conclusions,' said David. 'But maybe a quiet word.' He sighed. 'Boys just whack each other about for that kind of thing.'

'I know. I think you have it easier.'

'Yes,' said David, moving away. 'Apart from the world wars and things. Do you think your cook would have any tea left over?'

Despite her disappointment, Maggie couldn't help feeling herself perk up.

For once, Simone skipped supper. Her face was flaming. She'd seen the way Miss Adair had looked at her. Accusingly. Like, 'you're the poorest girl in the school. It must have been you.' She'd felt the guilty blush steal over her cheeks. Fliss and Alice, too, had given her such a hard look when Fliss had realised her watch had gone. She'd wanted to shout at them that it wasn't her, that she would never do that, but she couldn't. The words wouldn't come; it was as if her throat had seized up. Now they would definitely think she'd done it; that she was jealous of Fliss just because she was pretty and popular and all of those things. Which she was.

Only Imogen was in the room, studying quietly with her back to the door. Simone undressed quickly, threw herself under the blankets and cried herself to sleep as quietly as she could.

*

Fliss was the centre of attention at the table, as people jockeyed for position to tell her how sorry they were about her watch and try and remove themselves from suspicion.

'Who do you think it was?' asked one of the Tudor girls.

Alice looked around. 'Well, don't think I mean anything by this or anything,' she said. 'But have you noticed the one person who's not here?'

The children had bolted their food and moved on to the television lounge by the time David and Maggie had finished clearing up and everything was dark in the cafeteria. Mrs Rhys, the cheerful cook, had left two covered plates of sandwiches, scones, cheese and fruit out, and the urn was still plenty hot enough for tea.

'It's still going to be a good concert,' said David, his hand on her shoulder as they walked over to the deserted tables. 'Don't worry about it.'

Maggie stiffened instantly when she felt his hand, and nearly dropped her scones. 'I know,' she said. 'I just want everything to be all right, you know?'

They sat down, not facing each other, but corner to corner, their heads nearly touching. She wanted to lean forward, breathe him in, but didn't dare.

'I know,' he said, and for an instant, Maggie thought he was going to take her hand, in the darkened, deserted meal hall. The space between them was charged; she was sure she could see sparks leaping between their fingers. Her heart beat faster.

It was so strange. She'd got so used to her and Stan over the years, and had worked with so many female teachers, she hadn't really thought much about other men, apart from in an abstract, Brad Pitt kind of a way. It was strange how

141

quickly this tall, skinny dark-eyed man with the manic grin had got into her head.

There was a pause, which turned into a long, loaded silence. And suddenly, she knew. Suddenly, they were staring at each other in the deserted hall. David turned his gaze on her and she returned it. For once, the noisy school had fallen completely quiet. Maggie was aware of her breathing; and of his, and she wondered, as time seemed to slow down and take on a fluid quality, if he would be rough, or smooth, or both, and, almost as if it didn't belong to her, she felt her own hand stretching out to clasp . . .

'SIR! SIR!!! LLEWELLYN'S PUSHED MIKE JUNIOR'S HEAD DOWN THE LOO AGAIN!'

'I DIDN'T! I DIDN'T! OR AT LEAST I WAS SORELY PROVOKED!'

Six boys burst into the hall like a small angry torrent of beavers. Maggie pulled her hand back immediately as if she'd been touching something hot. David gave her a quick glance – was it annoyed? Regretful? She couldn't tell – and stood up.

'What? What's all this? No, on second thoughts, I DON'T want to know. Come on you savages, back to the prison pit where you belong.'

He turned to Maggie, and the look in his eyes was completely unfathomable.

'I'd better go and round up the rest of this sorry crew before they unleash the dogs of war all over your nice hall.'

Maggie forced her lips into what she hoped was an unbothered smile and nodded vehemently.

'Definitely. Definitely. Of course. Right. Bye then.'

Chapter Nine

The days passed, and the thief did not come forward. Although it had been the talk of the school, the chatter started to die down a little. But Simone was well aware it centred on her, and stalked the halls with her head down and her eyes red. Maggie decided she really must have a word with her, although she'd been putting it off. There had been no more cosy book swaps, either. She needed to find out what was up, she was neglecting her duty. But everyone was just so busy at this time of year.

At least nothing else had gone missing. A note had gone round the entire school, warning the pupils that there might be a thief on the loose, that valuables should be given to Matron and locked away, and that anyone with any information should come forward. No one had.

Meanwhile, Maggie had a more pressing problem on her hands. Stan was on his way. He was coming down for the week of the concert, then they could drive back up home together. The idea was he could see the Christmas show and a bit about her life, and hopefully they could spend a little bit of time together and get themselves back on track. Every time she thought about it, she felt so nervous. Partly because of what he might have been getting up to. And partly because of what had crossed her own mind. David hadn't emailed her since the rehearsal. Although disappointed, she'd realised immediately what this meant – that there was nothing going on, just her slightly feverish imagination. It must be true what they said about girls locked up in boarding schools. And it was absolutely ridiculous behaviour; getting a silly crush on some teacher across the way, who probably got crushes from every child he ever met, girl or boy, she thought firmly. It was ridiculous and completely unprofessional; they were working together, and they had to stop it getting out of hand.

She and Stan had been together seven years. That was worth fighting for. And the idea of Stan cheating on her was the real issue, not distracting herself from her sadness by a dangerous flirtation.

The train from Glasgow took a long, long time to wind its way down the entire country and finally into Exeter. Maggie was standing at the barrier and saw Stan disembark a long way down the train. He was brushing a lot of pastry crumbs from his hoodie. Maggie looked at him as if through the eyes of a stranger. He looked the same as ever – long and skinny, except with an oddly protuberant pot belly that made him look a bit pregnant; spiky, gingerish hair, pale skin. He carried a large sports bag and a copy of *Top Gear* magazine – surely it couldn't have been all he'd brought to read for a ten-hour train trip. Or maybe it was.

It seemed to take for ever for him to make it to the gate. All around were couples falling into each other's arms, running up and crying with happiness and relief.

'Hey,' said Stan, looking nervous.

'Hey,' said Maggie. She wished she was running into his arms, but somehow she couldn't make herself. It would be stupid. Starting a relationship at school meant you never got over-demonstrative.

She didn't know how to broach the subject, but she couldn't just dive in straight away.

'How was your trip?'

'Good,' said Stan. He burped. She smelled lager. 'You look posh.'

'Do I?' said Maggie. Veronica had very kindly mentioned that a friend of hers owned a boutique in town and offered a discount to school staff. Claire had taken her shopping, and together they'd spent rather a lot of money (Maggie was finding that without paying accommodation, food, petrol or going-out costs she was able to save a huge amount of her salary) on some new basics for her – two beautiful wool skirts, some plain white, well-cut shirts and a heart-stoppingly expensive cashmere jumper. The plain clothing accentuated Maggie's good legs and beautiful dark hair, which she had tied back more loosely, after Claire had insisted on pulling just a couple of fronds round her face.

Stan could see that she looked well. His heart sank. If she'd looked fat, or sad, or lonely or any of those things. But it was patently obvious that she was doing just fine down here without him. Better, if anything. He knew it.

They stood there a tad uncomfortably for a moment, then Maggie leaned forward and kissed him awkwardly on the cheek. Stan turned his face so that the kiss could hit his mouth, but he didn't quite make it in time, so it ended up a rather awkward mishmash.

'Ehm. So. Have you crashed my car yet?' he said, as they disengaged.

'It's our car!' said Maggie. 'And no, of course not.'

Stan heaved his bag into the boot, and climbed in the driver's seat.

'Eh,' said Maggie.

'What?'

'Well, have you been drinking?'

'I had a couple of lagers on the train, but nothing . . .'

'I think I'd better drive,' said Maggie. 'Plus, I know the way, remember?'

Stan didn't want to get out of the car and feel like an idiot, but he supposed she did know the way.

'OK' he said, ungraciously, and moved round to the passenger seat, heaving a sigh.

They left the ring roads of Exeter behind them quickly enough, followed by the motorway, and eventually left the main roads to start the climb towards the cliffs of Downey House. Early snow had stayed on the tops of the hills and the views over the sea were quite starkly beautiful. Maggie took quick glances to her left to see if Stan was taking them in or even noticing them.

'It's scenic, isn't it?' she asked eventually.

'Hm,' Stan grunted, non-committally. 'I thought you hated the country.'

'So did I,' said Maggie. 'I'm quite surprised with myself.'

'Hm,' said Stan.

Maggie couldn't believe she was feeling so disloyal, but as she parked the car – at least Stan had shown a mark of surprise when he'd seen the towers emerging from behind the hills – she was wondering if he should have come at all.

'Fuck me,' he'd said. 'It really is a fucking castle, isn't it?'

Maggie looked at it affectionately.

'Yes,' she said. 'And it's starting to feel like home.'

'Thought as much,' said Stan, ungraciously.

This wasn't going right at all, thought Maggie. She needed to get over the horrid panicky feeling she'd had when she'd got that text, and remember her priorities. She was Maggie Adair. From Govan. Who'd fallen in love with

Stan when he was seventeen years old. He was her best friend. Her lover. Her Holy Cross saviour.

She cast her eyes to the left. He was sitting in his Celtic top, looking so awkward and nervous. She felt her heart soften towards him. Of course it was a new environment. Of course he was nervous. Hadn't she been, the first time she'd rolled up the gravel drive in their small, unimpressive car? The school was designed to impress; to be the best. Stan was intimidated, and she should be careful of his pride.

'Hey,' she said, reaching over and grabbing his knee. 'You know, they're all a bunch of English arseholes.'

'Yeh,' he said, glancing down at her hand on his leg. He felt bony, warm, reassuring somehow. 'I know. I had to hear them shouting all the way down on the train. No wonder I drank so much lager.'

Maggie nodded. The smell was noticeable in the small car.

'I really need to take a wazz,' said Stan.

'We're here,' said Maggie, opening the car door. Her heart suddenly skipped a beat. There, crossing the car park and looking distracted, in a tweed jacket with a long stripey scarf blowing out behind him – he couldn't have looked more like a fey English type if he tried – was David.

'MAGGIE!' he hollered, as she emerged from the car, Stan slightly crossing his legs as he levered himself out the other side. He came striding over, Stephen Daedalus bouncing excitedly when he saw Maggie there, tail wagging furiously.

'Thank God,' said David, looking slightly breathless. 'We need you. It's an emergency.'

'What?' said Maggie.

'Forters junior has put his back out doing water polo. He can't stand up for the concert.'

'But it's tomorrow!'

'Yes, I know that.'

Maggie thought as quickly as she could. His lovely piece, ruined. Who did she know . . .

'I think I have just the person,' she said, internally rolling her eyes at how she was going to have to crawl to Alice now, and completely underscore the girl's original strongly held belief that she should have been the star all along.

'Trebizon-Woods,' she said. Stan looked at her as if she was speaking a foreign language.

'Will she learn it in time?' said David. 'You know what my lot are like, you have to hide the verses in porn mags and Yorkie wrappers.'

'Oh, she knows it,' promised Maggie. 'She may be a tad reluctant to do it for me, but hopefully sheer ego and vanity should shine through. I'll flatter her a lot.'

'EXCELLENT,' hollered David. Then he turned his penetrating gaze on Stan, who was standing and looking increasingly awkward.

'Hello! Who are you?' David stuck out his hand. Stan didn't stick out his. David shoved his back in his pocket. 'I'm David McDonald. Maggie's opposite number at the boys' school.'

'I thought there were only girls here,' said Stan, in a rather uncomfortably bleating tone.

'Oh, yes, yes, that's right . . . I work on the other side of the hill.'

'Oh,' said Stan.

'And you are?'

Maggie felt ashamed of how embarrassed she was. Of Stan, in his nylon Celtic football shirt, covered in McCoy's crumbs, with his dirty jeans, pot belly, short haircut. She hated feeling like she was seeing them through David's eyes. Partly because she also suspected that David wouldn't judge people on what they wore; it wasn't his thing at all.

'I'm Stan. I really need to go to the toilet.'

David's eyebrows arched temporarily. 'OK. It's all girls' loos up there, but maybe Miss Starling wouldn't mind if you attacked her rhododendrons.'

'David.' Maggie shot a look at him. This was not the time for dry English humour. Stan looked miserable.

'Stan's my . . .'

She was scarcely conscious of the pause until it had happened.

'Boyfriend,' said Stan, sullenly. It sounded strange coming from him. He'd seemed so reticent in the first place. 'I'm her boyfriend.'

'Ahh!' said David, looking back at Maggie and then to Stan. 'Lovely!'

Maggie bit her lip. She didn't want Stan to realise that she'd known David for a while and had never mentioned him.

'Yeah,' said Stan.

'There's a loo over here,' said Maggie. 'I'll speak to you later, David. I'll have a word with Alice and get back to you, but I'm sure it'll be fine.'

David nodded and retreated, looking rather thoughtful.

Maggie showed Stan up to her rooms quickly, ignoring the sizing-up glances from the girls she passed and trying not to think about whether or not they'd gossip – of course they would. She wondered how many men in football shirts arrived here. None of their fathers or brothers, that was for sure. Stan, whilst moving reasonably swiftly, kept stopping on the stairs to look at things: portraits of old girls, chandeliers, panelled doors. He whistled softly to himself.

Finally they reached the little suite in the East Tower. Stan couldn't stay there, of course, not without all sorts of criminal records checks and so on, but he could have a look around. Maggie had tidied up and laid a new bedspread over the bed. It didn't make it look any more like a double than it had done previously, but it cheered things up a little. She'd also added flowers, and bought some lager for the fridge.

'I'll just have a wazz,' muttered Stan. Maggie stood, staring out of the window, feeling suddenly helpless.

Five minutes later Stan came back out. He'd brushed the crumbs off his shirt and eaten some toothpaste. 'Hey,' he said quietly. Maggie didn't turn around, just kept staring out of the window. 'I didn't know there were men around here at all.'

'He's just a teacher at the school across the hill,' said Maggie dully. 'We have to work together.' She turned round to face him. She could see it in his face. He looked guilty. 'Stan,' she said.

Looking at him for the first time in a while she suddenly saw him again. Seventeen and long and skinny, pretending he wasn't waiting for her outside the dinner hall. The leap in her heart as she'd seen him there; trying to hide her French jotter, which had his name scribbled all over the back page. His slow creasing smile as his mates joshed him, but he had stayed and waited for her anyway.

The bedroom felt colder than ever.

'I didn't do anything,' said Stan sullenly, staring at the floor. 'She wanted to, but I didn't.'

'So there was a "her",' said Maggie, feeling her blood run cold. 'And you told "her" it was a great night.'

'I didn't say I wasn't thinking about it. I said I didn't do anything. And you can believe me or not.' Stan ended on a defensive flourish. Then he looked up at her to gauge her face.

'I missed you,' he said simply.

150

Maggie felt her prejudices about him, her worry about how he came across, amongst her new life, her worry about whether he really cared for her or whether he was quite pleased to have the place empty for a bit . . . all of that faded away as she saw her spiky-haired Stan right there; his cocky funny side gone, and all because he loved her and missed her. She felt . . . love, mixed up with feeling a bit sorry for him.

She stepped forward. She believed him. It was as simple as that. Some woman would have come on to him, and he'd have done his best to back down from it. There might even have been some snogging, but she could deal with that. After all . . . and she banished the thought of David from her mind. She put her hand up to Stan's cheek.

'I missed you too,' she said.

'Naw you didn't.' He indicated all around. 'Not now you're living in a fucking castle with *David*.'

Maggie stepped forward. 'Sssh,' she said. Stan looked at her, half suspicious, half hopeful, as Maggie stepped towards him. 'Want to go out and do something that is totally banned in a girls' school?'

After a mostly successful reunion afternoon at the local B&B, Maggie needed to get to the dorms; there was a rehearsal after supper and she had to catch Alice. She wasn't particularly looking forward to it, but there it was. Simone and Imogen were there finishing their prep. Fliss and Alice were reading about Britney Spears in a gossip magazine.

'Alice, can I see you for a minute?'

Alice heaved a sigh that was a tad too grown up for a thirteen-year-old, then brightly announced, 'Of course, Miss Adair,' so she couldn't get into trouble for it.

Maggie took her outside.

'Simone seems to be happier,' said Alice, in that irritatingly adult way she had.

'It's not about Simone,' said Maggie. 'One of the Downey boys has had to drop out, and we need someone who can perform the T. S. Eliot.'

Alice's eyes lit up, but she tried not to look too eager. 'Yes?'

Maggie rolled her eyes. 'And Mr McDonald and I thought you might like to take it on.'

Alice pretended to look as if she was thinking it over. Maggie smiled; she was pretty good.

'Well, it is a lot of extra work.'

'Fine,' said Maggie, 'I'm sure Simone would be happy to do two.'

'No! I think, I think I can fit it in.'

'Good,' said Maggie. Then she relented. 'Well done, Alice. I'm sure you're going to be very good.'

Alice nodded. 'Is that your boyfriend, miss?' she asked. Not much didn't get round the school in about ten seconds, Maggie thought ruefully.

'Is that your business, Alice?' she said sharply, deeply regretting bringing Stan up the main staircase rather than sneaking him in the fire escape door.

'No, miss,' said Alice, delighted she'd obviously struck a nerve and looking forward to spreading it round the class.

'Well, on you go then. And finish your prep before you start on *Heat*, OK?'

Alice re-entered the dorm smiling broadly to herself.

'What?' said Fliss, suspiciously. She had wondered if there was any updating on the thieving. Nothing had gone missing in the last week or so and it all seemed to have settled down.

'You know we were trying to work out what you're going to do at the Christmas concert?'

Fliss felt again the big ball of anxiety in her stomach. She was horribly nervous about doing something really terrible. On the other hand, she had to get out of this school, she had to. Get back home again, go to Will's party; see Ranald, go to a proper school. She just had to steel herself and do something really bad once. It did make her feel horribly nervous and anxious, though, and was keeping her awake at night.

'Well, you just got better back-up. I'm on too.'

Fliss jumped up. 'That's brilliant! That's great news.'

Simone overheard and shrank a little inside. When it was just her and Fliss at rehearsals, Fliss wasn't that mean to her. A little quiet and distracted maybe, and friendlier to the girls from the other houses than to her, but not horrible, and sometimes she'd even walk her back to the dorm, though she never mentioned this to Alice. Fliss was someone Simone would like as a friend. She was glamorous and quite funny, nothing like as sullen as she pretended to be in class. If she could just get to know her, Simone thought she could really talk to her. If she could just get to know anyone. Simone sighed and went back to the letter she was sending her parents. They didn't have a computer, so she couldn't email and Skype like everyone else. On the other hand she did get a lot of letters in the post, which made the other girls jealous. She'd told her mother to stop sending cake, and thankfully she had.

'I am having a good time here,' she wrote out carefully. 'Everyone is very friendly and I get on well with everyone.'

Well she couldn't write the truth. Even isolation was better than being plucked out and sent back to her old school.

*

The dress rehearsal for the concert went badly, which, as much as David said it was tradition, shook Maggie up a little. Lights didn't cue at the right time, the orchestra was all over the place, and Simone lumbered on at completely the wrong point, bursting into tears when this was pointed out to her for the second time. Alice was word perfect already, but Fliss was suddenly strangely jumpy and nervous. The weather had turned frightfully cold, and David said Stephen Daedalus could smell snow and was refusing to leave the house. Maggie wondered if he was right. It didn't snow much in Glasgow; too built up and too near the sea, and when it did it hardly lay on the ground before it got dirty and snarled up with cigarette butts and footprints.

Stan had spent his days holed up in her rooms watching television. In vain she'd tried to interest him in taking walks around the local area; visiting the beautiful, windswept beaches, or the quaint villages. He'd been happy to go to the local pub every night and eat their microwaved lasagne and drink the local beer whilst complaining it wasn't Eighty Shilling.

Oddly, though, Maggie was finding she didn't mind. It was just Stan, doing what he did. It was comforting. And they had fun together, taking part in the pub quiz with Claire (the English league football round stumped them all), chatting about her friends and family and what everyone was up to, then retiring to the B&B which, perhaps through enforced intimacy and the fact that Stan couldn't eat in it, meant they were making love more often than ever.

It was only now that Maggie realised how lonely she'd been. All the silly fantasising about David was clearly just that, the imaginings of a lonely woman who'd let her imagination run away with her; no better than the girls she taught. This was where she belonged, sipping beer and laughing at Stan's impersonation of his boss at the distribution plant. She must just stop thinking about David, that was all. And she could tell Stan was happy too. It wasn't so unlikely that other women fancied him, after all.

It did snow, huge choking flakes through the night. The girls woke with yelps of excitement and a festive atmosphere ran through the school quicker than lightning. Mrs Rhys took the nod from the grounds manager, and decided to make bacon and eggs rather than the weekday porridge (or gruel, as the girls referred to it). Some of the parents who were coming to the concert were staying a couple of days, to take the girls home from school in the car, though most would take the London train on which the school had a block booking. Though many girls had gone home at half-term, some hadn't seen their mum and dad for twelve weeks and were quite beside themselves. There was a flurry of nerves and packing and huge excitement as the delicious smell of cooking sausages wound its way up the stairs.

Veronica went to her office early, a heather-coloured cardigan from Brora pulled tightly round her shoulders. This was not ideal at all. The snow would affect the roads, which would mean the parents would be late, the concert would overrun horribly and everything would be out of sync. She hated disorder. Not only that but the inspectors were coming back to watch the concert. She shook her head. This wasn't *High School Musical*, the film every single girl in the school had suddenly gone mad for last year and even got up a petition to go and see. It wasn't a performing arts college. The quality of the music teaching was one thing, but turning her girls into a troupe of showboats was extremely far away from her original aims.

She leafed through her paperwork. Very few girls were staying over the Christmas break; just one whose parents were diplomats in a country currently going through some upheaval, and an Australian fourth former, Noelene, who got horribly unhappy in the winter months. Veronica couldn't understand the parents sending her so very far away. Getting an English education was one thing. Getting it whilst your parents were sunning themselves by the pool was quite another.

There was a knock at the door, interrupting her train of thought. Miss Prenderghast popped her head round.

'It's Patricia from the Inspector's commission – with a new inspector too,' said Miss Prenderghast. She lowered her voice. 'It's a *man*.' Veronica raised her eyebrows. The men in this line of work tended towards the very pernickity, finicky types brandishing a large manual of health and safety practices. Not, frankly, ideal.

'All right, Evelyn, thank you. Send them in please,' she said.

Pat bustled in, all frenzied seriousness as usual, as if someone had just deliberately said something to upset her.

'Merry Christmas,' said Veronica, conscious of the fragrant holly and mistletoe lining the fireplace. Pat raised her eyebrows.

'Do you know, many schools prefer to inclusively celebrate Winterval now? So that no child feels left out?'

'Christmas leaves no one out, Patricia,' said Veronica, wondering what would constitute a safe nicety.

Her eyes moved upwards to look at the man who followed her in. He looked quiet, neat and tidy in a grey suit. Quite young for an inspector; not yet forty, she would say.

'Veronica Deveral,' she said, holding out her hand. The man seemed to look at it curiously before he took it.

'Daniel Stapleton,' he said. Then he shook her hand quite forcibly, staring into her face.

Veronica sighed inwardly. Were any of these inspectors quite normal? He probably learned 'keep eye contact' on some money-wasting training course. 'Welcome to Downey House,' she said.

'Thank you,' he said, his voice sounding a little trembly and nervous.

'Coffee?'

'Yes please,' he said, glancing nervously at Pat. Pat nodded and said, 'Miss Prenderghast, do you think we could maybe get a couple of sandwiches?'

Veronica despised anyone treating her highly organised administrator as some sort of domestic servant, but Miss Prenderghast was already heading off to the kitchen as Pat took the seat nearest the fire.

'Now, for the concert tonight, we have several quality target initiatives that we'd like to see pushing the envelope . . .'

Sylvie ran into the common room, where the girls were talking nervously about the concert and the party, in particular what they were going to wear. Everyone was asking Fliss and Alice what the boys in the orchestra were like, what the readers were like, and in particular who was the tall boy they'd seen walk in in full high-collared dress uniform?

Besides that, of course, the main topic of conversation was Miss Adair's chav boyfriend. There had been great excitement when he'd been spotted in the main halls wearing a football top! The girls were full of excited speculation as to whether he'd ever been arrested and whether or not he was a football hooligan. Ursula and Zazie, a Moroccan girl from a wealthy family who spoke perfect French and English and had a usually mischievous sense of fun, had both expressed amazement that someone as old as Miss Adair would have a boyfriend at all, rather than some ancient husband stashed somewhere.

Fliss had found her nerves all shot; she'd hardly slept the previous night. But she and Alice had talked it through; they were going to do it. She was going to do it. In front of everyone. She was going to ruin the concert and go home. Then she'd sneak out to Will's band and then ... well she didn't know what would happen after that, but it didn't really matter. No more stupid classes. No more stupid Miss Adair on her back all the time. No more stupid having to share a room with Imogen and fat Simone. No more having to listen to Hattie's boring stories about being a prefect, blah blah blah. She'd be back where she belonged. And once Mum and Dad got over being a bit pissed off they'd be pleased, she was sure of it. Pleased to have her back, just her on her own, no stupid sister. It would definitely be worth it. But oh my goodness, the nerves. She tried to concentrate on what the other girls were asking her – about Jake, the lanky pretty boy from the boys' school, who was reading the Betjeman. Not her type. Her type was only Will. Will. Even saying the name made her heart flutter, and steeled her resolve.

Anyway, here was Sylvie tearing in. She was meant to be dancing, but was looking as scatterbrained as usual.

'I've lost them!' she was saying.

'What?' said Alice.

'My earrings! I have special silver earrings that go with my Dickens outfit. And I can't find them! But I'm sure they were in my desk drawer.'

The noisy common room went quiet. It was common knowledge that Fliss had lost her watch. Most of the girls had hoped it was a mistake or a one-off. Now it looked as though there was a serial thief amongst them.

Sylvie was nearly tearful. Normally nothing troubled her, so to see her upset was very unusual. She looked around.

'I know they were there because I tried them on last night for rehearsal. So it was someone who's been around the dorms since. I didn't lose them. So if it was one of you . . .' Her voice choked up. 'I hope you're proud of yourselves.'

Simone, crouching in the corner with one of the books Maggie had lent her, stiffened. Then Alice picked up what Sylvie was saying.

'Yes,' she said. 'I know not everyone has lots of money at this school. And people shouldn't be judged on how much money they have. But if you don't have much, you should-n't take other people's things. I'm not accusing anyone. I'm just saying.'

The whole room went silent. Simone felt every eye on her.

'Anyone got anything to own up?' said Alice. Nobody said anything. 'Anyone?'

Simone felt herself get to her feet. Her face was flaming, a bright, bright red colour she could feel. She wanted to make it clear; to show people and tell them that it wasn't her, she wasn't a thief; all the girls in her old school had gone stealing all the time and she'd thought it was disgusting. But the words wouldn't come out. Her throat was completely choked up.

'Just . . . shut up!' she half-screamed at Alice in a high-pitched tone. 'SHUT UP!'

And she pushed her way through the girls and left the room.

All the girls were hanging out of the windows as the first cars started to pull up, snow on their roofs, into the allocated car spaces. Sixth formers were out in padded jackets to direct the traffic, along with the grounds staff. The forecourt was lit up with fairy lights, and a huge Christmas tree stood in the middle of the cobbled quad. The school looked as beautiful as it possibly could, thought Maggie, waiting for Stan to make his way up from the village. He'd taken the car, although walking would obviously have been slightly healthier for him, but she didn't want to argue.

She was wearing a new dress that she'd bought. It was a deep, Christmassy red, that reflected well against her dark hair and brought out the pink in her cheeks. Pulled tight around her waist, and with a pair of magic knickers on, she looked good – pretty, but not so vampy that any of the girls' families would feel uncomfortable around her.

The girls were in uniform for the concert, but were doing their best to bend the rules for the visit of the boys' school, so there were ribbons in the hair, illicit skirt turning-up and barely traceable make-up everywhere. Yelling and running, normally completely *verboten* in the inner sanctum of the school, was breaking out all over. Usually very conscious of the feelings of the pupils who did not have parents coming, Veronica found this difficult, but didn't forbid it. Just because some were unhappy didn't mean you had the right to make everyone so.

Finally, quite a while after the scheduled six p.m. start, the heavy, old red curtains of the packed theatre opened, and Veronica walked out.

'Welcome everyone,' she said, 'particularly those of you who have come a long way. We've been very proud of our girls this term and I know that next year, as we move towards the summer, they will work harder than ever.'

There were some theatrical groans at this, as the students knew they were far enough away from their austere head-mistress to risk a little gentle heckling.

'But Christmas is a festival. Wherever you are from, and whatever your beliefs.'

Pat's head, from where she was sitting in the audience scoffing Haribo, popped up at this.

'Northern European countries have always celebrated the depths of winter, the very nadir of the year, with celebration, dancing, warmth, food and light. We in the Christian tradition also celebrate the birth of the infant Christ, but there are many winter traditions that surround us, and all exist to wish us peace and prosperity at this cold time of year. So on behalf of my girls, and Dr Fitzroy, who has so kindly lent us some of his boys to make up the orchestra and some of the readings, may I wish you peace and joy from all at Downey House.'

The applause was loud as Alice, looking beautiful and very meek – Maggie mentally shook her head – came out with Lars, a cellist from the upper school. The idea was to interplay the poem with a strange, eastern melody and it worked beautifully. Maggie felt a shudder go up her spine as Alice, having been told to downplay her reading, came to 'This birth was hard and bitter agony for us' and the refrain was subtly echoed in the music. There was no doubt Mrs Offili had done a wonderful job.

After that, there was dancing from the older girls, and the choir, which was nearly of professional standard, all sang except for the back-row altos, Maggie made a mental note, who were standing far too close to the boys and four of them were red-faced and sniggering about something. They weren't in her group, but she might have a word with Miss Starling.

Backstage, the mood was giggly and tense amongst the soloists. Astrid was in a world of her own with her clarinet, tapping out melodies in the air when she was meant to be putting make-up on (the girls took this performing privilege very seriously). Clarissa Rhodes, school star, was singing a version of the Carol of the Bells which, it was rumoured, had made Mrs Offili cry. As usual, she didn't think she was good enough and was nervously checking the sheet music.

Alice had bounced off the stage to a mass of warm applause, and was making a terrible job of hiding her delight. Now her part was over, she could content herself by basking in how much better she'd been than everyone else. Simone was in a corner by herself. Nobody had offered to put her eyeliner on, or a bit of lip gloss. She looked terrible; her eyes were red and dark-rimmed from lack of sleep; her hair was a mess and if anything she'd put on weight again.

Fliss was also standing alone, her heart beating at an alarming rate. She'd have been nervous about performing anyway, but this hadn't really sunk in until she'd peeked out of the red curtains and seen how many people were out there; hundreds and hundreds. She couldn't even see her own mum and dad.

'There's still time not to do it,' said Alice, who was hoping very much that Fliss would. They'd cooked up the plan together in the alcove late at night. 'I wouldn't tell anyone.'

Fliss shook her head. 'No,' she said. 'I have to do it. I have to get home. And this is the best way that doesn't involve hurting anyone.' She glanced over at Simone. 'Or stealing stuff.'

At the sound of the 'stealing' word, Simone had raised her head, then she buried it again. Maybe the best thing she could do would just be to tell her parents that she didn't want to go back to Downey House, that it hadn't suited her after all, that she'd been wrong. But then they'd send her back to St Cats. There wasn't a solution. She was trapped.

She tried to focus on her piece. Her hands were shaking. She mustn't forget it. She mustn't.

The Tudor first years finished their pageant – a series of rhyming couplets they'd written themselves about Christmas down the ages. It was good, thought Maggie. She should have done something like that. It was sure to have impressed Miss Starling.

'Hello,' said a voice in the wings. 'Nervous?'

Maggie turned round to see David standing there, looking tall and handsome in a velvet jacket which should have looked odd and dated but actually rather suited him.

'No,' she started to say. 'Actually . . . yes. For them, of course.'

'Of course,' said David. 'You look very nice.'

She felt herself blush; she hadn't thought he'd pay attention to things like that.

'Thank you,' she said. She'd managed, whilst Stan was there, to mostly wean herself off thinking about him. But she did wonder, once again; was this man gay, single, or what? It wasn't a conversation they'd ever had.

They stood in silence for a while, watching Clarissa sing the Carol of the Bells. At first her high voice rang out accompanied only by a single bell. Then, as the choir came in on the ding-donging, Maggie felt the hairs on the back of her neck rise. Finally, the entire orchestra and choir together sang to the rafters the triumphant, 'Merry merry merry merry CHRISTMAS'. It was stunningly beautiful.

'Wow,' Maggie said breathlessly. She realised, with sinking heart, how aware she was of David right next to her. Maybe it hadn't gone away at all. Maybe it was just lurking, to catch her out.

'Yes,' he said, turning to look straight at her. She caught her breath.

Then suddenly the quiet intimacy of the moment was lost completely as the horde of the choir pounded off through them like a flock of clumpy-shoed gazelles, to cheers from the audience. It was hard to find a quiet moment in a school. Maggie checked her programme and realised she should be herding on Felicity.

'I have to go,' she muttered, almost apologetically, feeling her heart pound.

'Of course; me too,' said David, looking very awkward.

Maggie darted off in the direction of the dressing room. 'Come on, come on,' she chided Fliss, who was standing there looking slightly ill. 'Don't worry, you're going to be great.'

Felicity was the last act on before the interval, after which there was the senior ballet and play to get through, with Simone's monologue opening the second half. They were running late, though not ruinously so.

'Come on. You're not too nervous are you?'

Fliss couldn't work out why Miss Adair was being so kind to her, even offering her a glass of water. Everyone at this school was horrid, except for Alice. That was why she was leaving. She was going home. That was it.

'You'll be wonderful,' said Maggie, surprised Fliss was so pale and terrified. Most of the girls had reasonable poise in front of their peers; part of a class that had told them since birth they were more than good enough. But here she was, practically having to throw her on stage.

There was a silence from the auditorium now, just an expectant rustling of programmes. Fliss closed her eyes.

'OK,' she said. Then she walked on to the stage.

The lights were so much in Fliss's eyes at first she could scarcely see a thing. In a way that was quite good. People looked further away; she couldn't distinguish who was who. But it did make her realise the scale of the occasion.

She stepped up to the microphone. It was set to Clarissa's height, far too tall for her, and no one had brought it down, so she had a very awkward moment fumbling for it. Maggie, watching from the wings – David had vanished – felt embarrassed that she hadn't arranged for someone to fix it for her. Oh well, sympathy would be on her side. She would deliver Jo's speech and just as it ended the orchestra would join in with some jaunty American turn-of-the-century melodies to play the audience out into the main hall where there was exceedingly weak mulled wine for the grown-ups and sixth formers, and squash for the rest.

Fliss gave up her struggle with the microphone stand and decided just to hold the mike instead. She bit her lip and stepped forward. 'Eh,' she said. Immediately the microphone let out a howl of feedback. People were starting to sit up and take notice. There hadn't been much in the way of hopeless amateurs so far. Everyone was too good. For the bored younger brothers and sisters in the audience, as well as those members of the school not involved, a little diversionary failure couldn't come soon enough.

'There's a few things I want to say about this school before I start,' said Fliss, but her voice was wobbly and not quite close enough to the mike.

'Speak up!' shouted a voice from the back.

Suddenly Fliss saw red. 'This school is crap!' she yelled into the microphone. 'The food is crap and the teachers are crap and you're all being ripped off!'

A thrill of delighted rebellion rushed through the younger (and some older) members of the audience.

'First of all, there's the COMPLETE unfairness of the mobile phone locking scheme. That is a complete attack on human rights. And some of the teachers can barely speak English. Our English teacher is almost impossible to understand. Why should we have to suffer through that?'

Maggie had a quick intake of breath and moved towards the stage.

'Not to mention the horrible PE changing room where there's still communal showers like this was 1980 or something.'

Some of the fathers' eyebrows were raised at this.

'SO . . .' And at that, Fliss ripped open her shirt. The entire audience gasped as the buttons popped off and, underneath it, saw she was wearing a white T-shirt, crudely scrawled with the words DOWNEY HOUSE SUCKS.

Fliss, realising she'd captured the attention of the audience, stepped forward to continue the litany of injustice, before ending it on a chant she hoped would be taken up by the entire school – DOWNEY HOUSE SUCKS! – until someone ran on stage to drag her off. That English teacher most likely. That should do it.

Sure enough, Maggie, who'd hardly been listening until her name came up, so conscious was she of where David was, now made to run on stage. Mrs Offili was already on her feet to start up the orchestra in order to drown out the noise. But right then, Fliss took one last step forward to emphasise her point . . . and dropped out of sight completely.

The orchestra didn't sit in the orchestra pit for the first half of the show; they went on the stage, so that the proud parents could pick out their daughter, the second bassoonist. They would go down there once the ballet started, but for the moment it was empty. Which could be seen as good luck, mused Veronica later, as she tried, and failed, to see an upside, as it meant Felicity Prosser broke only her own ankle and didn't injure anyone else.

The kerfuffle and yells which broke out as Felicity dropped from the stage were enormous and what had happened ran through the school at the speed of light. Most of the parents assumed the girl had been drunk, and wondered how alcohol was obtainable on the premises – and to such a young girl too. Veronica ordered the orchestra to play on and for the interval to continue as planned; of course, there was only one buzz in the air.

Maggie was third on the scene, to find David and Mrs Offili already there ministering to a white-faced Felicity, who had tears streaming down her face from the pain.

'What the hell!' she started shouting at her, her own shock and worry about her pupil coming out too clearly in her voice. 'What the HELL was that?'

David turned round from where he was looking at Felicity's ankle. 'I think we need to get her to a hospital,' he said. 'I can drive her if you like.'

Maggie felt herself instantly reproved, and bristled. 'She needs to get to a hospital because she was pulling some ridiculous stunt and it's her own fault. What on earth were you *doing*, Felicity?'

Fliss couldn't breathe for the pain. The pain in her leg and the shocking and terrible recriminations she felt raining down on her head from all the people in the hall. There was a ring of people around her as all the curious individuals came to nose about. She could hear her mother's voice saying loudly, 'Where is she? What happened? What's happened to her?' and the crowd parting to let her through.

Suddenly what had seemed like such a good, rebellious idea in the dorm with Alice seemed like the worst idea ever.

What had she been thinking? Making an idiot of herself in front of the whole school? And now, her ankle really, really hurt. She felt cold inside, worrying if something was really wrong with her.

The handsome English teacher from the boys' school was looking at her in a concerned way and had covered her up with his jacket, which wasn't too bad until he prodded her foot, and Miss Adair was shouting at her, but that was nothing unusual. For a second she wondered if she could make herself faint, but as her mother and outraged-looking sister pushed through the crowd she realised there was no making about it, and she dropped clean away.

The next thing she knew she was on a bed in the sanatorium. The first person she saw was Matron who told her she was going to be fine, but she needed to go to hospital to get her ankle seen to.

Her parents and Hattie were there too, looking confused.

'But why?' her mother was saying. 'Why?'

Miss Adair was right behind her, still looking furious, as was Miss Starling. The teacher from the boys' school looked concerned. Fliss wondered if he'd carried her into the sanatorium.

She looked down at her swollen throbbing ankle.

'I just wanted to go home,' she said, tears pouring down her cheeks.

The father of one of the pupils, a surgeon, came and gave his professional opinion on Felicity's ankle – that he believed it was indeed broken – and she was packed off to casualty in Truro.

Veronica was in two minds. She should perhaps call off the show. On the other hand, there were a lot of parents who'd paid a lot of money and come a long way to see their children perform, and she didn't want the antics of one to ruin the evening for the rest of them. And she disliked quitters. She came to a decision.

'Ladies and gentlemen,' she announced in the grand hall, where quite a few parents were getting stuck into the mulled wine. 'I do apologise for the behaviour of one of our younger girls. She's very new here. But all our other wonderful girls and boys are here and ready to perform for you, so if you'd like to retake your seats . . .'

There was a general mutter of approval, particularly from parents who hadn't yet seen their own offspring, and a loud tut from Pat, who was, no doubt, Veronica reflected, judging how much she could escalate the incident in her own report, for health and safety reasons.

Simone, trapped in her own misery backstage, had hardly noticed the commotion, only that everyone had disappeared and left her on her own, which was hardly unusual. Now they came back in dribs and drabs whispering excitedly – 'She was drunk! She called everyone a bastard!' to one another so she gathered something had gone terribly wrong with Fliss's piece. It would probably make her more popular than ever, Simone found herself thinking meanly.

'Simone,' said Maggie, somewhat wild-eyed. She was ashamed of her outburst before, shouting at a sad, injured girl in front of David. 'Do you think you can go on and do your piece without managing to jeopardise the entire school?'

Simone nodded behind her owl glasses, not quite understanding.

'OK, on you go then.'

The orchestra had just about calmed down enough to play a Grieg interlude, introducing the Dickens as Simone walked on. The audience was now upright and expectant, hoping that she would do something equally unexpected.

'Marley was dead, to begin with,' said Simone, launching into the speech she'd rehearsed a thousand times in her head.

And she was good. Very good. Not even her mother standing up and filming in the middle of the front row, in direct contravention of instructions, as well as of the people behind who wanted to see, could stop her. She was clear and her London accent added a veracity to the words, and as she came to a close, the senior girls, who were dancing a piece based on the book, fluttered on like a clutch of Dickensian fairies, in tasteful rags and smocks, to hear her intone how 'the candles were flaring in the windows of the neighbouring offices, like ruddy smears upon the palpable brown air. The fog came pouring in at every chink and keyhole . . .'

The applause was massive and heartfelt, particularly from the staff and those pupils who didn't want to see the school made a laughing stock of by a pushy middle-schooler. Maggie found herself grinning with relief, before she went off to check with the hospital. And Veronica couldn't help being quietly pleased and surprised at her awkward little scholarship girl. Would she yet surprise them all?

Maggie had called the hospital – Felicity's parents had taken her in their car, and Matron had followed on behind. All would be fine. The corridor was empty and quiet, as the audience was entranced by the seniors' ballet (some of the fathers perhaps a little more than they ought to have been). She wondered briefly where Stan was and what he made of all this. Then out of the shadows stepped David.

Maggie felt her heart flutter. Oh, this was ridiculous, she had a huge disciplinary crisis on her hands, and, who knows, the parents could take it into their heads to sue the school, and where would they be then?

'Is she OK?' asked David. Maggie nodded; Matron had responded briskly that they were putting her in plaster and she'd be right as rain.

'Her parents will take her home whilst we sort out what to do.'

'Just a little bit of teenage rebellion,' said David.

'Just a bit,' said Maggie. 'Quite a big bit though.'

David looked at the floor. 'Look, Maggie, I think . . .'

He seemed awkward and looked up again. He was standing right underneath some mistletoe.

'Ah,' he said, noticing it, but not stepping away. 'The thing is, Maggie . . . God, this is bad timing. Well. Uhm. Too late now. Uh, I really like you.'

Maggie stopped short and looked straight at him. Her heart was pounding in her mouth. Surely not, with Stan here and everything. She couldn't. He couldn't. It wasn't right. It wasn't even legal on school grounds.

But suddenly she thought she wanted to kiss David McDonald more than anything else in the world, even as she could hear the orchestra play the Coventry carol next door.

David tried again. 'There's something I should have . . . it's very important that our relationship remain professional.'

Maggie felt her heart drop like it was in an elevator shaft. Of course it was. Of course. What an idiot she was. David was looking at her, but it was hard to read his expression. Almost as if he found this painful too.

'I think it's for the best, don't you?'

Inside Maggie wanted to scream, NO! No! I want you! Instead, she just nodded her head and said, 'Quite! I'm sorry, I didn't realise we'd gone beyond the normal bounds . . .'

'No,' said David, shaking his head vehemently. 'No, of course we haven't.'

Without being able to consciously help it (or so she told herself), Maggie found herself glancing upwards at the mistletoe, and then back towards David. He seemed to move towards her – was he? Did she? She found herself compelled to move forwards. Her gaze was fixed on his dark eyes. Was she really going to move straight into his arms? What if they were discovered? The school really couldn't have any more scandal tonight. But to feel his lips on hers suddenly seemed more important than any rule; any job she could possibly have. She felt drunk with longing; she wanted him more than she'd ever wanted anything. Shocked by the power of her feelings, she stepped forward. It felt as though the music dropped away; the snow outside rendering every-thing silent and still.

'David,' she breathed.

'David!' she heard.

It was a loud, friendly voice and it came from a blonde woman who'd just entered the passageway. She was pretty and fresh looking.

'Hello!' she said cheerily, putting out a hand to Maggie as she came forward. She came up to David and took his hand.

'I'm Miranda.' She turned to him. 'Ooh, look, mistletoe. Do you think it would be *dreadfully* naughty to kiss in school? This is where I learnt after all.'

'Hi! I'm David's fiancée,' she added to Maggie, as if the ring on her finger and her stance of ownership could have left anyone in any doubt.

Chapter Ten

It was not the happiest of Christmases. Glasgow was covered in a grey sludge which, Maggie felt, reflected her own state of mind. She felt so stupid, so ashamed and so damn cross! OK, she'd never mentioned Stan, but – a *fiancée*? So, David probably had lots of girls crushing on him every year without a *teacher* embarrassing herself. Was she, a woman with a boyfriend, really going to snog another, engaged teacher, in the school when all the parents were there? Thinking about it made her shiver with horror. What on earth had she been thinking? What was wrong with her?

Stan thought she was sad because she was realising how much she missed Glasgow and all her friends. He was being incredibly nice to her. Maggie had thought guiltily that maybe he suspected something was up, but, no, he hadn't mentioned David – he'd hardly mentioned the school at all, just arranged nights out at the pub with their friends and lots of trips round to her mum and dad's. She was grateful for the distractions and touched at Stan's kindness – long distance relationships really were difficult. Maybe it was time to see if he'd like to come and work closer by. Stop her getting fixated on someone like a teenager who still had posters up in her bedroom.

And it was nice to get looked after by her mum and dad,

and watch telly late, and play with her nephews and come and go as she pleased without having to worry about being on show all the time. That was the thing about Downey House, and she'd never anticipated how much of a burden it could be; to eat communally, work communally; to see the same faces all day every day was quite wearing, more so than she'd realised. It was nice, after all, to slump around the house in pyjamas, playing music loudly and watching television with Cody and Dylan.

'I thought we'd go out on New Year's Eve,' said Stan, as she sat polishing off the Quality Street in front of the *Doctor Who* Christmas special they were watching for the fourth time.

'Oh yeah,' said Maggie, not really paying attention. 'Is Jimmy having another party?'

'Neh, thought we'd go out for dinner, something like that.'

'OK,' said Maggie, surprised. Going out for dinner wasn't a very Stan thing to suggest. He was improving.

New Year's Eve was, as ever, utterly freezing and bitterly wet. Maggie started regretting their plan almost immediately as they waited for a bus, having tried and failed to catch a cab into town. The restaurant was filled with large groups of noisy people shouting and bursting balloons at one another whilst wearing party hats, and the frazzled waiter moued apologetically as he showed them to a cramped table for two buried in the corner. Stan immediately ordered a bottle of champagne, which was very unlike him. Maggie gave him a sharp look. They were doing a little better financially as Maggie's job paid more than her old one, and she was spending a lot less. But still, this was a bit recklessly extravagant, and they should really . . .

'Maggie. Maggie!'

Stan had to say her name twice before she responded. When she looked up she saw he was kneeling on the floor.

Oh my God! Why hadn't she noticed he was wearing his only suit?

'God, I meant to do this at the end of the meal, but I'm sweating like a pig, and I don't think I can hold it in, so . . .'

Maggie stared at him. What was he doing? Oh God. This was the last thing she'd been expecting. The other, red-faced, drunken people in the restaurant had started to look round, after someone caught sight of what was going on. She shook her head in amazement. Well, David wasn't the only person who could be engaged after all.

'So, my lovely Maggie . . . you've had your time away, and I've missed you horribly and we've had our ups and downs, but I really really want you to be mine for ever, so, uh, will you marry me?'

Somebody woo-hooed in the restaurant, but everyone else had fallen suddenly, eerily silent; even the waiters had stopped scurrying around. Stan looked up from where he was kneeling, and fixed Maggie with his kind blue eyes.

'Well?'

Fliss was, in the end, only rusticated. That meant, as Hattie had pushily explained, that she was suspended but without it going on her permanent record. It was only for the last three days of term. The school saw her broken ankle as quite punishment enough and had given the lightest penalty. Had she managed to deliver more of her speech, it had been made extremely clear to her in a conversation with Miss Adair, Miss Starling and Dr Deveral, which her parents attended – a meeting Fliss would never be able to think of again in her life without feeling the most deep and intense shame – then things could have been a lot worse.

Of course she had not made it to Will's Christmas party. Or any Christmas party. Her mother was more sympathetic, but her father's disappointment was clear to see in his face. She hated making him so miserable. Hattie, of course, was triumphant and made a show of being extra helpful by bringing her books and extra study guides to help her catch up. Only Ranald, licking her face every day like he couldn't quite believe she was home, gave her any succour.

Now, her cheek and rebelliousness felt a bit stupid and immature. Getting bad marks on purpose? Fliss thought, with a creeping sense of contrition. Did she really do that? What must the teachers think of her, even that horrid Miss Adair.

After a muted Christmas – the grounded and incapacitated Fliss opened her new clothes without much pleasure, knowing her opportunities to wear them were severely limited – and oddly stilted visits from her friends, who were full of the new shopping centre, and the new boys at the school and teachers whose names she didn't know, she was staring out of the window at the sleet driving into the orchard, whilst failing to take her usual comfort in rereading *What Katy Did*, when both her parents entered her room at the same time and sat down. Fliss looked up at them nervously. Being grounded was one thing. Getting another lecture on how badly she'd let everyone down and how she'd disappointed them was quite another.

So she was surprised when her mother took her hand.

'Felicity,' she said. 'Your dad and I have been talking. We didn't . . . we didn't realise you were so unhappy.'

'I wasn't unhappy all the time,' said Fliss, grudgingly. She'd had a lot of time alone in her room to think about things. She glanced at her father, but his eyes were downcast.

'We've talked about it, and we've decided,' continued her mother. 'We'd like you to see out the year. And then, if you still really hate it . . . well, we can talk about it then.'

'I want you to give it a proper shot,' said her father, his voice sounding gruffer than usual. 'To see it through. None of the best things in life are easy right off the bat, Felicity.'

'And we paid the fees up front,' said her mum, like that was important. 'I've spoken to the school. You can go back on your crutches with your plaster, they can manage that. You will apologise to everyone involved in the concert for the upset you caused. Then it will never be spoken of again. But if you as much as breathe out of line . . . I'll be furious. I want you to try, Fliss. Try your absolute hardest, OK?'

Fliss nodded, grudgingly. She'd expected a lot worse. Her book was easier to read now, after her mother had kissed her on the cheek and both parents had gone off to the RSPB Christmas ball. Till the summer. She could wait.

'If I have to listen to that BLOODY' – Joel, trying out the word in case it counted as swearing – 'Dickens garbage one more time do you think I am going to be a) a little bit bored, b) extremely bored or c) so bored I'm going to have to kick myself in the head?'

'You should be proud of your sister,' said Mrs Kardashian. Simone had been made to perform her extract in front of every set of relatives and friends her mother could muster to showcase her privately educated daughter.

The relief of being home, where nobody watched what she ate, or made sly remarks (apart from Joel, and she could cuff him) or accused her of being a thief, almost made her want to cry. She revelled in the very smell of home; of food cooking and her mother's perfume. Seeing her own bedroom made her sink down with relief.

But her parents' pride in her and her accomplishments was so strong.

'Shy, but with excellent imaginative and intuitive skills,' Maggie had written on her report card. The fact that Simone's spelling and punctuation were behind, thanks to years of noisy undisciplined classrooms, she'd put aside with the aim of trying to boost the girl's confidence. She still didn't know how to broach the subject of stealing. She'd have to do something about that in the new year.

'A pleasure to teach,' Miss Bereford the maths teacher had added. Mrs Kardashian had brandished that report at everyone from the postman upwards. So Simone swallowed her feelings and tried her best to smile and take things in good humour, even as her mother tried to get her to wear her school uniform to church.

It was only towards the end of the holiday that Simone's nerves started to bunch up again in her stomach. She was eating more, she realised. Packing her suitcase was torture. Even the thought of having to walk into that dorm again; to hear the whispers and giggles of the other girls instantly silenced as she entered. Of another lunch or supper sitting alone at the end of the table, excluded from the conversation. The thought of it made her queasy. The night before she was due to catch the train she went upstairs to finalise her packing, taking a packet of Hobnobs with her as she went.

Her father came in to find her weeping over her new chemistry textbook.

'Hey, what is it, *scumpa*?' He chucked her gently under the chin, which made her cry even more. 'It's not the school, is it?' he said, sitting down on the bed. Simone wanted nothing more than to throw herself in his arms and tell him everything; about the teasing, and remarks, and the loneliness; the huge, massive, crushing loneliness.

But what for? He'd sacrificed a lot to come to this country; to see his children do well. In Romania he could be an engineer. Here he could drive a cab. He had sacrificed his own hopes and ambitions for her. She couldn't tread on his dreams, even though she knew at some level how much he hated her being away from him and thought the fancy school would carry her even further away.

And to go back to her old school. How would that be better? How would that help anything at all?

'It's nothing,' she sniffed. 'I'm glad to be going back. I'll just miss you all, that's all.'

Her papa took her in his arms and gave her a long squeeze.

'We miss you too,' he said, patting her back and rubbing his own eyes. 'We miss you too. And we love you, *iubita*. You're making your mother so proud, you know? You're making all of us proud, even that *obraznicule* brother of yours. Never forget that.'

Veronica usually saw in Christmas with the minimum of fuss. She liked to keep busy. Jane was a good companion in this respect; she minded her own business and chose to discuss history rather than pry into anything personal. Veronica wondered about Jane herself, and her own preferences, never voiced, but she wouldn't dream of raising it. And the weather was clear and bright and warm in the Greek islands, where they ate moussaka and visited the ruins and in the evening put cardigans on their shoulders and strolled through villages, looking for the most authentic tavernas. It had not, flighty teenagers notwithstanding, been a bad year, on the whole. Applications were up, and the new English teacher, whilst hot-headed on occasion, certainly seemed enthusiastic and worked hard; two qualities, Veronica often felt, that compensated for the occasional practical deficiency, though June Starling didn't always agree. Now, she only had this wretched assessment to get through and everything would be clipping along quite nicely.

Maggie took a deep breath. They could sort out the geography later. OK, her new job had its tough moments – and she wouldn't mind never seeing David McDonald again – but she didn't want to give it up straight away; there was still so much to learn she could bring back later. Stan could even find something in Cornwall; he liked the pubs well enough. Anyway, it was something they could discuss. And they had plenty of time; there was nothing wrong with a long engagement.

Gosh, she also found herself thinking. Here I am. Being proposed to. How extraordinary. She was even more surprised at not having guessed it was coming. After all, they had been together a long time. But they'd had such a difficult year. She looked at Stan's scruffy, loveable face.

As the restaurant diners, almost as one, leaned closer, she let a huge smile break out.

'Of course,' she said, only a tiny part of her mind wondering if this was quite right. 'Of course!'

And the room let out a huge round of applause.

Chapter Eleven

The weather was sharp and cold as the cars rolled up for the spring term. Faces were solemn; this term there was sport outside in the freezing cold; mock exams for the older girls. Maggie examined the little shiny half-carat ring they'd chosen in Laings on her finger for the thousandth time and vowed that there was going to be no more nonsense of the Felicity/Alice variety – she was going to split up the troublemakers and put everyone's nose to the grindstone. She didn't care that they sniggered at her and that the girls didn't accept her. She was going to make them work. It was a broad syllabus and she wanted to prove to Veronica, to Miss Starling, to the assessors and everyone else that she was capable. No, better than capable: a good teacher.

Claire was the first to pounce when she arrived in their little suite of rooms, amazed at how pleased she was to be back there again.

'*Qu'est-ce que c'est?* What ees that on your finger!!!' she exclaimed, as soon as she heard Maggie arrive. Maggie beamed and stretched it out. They had phoned her parents, Stan's dad, and everyone they knew as soon as Stan had got up off the ground, looking as pleased with himself as if he'd just won the lottery. Everyone's happiness was so strong and palpable she'd found herself getting swept along in the champagne, and the hugs and the planning. She needed to have a conversation with Stan about maybe him moving to Cornwall for a couple of years, just while she got the experience she needed at Downey House, then they could go back to Glasgow, she'd find a school that needed her and everything would be just fine. All the talk was of where, and when, and what it would be like and who would come. They hadn't set a date yet, there was too much to discuss and they only had a few days before Stan was back at work and Maggie was already making plans to go back south.

'But it won't be for long, love, will it?' Stan said hopefully, tucking into pizza on their last night together.

'Well, I think I need to be there a bit longer than three months,' said Maggie, carefully folding up her new soft grey jersey dress, just like one Claire had, that she'd picked up in the January sales. 'I need to get a good reference, then I can work anywhere. I should stay for at least two years.'

Stan made a grumpy face. 'You don't want to get married for *two years*? I thought you girls were always desperate to get down the aisle.'

'Well, we could do it next summer. This summer is probably too early anyway, everything will be booked up. And it will give us longer to save up.'

Stan looked at her. 'Yeah? You want a big do?' He didn't seem the least bit put out by the prospect.

'I don't know,' said Maggie. 'We could just slip off to Vegas if you like.'

'Yeah, get married by Elvis. In a cadillac,' said Stan, his eyes gleaming. 'Neh. It would break your mother's heart.'

He was so thoughtful, she thought.

'Stan,' she said. 'Are you sure you couldn't look for work in Cornwall? They have newspapers there too, you know. And fish suppers.'

Stan looked perturbed. 'But I like it up here. All my friends are here. And my family. You're the one that wants to go down and ponce about amongst English folk.'

'I know,' said Maggie. 'But I thought you'd like us to be together.'

'Yuh,' said Stan. 'That's why I asked you to marry me. Come home. Let's get a wee house in Paisley. It'll be good.'

'I know,' said Maggie. And it would. It would. She just . . . 'I just think I should see this job out, OK? It's a great opportunity for us. For setting up our future.'

'I miss you,' said Stan.

'I know,' said Maggie. 'I miss you too.'

'And that school of yours is full of mad folk. What about that weirdo, the bloke teaching English?'

'David's not weird! He's just different.'

'I didn't think they let blokes like that teach in boys' schools.'

Maggie looked at him in exasperation. 'I'm going to pretend I didn't hear that.'

Stan smiled. He liked winding her up.

'Was eet *romantique*?' asked Claire, as they sipped tea together and watched the cars draw up.

'Well, it was in a restaurant,' said Maggie. 'And there were about a hundred pished folk watching. But it had its moments.' She smiled to herself at the memory.

'*Bof.*' Claire had finally confided in Maggie that she was having an affair with a married man but she wouldn't tell her where. She often vanished on weekends and in the holidays, and came back slightly sad, if suntanned, and with a fabulous new pair of shoes every so often. Maggie was convinced she'd winkle it out of her sooner or later, but for the moment, Claire was content to dive on Maggie's romantic news.

'So what are you going to do?'

'Well, nothing yet,' said Maggie. 'I think I'd like to have a long engagement.'

'Oh yes, like Monsieur McDonald.'

Maggie stopped with her teacup halfway to her mouth. Claire had known? Why hadn't she mentioned it? Well, she supposed it wasn't really her business. She had never discussed David with Claire; was too afraid of a giveaway blush if she so much as thought of his name.

'Oh yes, I met his fiancée.'

'She works in Exeter, I theenk,' said Claire. 'Does not visit very often. I sometimes think that he is lonely. The other teachers at the boys' school, they are very old, don't you think? Apart from Monsieur Graystock, *bien sûr*.'

Maggie hadn't met the classics professor, but had heard Claire mention him. She'd spied him from afar at the concert; he was tall, aristocratic and distracted looking, and she hadn't given him much thought. But then, Maggie had never had much thought to spare for the other teachers at Downey Boys.

'So why aren't they married?' she asked.

'*Je sais pas*,' said Claire, shrugging. 'I heard she wanted him to move to the city, but he does not want to go and move Stephen Daedalus . . . it is true,' she said, wrinkling her nose. 'The English and their dogs.'

Maggie would have added something about the French and their mistresses, but didn't feel it was entirely appropriate. But that was interesting about David. Pulled in different directions, just as she was. She instantly dismissed all thought of him from her head. That was pointless, and supremely silly. And she was an engaged woman now, with someone at home who loved her very much.

'We should get changed for supper,' she said. 'I'm sure the girls are going to be *thrilled* to see us again . . .'

'And a hardworking term too,' said Claire. 'I am going to be *slavedriver*. I want those *petites rosbifs* to stop just one time from mangling my beautiful language until it sounds like peedgeons fighting. Do you think it can be possible?'

'Definitely,' said Maggie, as the two friends headed for the stairs.

Fliss was nervous as they pulled into the gravelled forecourt once more. She had promised her parents she'd behave, but was worried about how her teachers would be with her – particularly the hated Miss Adair, who hadn't shown the least bit of sympathy over her ankle. She'd promised faithfully to raise her marks; they could hardly get any lower. She swung her plastered ankle out of the side of the car, and waited for Dad to help her out. She was only limping slightly now, with a stick, and it didn't hurt at all, except when it was itchy. Would the other girls shun her for messing up the Christmas concert?

She needn't have worried. From the moment Alice spotted her from the dormitory window, and ran down with a scream of excitement, Fliss was enveloped in a mass of girls eagerly asking her what it had been like at hospital, asking to sign her plaster, and, mostly, sighing over the romance of fainting and being carried to the san by dashing Mr McDonald, just like Kate Winslet in *Sense and Sensibility*, or Keira Knightley in *Atonement*. Fliss was very peeved she couldn't remember a bit of it.

'Are we really sure she hates that school?' said Fliss's father as they drove away, scarcely noticed by their popular offspring, both completely submerged in chums.

'Let's just see at the end of the year, shall we?' said her mum.

*

At least there was a heavy workload this term, thought Simone, the only person pleased at the prospect. She could bury herself in books and nobody would notice. The fuss about stealing seemed to have died down for now. Maybe those things really had just gone missing after all. She would ignore the accusatory glances, ignore everything except concentrating on work and passing exams. She was going to make her dad so proud. Even prouder than he was already. Remembering her family's love provided a small candle of warmth inside her.

'Yes?' Veronica looked up at the door, as Daniel, the new assessor, knocked and slipped into the office without Pat. She was surprised, yet again, at his youth and wondered why he'd chosen this job.

'Hello,' she said pleasantly. 'Tea?'

'No, thank you,' he said. 'I think Patricia is on her way.'

She nodded. Then they both spoke at the same time.

'So,' she said.

'Well . . .'

They both smiled.

'You go,' he said.

'I was just wondering what brought you into this line of work?' asked Veronica. 'Sorry if that's a personal question.'

'No, not at all,' said Daniel. 'I'm really a teacher, I'm just on secondment.'

'Oh yes? Where do you teach?'

'I teach history in a grammar school in Kent. But this offered some travel, a chance to look at practice in independent schools. See what good ideas we can come away with.'

'That's not always how assessors see it,' said Veronica, smiling wryly.

'It's how I see it,' said Daniel firmly. 'And I was looking

forward to seeing the famous Downey House . . . and meeting you. You've quite a reputation.'

Veronica knew and disliked this, even though it was good for the school.

'It's not about me,' she said. 'It's about the girls.'

Daniel smiled and nodded.

'Sorry I'm late,' said Pat, breezing in without knocking, and not sounding sorry at all. 'Terrible traffic.'

Veronica refrained from commenting on the fact that there was never any traffic on the quiet country road that passed by the school.

'Shall we begin?' she said.

Maggie took a deep breath. All right. So things hadn't gone brilliantly with Middle School 1 last year. But it was time for a new start for all of them. Then she winced. Oh no, she still had to deal with Felicity. She'd had her punishment, but Maggie still had absolutely no doubt that Alice Trebizon-Woods had been involved at some stage, and now she really had to split them up.

'Alice, Felicity,' she said, feeling the eyes of the class on her. It hadn't escaped her notice that Felicity had been lionised for her act of defiance. 'Felicity, I know you paid the price for your little prank at the Christmas concert' – a ripple ran through the room – 'but nonetheless. I don't want you two sitting together any more.'

'But . . .' started Felicity, before remembering crossly that she'd promised her parents she'd behave herself and that that was her new route home.

'Uh-uh,' said Maggie, stopping her. 'I don't want to hear it. I want heads down this term. We have a lot of work to get through, and I want everyone applying themselves. And I mean everyone, including you, do you understand?'

'Yes, miss,' said Fliss in a small voice, making a token attempt to hide the resentment in it. She picked up her books and moved to the only spare seat in the room, inevitably next to Simone, who gave her a half-smile and nothing more.

'Right. Class,' said Maggie. 'We're going to ease into the new year gently with "The Crystal Set". Here, pass copies back.' She felt herself stiffen. Why did she feel like such a martinet with this class? Such a grumpy, chippy drudge?

'Miss!' said Sylvie suddenly, out of the blue. 'Is that an engagement ring?'

Maggie glanced up. She'd forgotten that kids didn't miss a thing, and was still very conscious herself of the new ring on her finger.

'Yes it is, Sylvie,' she said, a half-smile crossing her lips. Their campaign of animosity forgotten, all the girls craned their necks to see it, apart from Fliss and Alice, who were sulking.

'Are you getting married, miss?' Sylvie sounded amazed that someone her age could possibly have met a chap.

'That's what being engaged means, yes, Sylvie.'

'Where are you getting married, miss?'

'What's he like?'

'What is your dress going to be like?'

'Was he that skinny bloke that looked like one of the Arctic Monkeys?'

The questions came from all over the class.

'All right, all right,' said Maggie, trying to hide her pleasure. 'I am marrying my long term boyfriend, who lives in Scotland, and yes, he came to the Christmas concert, which he found quite the eye-opener.'

There was a little bit of laughter at this.

'We aren't marrying for a long time, so we haven't made any decisions about the wedding, and I'll be staying on for the moment. OK? But thank you for your good wishes. Now, heads down please – Simone will you start reading?'

'Just as the stars appear . . .'

Maggie was still conscious of Felicity and Alice gazing daggers at her. But it was a chink, surely.

Term continued to improve. There was more snow on the ground, and it was the season for tough cross-country runs, which most of the girls despised, but it gave them pink cheeks, resistance to bugs and a healthy appetite, so Miss James maintained the practice in the face of the annual onslaught of suggestions for figure skating, trampolining, salsa dancing and the like.

The senior girls were taking their examinations for Oxford and Cambridge and starting to worry about boards, but for those further down the school, worries mostly centred around the sports team trials.

And Maggie found she was feeling a little happier. She enjoyed the teaching more now she was focusing fully on that. OK, so maybe she wouldn't – couldn't – ever be fully accepted here, in a world that was so different from that she knew. But if she and the girls could see past their mutual antipathy, they would find that she could teach them successfully. Perhaps, she thought, in her gloomier moments, she could be like Miss Starling. Respected, if not adored like Mrs Offili, or even Miss James, however much they complained about her.

Stan didn't manage to get down to see her, but the weight and suspicion had lifted from their conversations; devoid of the jealousy and insecurity Stan had felt before Christmas, and the mistrust she had had, they could chat lightly about their days, without focusing too much on when and whether Maggie was going to leave.

'After all,' Stan had said, 'you'll be wanting a babbie after that. So, it makes sense.'

'I'm only twenty-five,' Maggie protested. 'There's lots of time for all that. Let's put some money by first, then we'll be set up.'

'Are you saying I don't make enough money?'

'No, it's not like that . . .'

So they'd move on to other topics less likely to bring sensitivities out in the other.

'Getting married are we?' June Starling had said, without much in the way of enthusiasm. Maggie wondered if June had ever had a boyfriend. It seemed hard to imagine it; June Starling seemed to have been born forty-five years old. Perhaps, thought Maggie tragically, she'd had someone who'd been killed and it had soured her for romance ever since. Or maybe it was just because she was mean.

'Will you be leaving us, or . . .?'

'Oh no,' said Maggie. 'I'm staying.'

She wondered whether this were true.

Daniel took to taking tea with Veronica every time he came in for an assessment day.

'Is this because you appreciate my company, or because you're digging for dirt you can write up later?' she'd asked him, only half in jest, but he'd put his hands up and apologised and promised to stop coming.

'I didn't mean that,' she'd said. In fact, he was easy company, and certainly more pleasant to spend time with than Pat and Liz. He set out his plans for teaching and changes in it, as well as showing her pictures of his family – he had a pretty teacher wife at home in Kent, two boys and a beautiful baby girl, Eliza, whom he adored and could rarely wait to get back to. Veronica wondered if he was casting about for a job. If he was, she'd have to see what she could do.

Still stung by the memory of the way she'd behaved the previous year, Maggie wasn't consciously staying out of David's way . . . all right, perhaps she was. It was some weeks before she ran into David, down in the village shop as she was picking up, to her shame, some Maltesers (she disliked using the tuck shop, and it was going to be stopped for Lent anyway) and a clutch of gossip magazines. The shop was run by a friendly couple, who sold practically everything and were good at not passing over contraband to the girls. She was putting her change away when she heard a familiar friendly voice behind her ask for six panatellas and some dog treats.

Scooping up her magazines as if they were pornography (which they probably were to him; and how could she expect to teach *Clarissa* to her fifth formers next term if she kept putting off starting it?), she wished she'd put on lipstick as she turned round, determined to seem bright and breezy.

'Hello,' she said, so brightly it sounded to her ears fake and forced.

David looked a bit taken aback. So he should, she thought, crossly. She couldn't possibly have imagined all of it, could she? Mind you, could she? What had they done, really, when you thought about it? Nearly hold hands once? Have him say 'I like you, but . . .'? As the days went by, and the reality – that she was marrying Stan – fell more into place, she wondered if she'd made the whole thing up in a Cornwall/new-job-induced frenzy.

'Oh, hello,' he said. Then, as if he couldn't help it, his irrepressible grin broke out. Her heart skipped, and she told it firmly to stop.

'I wasn't buying cigars.'

She smiled back at him.

'I wasn't buying gossip magazines.'

'You *weren't*?'

'Why are you trying to make me feel guilty? Since when do gossip magazines give you *cancer*?'

'An occasional treat,' said David.

'Me too,' said Maggie. She thought of her stuttered hellos to Miranda at Christmas, his pretty blonde fiancée who was something high up in a shipping company in Portsmouth.

David had been warning her to back off, and she wanted to assure him that she'd got the message.

'Did you have a nice Christmas?' he asked now, leaning down to give Stephen Daedalus a treat. The dog was already licking Maggie's hand, delighted to see her again.

'Great,' said Maggie, pleased at the opportunity to mention it. 'Stan and I are getting married!'

There seemed to be a brief instant before David's grin spread over his face again, as he held the door to let her out before him.

'That's wonderful news!' he said. 'A wedding. What a wonderful thing.'

'Two weddings,' said Maggie. 'If you count yours.'

'Yes,' said David. 'Uh, I hadn't realised you hadn't met Miranda before. She's away a lot.'

'She's great,' said Maggie, determinedly light of tone.

'Yes, she is.'

It was a lovely cold sunny afternoon and Maggie, wrapped up warm in a red beret and scarf, had been planning on walking back to the school. It did seem absurd for them to be heading the same way and not go together.

'Are you heading back?' asked David. Maggie nodded.

'Perhaps,' he said, 'we could enjoy our occasional treats on the way.'

Maggie smiled. 'I'd have thought a pipe was more your style.'

'I did try it. Bit affected,' said David. 'I felt as if I should be keeping lookout for the hound of the Baskervilles.'

'But cigars . . . are you celebrating something?'

David shook his head as they struck out for the cliff path, leaving the pretty pastel village behind them.

'Nope. Except for it being Saturday . . . do you mind?' He took out a book of long matches.

'Not at all,' said Maggie. 'I rather like it actually. My granddad used to smoke the little stubby ones. I missed the smell when he died.'

'Of throat cancer,' said David.

'Old age,' said Maggie. 'He was ninety-three.'

'Excellent. Now, what about your treat?'

'Would you like a Malteser?'

'I'm not sure they go.'

'Oh. Would your dog like one?'

'Definitely not. Stephen Daedalus?'

The dog came flying back in order to chase a stick David threw for him in the air. I do not fancy this man, ordered Maggie to herself, as he unfurled his long body and ran, thin as a reed and looking like an over-excited teenager, with his ridiculous cigar between two fingers. But at least they seemed to be over their awkwardness. In fact, it was as easy as ever to be with him, as he chatted about books he was reading, gave her some pointers on getting in to *Clarissa* and made her laugh telling her about the camp adult pantomime he'd unwittingly taken his nephews to, then spent two hours afterwards trying to explain the double entendres. He is fun, Maggie told herself. Good company. A little peculiar, like Stan said. But fine.

*

Everything went smoothly until the middle of February, when the entire area was hit by a freezing patch. The snow came down full force and made the road impassable for two days until the plough had reached them, something that had caused much hysterical excitement amongst the girls, with the more impressionable genuinely believing they would be reduced to eating corpses and barricading the cellars against wolves. Once this hysteria passed, however, it was business as usual – until Astrid Ulverton's clarinet went missing.

Chapter Twelve

Maggie and June Starling had discussed the missing items before, of course. It was so sporadic and so difficult to prove – teenage girls were notorious for losing anything that wasn't nailed down – and in the end they had decided not to launch into serious further action with either Fliss's watch or Sylvie's earrings. Things did get lost, and as they weren't allowed to search lockers without good reasons for their suspicions, they had merely appealed for the culprit to come forward, without much hope of success.

This was different, however. Everyone in the school knew Astrid was married to her clarinet. It was worth a lot of money, and Astrid rarely let it out of her sight. It slept on her nightstand like a favourite teddy bear and the usually strict rules on instruments in the dorm were occasionally bent for Astrid in those difficult times when inspiration struck and she was trying to get down a new tune – her roommates, Sylvie, Ursula and Zazie, were fairly tolerant on the issue.

But Astrid had left her clarinet on the bed and the door open whilst going for a shower the previous evening. The dorms were just off the common room, with plenty of girls from the first two years popping in and out. It could have been anyone. But one thing was for sure; it hadn't dropped down behind a bed or been mislaid.

Astrid was red-eyed from crying as she stood in front of Miss Starling, Maggie by her side. Veronica had been alerted but didn't want to interfere at this early stage.

'And you've looked everywhere?' said Miss Starling, sternly. 'You can't possibly have lost it?'

'I couldn't have,' said Astrid stoutly. 'I know exactly where I put it. I never leave it alone.'

'What on earth would someone want with a clarinet?' wondered Maggie. 'It's not as if they can play it without giving themselves away.'

'It's not about that,' said Miss Starling. 'It's about power, and upsetting people. Do you have any enemies, Astrid?'

Astrid looked as if she was going to burst into tears again.

'I don't *think* so,' she said. In fact it was true; nearly everyone liked Astrid. Her talent was too natural and extraordinary to attract jealousy.

'We're going to have to interview them all,' said Miss Starling after she'd been dismissed. 'Scare the heebie-jeebies out of them. Threaten the police. We should be able to see after that . . . I hope. I hate stealing,' she said, thumping the desk to emphasise her point. 'Of all the shady, underhand, sly things to do, it's the worst. I hate to think of a Downey's girl even being capable of it.'

Maggie nodded, seeing the teacher's dedication to the school. 'Shall we get just the Plantagenet girls, or do we want Wessex, Tudor and York as well?'

'Anyone who could have been through that common room,' said Miss Starling. 'So just the locals, I suppose. First years first, they're by far the most likely. Let me see Felicity Prosser too, and that other girl who lost something.'

Maggie nodded, and went off to tell the year-group, with sinking heart.

*

Now the novelty of her being back and her injury had worn off, and since she couldn't join in the sports or walks or drama, Felicity was bored. And she was having to apply herself to being good, which was, as Alice kept pointing out, much duller than before. So when the investigation was announced, she was quite excited; partly because something different was happening and, because of her watch, she didn't think she was going to fall under suspicion. It was quite interesting to see trouble when she wasn't allowed to be part of it any more. Staying on the right side of Miss Adair had been tiresome.

The girls were sent in one by one to face the inquisition. Miss Starling favoured long silences that the girls could then fill, hopefully in an incriminating fashion. Even the most innocent of girls would find their conscience pricking, wondering, if only for a split second, if perhaps they *could* have done it in a moment of madness. Simone was trembling with fear as she entered.

'Hello,' said Miss Starling sternly. Maggie had briefed her that Simone was a likely candidate – she'd been in the vicinity of each incident and had good reason to despise the classmates who'd done so little to welcome her, even oblivious Astrid. As she did so, Maggie felt a quick stab of guilt that she had failed in her pastoral role towards Simone, who seemed more pasty and miserable than ever. They'd had a few late-night tea and reading sessions, but Maggie had never quite found the words to get Simone to open up to her, and it had always been easier to chat about books than about how she was actually feeling. Now, seeing the miserable girl in front of her, she felt more of a misfit in this school than ever – she couldn't get on with the posh kids, but couldn't help the normal ones.

'Now you understand that we are talking to everyone?' Maggie began tentatively. Simone nodded, not trusting her voice. She had tried to work out what would be the best way to behave so that they realised she was innocent, but she didn't know how. It was like when she was being teased by Estelle Grant. It didn't matter what she said, whether she answered 'yes' or 'no' to the question 'are you a retard?'. They were going to tease her and taunt her regardless, and talking just made everything much worse. The only way she'd found to get through those sessions was to act like a tortoise: retreat entirely into herself and try and wait it out until everyone left her alone.

'Did you take Astrid Ulverton's clarinet?' said Miss Starling, peremptorily.

Simone shook her head, still staring at her lap.

'Speak up child,' said Miss Starling. 'Did you take it, yes or no?'

Simone wasn't going to get the words out and didn't even try; she shook her head again, tears forming at the corner of her eyes.

'It's all right,' said Maggie, playing good cop. 'Simone, if you have something to tell us, it's always best to get it off your conscience.'

There was a long silence. Simone simply couldn't speak. Miss Starling looked at Maggie over the top of her spectacles.

'You can go for now,' she said eventually to Simone, who scurried out.

'Well, I don't like the look of that,' she said to Maggie when Simone had gone.

'She's horribly shy,' said Maggie, looking worried. 'I thought she might be improving, but ... it's taking her longer to settle in here than I thought.'

Miss Starling shot her a sharp look. 'Yes, it can take people a while to settle in,' she said, leaving Maggie wondering exactly who she was talking about. 'Well, anyway, if she's stealing she won't have to worry about being here for much longer. Now who's next?'

'Alice Trebizon-Woods.'

Miss Starling sniffed. 'She'd tell you black was white, that one, and not bat an eye.'

Maggie privately agreed, but didn't want to mark her down in front of Miss Starling, and certainly Alice, with her large brown eyes and butter-wouldn't-melt manner made a very convincing job of knowing nothing about the thefts.

'I feel so bad for Astrid,' she said sincerely. 'That clarinet is her life.'

Maggie wondered why, despite the fact that she agreed with Alice, she still found her manner so irritating.

'We all do, Alice,' she said. 'That'll be all.'

There was nothing for it. Veronica detested these situations, but there was no way to get to the bottom of things otherwise. She would have to order a search, and if that didn't work they'd have to consider getting the police in. Parents would be furious if they didn't think absolutely everything possible was being done. They didn't encourage pupils to bring expensive items to school, but it was impossible to stop them, and most of the girls had laptops and mobiles. With a heavy heart, she gave Miss Starling the word. It was more work for the teachers too, and stress as they tried to tell who amongst their girls was the bad apple. She hoped fervently that it wasn't Simone, the scholarship girl, but the omens didn't look good. Which was a shame; she looked set to do very well in all her courses, with a particularly excellent showing in maths and physics; exactly the kind of girl who ended up a credit to the school.

Wednesday afternoon was put aside for the search. This

was normally a time for school sport, and the fact that it was being set aside annoyed Miss James, who disliked being regarded as a second-class subject. When the girls found out, however – Miss Starling and Maggie had to pounce on the dorms shortly after making the announcement at lunch, obviously requiring an element of surprise – they didn't, on the whole, mind. They were tired of chilly lacrosse, the dreaded cross-country runs, and changing rooms that never seemed to heat up properly.

It was a terribly freezing day; unseasonably cold even for February, with icy winds blowing down from Siberia; the type of wind that found its way inside your clothes, that blew icy swirls of sleet around you and made you lean into it as you walked.

The girls were to go and sit on their beds as the search took place. Every girl's locker and wardrobe was to be taken apart; their beds and bags thoroughly rummaged through.

It was an unhappy affair; Maggie felt like a jailer, and the girls all felt under suspicion, which they were. One by one the dorms were completed until, with heavy heart, Maggie entered Simone and Fliss's room. She was crossing names off a list and started nearest the window. Alice's clothes were much more neatly folded than her own, Maggie found herself thinking. Next was Fliss, who gave Maggie her usual pout, but none of her usual cheek.

'If you can find my watch I'd be very grateful,' she said, and Maggie nodded silently.

'We're doing everything we can,' she said. There had been no point in searching the bed of sad-eyed Astrid, but for the sake of propriety they'd had to do it anyway.

Finally they came to Simone's. She barely looked up as Miss Starling bent down and looked in her bedside cabinet.

There were lots of books, and chocolate wrappers, which Miss Starling handled with some distaste.

'You know the rules on eating in the dorm?' she asked sternly. Simone nodded.

'It's dirty and it's dangerous,' she said. 'You could be encouraging rats, anything.' The other girls in the dorm looked slightly nauseated. It must be secret eating still, thought Maggie. Once again she regretted bitterly being so caught up in shows, and Stan, and David, and getting along at the new school, that she'd left behind the one pupil who really really needed someone. She had failed, it seemed, in so many ways. One student injuring herself, another . . .

Her regret deepened even further a minute later as Miss Starling, her hand under Simone's bed, made a gesture of surprise, then pulled out, one by one, Astrid's clarinet, Fliss's watch and Sylvie's earrings.

There was silence in the room.

'Felicity,' said Miss Starling. 'Is this yours?'

'My watch!' shouted Felicity in delight, hobbling over. 'Thank God. I hadn't told my mum yet.'

She frowned, looking at Simone, whose mouth was hanging open. 'Uh, maybe it could have fallen under the bed by mistake?'

'Unlikely,' said Miss Starling, in a tone as cold as the weather. 'Someone get Astrid Ulverton and Sylvie Brown for me, please, would you?'

She made the girls identify their objects, which they did, quietly, unable to look Simone in the eye, and then sent them on their way.

'Simone,' she said to the girl, who was sitting there, red in the face. 'Could you come down to my office please?'

Numbly, Simone followed the two teachers out of the

door. They walked slightly ahead, glancing at each other, then admonished her to sit and wait whilst they went inside.

'I'll just call Veronica,' said June Starling when they got to her office.

'Yes,' said Maggie. 'Oh, it's such a shame. It really is. I feel so responsible. If I'd got more involved with her earlier . . .'

June regarded her over the tops of her spectacles. 'I heard you let her come and visit you in the evenings and borrow your books.'

Maggie twisted uncomfortably. 'Oh, that was nothing. I should have talked to her more. It's my fault. I should have—'

'I suspect it was rather more than nothing to Simone. It was kind. Unfortunately,' she continued, shuffling her papers, 'in some cases, kindness is not enough.'

She picked up the phone to call Veronica, who had been anticipating the call all morning and suggested with a heavy heart they come and see her. She was disappointed in her young teacher. She'd been given special responsibility to keep an eye on their new pupil, and clearly hadn't done so.

As they left the office to cross the great hall, however, Maggie noticed immediately what took June Starling a second or two to process. Simone had gone.

At first, they only searched around the corridors, not wanting to sound the alarm or to get anyone. But it became clear, very quickly, that Simone was not in the building, and no one had seen her.

'I'll call the police,' said Miss Starling.

'I'll go after her,' said Maggie immediately. 'She must have run out. It's perishing out there, it's below freezing. She doesn't have a coat or anything.'

June nodded. 'Take Harold.' She meant the head care-taker. 'And make sure you wrap up too.'

'I've got my phone,' said Maggie. 'Call me immediately.'

Miss Starling got on the telephone to make the arrange-ments as Maggie dashed to her room to find her coat. Simone couldn't have got far, she wasn't sporty and the weather was cruel. And Maggie knew the crags quite well now. She also grabbed Simone's coat from her dorm, ignoring the concerned faces of the girls inside, so that the girl would have something warm to put on when they caught up with her.

Harold joined her at the doors, looking worriedly at the sky. It was cold as all hell out there, and the clouds were so low it felt as if it was getting dark already, although it was just past three o'clock.

'Reckon more snow's coming, miss.'

'I'm sure we'll find her in no time,' said Maggie, hurrying ahead, and hoping that was true.

Simone was nowhere to be seen around the road, and the coastal path seemed the obvious route to follow.

Once on top of the cliffs, the full force of the wind hit them in the face. Visibility was decreasing all the time, with the first light flakes dusting them from above. For the first time Maggie felt a sense of genuine fear. Someone could seriously get into trouble out here. She moved over to the cliff's edge and peered over. Surely she couldn't . . . she wouldn't have . . . she was such a careful girl, surely she wouldn't do anything so madly impulsive?

Once again she scanned the horizon. There was no sign of another living soul . . . except one. A dark figure heading towards her. At first Maggie's heart leapt, but then she realised that it was a man's outline, not a teenage girl's. Her heart rose slightly, however, when she realised it was David, rain or shine, out walking Stephen Daedalus. She waved her arms so he would see her through the rapidly thickening snow and walked towards him.

'I thought I would be the only person mad enough to be out on a day like today,' said David. 'Of course it's my dog that's mad, not me . . . what's the matter?' he said, as he saw her face.

Rapidly Maggie explained. David's face grew worried.

'She's out without a coat? In this?'

'Well, there are people searching the school, but she doesn't seem to be there.'

Harold had made it as far as the headland now, and was turning back, shaking his head.

'I'll call in the teachers from our school, co-ordinate a wider search,' said David.

'The police are on their way,' said Maggie. 'Is there time?'

It was a proper blizzard now. The temperature seemed to have dropped even further. David sighed as they crossed over the cliff path, checking through the gorse on the other side.

'SIMONE!' they yelled periodically, though their voices were swept away on the howling wind, which seemed to rip the very breath out of them. 'SIMONE!!!!'

'I can't see any sign of her on the beach,' said Harold, returning to them. Maggie felt her fingers grow cold in her pocket. 'Has someone headed for the village?'

Maggie checked her phone. There was a text message from the school. No one had seen her in the village, and the police were on their way with their dogs.

'Dogs!' she exclaimed excitedly. Her fingers had felt numb as she'd tried to read the text, and she wanted desperately to plunge them back into her pockets.

'What?' said David. 'Oh, what do you mean?'

'Can Stephen Daedalus do tracking? I just remembered, I've got Simone's jacket in my pocket. Could he smell it and find her?'

David looked excited. 'I don't know, but it's worth a shot.'

He bent down. 'Now. Stephen Daedalus. I have a very important job for you.' He took the coat from Maggie's outstretched arm. 'Can you find her? Can you, boy?'

Stephen Daedalus wagged his tail and looked at them expectantly.

'Sniff this! And go find her! You know you can do it! Good boy!'

The dog sniffed excitedly, then looked up at them again, as if to say, that was nice, but what's the next game?

'Go find her,' shouted David. 'Come on! You can do it!'

Stephen Daedalus took one more sniff of the jacket.

'It's not going to work,' said Maggie, who was feeling that standing still was a terrible idea, for Simone, and for them in this unholy weather. 'Come on, let's just keep going.'

'Hang on,' said David. He slowly drew the coat away and handed it back to Maggie. Then he stood up.

'On you go,' he said. 'On you go, good dog.'

And suddenly Stephen Daedalus sat upright, sniffing the air. Then he turned tail and plunged into the undergrowth.

Maggie and David looked at one another.

'Shall we follow him?'

'His father was a hunting dog,' said David. 'And do you have any better ideas?'

Harold had already set off in swift pursuit.

Later, when she looked back, Maggie couldn't remember how long they'd spent following the dog through the moors. All the world had become white and cold, with the sky and the ground hardly demarcated at all.

Harold had a torch, their only source of light as the darkness swept across the crags like a wave. Perhaps it wasn't even that long, but it felt like days following the trail, as David took her hand and helped her up difficult inclines, or across iced-over streams. They were further and further away from the school, its warm lights mere dots on the horizon; ahead was the Irish Sea and little else.

None of them dared to say what they thought might be true; that the dog had no idea where it was and could render them as lost as Simone. Maggie tried to check her phone – fumbling with her gloves and dropping it on the ground – but they'd gone out of range of a signal, so they had no way of knowing whether she'd been found or not. There was no sign of the police.

Finally, as the night was becoming truly black, with no moon visible behind the clouds to help light their way, and all of them terribly puffed from rushing after the dog, Stephen Daedalus stopped short of a copse, and started to bark loudly, the noise startling all three of the search party.

Maggie, who had felt her brain go dull in the everlasting white-out and was full of horrible fears she couldn't express, suddenly got an adrenalin rush of energy as they all hurried forward.

Under the overhang, barely protected from the howling wind and snow, curled up in a ball and shivering uncontrollably, only her thin school shirt protecting her from the howling gale, was Simone.

'Good dog! Good dog!' David was shouting in a completely hoarse voice as he launched himself forward, first with Simone's coat, then his own. Maggie and David sat on either side of the girl, all of them huddling together for warmth as Harold, who knew the moors so well, dashed back for help. Even Stephen Daedalus came up and sat across them all, and his panting warmth was extremely welcome; Maggie made sure Simone's hands, frozen into claws, sank into his thick fur.

'Leave me alone. Leave me alone,' was all she was saying, as she rocked back and forward.

'Don't go to sleep,' David was telling her. 'Don't go to sleep, Simone. Stay awake. We'll sort all of this out.'

Maggie was colder than she'd ever been in her life, but took some comfort from the three of them huddling together.

'Should we try and get moving?' she said to David, who looked unsure.

'I think we should heat her up first before we start moving,' he said. Maggie agreed, remembering that she'd read somewhere that they should take off their clothes to provide body heat, and reflecting dimly through her frozen brain that this was the kind of thing she'd ideally once have liked to do with David without a) Simone, b) a howling storm or c) Stephen Daedalus. This meandering train of thought, however, was interrupted by a huge noise that rose above the storm, as a floodlight bathed the area and the copse; the snowflakes ploughing through the light beam.

'We have you on our heat sensor,' came a voice over the loudhailer. 'Please stay where you are.'

Stephen Daedalus quivered and buried his nose in David's knees. But David and Maggie's hearts leapt: Harold must have got back in time after all. Because what they could hear was a helicopter.

Chapter Thirteen

After being briefly checked over at the hospital and declared fine, both Maggie and David were free to return to the school. From the corridor, watching David be charming to the nurses as he buttoned up his clean blue shirt, Maggie called Stan on her mobile, even though she knew it was forbidden.

'WHAT?'

Maggie squeezed her eyes tight shut. She didn't want to have to explain it again.

'What do you mean you lost one in the snow?'

'It wasn't quite like that,' she implored. 'And everyone's fine now. It'll be OK.'

'It'll be OK when you drive to Exeter Airport and catch the next flight home to Glasgow.'

'I can't, Stan. I have to stay and face the music. Simone was my responsibility. And I failed her.'

'That bloody school failed you!' said Stan. 'They let the pupils treat you like dirt, and now they blame you for some maniac running away!'

'It's not like that,' said Maggie. 'Honestly, Stan.'

She caught David out of the corner of her eye looking at her enquiringly, as if asking if everything was all right. She tried to make a reassuring expression at him.

'I have to go,' she said.

Stan let out an exasperated sigh. 'So, I don't know when I'm seeing you, then, is that right? You've half died on a mountain but, you know, the *school* is more important.'

'It's my job,' said Maggie simply, and hung up the phone. She had a sneaking suspicion Stan was right. Maybe she should just go home. She was probably going to get sent home anyway, after this fiasco. But Stan couldn't, didn't understand . . .

'Are you all right?' said David, coming out of the treatment room. Maggie bit her lip in case she betrayed her feelings.

'The kids get under your skin, don't they? Can you imagine what having your own would be like?'

Once again she was grateful to him for striking the right note, even as she knew she had to face the music alone.

'Terrifying,' she said, and they went outside into the freezing night, where Harold was waiting for them, in the battered old Land Rover that even a snow storm could scarcely stop.

Simone was being kept in overnight as a precautionary measure. After being wrapped in silver blankets, she'd been heated up in an extremely hot bath, but so far there were no signs of hypothermia or frostbite; just a touch of exposure. The doctor did say, however, that it was lucky they'd found her when they did.

Maggie had offered to stay with her, but no one was allowed to stay overnight. Matron would be over first thing to collect her. Her parents would be driving down through the night from London.

It was well after ten by the time Harold drove them up the familiar driveway; but every light in the school was burning, and the girls were outlined at the windows.

Veronica was standing in the great hall, where the fire had been lit – outside of Christmas, an unheard of concession. An exhausted Maggie entered, head bowed, ready to take whatever Veronica could throw at her – could it be as bad as dismissal, she wondered, to lose a vulnerable pupil? Stan would be seeing her sooner than he thought. And the girls here would hardly miss her, after all.

So Maggie wasn't expecting the round of applause that rose up from the line of girls waiting on the great stairs.

'What?' she said, looking round. David, standing just behind her, smiled to himself.

Miss Starling stepped forward. 'It was very brave and clever of you to go out as you did, and to think of using Stephen Daedalus. No one could have predicted that Simone would bolt as she did.'

Maggie felt her cheeks flare. Praise from Miss Starling was not something she was used to.

'I'm so sorry the situation got so out of hand,' she said. 'It's my fault. I should have realised she was so unhappy she was stealing . . .'

Veronica stepped forward too, shaking her head. 'No, it wasn't. Simone wasn't the culprit at all.'

Maggie's eyebrows shot up.

'It was Imogen Fairlie. She shared a dorm with Simone, Felicity Prosser and Alice Trebizon-Woods. She'd felt ignored and was trying to be the centre of attention, then when the searches started, lost her nerve and panicked. We've spoken to her parents. This isn't the first time, apparently. They're going to take her home.'

'Oh,' said Maggie, her heart suddenly going out to silent, no-trouble Imogen. What a dreadful cry for help – another one she seemed to have missed completely. 'Does she have to . . .?'

'Yes,' said Veronica, firmly. 'There are some things I simply can't tolerate in a Downey girl. Making a bid for attention is one thing. Cowardly letting another girl take the blame is something else altogether.'

Veronica noticed David hanging back.

'And thank you,' she said directly to him. 'From all of us.'

David looked embarrassed. 'It wasn't me,' he said. 'It was Stephen Daedalus. And Maggie, of course.'

'We were all very lucky you were there,' said Veronica simply. 'Now, please, both of you, come to my study. I think we all need a night cap.'

She turned round to the girls on the stairs.

'I certainly know I owe Simone Kardashian an apology. Please look in your consciences and see if you think you do too. And now, bed, everyone! It's an ordinary day tomorrow and I don't want to hear another sound out of any of you.'

For once, though, Dr Deveral's word was not taken as law, as the girls dispersed, chattering excitedly like birds.

Maggie had a long hot bath, accompanied by some of Veronica's excellent whisky, and slept in late the next morning, not even hearing the bell. Ordered by Miss Starling, the catering staff had made a large cooked breakfast for everyone. Maggie went to the san at eleven.

Simone was sitting there alone, without her parents, who had got trapped in the snow and had to spend the night in Devon.

'Simone,' said Maggie, 'I'm so sorry all this happened to you. But why couldn't you just tell us it wasn't you? I was there, wasn't I?'

Simone looked down. 'Nobody believed me. Everyone thought it was me.'

'Well, everyone was wrong,' said Maggie. 'Me included.'

'I'd have thought you might have understood,' said Simone. Maggie knew what she meant. They came from the same world. They knew what it was like out there.

'I know,' she said, feeling ashamed. 'I should have. I'm sorry.'

Simone shrugged.

'Do you want to come to class? I know the girls would like to see you.'

Simone looked white. 'Do you think?'

Maggie nodded. 'Definitely. They're not all bad, you know.'

Simone gave a half-smile.

'Come on,' said Maggie. 'I think it would do you good. Even if your parents do want to take you home.'

Simone thought about it for a moment, then consented.

Miss Starling was letting the Plantagenet girls watch a video of *Love's Labours Lost*. She hated letting the girls watch DVDs, thought it morally corrupting, but you couldn't swim against the tide for ever, and she had her own class to teach.

When Maggie opened the door, however, all thoughts of the video were gone. The girls stared at Simone, who instantly wondered if she'd made a mistake and that this was a really bad idea. So did Maggie. Acceptance from other children was an impossible thing to force. Maybe her running away made her even weirder in their eyes. Plus, of course, they'd have to get over their distaste for her to even say anything.

She paused the video, and for a time everyone was quiet. Then, suddenly, little Fliss Prosser, her supposedly worst pupil, stood up.

'Uhm,' she said, looking at a loss for words for once. 'I just wanted to say. And I don't speak for everyone or anything, but, err. Simone. I'm really really sorry I thought you were stealing. It was a mistake, and I'm dead ashamed. Right.'

And she sat down again, cheeks pink. Maggie was impressed. She didn't think Fliss had it in her.

Then Astrid stood up too.

'I'm sorry,' she said. 'I should have known you wouldn't take my clarinet.'

All the other girls mumbled apologies in agreement after that, and Sylvie stood up and asked Simone to tell them what it was like being lost in the snow. Maggie looked at Simone and asked if she would tell the story, and then, the most surprising thing happened. To Maggie's complete astonishment, at first falteringly, but then with more of the confidence that she'd shown at the Christmas concert, and the humour she'd suspected from their meetings, Simone began to tell the whole story: about how she couldn't decide whether to bolt or hide when she was waiting outside Dr Deveral's office; how she'd run and really quickly realised she had no idea where she was because she'd missed so many of the cross-country runs; how she'd thought Stephen Daedalus was a wolf come to eat her, and the helicopter sounded like an alien spaceship, which was when she really did think she'd died and that the scientologists were right after all.

Listening to this Maggie realised something with amazement; Simone was funny. Hearing the girls crack up, and her good comic timing and pauses, the entire class saw a new side to the previously timid girl. At the end of her account, when she said precisely what Maggie had been thinking – that she was slightly hoping Mr McDonald would go bare-chested with her so that at least she would know what it was like before she died, Maggie was laughing too, and there was a large spontaneous round of applause as

Simone took her seat back next to Fliss, who even put her arm round her and gave her a squeeze. 'Brilliant,' she said audibly. 'Much better than my ankle.'

'I think so,' said Simone. 'Though the next person is really going to have to cut off a leg or something, to get Mr McDonald's attention.' The class cracked up again, except for Alice, who donated a rather wan smile. She knew, more than anyone, that she owed Simone an apology, but was finding it rather hard to choke the words out.

'OK, OK everyone, settle down,' said Maggie, but she found it hard to hide her delight. More than just Simone, she could feel a mood in the class; a relaxing; a genuine sense that they were all working together, were all on the same side.

'And more of *Love's Labours Lost* later; I think we'll take a quick look at a poem more germane to our current situations – quickly please, Fliss and Simone, could you turn to page 271 in *Poetry Please*, and start reading "Stopping by Woods on a Snowy Evening".'

And without hesitation or fuss, thirteen girls immediately did so.

Amazingly, Simone's parents, once they'd got over the terrible shock, were persuaded (almost entirely by Simone herself) that the whole thing had been a very minor, and not at all dangerous misunderstanding. Veronica, mindful of the school's reputation, and the possibility of their suing, did not discourage them from this apprehension.

It may have helped that their first view of Simone, as she came downstairs, was of her surrounded by other girls, arm in arm with Felicity, both of them being interrogated for more details of their run-ins with Mr McDonald. Simone, carrying her bag, said something and everyone laughed. Mrs

Kardashian looked on in pride. This was exactly how she'd always imagined Simone being: happy, pleased, surrounded by other, nice, girls. She wouldn't, she reflected, have wanted to take Simone home now if she'd had a leg gnawed off by the school's own timber wolf. Simone and her father might think she didn't have a clue as to what was going through her beloved daughter's head, but she certainly did, and had been equally certain that her instinct was the correct one. Which didn't stop her screeching, 'FETITZA' over the tops of everyone's heads.

Suddenly, though, Felicity thought, Simone's mum didn't look so weird. She looked just more colourful; a bit exotic. Maybe even a bit more fun than her own stodgy parents. She swallowed this thought at once; it was disloyal.

Simone didn't care and went straight up to her parents and gave them a huge hug.

'I'm so pleased to see you,' she said.

'And you,' said her father, gruffly. 'What happened to you? Are you all right?'

'I'm fine,' said Simone. In fact, she looked better than fine. She looked happy. There was a rosiness to her cheeks and a bit of a sparkle in her eye, for the first time in a long time.

'We were so worried, *fetitza*,' said her mother. 'Even Joel was upset.'

'Where is he?'

'He wanted to go with his friends to some warcraft thing,' said her father, who had even less idea about Joel's hobbies than she did.

Simone had special dispensation for a sick day, but as she wasn't feeling particularly sick – the lucky effects of being fourteen, Matron had said, exhorting her to watch her chest and not go swimming – she went into Truro with her mum and dad, and they bought her a new pair of jeans at Gap and took her to Pizza Express for lunch. Simone had rarely been happier.

And even after her parents returned to London, and the big thaw finally arrived, flooding the games fields in the far corner of the school grounds, and turning every trip outside into a muddy morass, things were still looking up. Both Fliss and Simone were signed off games for the foreseeable future and were spending PE sitting on the sidelines, sewing up netball vests, which was horribly dull, but gave them quite a lot of time to chat.

Fliss, to her amazement, was discovering that Simone, the kind of person she'd never have looked at twice for having as a friend, was actually funny, kind, and really good to spend time with. All the time Fliss had had her down as a shy waste of space, she was, whilst shy, using the time to observe people and places around the school and was, in her own way, every bit as cheeky as Alice. Sitting together in English also helped, and soon they were sharing homework, as Fliss had so far to make up her marks after her disastrous first term.

Alice didn't like the new situation at all. In fact, she hated it. It was bad enough being one of three. Being one of three to a big fat boufer was just stupid. Plus, she missed the old Fliss, whom she could coax into bad behaviour. The new one was a total goody-goody. She hadn't forgotten about the trick she'd promised to play. She was just going to have to make it pretty darn spectacular. That should get the focus back in its rightful place.

Stan seemed far more worried than Simone's parents, which was touching in a way, but also slightly irritating to Maggie, who was still on a high from being treated as a heroine, rather than the disciplinary she'd expected. Stan took the tortuously long train down the next weekend.

'What for?' asked Maggie, as she went to pick him up, the tip of her nose pink – the only relic from her expedition.

'What do you mean? You could have been killed. I want to have a word with that headmistress of yours.'

'It wasn't her fault,' said Maggie. 'Simone unpredictably ran out, then I ran out. Anyway, everything ended up fine.'

'Yes, by luck,' said Stan. 'And of course that poncey English teacher was involved.'

'And we're lucky he was there,' said Maggie. 'Come on. I've got two free days and I don't even want to look at marking. Shall we go and visit a tin mine?'

They did so, but it wasn't an entirely comfortable experience, even though they did hold hands. Finally, they arrived, slightly chilled from the still-frosty air, in a local tea room with steam rising onto the floral-curtained windows.

'This is the best bit of sightseeing,' said Maggie. 'Shall we have scones?'

Stan sat down. 'Thing is, Maggie, I've been thinking.'

'Yes?' said Maggie, looking round for the waitress.

'I know we were talking about you staying here for another year maybe, for your career, before you come home?'

'Yes?' said Maggie, uncertainly. Two lower sixth formers, on a weekend pass, had arrived just behind them – Carla's tea shop was very popular. They had sat down self-consciously, still trying to look nonchalant in the outside world, but Maggie could tell they were craning their necks desperately to try and overhear Miss Adair and her fiancé.

'Well, after everything that's happened . . . Please. I'm sick of asking. But won't you think about coming home? Nobody would blame you for leaving now.'

'They'd think I was a coward,' said Maggie, ordering tea and two rounds of scones with jam and tea, hoping they could keep this light.

'You're obviously not a coward,' said Stan. 'You should be getting some sort of award. Anyway. If you came home, you could find a job locally and we could think about buying a new place to live. You know, before the wedding.'

Maggie hated feeling so torn. Of course she wanted to go home with Stan one day; he was her partner, wasn't he? Her other half? She watched him as he piled jam on, ignoring the butter and cream as semi-nutritional by-products. At least she'd remembered not to get the raisin scones.

'But,' she said, then stopped and lowered her voice. 'You know.' And as she said the words, she knew they were the truth. 'I love this job, Stan.'

There was a long pause after that, as Maggie reflected on it.

'More than you love me?' said Stan finally, stirring sugar into his tea and not looking at her.

'Of course not! We've been through this! But I made a commitment and want to follow it through; why is that so hard to understand?'

Stan stared at her. 'Because we're getting married and I don't want you at the bloody dog-end of the country, getting half-frozen to death. Why is that so hard for you to understand?'

Suddenly, the atmosphere between them, which since the New Year had been so joyous and exciting, seemed to turn sour. It felt, on this issue at least, as if there was nothing more to be said. They seemed to be at something of an impasse. They ate their scones and drank their tea in silence, as quickly as possible. Maggie was acutely aware of being watched by the girls, no doubt vowing they would never be in one of those couples that sit silently in restaurants. Well, thought Maggie mutinously. They could see how they liked it when they got there.

'Shall we go?' she said, as soon as she'd swallowed her last mouthful. Stan merely nodded, but as they left, reached out to take her hand in a conciliatory fashion. She took it. They were friends again, but no closer to a resolution.

As they trudged up the wet lane, she heard a commotion from the local meadow. Glancing up, she saw David and his fiancée. They were throwing a frisbee for Stephen Daedalus, and David was laughing his head off. The weak winter sunlight reflected off Miranda's blonde head.

That's what I want, Maggie found herself reflecting wistfully. When was the last time Stan and I just had a really good laugh?

'Gaw, they must be proper freezing,' said Stan, who of course had refused to wear a scarf or a hat. 'Nutters.'

Just as he said this David caught her eye and waved. Both of them came over, leaning across the ancient stone wall that divided the field from the old cart track road.

'Hello hello,' he said cheerily. 'How are you, Stan? The heroine's consort.'

'Hardly,' said Maggie, rolling her eyes, and giving Stephen Daedalus a quick rub.

'It's amazing what you guys did,' said Miranda, widening her eyes. 'I couldn't believe it when I heard. It was on the radio and everything.'

'Yes, you can imagine how thrilled the head is about that,' said Maggie. '*Not* very. It was all Stephen Daedalus anyway.'

'How's our young Simone?' asked David.

'Oh, she's good. Between her and Felicity Prosser, they're having quite the time being the ones who got most snuggle-up rescue-time with you,' said Maggie, realising the light

219

tone she'd meant to bring to the comment sounded a bit silly when she tried it out loud.

'Christ,' said David. 'Back to the boys for me. Or does that sound even worse?'

'It does,' said Maggie grinning, and grateful to be rescued.

'Darling, let's go in, I'm freezing,' said Miranda testily.

'Yeah,' grunted Stan. Maggie had rather been enjoying a little sunlight, however pathetic, and David looked disappointed, but immediately deferred to Miranda's wishes.

'Absolutely. Fancy scones in the village?' he asked the whole group. Maggie found herself full of regret that they had to say no, they'd just had some, and it was all she could do not to turn her head as they waltzed off towards the village, David pontificating on something as usual.

'He's a right weirdo,' said Stan as they went on. 'Can't shut up.'

'Some people are just like that though,' said Maggie, as they came to their hotel, feeling thankful that Stan had never had a suspicious nature. 'They can't help it.'

'Can't bloody put a sock in it, more like,' growled Stan. 'What's wrong with a bit of peace and quiet anyway? Won't want to hear much from you when we're married.'

'You're joking.'

He took her in his arms. 'Course I'm joking, you dimwit. Come here.'

And his kisses tasted good, of tea, and jam. But still, nothing was decided.

Chapter Fourteen

Easter was shaping up to be a much quieter term, thought Veronica, then she admonished herself firmly for thinking so: she'd made that mistake before. She looked with some pleasure at the daffodils ranging over the hills. That was spring down here; every single day something new burst into life, and the landscape changed all over again. Not at all like the dark grimy northern city where she'd grown up. She was reflecting on this when there was a knock on the door again. It would be the assessment team. They were finishing up. Liz was back, after her three months off for stress, and this would be their final session before they went to write up their report.

She hoped it would be a good one. Daniel had seemed much more sympathetic to her aims . . . In fact, she was surprised to see, Daniel was standing at the door on his own, Miss Prenderghast smiling apologetically behind him – she definitely had a soft spot for the young man.

'I thought you weren't due for another twenty minutes,' said Veronica, indicating the pile of applications she'd been working through. They were always over-subscribed, but this year their over-subscriptions seemed a little down. She'd have to go through the figures properly with Evelyn.

'No,' said Daniel. He looked nervous, as ill at ease as he

had done the first time he'd arrived, now over three months ago. 'I wondered if I could have a word about something?'

'Of course,' she said, stepping back and welcoming him in. Perhaps he was going to finally ask her about a job. She'd be delighted; as always she was looking for good teachers, and despite the crush factor, it was good for the girls to have some men in the profession. Stopped them going into a frenzy when they hit university, and John Bart, the fiftyish physics teacher, didn't really cut it, with his head in the clouds the whole time.

'Can we sit down?' he said.

'Of course. Would you like tea?'

Daniel shook his head, although his throat was very dry. He fingered the papers in his lap. 'I just want to ask you something,' he said.

Veronica looked up, alerted by his tone of voice. 'Yes?' she said, quite briskly.

'Was your name ... was your name originally Vera Makepiece?'

Something happened to Veronica then. It was as if her entire self shifted a little. Her eyes went wide and she found that, despite years of rigid self-control, she seemed to have lost the ability to control her expression. She went to stand up, then sat down again ... it was most peculiar; she, who always knew what to do, suddenly didn't know quite what to do.

Nobody knew this. Not Jane, not Evelyn. Nobody. She hadn't been Vera Makepiece for over thirty years.

'What do you mean?' she asked, realising too late that a giveaway quaver was instantly noticeable in her voice.

'Were you born Vera Makepiece?' Daniel asked again. His voice had a tremor in it, just like her own.

Daniel looked at her with his large, grey, serious eyes, so

like her own. And somehow, instantly, she just knew. She knew. All the little chats; all the early morning cups of tea. They were all for a reason. He was gathering clues about her; trying to figure her out.

She fell back in her chair, completely unable to speak. Daniel's face worked, and he looked like he was going to lose control completely.

'Who ... who are you?' Veronica asked finally, after Daniel had managed, with a trembling hand, to pour her out a glass of water from the crystal carafe, refilled each morning, that sat on her desk.

There was a long silence, then Daniel let out a great long sigh, as if answering this question was going to take a huge load off his mind. He himself couldn't believe it. Several nights over the last few months he'd woken up bathed in sweat after dreaming of this moment; or hadn't been able to sleep at all, tossing and turning as Penny slept peacefully beside him, until the baby woke them both. He'd had a rough idea for many years but had never found the courage to do something about it before – but when the secondment place had come up, he'd felt it was meant to be. Now, sitting here, in front of ... her ... he wasn't so sure.

'I was adopted in Sheffield in October 1970,' said Daniel, simply. 'My given name was ...'

'James,' said Veronica.

'Yes,' said Daniel. 'I'm James.'

There. He'd said it, and got it out. Years of prevaricating, until finally he'd met this woman, this headteacher. And he could see she was quite intimidating and didn't suffer fools gladly. But he'd liked her, and been incredibly pleased when she'd seemed to like him too. How she would respond now ... well, he hadn't thought much further than this moment. His time here was nearly up anyway; if it all went badly, he could go back to Kent and forget all about it.

He realised he was kidding himself, of course. He could never forget.

'Ohhh,' said Veronica. Now she was giving up all pretence at reserve, or containment, or having any control over her emotions whatsoever. She made another attempt to stand up, and this time succeeded. 'Ohhh. Are you my . . . are you my . . .'

But the word 'baby' would not, of course, come out, and suddenly Veronica glanced at her hands. Tears – tears she had not shed for so long, and had sworn never to shed again – were dripping through her fingers and down onto her papers. When was the last time she had cried? She didn't have to ask herself the question. The last time she had cried was when she had held a little creature to her bosom, and the large lady had come and taken him away. After that, nothing, nothing on earth could hurt her enough to make her cry again.

Daniel didn't know if the tears were a good or a bad sign. He could feel himself wanting to cry; could feel himself as a little boy, asking his adoptive mother over and over again, 'But Mummy, you wouldn't leave your big boy, would you?' and his mother, who was a kind and patient woman, had held him and said, no, but they were very lucky, because they'd got to choose him, and he was the best one there was, and that they would never leave him.

'I'm so sorry,' said Daniel, 'to land this on you . . .'

There were agencies he could have used to act as a go-between, but he hadn't felt comfortable with the ones he'd met – they'd been very nice, but he hadn't liked them poking their noses into his private business. He was very like his mother in that respect.

'I just got confirmation through the post this morning . . .' Daniel raised his pile of papers, uselessly, as if Veronica would want to read them and check his credentials, 'And I didn't . . . I couldn't wait.'

Veronica shook her head. She couldn't fall apart. She couldn't. With near superhuman effort, she managed to page through to Evelyn and tell her to cancel her engagements for that afternoon.

Then she retook her seat and stared at Daniel in tearswept disbelief. Daniel was desperate for her to say something – anything – so he could get the least bit of a handle on what she was feeling. After all, he'd had years to plan this. His biggest fear, however – that she would simply say, 'Oh yes? The baby I had? Well, jolly good, nice to meet you' and send him on his way – was thankfully not being realised.

'Please,' Veronica said eventually, recovering some of her composure and making ample use of the large box of tissues she kept in the office for over-emotional teenage girls. 'Please. Tell me. Was the family . . .'

'My parents are great,' said Daniel carefully. 'They said you were very young.'

Veronica swallowed hard. One of the reasons she could empathise with the girls in her care was remembering how frightened, how young she had been then.

'I was,' said Veronica. 'I had no choice. And then, as time went on . . . I didn't meet anyone else I could form a family with. I couldn't have got you anyway. And then it was too late, and it would seem cruel, and I got a grant to go to university.'

She leant across the desk, her eyes suddenly burning with intensity, and gazed straight at him. 'But I never stopped thinking about you. I promise.'

'Thank you,' said Daniel, trying to swallow the lump in

his throat. Had she really? The idea that she would have thought about him all this time was ... well, was what he had to hear. That his mother – lovely though his adoptive mum had been – that his real mother had loved him too. He managed to swallow, and went on. 'My parents said you were very young and very frightened.'

'And my father was very strong-willed,' murmured Veronica. 'But you know. If it had only been such a very short time later, I would have kept you. Feminism came late to Sheffield, you know. It's so hard to explain to people now how much the world has changed.'

'Tell me about my dad,' said Daniel.

Veronica felt the knife twist in her heart.

'One day,' she said. 'You understand this has come as such a shock to me?'

Daniel nodded. They would have time, hopefully. There was no one named on the birth certificate.

They sat in silence, Veronica letting her gaze wander over his long nose, short grey hair – the similarities were unmistakeable now she looked at them. The thought struck her; thank goodness she had never found him attractive.

'So, you planned all this ...'

'Actually, no,' said Daniel. 'It was a chance remark; Pat got your name wrong and called you Vera. And I knew from the registrar that your own mother's name was ...'

'Deveral,' nodded Veronica. 'After the way my father behaved, I just wanted to get away from him ... it was such a long time ago.'

'Thirty-eight years,' said Daniel. 'So, I twigged, but then thought, it can't be, it just can't be, but then when the chance of the job came up, I took it, and then I saw you ... and being in the same profession. I mean, it was just too weird.'

'So you've been working with me all this time thinking I

might be your mother?' mused Veronica, shaking her head. 'It seems so very strange.'

'It was,' said Daniel. 'Especially when you were so kind to me. I wanted to tell you before, but it didn't seem fair till I knew for sure.'

There was a long silence.

Veronica knew she badly needed to go somewhere and cry; howl at the universe and screech at the injustice: that she should have created this person; a lovely person, but had missed it all. Every fall she could have kissed better; every sticky first day of term, with new pencil cases and trousers grown out of; making the football team; unwrapping Christmas presents; sending him off to college. It was as if a speeded-up version of the life they'd never had together flashed in front of her eyes, but she couldn't look at it; it was too painful.

And her own life hadn't been wasted, surely? Nonetheless, right now she had a fierce need to be alone.

'So what now?' said Veronica.

'I'll have to tell Mum and Dad,' said Daniel. 'They know I was looking for you . . . Penny will have to know too.'

'Of course,' said Veronica, although she had no idea what was proper protocol under the circumstances. 'Please . . .' She mustn't cry. She mustn't. But why could she feel him, the sense memory so strong, feel him as a baby in her arms as if it were yesterday, before they took him away?

'Please thank them from me, for the wonderful job they have done,' she managed to get out eventually.

'I will,' said Daniel stiffly, holding the emotion from his voice. 'And, once we've delivered the assessment, will I be able to come back and see you?'

'I would like that very much,' said Veronica.

*

Veronica sat still at her desk for a long time. She was in no fit state to see anyone. Her head was buzzing, absolutely full of conflicting thoughts. At the fore were two: one, how wonderful, how amazing; how very much Daniel was exactly what she would have wanted for a son. Happily settled, handsome, polite, with a good job. And she wondered to herself if she could have provided him with the stable home life and good example that had obviously worked so well for him. Very possibly not.

She also felt a cold hand at her neck. This . . . well, it wouldn't be ideal. For the school. For prospective parents. Who would want to send their child to the care of a woman who had abandoned her own child, however compelling the reasons? She thought of those awful stories she'd seen in the magazines Evelyn liked to read: 'I found my Long Lost Son on the Internet' and such like.

The idea of something so private becoming common knowledge, to be gossiped about and discussed by the girls at home . . . that was an insupportable thought too. But would Daniel wish for secrecy? He could already be out, spreading the news. She clutched her teacup so hard her knuckles went white. Surely not. No, of course not.

They would discuss it sensibly. Yes. She could gradually feel her breathing ease, get back under control. She must control herself, that was it. And perhaps she could meet his adoptive parents, thank them. And . . . she hardly dared to think it, hardly dared to breathe or admit to herself how great her longing was. But if she could meet his children . . . be involved with his two little boys and the little baby girl, Eliza her name was. Being their other grandmother . . . it was a desire so strong, it frightened her. Breathing out hard, she rose to stand at the window, the view of the cliffs and the sea normally one she found infinitely calming. Today, though, the choppy April waves and grey sky, filled with fast-moving clouds, reflected her own tempestuous mind, which couldn't settle.

To look at her, though, you wouldn't suspect a thing.

Chapter Fifteen

Post-Easter, the school seemed to divide in two. For half of them there were looming exams, barriers to be surmounted; for the eldest, university interviews and coming to terms with the next phase of their lives, whether that was travelling on a gap year, or moving straight into higher education. Hanging over this for the teachers was the huge pressure on results, which meant that their desire to help the girls and not make this time too difficult for them was compounded by the need to make this year the best ever; to beat other schools in their league and show Dr Deveral that everything was running as smoothly as ever (she had been uncharacteristically reserved lately). Clarissa Rhodes, expected to get an unprecedented six starred As, was frequently to be found mopping her eyes in the loos, even as she was being wooed by several top universities in the UK and the United States.

'I just can't help it,' she wailed to Maggie, who still felt slightly nervous teaching someone whose work was rather better than hers and whose legs certainly were. 'What if I don't go to Harvard and someone else comes along and discovers a successful alternative to OPEC?'

'There there,' said Maggie encouragingly. 'You are going to be just fine.'

Maggie felt a little sunnier too – she and Stan had managed

to get away at Easter. It was just a week in Spain, but she felt better for having a bit of colour, lazy days sleeping in without bells and fun nights drinking horrible local spirits and cutting it up a bit on the dance-floor, just like they used to when they were at school. It had been fun, good straightforward fun, and all the stresses of daily life and heavy conversations had been put behind them. Maggie knew many of the other girls had spent Easter in Mustique, or Gstaad or on safari, but sipping a ridiculous cocktail out of a coconut shell whilst inexplicably wearing a balloon crown, she and Stan laughing their heads off, she hadn't felt envious in the slightest.

It made such a change, at this time of year, when she had normally been in a frenzy trying to help the few children who were going to even turn up for their exams, versus those who started chafing at the bit to get outside as the days got longer and the sky clearer. It was a tricky balancing act.

Here, all the girls in her upper classes looked likely to pass, even Galina Primm, whose dyslexia was so bad it was often hard to tell what she was writing at all. But special arrangements had been put in place so that she could take longer and dictate her exam papers, which meant she shouldn't have any problem with the GCSE papers at all; it wasn't her brain that was at fault, just the wiring between her brain and her fingers.

And her lower class was, finally, falling into place. It was such a luxury to enter the classroom without worrying about Simone being in tears, again, or Alice and Fliss giggling and gossiping behind their hands. Knowing girls as she did, Maggie knew these acts of class solidarity rarely lasted for long but, in the aftermath of the stealing incident, and Simone's subsequent new-found and hard-won popularity, it was nice to see them all working well as a group.

So it was with a sunny heart she walked into class on a warm Wednesday morning in mid-May, wondering if it was time to give the girls some time off from the Ben Jonson they'd been looking at, and wondering if they'd all read Laurie Lee. If not, they'd like him.

This, and thinking about Claire, who'd become very quiet and clammed up about her love life lately, was what was going through her head, as she walked into the classroom, only to find all the girls with their noses jammed in horror against the glass windows on the eastern side of the building.

Alice had been planning her trick for months. She needed to gain back the respect of her classmates, many of whom thought she had been unjustly hard on Simone, but were too frightened of her sharp tongue to say so to her face. She couldn't bear all this lovey-dovey atmosphere in class. The fashion was for girls to walk arm in arm. Next they'd be giving each other bead bracelets. Alice sniffed. Well, this would wake them up, and give that common Glaswegian witch something to think about too.

It wasn't normal for Alice to feel the one sidelined, particularly for someone she didn't think much of. Normally girls looked to her for guidance, but now it was all sweetness and light and everyone spending most of the day speculating romantically about that stupid English teacher from the boys' school. Well, she'd show them.

It took a while to arrive – her grandfather, and frequent partner in crime, had had some trouble digging it up from his attic, but had managed it eventually. Miss Starling had asked her what was in the large parcel, but she'd looked wide-eyed and explained her grandfather had sent her a small stool, and that had seemed to satisfy her.

Fortunately there'd been heavy rain the night before. She'd risen silently at one a.m., when the whole house was asleep, creeping over to wake Fliss, who finally had the plaster off her ankle and was back to active service.

Fliss awoke to see Alice leaning over her with a torch, and nearly screamed out loud.

'What!' she finally managed to whisper.

'Larks afoot,' said Alice. 'Come on. Remember I mentioned our prank?'

Fliss searched her memory. Hadn't Alice forgotten all about that ages ago?

'Uh huh,' she said, slowly.

'Well, it's time,' said Alice.

Fliss sat upright. 'What do you mean?'

'It finally arrived. The thing I need. And it needs to be done now. So are you in or not?'

'I don't know!' said Fliss. 'I'm behaving myself now, you know. Any trouble and I'm going to get into absolutely serious s-h-i-t.'

'Does that include, you know, swearing to yourself,' said Alice sarcastically.

'No,' said Fliss. 'But I just don't want to . . . you know. Show myself up again.'

'OK,' said Alice. 'I promise I'll take all the blame if we get caught.'

'Blame for what?' came another voice. Alice rolled her eyes.

'Go back to sleep, Simone.'

'But I want to know.'

'Me too,' said Fliss, folding her arms and looking slightly mutinous. Alice sighed. Roll on next year when she'd be able to boss around the younger pupils.

'OK,' she said. 'I'm going to explain. But Simone, you can't

233

come. You just have to keep mum. Or, better still, you could be our "Credulous Stooge".

'All right,' said Simone. She was delighted not to have to go, but to be included at the same time. Then Alice explained the prank and it was simply beyond Fliss's powers not to go along with it.

'We'll need waterproofs,' she whispered.

'I've got it all sorted,' said Alice. 'Here, grab this mallet.' Fliss's eyes widened. But she did as she was told. And with Alice clutching the heavy box, they crept silently downstairs to the unmanned fire escape.

The night was mild, and lit brightly by the moon and the stars, but evidence of the recent heavy rainfall was everywhere; the mud was thick and glutinous and it was hard going in the socks Alice had insisted on, to minimise footprints.

'I've got it all mapped out,' she said. Fliss shivered; half of her wanted to collapse in hysterical laughter, half was just plain terrified.

'We'll never get away with it,' she whispered.

'It is our duty to try,' said Alice solemnly. 'Now, be quiet, get down in the mud, and start rolling.'

Two hours later they had made it back to the dorm unnoticed – Simone was lying awake, fearfully, and had thoughtfully stuffed pillows down their beds.

'In case Miss Adair came past,' she said.

'Smart thinking,' said Alice, surprised. They cleaned the dirt off as well as they could in the little sink in their bathroom; the macintoshes she'd borrowed from the gardeners' shed had gone back in there – a new coating of mud hadn't made much difference. The really important thing was that their footprints didn't show – only the huge, unmistakeable footprint of her grandfather's wastepaper basket, trophy of a century-old hunting trip in Africa . . .

'What's that?' timid Sylvie was saying, staring out into the mud, now lit up brightly by the spring sunshine. The light made the tops of the great marks sparkle.

Maggie could now hear an excited uproar from the other classes up and down the halls, as well as windows opening. The refectory had high windows, too high to see out of, but this side of the building the view went all the way to sea. She could see Harold and two of the groundsmen, just starting work, following something and looking puzzled. As she watched, one of them peeled off and ran up in the direction of Dr Deveral's office.

'What is it, for goodness' sake? Girls, get down.'

As she came up she could see them, right across the lawn, straight past the windows and heading out to the pond: a huge set of hoofprints, with three large stubby toes, set in a galloping motion.

'I thought I heard something last night,' said a voice behind her. She turned, and it was sensible Simone. 'Kind of like a rumbling. But I didn't think much of it. But now I think of it – it could have been galloping!'

'I did too!' said Felicity Prosser, her face looking full of colour suddenly. 'Kind of like a rumbling, bashing noise.'

Suddenly the rest of the class nodded and started loudly agreeing that they'd heard it too, until even Maggie was wondering if she'd woken in the night – surely not.

Now Miss Starling and Claire Crozier were both outside, being given details by the groundsmen, and Maggie turned to her class.

'Calm down all of you.'

'Calm down?' said Sylvie. 'There's a wild animal escaped from the zoo!'

'All the better reason for you to stay indoors then,' said Maggie. 'Let me find out what's going on.'

She stalked outside.

'This is ridiculous,' Miss Starling was saying.

'I know,' the gardener was saying. 'But there are no footprints or anything near it, and it's definitely rhinoceros.'

'That's absurd.'

'I went on a safari,' said the younger gardener. 'We were tracking them. They were exactly like that.'

'And where do the tracks go?' said Miss Starling.

'You know, there ees the safari park just at Looe,' said Claire.

'That's monkeys,' said Miss Starling.

'Perhaps they have expanded,' said Claire.

'Ring them,' said Miss Starling. She bent down to examine the marks. 'I can't imagine how they got here . . . did you hear anything, Miss Adair?'

Maggie shook her head. 'Though some of the girls are saying they heard rumblings in the night.'

Miss Starling stalked ahead following the markings. They were set, two by two on the diagonal, and deep in the mud, as if an extremely heavy animal had indeed been running. It was entirely mysterious. The undergardener took his hat off and stared at them.

'I tell you, I've seen rhinoceros tracks, and they look just like that.'

Behind them, some of the older girls had strayed into the grounds and were also following the tracks. Seeing their lead, more classes had come out to see what was going on. There was much squealing.

Miss Starling's mouth was pursed. The tracks went all the

way down to the pond, where there was a broken-down wooden bridge. This area was out of bounds to pupils, and anyway dank, unpleasant and hardly an attraction.

This morning, however, a huge part of the bridge was knocked through. It looked exactly as if a huge creature had barged through it, only to tumble into the watery depths below. The group stood there for a moment, staring into the pond.

'What a terrible thing to happen,' said the under-gardener. 'He must have been scared out of his wits.'

Maggie was busy wondering how she was going to explain to Stan that there were wild animals on the property as well as everything else. And would they have to evacuate the grounds now they'd found its final resting place? And would they have to dredge the pond?

She glanced at Miss Starling and was surprised to see her shoulders shaking. Surely she couldn't be that upset? Maybe she was a real animal lover.

Then she looked closer. Miss Starling's shoulders were shaking . . . surely it couldn't be . . . it couldn't be with *laughter*.

'Miss Starling?' she said, moving forwards. But it was true. The lady was rocking back and forth, her eyes moist, clutching her fist to her mouth.

'Are you all right?'

'I'm fine,' said Miss Starling. 'Tee hee hee! I mean, I'm fine.'

Claire and Maggie swapped incredulous looks. Then they started laughing too.

'That,' said Miss Starling, 'is a new one on me. And it's not often anyone gets the chance to say that.' She managed to compose herself in record time and looked around to see that they were being watched by a crowd of wide-eyed girls.

She marched up to them. 'There has been some damage here,' she said, sternly. 'If anyone believes they can assist to repair it in any way, please come and see me. In the meantime' – and her face was so straight, Maggie could fully believe she had imagined the last five minutes – 'I recommend nobody drink from the pond until we get it fully drained. Now, everyone back to class *immediately*.'

Alice, Fliss and Simone lay breathless on the floor of their dorm. Every time they felt they couldn't possibly laugh any more, it was too painful, someone would recall the look on Maggie's face when everyone mentioned hearing the noise, or the under-gardener's scientific insights into hoofprints, and they'd all set off once more.

'I said I'd get that Miss Adair,' Alice would howl again, and the hysterics would rise again.

When their sides actually hurt, there wasn't a breath left in them, and Fliss thought she was going to throw up, Alice finally rose.

'OK,' she said. 'Off to face the music.'

'Are you going to own up?' said Fliss, impressed.

'God, yes,' scoffed Alice. 'Of course, who do you think I am, Imogen? My granddad said if I could pull it off he'd pay for the fence.'

'I'd like to meet your granddad,' said Simone, wonderingly.

'Oh, maybe you will,' said Alice carelessly, and Fliss's heart leapt, recognising in it a simple acceptance of her new friend.

'They won't send you down, though, will they?' said Fliss, suddenly worried.

'Unlikely,' said Alice. 'I didn't actually do anything too bad, and that bridge needed demolishing anyway. Few detentions,

I think. Which will be well worth it. And I won't mention you guys, don't worry.'

'Thanks,' said Fliss.

As it turned out, Alice was exactly right. Miss Starling was less strict than her usual self, and Alice merely received lines and a sharp telling off. The rhinoceros-foot wastepaper bin was ordered home to its rightful owner, and although everyone in Middle School 1 knew that Alice was behind it – and treated her with reverence and incredulity because of it – it also somehow made its way into Downey House folklore that, one night, an escaped rhinoceros had run through the grounds and drowned in the pond. It was to keep generations of Downey juniors well out of reach of the water.

The other positive outcome was that Simone's willingness to support the prank cemented the girls' friendship in the dorm. Three was never an easy number, and Simone would always have a residual distrust of, and admiration for, Alice's quick wit and sharp tongue – but the three girls were now inseparable.

Chapter Sixteen

If it hadn't been for Alice and Fliss, Simone would never have gone up for the hockey team. But they encouraged her, and it wasn't as if she was going to need too much time to study for end of term exams – she'd done so much work throughout the year, it would really just be a case of going in and writing down the answers.

All year Miss James had been putting them through their paces in various sports. Unlike most games mistresses, she wasn't keen on forcing girls into teams too early. It took some girls a while to find their feet and confidence; telling a girl she couldn't do sport too early was likely to put her off for life, and she would probably finish her career on the games field hanging around the goal chewing nonchalantly and gossiping with chums.

So she tried different sports; shook up teams, encouraged everyone to play every position. Obviously some were stronger than others, but rotating often showed unexpected skills, and some girls found, for example, some talent in trampolining where they'd failed elsewhere.

In summer term, however, there were special netball and hockey play-offs between all the houses and that's where it got really serious. Not everyone had to try out, but there was kudos, time off other classes, and the chance to travel to other schools in later years if you made the team, so competition was fierce.

Try-outs were late in May on a Saturday morning. It was shaping up to be another lovely day. Seniors, bored with their A-level revision, glanced fondly out of their study windows, remembering past try-outs from their first year as if it were a lifetime ago.

'Right everyone,' said Miss James. She had her usual brisk manner, but no one could prevent the nerves from getting through. Fliss was sitting out this year, despite loving netball; it wasn't worth risking the ankle just yet, but she firmly hoped she'd be allowed to play next year. Alice wasn't auditioning at all, she thought sport was stupid. But Simone was there, making a feeble attempt at warming up, and her friends had gone to cheer her on.

'This is going to be super embarrassing,' she said at the sidelines. 'Andrea runs like the wind, and Sylvie is totally brilliant. They're all going to laugh at me.'

'They're not,' said Fliss. 'You're great at hockey.'

'I suppose I could stop the ball with my thighs,' said Simone. 'They're bigger than the net.'

'Is that legal in hockey?' said Alice.

'Maybe I could sue them for not letting a person of unrestricted growth play,' muttered Simone. Alice laughed, but Fliss didn't like Simone's habit of always putting herself down. Maybe if she got in the team she could drop a bit of weight anyway, and it wouldn't be such a problem.

'Go Simone!' she said. 'Go for it!'

Simone raised her eyes to heaven. 'Will you look after my glasses? I'm much more aggressive if I can't see what I'm doing.'

Miss James ran them around for a warm-up which didn't do Simone's cause much good – she was puffed out almost before they had to zigzag in amongst the mini traffic cones. And when it came to shooting at the goal, star shots Ursula and lanky sporty Andrea were streets ahead. But at Simone's turn in goal she stolidly and carefully blocked every shot, and Miss James made a mark on her paper anyway.

Maggie was delighted to see Simone's name up on the team list the following morning. Simone hardly ever came to see her now, only infrequently to change a book.

'I'm not reading so much now,' she'd said last time. 'I'm so busy.' Then she'd blushed. She'd be rather pretty if she could drop a little of that weight, thought Maggie. Then she had to get on. There were final assessment sheets to be dropped off – the assessors were counter-marking the mock examinations, which had made everyone terribly nervous – end of term exams to be set for the juniors, and exam supervision to be arranged for the seniors. The end of term concert she wasn't involved in. Probably just as well. The less time she spent with David McDonald the better. And anyway, she'd managed to persuade Stan to come down for sports day, tempting him with sunny weather and the promise of walks on the beach with frequent ice cream stops. She was sure if he just spent some time in Cornwall he'd learn to love it too.

Maggie sometimes surprised herself by thinking how much she'd forgotten now her once fierce ideals about returning to the poorer areas of her homeland, though she knew somewhere in her heart that she would have to – one day. Anna kept reminding her about it, telling her how Dylan and Cody's local park had been closed down due to council cuts and how they were driving her crazy kicking about the house all day. Maggie felt guilty and vowed to get them down here too, maybe when the Scottish schools broke up, earlier than the English ones, to let them, too, run about in the fresh air; play on the crags and the beach, jump in the enormous swimming pool. It wasn't, she knew, the solution.

Veronica waited for the final assessment meeting with some trepidation. Even the idea of being in the same room as Daniel again made her feel nervous. She was desperate just to stare at his face, even though she realised how peculiar this would be.

Pat and Liz had not been best pleased to have their previous meeting cancelled and were huffy and self-important when they turned up, fussing about with unnecessary flip charts and bar charts. Present, in the small lecture auditorium, were Veronica, Miss Starling, and three representatives of the board of governors, who were normally very hands-off: Dame Lydia Johnson, a local JP, Digory Gill, a local council officer, and Majabeen Gupta, a paediatrician from London who had a holiday cottage there and had sent all three of his girls through the school. The report, once it was bound, would go to every governor, every teacher, and from then on to every parent who requested it. It had been such an eventful year, Veronica reflected ruefully. She hoped it wouldn't have a negative impact on their score.

'Now,' said Liz, looking officious in a white polyester shirt which strained over her large bosoms. It was lucky she'd never attempted to button her suit jacket; it was very unlikely she'd succeed. 'When we approached this task, we used the 1989 matrix inversion schedule, as popularised by McIntosh and Luther, in the Northern Schools Initiative of 1991.'

Veronica glanced briefly at Digory. He was not one for jargon and tended to either complain through it or fall asleep. From the looks of him this morning, it might well be the latter.

'First we looked at how effective, efficient and inclusive is the provision of education, integrated care and any extended services in meeting the needs of learners,' droned Liz. 'We found that in many circumstances there were some problems with developmental acquisition of the proper non-discriminatory religion, disability, difference and gender instruments.'

Even Veronica was finding it hard to understand what she was talking about, and she had a PhD in economics. Perhaps a PhD in horrible waffle would have been more appropriate.

Over the space of the next forty minutes, however, it transpired that Pat and Liz had decided the school was not socially-minded enough, did not include enough work on environmental issues and wasn't inclusive. Veronica mentally struck this from her head. Inclusive wasn't, sadly, their business. They had girls here from every part of the world, from every race and religion, although she was well aware that the one thing they all had in common was that their parents were wealthy, and believed in educating girls. But her job was only to teach them to be tolerant and kind, not slavishly trying to right wrongs.

It didn't really matter, though, as she was hardly concentrating. She was watching Daniel. Her son, Daniel. She couldn't even believe the words as she thought them. 'My son Daniel.' She'd hardly slept since he'd been to see her.

Daniel was sitting, looking grave and making notes on a piece of paper. Veronica hoped he would stay behind so they could have lunch together, and she could ask him about his parents. Daniel felt nervous too. What was expected of him now? he wondered. Maybe it would be all right if they just tried to get to know each other. What on earth were the others going to say when they found out he was Dr Deveral's . . . he couldn't keep thinking of her like that, it was ridiculous, but so was 'mother' so he'd have to keep think-

244

ing of an alternative. Anyway. What were people going to think when they found out? It was going to be strange for everyone.

'There are also some extreme safety and security issues at the school,' Liz was now saying, touching as if sensitively on 'breakouts' and 'injuries' as if they were much more serious than she could bring herself to mention. 'We have enumerated these at some length in our final report.' Digory did look like he was nodding off. Just as Veronica was thinking this, she noticed June Starling give him a sharp dig in the ribs.

'However,' said Pat, taking back the baton. 'There are some other matters to consider.'

Another sheet came up on the overhead projector. This Veronica understood immediately.

Attitude of learners
Attendance of learners
Enjoyment of learners
Involvement of learners
Attainments of learners

And lined up under those headings were the exam marks of girls from the last five years, and the projections for this year, which were higher than ever.

Everyone gazed at this slide for some time.

'So,' said Pat, somewhat reluctantly. 'We'll have some recommendations to make about truancy, safety procedures and some suggestions as to how to promote inclusivity . . .'

'Yes,' said Veronica, her heart beating slightly faster.

'But these aren't problems, however pressing, that are believed to be significant enough to affect the school's standing in the long run,' said Liz, sounding grudging. 'The girls, it seems, have spoken for you. And they like the school as it is.'

There was a pause.

'Well done,' said Daniel, who'd known the results in advance. He rose to his feet. 'It's a top score all round.'

And he came forward to shake Veronica by the hand. It was only when he did so that she realised how nervous she had been. As usual, she didn't betray herself by even a tremor. She's amazing, thought Daniel. You would never think they were more than just colleagues.

'Thank you,' said Veronica. 'Thank you so much everyone. And thanks for your hard work.'

Pat and Liz gave thin-lipped smiles.

'You'll get the full report in the post in eight weeks,' said Liz.

Eight weeks? thought Veronica, but she didn't say anything, except, 'Lunch?'

Daniel caught up with her as they walked round the outside of the building – it was such a beautiful day. He approached her nervously; Veronica turned, equally nervous, having walked on ahead alone in the hopes that he would come and walk with her.

'Hello,' she said, checking to see no one was near them.

'Hello. How are you? Are you well?'

'I'm well. Yes. I'm well. You know. It's strange and everything. What about you?'

Veronica looked at the nervous young man beside her. What must he be thinking? she thought. After all, he'd been through all the work of finding her. Was he pleased? Disappointed?

'Oh, you know,' she said, trying to carry off a little laugh. 'Starting to come to terms with the world being a little different to how I thought of it before.'

'Quite,' said Daniel. He wasn't sure if it was the right thing to do, but he touched her lightly on the arm. Veronica tensed up, realising this was the first personal contact they'd had in nearly forty years.

'Sorry,' said Daniel.

'Not at all,' said Veronica. He didn't remember when she'd held him; buried her face in his head and smelled his brand new, bloodied fresh-bread smell. She'd never forgotten it.

'I, er . . . spoke to Mum and Dad.'

'Oh yes?'

'They think I should go slow. You know. Take it a step at a time.'

Both his parents in fact had been a little worried that he'd tracked Veronica down and confronted her, but loved him too much to tell him. Daniel swallowed.

'But I'm happy to tell the world. I don't mind.'

Something in his tone made her think that suddenly he didn't sound like a thirty-eight-year-old at all, but like the little boy he must have been. She must remember that; he was not an adult when he was talking to her, not really.

Veronica smiled at him. 'Well, I understand completely your parents' reticence. Of course it's too early, we don't want to go broadcasting anything until we've got to know each other a little.'

She realised immediately by the way his face twisted that this wasn't what he'd been expecting.

'What do you mean?' said Daniel, suddenly feeling as if he'd just been snubbed. Why not? Why couldn't they be a family? Wasn't that the whole point of him telling her? His parents would be so welcoming too.

Veronica felt conflicted. For a moment she thought he was

going to turn round and announce it to the others behind them, which made her shiver with horror. And she'd been looking forward so much to getting to know him slowly, on their terms, without being a topic of gossip and intrusion for the rest of the world . . . surely that was best.

'I just meant, I understand that a more cautious approach . . .'

Daniel didn't understand this at all. He'd thought she was so pleased. 'You mean, you're ashamed of having an illegitimate son? In this day and age?'

'Don't be ridiculous,' said Veronica, stopping short and looking straight at him. 'Meeting you again has been one of the best things that has ever happened to me.' She took a deep breath. 'After having you.'

Daniel took this in. Wow. That was . . . that was so amazing, so what he'd hoped she'd feel and say. But then why on earth would they have to keep it a secret?

'But in my position . . .' went on Veronica.

Daniel stopped short. His face looked red.

'I see,' he said and started to head back to the others.

'No, no!' said Veronica, reaching out as if to hold on to him, but dropped her arms immediately. 'It's not like that at all. I want to get to know you so much, Daniel. I was hoping to meet your family one day . . . even, I was thinking, you know Mrs Sutherland retires next year from the history department, and I even thought you might be interested in coming to work here . . .'

But how could she say this and mean something else?

'But in secret?' said Daniel, rubbing the back of his head.

'Please, Daniel. I just . . . I just don't want to rush things.'

'Well, you've already offered me a job, but apart from that you don't want to rush things.'

Veronica looked down at her elegant hands, noticing

unavoidably, as she always did, the way the veins grew uglier and more prominent every year.

'I . . . I . . . I seem to be making rather a mess of this, don't I?' she said. What could she say to him to make him realise how important he was; how important this was to her?

Daniel couldn't believe this. She really would offer him a job but not tell anyone he was her son. After everything he'd done to find her. She said she wanted him but when it came down to it, it was just like before – she didn't really want to acknowledge him at all. He felt his ears going pink, felt once more like a little boy .

'I don't . . .' he said, then decided to leave before he said something he couldn't take back. 'Uh. I don't think I'll stay for lunch.' And he strode off towards his car.

As Veronica watched him go, she felt a piece of herself break off; plummet into blackness. Her boy . . . her boy . . .

'Are you all right?'

It was Majabeen, come up beside her.

'It's wonderful news, isn't it?'

'What?' said Veronica, trying to wrest her brain back from where it had gone, down the road with her only son. 'Oh, yes. The report. Yes, I suppose it is.'

'Come on, then. I think everyone wants to celebrate. Is that young chap gone?'

'Yes,' said Veronica, slowly. 'Yes he has. Let me just go and freshen up.'

Chapter Seventeen

End of term! There was a heady atmosphere in the dorms as the girls were getting ready to go home, or abroad on exciting trips. Astrid was spending the summer on the special programme at the Royal College of Music in London. Alice was joining her parents in Cairo. Fliss couldn't believe how much she was going to miss her friends.

'I'll only be in London,' said Simone. 'You can come and see me.'

'No, no, come to Guildford – you can ride my pony,' said Fliss. 'It'll be great.'

All exams were over, and all that was left was to slack off, lie tanning on the grass at lunchtime, and make plans for the summer.

'I am going to sleep till eleven o'clock every day,' said Sylvie, dreamily.

'Is that the most wonderful thing you can think of to do?' said Alice, but not in as sneering a tone as she'd have used before.

'Yes, actually,' said Sylvie, uncowed. 'I'm very sensitive to bells.'

Clarissa Rhodes was off to the Sorbonne, where she would take a vast number of high level courses, all in

French. Maggie had felt entirely embarrassed when Clarissa came by especially to thank her.

'Well done with that Rhodes girl,' she now said, banging loudly on Claire's door. Hearing no answer she popped her head round – Claire ought to be here by now.

She was lying full length on her bed, howling her eyes out.

'What's the matter?'

'Eet does not matter. *Tant pis! Je déteste les hommes.*'

'What, all of them?'

Sitting down, Maggie got from her that the affair with the married man had ended catastrophically, and that he had gone back to his wife, tragically just in time for the summer holidays.

'There there,' said Maggie, patting Claire on the back. 'At least you won't have to see him any more.'

'Ah have to see him ALL THE TIME!' said Claire furiously.

'Why? What do you mean?'

Maggie had always imagined Claire's paramour to be some rich glamorous Frenchman, like Nicolas Sarkozy, only taller, who bought her jewels and had a beautiful apartment in an *arrondissement*.

'Mais non, it's Mr Graystock.'

Maggie shook her head. 'Mr Graystock at Downey Boys? The classics teacher?'

She dimly remembered the lanky posh chap, but had hardly given him a second glance as it was, she remembered with some embarrassment, at the height of her David mooning phase.

'Isn't he a bit of a chinless wonder?'

''e ees BASTARD!'

Maggie stayed with her for some time, amazed at what

was going on under her nose at the school that she'd managed to completely miss.

It was still a lovely morning though. Many of the Downey Boys would be coming over to see their sports day, and vice versa. She'd make excuses for Claire.

And all her girls had done well in their exams. She was so proud of them, this term they'd really got their heads down. And now all that was left was the sports day, then back to Glasgow for eight glorious weeks. Her parents were incredibly excited already and had made all sorts of plans; Stan was still here and threatening to drive the Fiat Panda all the way back to Scotland, which was fine by her. Nothing else had been said, but she knew, she just knew deep down that she wanted to come back next year. She'd had a short interview with Veronica that had confirmed what she'd hoped very much – that it was working out for her at Downey House, and they'd like to keep her. She had accepted, telling herself she'd sort it out later. But she just didn't know how long Stan would take 'no' for an answer.

Frowning slightly, she wandered past the sports pitch to walk down and pick him up from the village. Lessons were cancelled today as the girls all dressed up in house colours, in preparation to fight it out on the hockey pitch and athletics field. The gardeners had done an amazing job; flower beds were blazing with June flowers, reflecting the colours of the houses – rose-pink for Tudor, white for York, surrounded by green wreaths for Wessex, and fresh blue and yellow broom for the Plantagenets. Fluttering bunting had been hung up along the running track and around the stall that would be providing much-needed barley water later. It was an amazingly hot day, butterflies thronging up from the long grass beneath her feet.

She hailed the familiar figure at the foot of the driveway.

'Well met!' she shouted.

David grinned back at her, but she thought he looked a little nervous, and there was no sign of Stephen Daedalus.

'What's up? Where's Stephen Daedalus? Are you here on school business?'

David looked uncomfortable and glanced around. He was wearing long baggy khaki trousers, and a grey collarless shirt; if he hadn't seemed so awkward he would have appeared cool and fresh in the summer heat.

They couldn't be seen from the school where they were, far away from the high towers, close to the copse. She moved closer towards him.

'Uh,' he said. It wasn't like David to be speechless. He couldn't be blushing, could he?

'Here's the thing.' he said. 'And I'm just going to say it, all right?'

Maggie found that she was holding her breath.

'I . . . I've broken up with Miranda.'

Maggie squinted at him. She felt her heart start to beat faster. Why was he telling her?

'Oh, I'm so sorry.'

'It doesn't matter. She didn't like having a lowly school-master for a beau, and didn't really bother to hide it too much. Always pestering me to go to Portsmouth and get a job there. Like it wasn't all right to be happy in your job if you didn't make that much money . . . anyway, forget that,' he said, taking a deep breath. 'I . . . I. Well. I think you're . . . Anyway. Huh. This is difficult. Anyway. Listen. I'm going on holiday. I'm going to walk the Cinque Terre. In Italy. It's gorgeous, apparently, and some friends have a villa down there and I'll be staying with them, and, well, of course you can't, it's totally stupid to ask. But if you wanted to come. You could. That's all. Right. Sorry.'

His dark eyes had been fixed on the ground throughout this speech, and Maggie could barely think straight. But did this mean . . . what? What did it mean?

She stood there, staring at him.

'I know. I'm sorry. I shouldn't have said anything. I'll go. Sorry. Sorry. I'm really sorry.'

And he turned round. Maggie couldn't take her eyes off him. David. Her David. He was walking on now, not looking back, towards the gates of the school, his shoulders bent. She couldn't bear to watch him so . . .

'DAVID!!!' she shouted, just as he reached the entrance, even though she didn't have the faintest idea of what she was going to say to him after that. But she so wanted to say his name.

His long body stiffened, and, very slowly, he turned around. She found herself staring straight into his eyes. Very slowly, and with a faintly incredulous look on his face, he started to walk back towards her up the hill. Maggie caught her breath. Oh my. Oh . . .

'HEY!'

They both froze, still several metres apart.

'Can I come through this door, or do I get arrested as a sex pest immediately? Useful to know, like,' said Stan, hovering just at the very edge of the gates. 'Thought I'd come and get you, but I forgot about the paedie bit where I can't come in.'

Stan was wearing odd-length shorts that seemed to stop halfway down his calves, like they'd been bought for a toddler, and his beloved Celtic top. Maggie stared at him. David was looking at her still, so intently.

'I've brought sausage sandwiches,' said Stan. 'Miss a meal here, you're stuffed.'

David dropped his gaze, shaking his head. Then he pasted on a smile.

'Stanley,' he said. 'Hi there.'

'Hello,' said Stan, not friendly or unfriendly. 'Come on love.' This to Maggie.

Maggie felt her head spin. Had she taken leave of her senses? What, was she just going to suddenly dump this man, her Stan, when she'd agreed to marry him only six months before? Had she gone crazy?

She tried out her voice experimentally. It sounded weird, like she was listening to it on tape. 'Eh, hello, Stan.'

Stan didn't seem to notice.

'Are they really going to let me watch all these foxy girls in sporty skirts?' he grumbled. 'I'm not sure this is such a good idea.'

Unable to stop herself, Maggie found herself going towards him. You do not, she told herself very firmly, confuse what is real with what is a fantasy. That is madness. Madness.

'Must go,' said David. 'Get the dog, you know.'

'I reckon he's married to that dog,' said Stan, watching him head down the lane. Then he took Maggie in his arms and kissed her. 'School's nearly out, eh? Nearly finished! Yay!'

'Yay,' said Maggie, slightly more quietly, then she buried her head in his shirt, taking in his familiar scent.

'Steady on,' said Stan. 'I don't want your terrifying Miss Starling having my guts for garters. And she would too. She'd claw them out with her bare fingernails, and smile while she did it.'

'She's not that bad,' said Maggie.

'Not that bad? After everything you've told me . . .'

And Stan followed a very thoughtful Maggie up the hill.

Simone was nervous as she got ready in the blue and yellow polo shirt they'd had specially made up. All she had to do, she knew, was stand in the goal and do as well as she could. But it was one thing being surrounded by her own form, who supported her and had grown to like her. Girls from other classes, older girls were watching now. She bit her lip. Well, it was too late now. Fliss was plaiting her hair to keep it out of the way.

'And don't let them go for your glasses,' she was saying.

'No,' said Simone.

Miss James got her teams together. Two ten-minute halves for six-a-side teams per game; York versus Tudor first, then Plantagenets v Wessex, followed by a play-off.

The whole school was out on the benching, in a festive mood; the senior sports coming up later. The little ones' hockey tournament was always fun, the older girls shaking their heads in disbelief that they were ever so small and immature, and laughing if things got aggressive, as they could do.

Miss James blew her whistle as the whites and pinks faced off. The game was fast and furious played with this number of players in such a short time frame, and it took a while to get a goal on the table. But at the eighth minute, Eve McGinty, a tough-faced girl from Tudor, whacked one across the goal line, followed in the second half by two more. She was clearly a formidable opponent, and York retired sulkily.

'Go, Simone,' shouted Fliss, as she stood up to get on the pitch. Everyone, it seemed to Simone, was yelling.

Maggie was watching, trying to clear her bewildered head. Had David really . . . suddenly she had a vision of them both, walking through Italy, eating in simple trattorias, getting brown with the sun and healthy with the exercise; spending balmy nights with sweet pink wine in little towns where whitewashed churches rang out their bells as the stars above swelled and the velvety soft nights washed over them with the scent of heavy lilies . . .

'You all right?' said Stan, nudging her. 'This fat girl's one of yours, isn't she?'

With effort, Maggie pulled herself back. And indeed, it was wonderful to see Simone out there, blocking, passing the ball back and forward, hearing the shouts from the crowd.

No one, though, it seemed, could get in to score. It looked like being sudden death in the second half when, suddenly, Andrea broke through at the last moment and hit the little ball straight into the corner of their opponents' net.

The Plantagenet girls erupted into a bouncing mass of blue and yellow from their place on the benches, jumping up and down and hugging each other.

'Well done,' said Miss James, as they took five minutes before the final. 'Now, watch out for Eve McGinty. She's the best in the year. Simone, do you think you can stop her?'

Simone was getting her breath back and polishing her glasses, but she nodded nervously nonetheless. She'd felt very strange out there and was thankful that the ball hadn't really come too close to her goal.

That all changed when the next match began. There was no doubt that Eve was the star, and she went for the ball with all the aggression of a national rugby player. Simone saw the ball come straight for her, and, in a temporary loss of nerve, closed her eyes. The ball went straight between her legs and landed in the goal, glinting up at her.

There were roars from the Tudor side, and groans from the Plantagenets; even a couple of solitary boos. Maggie winced in disappointment for her, and again as Eve slammed the ball in two more times in that half alone. It was going to be a massacre.

Simone knew she was purple at half-time, partly with exhaustion, and partly with embarrassment.

'Would you like me to take you off?' said Miss James.

'She'll be all right, won't you Simone?' said Andrea.

And at that, Simone felt her confidence rise a little. If tall, capable Andrea thought she could do it, there was no reason not to.

'I'll do my best,' she said.

'Well, do better than that,' said Andrea, spitting out her orange peel. 'Do your job. Block these bloody goals.'

And my goodness, she did! Simone was everywhere over the back of the pitch; feinting, blocking, and whacking the ball back with gusto. Even the most indifferent of pupils, who thought sport was a complete waste of everyone's time, were riveted by the chubby commando of the hockey pitch. As Eve's frustration started to show, Andrea went for her, allowing little Sylvie to slip in at the last moment and pocket one. Goal! In the ensuing kerfuffle, Andrea went headlong in again and scored almost immediately. Goal!

Almost roaring with frustration, Eve ploughed down the field with the ball, heading straight, it seemed, for Simone's glasses. Everyone waited for Simone to move. But she didn't. She held her ground, and as Eve whacked the ball with full force straight at Simone's left side, Simone merely leaned over and planted her stick on the goal line. And WHACK, the ball was off and back in the game; picked up by Ursula, passed to Sylvie, who as usual was dancing unnoticed right up at the front line, and one more was in. GOAL!

The Plantagenet girls were on their feet now, shouting and roaring like little savages. There were two minutes of the game left as Miss James threw the ball back into play. Tussling at the front was absolutely vicious, and ankles were whacked willy-nilly as both sides fought for their lives. But the ball wasn't getting anywhere up or down the field – the girls were all over it, any concept of tactical play gone completely. Finally, desperately, Eve McGinty made a huge swing at it.

The hit connected, and the ball flew through the air, as the girls all stopped to follow its parabola. Once again Simone saw it. And she did not close her eyes this time, but said to herself, 'DO YOUR JOB.'

Whereupon, with tremendous skill, she trapped the ball and hit it full flight across the pitch, straight to Andrea, who putted it gently into the back of the net just as the whistle blew.

The noise levels were absolutely extraordinary. Miss James was grinning like a Cheshire cat; nobody could say sport was unimportant now! Maggie, to her surprise, found herself not thinking about David for the moment, but standing up in her seat, unapologetically cheering the Plantagenet girls' victory. The team were now surrounded by the rest of their classmates, jumping up and down and screeching with excitement, a mass of colour in the blazing sunshine. Miss Starling was shaking her head at the noise. Maggie rushed down to congratulate them – she couldn't help it – and was touched and heartened by the warm welcome the girls gave her.

'All right,' said Stan, when she returned to her seat in the stands – the middle school second year were about to start on their javelin throwing.

'All right what?' said Maggie, still pink with happiness.

'All right. You were right,' said Stan.

'What?'

'You were right. It is good for you here. You do belong.'

This was so unexpected, Maggie just stared at him.

'Lots of people have long distance relationships for a bit – ours has been going all right, hasn't it?'

Maggie felt a surge of guilt that she squashed down as far as she could.

'Yes.'

'OK. I'll stop bugging you. You stay here and . . . well, we'll see in a year or two, yeah?'

Maggie would have liked to hug him, but it was rarely advisable when surrounded by pupils. Instead she squeezed his leg, hard. Inside she was a mass of contradictions – but women were like that, weren't they? she told herself. Weren't they?

'Thank you,' she said. 'Thank you.'

'So, anyway,' said Fliss's mum, as they drove back up the motorway. They were heading straight for Gatwick for a couple of weeks in France, even though Fliss would rather have gone back to Surrey to catch up with her old friends. Oh well, it wouldn't be for long.

'And then we never thought Simone was going to be one of us, but then it turned out she's OK really, then she helped me out a lot with my English, so I think my marks are going to be really good now, I mean, the exam was totally easy and everything, but she's all right that teacher, and I'm going to definitely try out for the team next year, my ankle's completely fine, and next year you get to travel and play other schools, and . . .'

'So,' said her mother when she could get a word in edgeways. 'We did say we were going to look again at whether you wanted to stay on at Downey House.'

'Oh,' said Fliss. She'd forgotten about that. Then she saw her dad at the wheel, smiling.

'I suppose it's OK,' she said.

'I knew it!' crowed Hattie triumphantly. 'I knew she'd think it was the best school in the world.'

'Shut up, swotto,' said Fliss.

'Shut up yourself.'

'No, *you* shut up.'

Veronica took a final turn around the empty classrooms before leaving the buildings in the capable hands of Harold Carruthers for the next few weeks. It was amazing how still the place felt; all the eternal noise and bustle and colour of four hundred girls, bursting with life, vanished overnight.

Dust was already settling on the desks and the radiators and work peeling from the walls, and the school had a characteristic, slightly deadening smell of old ink and gym shoes, as if it knew its rightful inhabitants were missing.

She wondered, as usual these days, about Daniel. She'd written to him once or twice, hoping to hear from him, but she hadn't. She'd poured her heart out into those letters; telling him exactly what he'd always meant to her and what she hoped he could mean in the future. She could only hope it was enough. Losing a child once had been bad enough . . . losing him again would be such a heavy burden to bear.

She went through classroom after classroom, running her hands across the desks, checking that there were no left-behind apple cores or milk bottles or anything that could cause them problems at the start of the new year. It had been an eventful time. With some good new people, and sad losses. But sometimes she felt she loved the school most of all when it was empty, with only its faint scent and her own quiet footsteps to remind you that its halls were once full of laughter and chatter and young minds being formed. And if she half-closed her eyes, she could almost hear an echo of singing, from far away and down the hall . . .

We are the girls
The Girls of Downey Hall
We stand up proud
And we hold our heads up tall
We serve the Queen
Our country God and home
We dare to dream
Of wider plains to roam
We are the girls
The Girls of Downey Hall.

Maggie's Poems

The Choosing

We were first equal Mary and I
with the same coloured ribbons in mouse-coloured hair,
and with equal shyness
we curtseyed to the lady councillor
for copies of Collins' *Children's Classics*.
First equal, equally proud.

Best friends too Mary and I
a common bond in being cleverest (equal)
in our small school's small class.
I remember
the competition for top desk
or to read aloud the lesson
at school service.
And my terrible fear of her superiority at sums.
I remember the housing scheme
Where we both stayed.
The same house, different homes,
where the choices were made.
I don't know exactly why they moved
but anyway they went.
Something about a three-apartment
and a cheaper rent.

But from the top deck of the high school bus
I'd glimpse among the others on the corner
Mary's father, mufflered, contrasting strangely
with the elegant greyhounds by his side.
He didn't believe in high school education,
especially for girls,
or in forking out for uniforms.

Ten years later on a Saturday –
I am coming home from the library –
sitting near me on the bus,
Mary with a husband who is tall,
curly haired, has eyes for no one else but Mary.
Her arms are round the full-shaped vase that is her body.
Oh, you can see where the attraction lies
in Mary's life – not that I envy her, really.

And I am coming from the library
with my arms full of books.
I think of the prizes that were ours for the taking
and wonder when the choices got made
we don't remember making.

Liz Lochhead, 1970

Daffodils

I wandered lonely as a cloud
That floats on high o'er vales and hills
When all at once I saw a crowd,
A host, of golden daffodils;
Beside the lake, beneath the trees,
Fluttering and dancing in the breeze.

Continuous as the stars that shine
And twinkle on the Milky Way,
They stretched in never-ending line
Along the margin of the bay:
Ten thousand saw I at a glance,
Tossing their heads in sprightly dance.

The waves beside them danced; but they
Out-did the sparkling waves in glee:
A poet could not but be gay,
In such a jocund company:
I gazed – and gazed – but little thought
What wealth the show to me had brought:

For oft, when on my couch I lie
In vacant or in pensive mood,
They flash upon that inward eye
Which is the bliss of solitude;
And then my heart with pleasure fills
And dances with the daffodils.

William Wordsworth, 1804

The Silver Tassie

Go fetch to me a pint o' wine,
An' fill it in a silver tassie,
That I may drink, before I go,
A service to my bonnie lassie.
The boat rocks at the pier o' Leith,
Fu' loud the wind blaws frae the ferry,
The ship rides by the Berwick-law,
And I maun leave my bonnie Mary.

The trumpets sound, the banners fly,
The glittering spears are rankèd ready;
The shouts o' war are heard afar,
The battle closes deep and bloody;
But it's no the roar o' sea or shore
Wad mak me langer wish to tarry;
Nor shout o' war that's heard afar:
It's leaving thee, my bonnie Mary!

Robert Burns, 1788

The Journey of the Magi

'A cold coming we had of it,
Just the worst time of the year
For a journey, and such a long journey:
The ways deep and the weather sharp,
The very dead of winter.'
And the camels galled, sore-footed, refractory,
Lying down in the melting snow.
There were times we regretted
The summer palaces on slopes, the terraces,
And the silken girls bringing sherbet.
Then the camel men cursing and grumbling
And running away, and wanting their liquor and women,
And the night-fires going out, and the lack of shelters,
And the cities hostile and the towns unfriendly
And the villages dirty and charging high prices:
A hard time we had of it.
At the end we preferred to travel all night,
Sleeping in snatches,
With the voices singing in our ears, saying
That this was all folly.

Then at dawn we came down to a temperate valley,
Wet, below the snow line, smelling of vegetation;
With a running stream and a water-mill beating the
    darkness,
And three trees on the low sky,
And an old white horse galloped away in the meadow.
Then we came to a tavern with vine-leaves over the lintel,
Six hands at an open door dicing for pieces of silver,
And feet kicking the empty wine-skins,
But there was no information, and so we continued

And arrived at evening, not a moment too soon
Finding the place; it was (you may say) satisfactory.

All this was a long time ago, I remember,
And I would do it again, but set down
This set down
This: were we led all that way for
Birth or Death? There was a Birth, certainly,
We had evidence and no doubt. I had seen birth and death,
But had thought they were different; this Birth was
Hard and bitter agony for us, like Death, our death.
We returned to our places, these Kingdoms,
But no longer at ease here, in the old dispensation,
With an alien people clutching their gods.
I should be glad of another death.

T. S. Eliot, 1927

Christmas

The bells of waiting Advent ring,
    The Tortoise stove is lit again
And lamp-oil light across the night
    Has caught the streaks of winter rain.
In many a stained-glass window sheen
From Crimson Lake to Hooker's Green.

The holly in the windy hedge
    And round the Manor House the yew
Will soon be stripped to deck the ledge,
    The altar, font and arch and pew,
So that villagers can say
'The Church looks nice' on Christmas Day.

Provincial public houses blaze
    And Corporation tramcars clang,
On lighted tenements I gaze
    Where paper decorations hang,
And bunting in the red Town Hall
Says 'Merry Christmas to you all.'

And London shops on Christmas Eve
    Are strung with silver bells and flowers
As hurrying clerks the City leave
    To pigeon-haunted classic towers,
And marbled clouds go scudding by
The many-steepled London sky.

And girls in slacks remember Dad,
    And oafish louts remember Mum,
And sleepless children's hearts are glad,

And Christmas morning bells say 'Come!'
Even to shining ones who dwell
Safe in the Dorchester Hotel.

And is it true? and is it true?
　　The most tremendous tale of all,
Seen in a stained-glass window's hue,
　　A Baby in an ox's stall?
The Maker of the stars and sea
Become a Child on earth for me?

And is it true? For if it is,
　　No loving fingers tying strings
Around those tissued fripperies,
　　The sweet and silly Christmas things,
Bath salts and inexpensive scent
And hideous tie so kindly meant.

No love that in a family dwells,
　　No carolling in frosty air,
Nor all the steeple-shaking bells
　　Can with this single Truth compare –
That God was Man in Palestine
And lives to-day in Bread and Wine.

John Betjeman, 1951

The Crystal Set

Just as the stars appear, Father
carries from his garden shed
a crystal set, built
as per instructions
in the *Amateur Mechanic*
Mother dries her hands. Their boy
and ginger cat lie beside the fire
He's reading – what – *Treasure Island*
but jumps to clear the dresser. Hush
They tell each other. *Hush!*

The silly baby bangs her spoon
as they lean in to radio-waves
which lap, the boy imagines,
just like Scarborough. Indeed,
it is the sea they hear as though
the brown box were a shell. Dad
sorts through fizz, until, like diamonds
lost in dust: 'listen, ships' Morse!'
and the boy grips his chair. As though
he'd risen sudden as an angel to gaze down, he
     understands
that not his house, not
Scarborough Beach, but the whole
island of Britain
is washed by dark waves. *Hush*
they tell each other. Hush.

There is nothing to tune to
but Greenwich pips
and the anxious signalling

of ships that nudge our shores.
Dumb silent waves. But that
was then. Now, gentle listener,
it's time to take our leave
of Mum and Dad's proud glow, the boy's
uncertain smile. Besides,
the baby's asleep.
So let's tune out here
and slip along the dial. *Hush.*

Kathleen Jamie, 1995

Stopping by Woods on a Snowy Evening

Whose woods these are I think I know.
His house is in the village, though;
He will not see me stopping here
To watch his woods fill up with snow.

My little horse must think it queer
To stop without a farmhouse near
Between the woods and frozen lake
The darkest evening of the year.

He gives his harness bells a shake
To ask if there is some mistake.
The only other sounds the sweep
Of easy wind and downy flake.

The woods are lovely, dark, and deep,
But I have promises to keep,
And miles to go before I sleep,
And miles to go before I sleep.

Robert Frost, 1922

I went to a very ordinary school that wasn't very nice at all. There was a lot of shouting and horrible remarks and fighting and belting going on (and that was just the teachers).

So that probably explains why I have always loved boarding school books so much. Malory Towers, St Clare's, Frost in May, the Chalet School books, What Katy Did at School, Jane Eyre . . . even Harry Potter when he came along. It seemed so exotic, so much fun.

Of course, when I met girls later in life who really had been to boarding school, they said it wasn't at all like that really, but I remain convinced that they were just trying to spare my feelings.

As an adult I found I still wanted to read these books — with, perhaps, some more adult themes, and maybe even — gasp! — some private lives for the teachers — but I couldn't find what I was looking for anywhere. So I have had to write them myself, and this is what you hold in your hand.

Jane Beaton

RULES

Second Year at Downey House

For my father. A great teacher,
and an even better dad.

Acknowledgements

Thanks to the board; W. Hickham; every teacher (and pupil!) who took the time to write to me and tell me a little bit about their life; Ben Ward, for finding David's poem; and my beloved Beatons, large and small.

Characters

Staff

Headteacher: Dr Veronica Deveral
Administrator: Miss Evelyn Prenderghast
Deputy Headteacher: Miss June Starling
Head of Finance: Mr Archie Liston
Matron: Miss Doreen Redmond

Cook: Mrs Joan Rhys
Caretaker: Mr Harold Carruthers

Physics: Mr John Bart
Music: Mrs Theodora Offili
French: Mademoiselle Claire Crozier
English: Miss Margaret Adair
Maths: Miss Ella Beresford
PE: Miss Janie James
Drama: Miss Fleur Parsley
History: Miss Catherine Kellen
Geography: Miss Deirdre Gifford

Pupils

Middle School Year Two

Sylvie Brown
Imogen Fairlie
Simone Kardashian
Andrea McCann
Felicity Prosser
Zazie Saurisse
Alice Trebizon-Woods
Zelda Townell
Astrid Ulverton

Chapter One

Maggie was dancing on a table. This was distinctly out of character, but they *had* served her cocktails earlier, in a glass so large she was surprised it didn't have a fish in it.

Plus it was a beautifully soft, warm evening, and her fiancé Stan had insisted on watching the football on a large Sky Sports screen, annoyingly situated over her head in the Spanish bar, so there wasn't much else to do – and all the other girls were dancing on table tops.

I'm still young, Maggie had thought to herself, pushing her unruly dark hair out of her eyes. *I'm only twenty-six years old! I can still dance all night!*

And with the help of a friendly hen party from Stockport on the next table, she'd found herself up there, shrugging off any self-consciousness with the help of a large margarita and grooving away to Alphabeat.

'Hey, I can't see the game,' Stan complained.

'I don't care,' said Maggie, suddenly feeling rather freer, happy and determined to enjoy her holiday. She raised her arms above her head. This was definitely a good way to forget about school; to forget about David McDonald, the English teacher she'd developed a crush on last year – until

1

she'd found out he was engaged. To just feel like herself again, instead of a teacher.

'Isn't that Miss Adair?' said Hattie.

They'd been allowed down into the town for the evening from the discreet and beautifully appointed villa they'd been staying in high on the other side of the mountain. Her younger sister Fliss turned round from where she'd been eyeing up fake designer handbags, and glanced at the tacky-looking sports pub Hattie was pointing out. Inside was a group of drunk-looking women waving their hands in the air.

'No way!' exclaimed Fliss, heading towards the door for a closer look. 'I'm going in to check.'

'You're not allowed in any bars!' said Hattie. 'I promised Mum and Dad.'

'*I promised Mum and Dad*,' mimicked Fliss. 'I am fourteen, you know. That's pretty much the legal drinking age over here.'

'Well, whilst you're with me you'll obey family rules.'

Fliss stuck out her tongue and headed straight for the bar. 'You're not a prefect now.'

'No, but we're in a position of trust, and . . .'

Fliss stopped short in the doorway.

'Hello, senorita,' said the doorman. Fliss had grown two inches over the summer, although to her huge annoyance she was still barely filling an A cup.

Maggie and the girls from Stockport were shimmying up and down to the Pussycat Dolls when she saw Fliss. At first she thought it was a trick of the flashing lights. It couldn't be. After all, they'd come all this way to leave her work behind. So she could feel like a girl, not a teacher. So surely it couldn't be one of her—

2

'MISS ADAIR!' shrieked Fliss. 'Is that you, miss?'

Maggie stopped dancing.

'Felicity Prosser,' she said, feeling a resigned tone creep into her voice. She looked around, wondering what would be the most dignified way to get down from the table, under the circumstances.

Normally, Veronica Deveral found the Swiss Alps in summertime a cleansing balm for the soul. The clean, sharp air you could draw all the way down into your lungs; the sparkle of the grass and the glacier lakes; the cyclists and rosy-cheeked all-year skiiers heading for higher ground; the freshly washed sky. She always took the same *pension*, and liked to take several novels – she favoured the lengthy intrigues of Anthony Trollope, and was partial to a little Joanna for light relief – and luxuriate in the time to devour them, returning to Downey House rested, refreshed and ready for the new academic year.

This year, however, had been different. After her shock at meeting the son she gave up for adoption nearly forty years ago, Veronica had handled it badly and they had lost contact. And although there were budgets to be approved, a new intake to set up and staffing to be organised, she couldn't concentrate. All she seemed to do was worry about Daniel, and wonder what he was doing back in Cornwall.

She was staring out the window of her beautiful office, before term was due to start, when Dr Robert Fitzroy, head of Downey Boys over the hill, arrived for their annual chat. The two schools did many things together, and it was useful to have some knowledge of the forthcoming agenda.

'You seem a little distracted, Veronica,' Robert said, comfortably ensconced on the Chesterfield sofa, enjoying the fine view over the school grounds and to the cliffs and the sea beyond, today a perfect summer-holiday blue. They weren't really getting anywhere with debating the new computer lab.

Veronica sighed and briefly considered confiding in her opposite number. He was a kind man, if a little set in his ways. She dismissed this thought immediately. She had spent years building up this school, the last thing she needed was anyone thinking she was a weak woman, prone to tears and over-emotional sentimentality.

Robert droned on about new staff.

'Oh, and yes,' he said, 'we have a new History teacher at last. Good ones are so hard to find these days.'

Veronica was barely listening. She was watching the waves outside and wondering if Daniel had ever taken his children to the seaside for a holiday. So when Robert said his name it chimed with her thoughts, and at first she didn't at all understand what she'd just heard.

'Excuse me?'

'Daniel Stapleton. Our new History teacher.'

'Mom!'

Zelda was throwing ugly things in her bag. Ugly tops, ugly skirts, ugly hats. What the hell? School uniform was the stupidest idea in a country full of stupid ideas.

'Did you know I have to share, like, a bathroom? Did they tell you that?'

Zelda's mother shook her head. As if she didn't have enough to deal with, what with DuBose being so excited about the move and all. Why they all had to go and up sticks and live in England, where she'd heard it rained all the time and everyone lived in itty-bitty houses with bathrooms the size of cupboards . . . well, it didn't bear thinking about. She doubted it would be much like Texas.

4

'Don' worry, darlin',' DuBose had said, in that calm drawl of his. He might get a lot of respect as a major seconded to the British Army, but it didn't cut much ice with her, nuh-huh.

'An' we'll get Zelda out of that crowd she's been running with at high school. Turn her into quite the English lady.'

A boarding school education was free for the daughters of senior military staff on overseas postings, and Downey House, they'd been assured, was among the very best.

As Mary Jo looked at her daughter's perfect manicure – they'd been for a mommy/daughter pamper day – so strange against the stark white of her new uniform blouses, she wondered, yet again, how they would all fit in.

Simone glanced at Fliss's Facebook update – *Felicity is having a BLASTING time in Spain!* – and tried her best to be happy for her. The Kardashians weren't having a holiday this year. It just wasn't practical. Which was fine by Simone, she hated struggling into her tankini and pulling a big sarong around herself, then sitting under an umbrella hiding in case anyone saw her. So, OK, Fliss might be having great fun without her, and Alice was posting about being utterly miserably bored learning to dive with her au pair in Hurghada, and she was jealous and she did miss them – but she was doing her best to be happy for them.

Thank goodness she'd been invited to Fliss's house for the end of the holidays, so they could all travel back together. Simone had tried not to let slip to her friends just how much she was looking forward to it – and even worse, to admit how much she was looking forward to going back to school.

It had been a long seven weeks, with not much to do but read and try to avoid Joel, her brother, who had spent the entire time indoors hunched over his games console.

5

She'd spent the summer dreaming of school and reading books whilst eating fish finger sandwiches. Her mother had tried her best to get her involved in some local social events, but it wasn't really her thing. She winced remembering an unbelievably awkward afternoon tea with Rudi, the ugly, gangly teenage son of one of her mother's best friends. His face was covered in spots and his hair was oily and lank. They were shuffled awkwardly together on to a sofa.

Simone's misery on realising that this was the kind of boy her mum thought she might like was compounded by the very obvious way Rudi looked her up and down and made it clear that he thought he was out of her league. She cringed again at the memory.

'You go to that posh school then,' he'd muttered, when pushed by his mum.

Simone had felt a blush spread over her face, and kept her eyes tightly fixed on her hands.

'Yeah.'

'Oh. Right.'

And that had been that. It was pretty obvious that Rudi, over-stretched as he was, would much rather be upstairs playing Grand Theft Auto with Joel.

Simone sighed. It would have been nice to go back to school with at least some adventures to tell Alice and Fliss. Still, maybe she could share theirs.

'Tell me about her thighs again,' said Alice, leaning lazily on shady manicured grass, watching tiny jewel-coloured lizards scrabble past and running up an enormous bill on the hotel phone.

'Jiggly,' said Fliss, under a cherry tree two thousand miles away in Surrey, tickling her dog Ranald on the tummy. 'Honestly, you could see right up her skirt and everything.'

'I never really think of teachers having legs,' mused Alice. 'I mean, I suppose they must and everything, but . . .'

'But what, you think they run along on wheels?' Fliss giggled.

'No, but . . . oh, it's so hot.'

'FLISS!' The voice came from inside.

'Oh God, is that the heffalump Hattie?' drawled Alice.

'I'm not going to answer,' said Fliss.

'FELICITY!' Hattie huffed into the orchard garden, her tread heavy on the paving stones. '*Felicity*.'

'I'm on the *phone*,' said Fliss crossly.

'Well, I have news.'

'Is she pregnant?' said wicked Alice.

'Ssh,' Fliss told her.

'Fine,' said Hattie, turning to go. 'So I guess you DON'T want to hear who's starting at Downey Boys this year?'

Fliss turned and looked at her.

'What are you talking about?'

'Just that I was down in the village . . . and was talking to Will's mum . . .'

And just like that, Alice was talking to an empty telephone.

'Come on.'

Stan was nuzzling her neck. 'Just one more cuddle.'

'I've got to pack!' Maggie was insisting. It wasn't too long before she had to go back and she wanted to be ready. Her clothes were strewn across the room, along with several books she'd wanted to collect to take back for her girls. Stan had a day off from his printing job.

Also, she felt nervous. Last year had been her probation year at the school. This year she'd be expected to perform.

'Cody and Dylan are quite something, aren't they?' asked Stan, moving away. Her two nephews had been playing with

7

them all day, and seemed to get more rambunctious every time.

'Quite brats, you mean,' said Maggie, who'd had to lift them bodily out of the biscuit tin at ten-minute intervals.

'Oh, they're just boys,' said Stan. 'That's what I used to be like. That's what ours'll be like.'

He tried to drag Maggie back on to the bed, but she resisted.

'Once you're Mrs Cameron, you're going to want little Codys and Dylans all over the place.'

'Yes, maybe,' said Maggie, extricating herself. 'But ours won't be allowed to do that to the neighbour's cat.'

Stan laughed. 'Boys will be boys.'

'I think that's why I only teach girls.'

Maggie softened. 'I do love Cody and Dylan, you know. I just worry – they're so crazy, and I know Anne is working all the time.' Anne, Maggie's older sister, ran a thriving hairdressing practice in Govan and was single-handedly raising her two sons. 'Sometimes I wonder what they're doing at that school.'

'Well, it was good enough for us,' said Stan.

Maggie gave herself up to his kiss, thinking about the rough Holy Cross where she and Stan had met, and where she'd later taught. It wasn't really a good school at all. Now, going back to Downey House for her second year there as an English teacher, she felt as nervous and excited as one of her girls when she thought of its four forbidding towers looming out of the hills over the sea. She fingered her new academic diary carefully.

'I suppose,' she said.

Fliss was nervous about having Alice to stay – she loved their large rambling house, but Alice was used to grand

8

residences, and she hoped it would be smart enough for her. She needn't have worried. Alice's parents being in the diplomatic corps meant they moved every couple of months. Anywhere that had a lived-in feel, with a calendar on the kitchen wall and family pictures scattered on every surface, was heaven to Alice.

Simone, on the other hand, was far more intimidated. Felicity's house was HUGE! The garden alone was about the size of a park. There were loads and loads of rooms. In their terraced house in London there was a front room, a back kitchen and three tiny bedrooms. She and Joel had to share when there were visitors staying, which was all the time.

Fliss's mum and dad were delighted to meet her friends, if a little intrigued by the chubby girl who could barely utter a word at mealtimes. Fliss was embarrassed too. Why did Simone have to act so frumpily all the time? Why couldn't she show people how fun she could be? What, did she think Fliss's parents would look down on her? That was insulting!

The first night there all three had sat up gossiping late into the night. Mr and Mrs Prosser had finally let Fliss start drinking coffee, which to Simone, used from childhood to thick sweet grounds you could stand a spoon up in, was no big deal, but it made the girls feel grown up.

Biggest topic of the night was, of course, Will Hampton. Fliss had had a crush on him for a year, ever since he'd started playing in a local band. In fact last year she'd nearly managed to get herself thrown out of school for trying to see him. And now he was going to be at the boys' school just over the hill from Downey House! Fliss could hardly contain her excitement.

'Well, we'd better see this chap,' said Alice. 'See if he passes muster.'

'He still sings in the church choir,' said Fliss.

'Well, that will do,' said Alice.

It was some surprise to Felicity's parents when the girls announced on Saturday morning that they'd like to go to church on Sunday.

Mrs Prosser raised a heavily botoxed eyebrow.

'*Church?*' she said, in the same tone as she might have said '*The casino?*' Hattie was on the youth guidance committee for their local parish, but she'd had to drag Felicity there under the threat of dire torture since she was nine years old.

'Why on earth do you suddenly want to go to church?'

Felicity pouted. 'To give thanks and all that.'

'Yes, I'd like to go too, Mrs Prosser, if that's OK,' said Alice, with her usual adult assurance.

'And me,' squeaked Simone, promising Jesus in her heart that she didn't really mean it by going to a protestant church.

Hattie harrumphed loudly, but Felicity tried to ignore her. Undaunted, Hattie harrumphed again.

'Are you trying to say something, Harriet?' asked her mother, unable to keep the sharp edge out of her tongue. She loved her eldest daughter to distraction, but she could be terribly pi.

'I wonder,' said Harriet. 'I do WONDER if the male voice choir is singing harvest festival this Sunday.'

Fliss instantly coloured, and Alice spotted it.

'Are they?' she said. 'Actually, it was my idea to go. I do like to give thanks.'

Fliss's parents glanced at each other.

'We'll all go.'

In the event, not even Hattie's hateful sniggering could spoil Fliss's view, and she stood rapt in the third pew, watching Will's dark head as he bowed to his hymnal. His band had broken up over the summer, but he still loved to sing. *Notice me*, Fliss begged in her heart. What was wrong with her? Was she too short? Too fat? In fact, Fliss was blonde and pretty, with delicate features that could often be overlooked for the more striking dark looks of her friend Alice, but at fourteen she couldn't see beyond a touch of puppy fat and the occasional pimple. With all her heart she wished she was as confident as pert, cheeky Alice, with her dark shining hair and neat figure. Even Simone had big breasts. What did she have? Nothing! Oh, how she longed to look like a model.

Afterwards they filed out, Simone bobbing and crossing herself when she thought nobody was looking. Normally Fliss couldn't bear her mother hanging around to talk to the vicar and anyone else she came across, but today she lingered anxiously, wondering if she could find the courage to ask Will about his move.

Suddenly her heart stopped as she caught his floppy brown hair – and he was growing so fast, he must be nearly six foot already and he was barely sixteen – as he came out of the beautiful old church, so in demand for weddings from people who'd never even lived in the village.

As if in a dream, she watched as he slowly walked towards her. She bit her lip nervously. He couldn't be, could he? He couldn't be coming to talk to her? She felt like she was sinking underwater. Could she speak to him? Could she?

He stopped in front of her, and Fliss found she'd lost her breath.

'Uh . . . hi . . .' she stuttered. She felt like the whole congregation was watching them.

'Hi,' said Will. He had an easy, smiling manner about him, which made you feel like you were the only person he'd been waiting to speak to all day. Of course, he was like that with everyone.

'Have a good summer?'

11

'Uh yeah.'

Fliss's heart was pounding. Why couldn't she say anything interesting? Make a joke, say anything?

'Cool,' said Will. He looked around, to where Alice and Simone were trying to hover not-too-closely. Wow. Fliss's friend was really really hot.

'Hey, those your friends?'

Fliss couldn't do anything but nod dumbly. Will walked towards Alice.

'Hi,' he said, putting out his hand. 'I'm Will. Do you go to Downeys? You may need to fill me in on all its evil ways.'

Alice gave him a curt look, hiding her massive curiosity. She could certainly see what Fliss saw in him. Out of the corner of her eye she caught sight of her friend.

'Oh, I'm sure Fliss can help you out with all that,' she said.

Will nodded his head.

'I'm sure,' he said.

'Oh come *on*, Fliss.'

They were four hours into the drive, and Alice had yet to persuade her friend she hadn't been flirting with Will on purpose. Hattie was smugly sitting up the front, reading a book about lacrosse. Simone was in the middle – she'd volunteered – trying to stave off the tension. And Fliss was staring out of the window, thinking about Will and also the last thing her mother had said before she'd left that morning: 'Now, Felicity, you *will* be careful with all that stodge they serve at school, won't you?' She'd leant down out of earshot of everyone else. 'You don't want to end up like Hattie, do you?' 'What's that?' Hattie had said crossly, bounding down the stairs like an inelegant carthorse, her boater, schoolbag, hockey shoes and tennis raquet unraveling in her wake. 'Nothing, my gorgeous girls. Have a wonderful term!'

12

Maybe she would avoid the stodge, mused Felicity. Maybe that would help.

Alice sat back with a sigh, just as the sleek Audi crested the hill and, for the first time, the girls caught sight of the turreted, castle-like building that would be home for the next nine months.

'School! School!' shouted both Hattie and Simone. Simone's spirits lifted fully. Even Alice smiled. It did look like something out of a story book, the four towers of the main houses – Tudor, York, Wessex and their own, Plantagenet – nestled in the hills, with the cliffs behind, leading down to the still turquoise sea.

Chapter Two

'*Mon dieu*,' was the first thing Maggie heard as she stepped down from the railway carriage – this year, Stan had won the battle for the car.

Just ahead, her friend Mademoiselle Crozier, the impetuous French mistress, was wrestling with an elegant suitcase which had discharged its contents on to the platform.

'Claire!' she yelled excitedly, but didn't reach her before the guard and three passing men had all stopped to help. Maggie reflected that she could probably lose a leg under the train wheels before she could attract the attention of three passing men, but put the thought to the back of her mind.

'Hello,' she called. '*Bonjour!*'

'Maggie!' Claire ran up to her and gave her a big kiss. 'Eet eez *disaster*!'

Actually, her case was now being tidily zipped up by the hefty guard.

'Here you are, love,' he was saying. 'Can I help you down to your car now?'

The man was so overweight it didn't look like he'd make it much past the platform, but Claire just gave him her widest smile.

'Thank you zo much! That eez perfect, thank you!'

The man blushed to the roots of his moustache.

'How do you do that?' said Maggie, as they set off down the platform in search of a taxi.

'Do what?'

'Be so French.'

'I know,' said Claire seriously. 'Truly, I am from Liverpool. I did spend a long time working on ze accent.'

'POPS! No!'

'It's all I could get, Zelda. Calm down,' said Zelda's dad.

Zelda stared at the hummer in dismay.

'Dad, did you know those things are, like, totally destroying the earth?'

'No, hun, that's my nuclear bombs. Come on, get in.'

Zelda pouted and went back to applying lip gloss, then she heaved herself up into the giant armoured car.

'AND we have to stop for gas, like, every ten minutes.'

Zelda's mother glanced at her.

'Are you sure you should be wearing so much make up? There's none allowed during semesters.'

Zelda gave her mother a long look.

'Mom. This is the sixteenth school you've sent me to. I think I know what I need on the first day, OK? Dad's got his armour . . . I've got mine.'

Veronica could almost feel the approaching coaches and trains and cars, as she went through the school for the last time. Everything gleamed: the cleaning staff had done a fine job. The polished wooden desks reflected the soft September harvest light through the high, newly cleaned windows set into the strong stone walls of the four towers.

The refectory, with its long tables soon to be filled up with laughing girls and clattering noise, seemed oddly still. The only sound was the tap of her own heels in the long corridor outside, lined with pictures of headmistresses past, as she moved towards her own office. It was filled with her personal treasures – she had never wanted the headmistress's office to be just a place of fear or punishment, but neither did she want the girls thinking of her as a friend. She wanted to strike a balance between formality and balm. The girls should know the right thing must be done – but that second chances were always possible.

Her excellent and efficient proctor Miss Prenderghast stuck her head round the door, brandishing a large pile of post.

'Sorry to bother you already,' she said.

Veronica smiled and asked after Evelyn's new bassett hound.

'And don't forget,' said Miss Prenderghast eventually, 'the teachers' meet is at Downey Boys this year. Tomorrow night.'

Veronica winced. She was dreading this. An annual cocktail party to catch up with the teachers, plan the year ahead and make the aquaintance of any new members of staff at their counterpart school. Which, this year, would include . . .

'Yes yes,' she said, somewhat impatiently, fiddling with her plain gold necklace. Veronica, in general, was not a fiddler. 'What else?'

Miss Prenderghast felt awkward in light of Veronica's evidently unsettled mood.

'And there's the School Trade Fair in March, but that's a while off yet.'

Veronica put her hand over her eyes. 'Ah yes. The schools fair.'

This was a trade fair for public schools – essentially, a selling job. Veronica couldn't bear it. She would much rather

her school and its results spoke for themselves, and anyone who wished could come and have a look around the facilities. She disliked standing on a cheap stall trying to lure in people with money.

On the other hand, there was no doubt about it. Downey's emphasis on all-round education in its most traditional sense – the rounding of an individual – was showing in its results, against schools whose exam sausage-machines did nothing but cram information as tightly as possible into stressed, overburdened children with nothing on their minds except getting a sports car for five starred A-grade passes. It looked, in the rankings, like they were slipping.

Veronica despised this push for results as reflections on parents often too busy to broaden their children's horizons themselves. She felt it too often led to drop-outs and break-downs at universities that encouraged self-directed learning, misery and bad behaviour in adolescents. However school tables were school tables, and she couldn't deny that they made a difference to what, in the end, however traditional, garlanded or revered, was still a business.

'Thank you, Evelyn,' she said. 'Another busy year.'

Miss Prenderghast smiled.

'We wouldn't have it any other way, Dr Deveral.'

The queue for taxis at the station was a mile long.

'Don't zey know we are teachers?' said Claire crossly, looking around for her friendly guard.

'I know, and I really want to check out the parents before they leave,' said Maggie worriedly. She wanted to meet the parents of the girls in her guidance class, now going into Middle School Two, just in case any issues she needed to be aware of had arisen over the long vac.

'Brr,' said Claire. 'I *never* want to see the parents. All they

17

want to tell me is of their villa in the Dordogne and how their child ees French genius and can I spend all my time with thees French genius. An you know,' she added sagely, 'she is not genius.'

As she talked, a silver Audi drew up and honked loudly. Maggie raised her head warily – normally cars honking at her belonged to teenage boys, out too late from her old school in Glasgow. Instead, a nicely coiffed blonde head stuck out of the car window.

'Maggie? Is that you?'

It took Maggie a second to recognise her. When she did, her heart skipped a beat. It was Miranda.

Miranda had been David's fiancée, although to Maggie they'd never seemed very well suited – although she knew her own feelings for the English teacher might have coloured this view. They had broken up in the summertime. Maggie had wondered if it might have had something to do with her, but it couldn't have done, surely. She hoped Miranda didn't think so. She couldn't help remembering David's face, at the end of last year, when he'd asked her to go on holiday with him. She'd done the right thing staying with Stan, though, of course she had. She hoped Miranda was OK.

'Uh, hi there!' she said, leaning down to the window. 'How are you?'

'Fine, fine,' said Miranda.

Oh well, she couldn't suspect anything then.

'On your way to school?' asked Miranda. 'Want a lift?'

Maggie shrugged. It would be useful. 'Can you take my friend Claire, too?'

'Sure!'

Miranda signalled and pulled over, and the women put their suitcases into the immaculately tidy boot. Maggie sat in front, still feeling nervous, even though technically she and David had never done anything wrong.

'Thanks for that, the queue is terrible.'

Miranda carefully pulled away. 'Yes, well, I'm going that way . . .'

She let her voice trail away as she looked out of the window. Maggie stole a glance at her. The antique ring on her fourth finger had gone.

They spoke in pleasantries until they had left the bustle of Truro behind and were heading out towards the country-side. Maggie, once again, after the tower blocks and heavy sandstone of Glasgow, appreciated its gentle beauty. Claire appeared to have gone to sleep.

'Maggie,' said Miranda finally, in a different tone.

Maggie felt her stomach lurch. Maybe Miranda *did* sus-pect something after all! Maggie told herself again she had nothing to feel guilty for, neither of them did . . . but as the nuns used to tell her at Holy Cross, there was sin in thought as well as deed.

'Uh, yes?'

'Have you . . . have you heard from David at all?' Miranda bit her lip. She looked pale; Maggie doubted she was used to asking for help.

Maggie shook her head. 'No, not at all. Didn't he go to Italy?'

'Yes, that's right, he said . . .'

Miranda signalled off on to the narrow country road and gave a half-hiccupy laugh.

'He is just so *damn* infuriating, you know?'

Maggie grimaced sympathetically.

'You know, he suggested maybe taking a break for a bit – we've been engaged for like a million years, we're obviously never going to bloody get round to it . . . And then, well, it just all came pouring out. I mean, it's OK for you, you guys are all teachers, so obviously it doesn't matter so much. But, you know, I'd just like a nice home, and someone with a bit of go-getting, you know? Some ideas and a bit of the get-ahead spirit. I mean, I work bloody hard, and I come home and there he is, nose buried in a book or messing about with that damn dog. I mean, is a bit of consideration too much to ask?' Her hands were gripping the steering wheel as her voice went higher.

'I don't *want* to work seventy hours a week when I have a baby, or live in some shitty rented flat all my life! I don't *want* to put everything I do to waste, just so he can get on with his precious boys! You can't believe the looks I get at the business group when I tell them he's a teacher. It's like that stupid old joke, you know? "Failed at everything? Try teaching."'

Miranda got a hold of herself and gave a short laugh. 'Sorry. I've just given you the same rant I gave him. And I know you're teachers too – sorry. I don't think you've failed at all, of course not.'

Maggie wasn't too sure about that.

But she could understand, a little, she supposed, Miranda's frustration. No doubt all her friends had blow-dried hair and nice manicures and husbands who worked in big cities for big pay cheques. She could see the attractions of an easy life. Though why it would make you throw over someone like David she could not comprehend.

'So . . . what's on your mind?' she asked tentatively.

'Well, he's annoying and distracted and always obsessing over something stupid and he never bloody stops talking. But . . . I don't know. I miss him. I'm not getting any younger. And the physical side is, well, it's kind of amazing. I just wish I knew what to do.'

Maggie very much did not want to hear about the physical side of things. Lifting her gaze, she felt her heart expand as, for the first time in two months, the four turrets of Downey House came into view. The car crunched expensive gravel under its smooth tyres.

'Oh, here you are,' said Miranda, looking up at the imposing building. She paused for a long time, then turned to Maggie.

'I'm not sure this is straight in my head.'

Maggie tried to look encouraging. 'Do you know what you want?'

'Don't be daft, I'm a woman in her thirties. Of course I don't.' Miranda attempted a watery smile, and Maggie felt her slightly forced friendliness melt into something more like empathy.

'I'm sorry,' she said, and meant it. She might think Miranda was crazy to pass up that man, but she knew what it was like to feel ambivalent about someone. She certainly did. And, odd though it may seem, perhaps she and Miranda could even be friends? After all, once upon a time they'd both liked the same man, so it wasn't as if they didn't have anything in common . . .

'Maybe I won't pop by the boys' school, after all,' said Miranda, placing her hands on the steering wheel. 'I obviously still have, uh, issues . . . Anyway.' She clasped her hands in her lap. 'I know you two are friends. When you see him, could you ask him to drop me a line? Please?'

'Of course,' said Maggie.

'And maybe we could go for a drink sometime? Girls' night out?'

Claire awoke with a start. 'Yes, please! So I do not keel myself!'

*

21

Zelda had a well-practised routine for starting new schools. First of all, find out if there were any more army brats just like her around. They normally understood each other. Failing that, hang back. Going in and trying to make friends was a sure-fire recipe for disaster, whereas if you were aloof and indifferent, they lapped it up. Not that it mattered, she'd be in Germany or Cyprus by next year, so, like, who gave a crap?

Now she threw herself on the spare bed in her assigned dorm, realising with some satisfaction that the other two girls were staring at her, wide-eyed. The dorm was two stories up – first years took the first floor – but otherwise conformed to a basic pattern: four beds, with their own side tables, and a corner sink.

Alice was still at her medical. Zelda patted her hair, which she'd back-sprayed until it was big – properly big. She didn't care if they were going to keep her in plaits for the rest of the year; today, she was having American hair.

'What kind of a shit hole is this anyway?'

The boyish blonde one spoke up immediately. 'I know. I protested about it last year. I nearly got kicked out actually.'

'Nearly, huh?'

'But I like it now . . . I mean, it's all right. It's a bit sucky.'

'So, what is it,' Zelda attempted a strangulated English accent, 'ginger beer and midnight feasts?'

'Are you American?' asked Simone eagerly. She'd never met an American before.

'Huh, well, guess my English accent isn't quite as good as I thought.'

Zelda threw her huge Louis Vuitton case on the bed. Fliss looked at it in horror; she thought it was vulgar. Simone thought it was amazing.

'It's not really midnight feasts, they're for kids,' said Fliss, trying to sound cool and unbothered though not particularly succeeding. Zelda was wearing a velvet miniskirt with long socks pulled up over her knees and a crisp white shirt with an Argyle-print, very tight tank top. Her bright yellow hair was backcombed over the crown of her head and she was wearing bright blue eyeshadow and a lot of pink lip gloss. She looked simultaneously a lot older and younger than her years, and very different from anyone the girls had ever met.

'Shame,' said Zelda. 'That's the only bit I was looking forward to.'

'My mum has sent me a big box,' chipped in Simone. Fliss wished she would get the puppy dog look out of her eyes. Come on, this girl wasn't *that* cool. 'We could have a midnight feast if you wanted.'

'Cool,' said Zelda. 'What else do people do for fun?' She took a long look out of the window and heaved a weary sigh. 'Push cows over?'

Maggie looked around her small suite of rooms, high in the west tower overlooking the sea, and gave a small sigh of contentment. It was odd, considering home was the ex-council house they'd bought in Pollock and made nice with a big telly and Ikea bits and bobs, despite far too many wires from Stan's Playstation, ideas for a surround-sound system which hadn't quite come off, and the trainers lining the hall. Here, the bare minimalism of the pale blue plaster walls, the small sofa with a delicate eau-de-nil print and the huge, gabled windows stretching out across the Irish sea felt calm and restful. And Claire, of course, was just through the other side of the study they shared. She unpacked carefully, not just tossing things around like she probably would at home, and remembered last year, when she had been so nervous.

This year was going to be different, she decided. She

wasn't going to feel out of her depth, or intimidated by the traditional surroundings of the boarding school. She was going to be calm, collected, never lose her rag—

There was a rap at the door.

'Miss Adair? Are you back? First assembly is just about to start, and I'd hate for one of my department to make a late showing.'

It was Miss Starling, Dr Deveral's second-in-command and Maggie's head of house, who always seemed to be telling Maggie off before she'd actually done anything.

'Yes, Miss Starling!' said Maggie, smoothing down her dark curls as best she could and heading for the door. Calm, elegant, inspirational . . .

Miss Starling was standing outside in the corridor, back straight as a poker, her fawn-tweed suit immaculate.

'Just got off the train, did you?' she asked Maggie. 'Shame you didn't have time to smarten up. Well, come on then, hurry up.'

'Yes, Miss Starling,' said Maggie, castigating herself as she usually did for speaking to her boss as if she were still a pupil. 'Uh, did you have a good summer?'

Miss Starling looked as if the question didn't make any sense.

'It was passable, I suppose. I've prepared a new review syllabus for your Middle School seconds I want you to take a look at.'

Maggie groaned inwardly. Miss Starling believed contemporary teaching to be namby-pamby in the extreme and believed that the girls should be spending their time memorising long screeds of Milton. Maggie didn't have anything against Milton per se, she just wanted to include and engage as many children as widely as possible; to build readers. And Milton wasn't always the way to do that.

'Yes, Miss Starling,' she found herself saying again, like a Victorian servant, as she trotted off at the deputy's fast pace down the corridor to the spiral stairs.

'She's going to be late!' Simone was fretting.

Fliss tutted. 'Matron will be checking her for tropical parasites again.'

Matron was stern and didn't suffer malingerers gladly, but to the truly sick she was a source of much balm.

Simone and Fliss – and Zelda, who had nothing better to do – were waiting for Alice, who was going to miss assembly if she didn't hop to it.

'She said she'd be here,' said Fliss, aware she was sounding childish. 'I wanted to show her my new Urban Outfitters dress.'

Zelda's ears pricked up. It looked like Alice was queen bee, which might be a bit more interesting than the fatso and the nervy blonde, who could be pretty if she wasn't dressed like a ten-year-old and tried a bit of make up on her pale, thin face.

'Where's she from?' enquired Zelda, world expert.

'Cairo at the mo,' said Fliss.

'Oh,' said Zelda. 'What's that like?'

Simone shrugged her shoulders. 'The country is, like, a total touchstone in bringing together East and West. It's geopolitically too imperative to be stable—'

'Hot,' said Fliss.

Simone swallowed hard. This may not be her old school, but still, her grip on popularity wasn't so strong she could go swotting it about all over the place.

When Simone, the lone scholarship girl from a poor background, had arrived the previous year, she'd hoped to find the pupils more sympathetic than at her old school, where she'd been relentlessly bullied for her studiousness and her weight. Instead, she'd found it just as cruel, with Alice, in particular, taunting her eating habits. Finally, falsely accused of stealing, she'd run away. Miss Adair and Mr McDonald – and his dog, Stephen Daedalus – had found her. Things had started to get a lot better after that and the girls were beginning to accept her, but she still felt insecure.

Just at that moment, a black-haired girl with dancing dark eyes and a mature air burst into the room.

'Bloody health certificate. I'm sure Matron wants to suck my blood.'

Fliss and Simone jumped up to go. Alice took a step back and regarded the newcomer coolly.

'Zelda Towrnell,' said Zelda, taking the initiative. Fliss watched the exchange nervously. Zelda, with her cool clothes and heavy make up, didn't look fourteen at all. Alice studied her, then appeared to make up her mind.

'Are you American? Whereabouts are you from?'

'Well, I was born in DC—'

'No way! My dad was posted there. I lived in Georgetown when I was seven.'

And they were off, chatting away nineteen to the dozen. Fliss turned away. Why did she have to be brought up in bloody boring Guildford, where everyone went to the same things and knew the same people and had visited Florida for Disneyland and that was it? She had thought they might be able to chat about her adoration of *High School Musical*, but that seemed silly and unsophisticated now Zelda and Alice were rabbiting away about bloody Jamba juice, whatever that was.

'We need to get to assembly,' she announced, suddenly conscious she was sounding like Hattie.

Alice and Zelda exchanged glances, and suddenly Fliss felt a cold hand clutch at her heart.

*

Veronica Deveral surveyed the large wood-panelled assembly hall, as four of her second years stumbled in late. She didn't mention it or pull them up. Miss Starling, recognising them as part of Maggie's guidance class, shot her a look. Maggie felt instantly cross with the girls – why did it always have to be her class showing her up?

Veronica simply paused in her short introductory welcome to new and returning students and waited till the girls had found seats at the back. Then, as if nothing had happened, she continued her talk, commending the young women in front of her to take part in the life of the school as fully as possible.

'I want you to work hard, play hard and think. Think about the kind of women you want to be, what you want to give to society and what you want to achieve in this life. We hope very much that Downey House can help you achieve it.'

She believed this, of course, wholeheartedly, but wondered too. With results becoming more and more important every year and grade inflation affecting A-levels, any school not churning out regular four A-starred medical students appeared to be slipping in standards. She took in the fresh faced, slightly anxious new girls, brown from holidays in Cornwall and Mustique, unusual-looking in the latest fashions they were allowed to wear on their first night. She wanted to take in these nervous girls and turn out poised young women, ready and prepared for everything the world could throw at them – not see them churned through some exam-passing machine and forced on to university courses and paths that wouldn't really suit them. Not everyone was a Simone Kardashian, she thought, her mind returning to the plump scholarship girl who'd topped the maths and science papers across the year before. The trick with Simone was to stop her working so hard and broaden her scope. But did league tables care about that?

Not a flicker of her concerns – or her trepidation at the teachers' cocktail party to follow – crossed her face, however, as she pleasantly exhorted the girls 'To try, to do. Winston Churchill once said, *I do like to learn, although I often do not like to be taught*. We understand that this can be true.' There was a scattering of laughter from the older girls. 'He also said, *Every day you may make progress. Every step may be fruitful. Yet there will stretch out before you an ever-lengthening, ever-ascending, ever-improving path. You know you will never get to the end of the journey. But this, so far from discouraging, only adds to the joy and glory of the climb*. And I hope you will also find this to be true of your time here.'

Maggie re-did her make up for the cocktail party. She had wanted to have a word with Fliss, Alice, Simone and the slightly alarming-looking new girl about their tardiness, but hadn't been able to find them after the assembly. Well, neither was it ideal to start term with a row, especially as she and Fliss had had their ups and downs the previous year, but they needed to know it had been noticed . . . Especially, she grimaced to herself in the mirror, by Miss Starling.

And now, of course, she had to see David. She hadn't allowed her thoughts to wander on to him at all during the summer. In Scotland, and on holiday, that was easy. Their minor flirtation had seemed like a mere silly dream, an adolescent infatuation easily confused because of her new circumstances. Back with her parents, Stan and her sister, she could be much more grounded in real life. They were planning their wedding for next summer, at the Sacred Heart in Govan, with a reception in the church hall and a very loud ceilidh band and disco taking them through the night. They couldn't afford very much, but it was OK, they could bung a bit of money behind the bar, and her dad would probably want to do a few songs, and they could have a buffet rather than a sit-down, that would save them quite a bit. And Father McSorley had christened Stan and her; had made their first communions, taken their nervous first confessions; confirmed them (Stan's new name John, as plain as he could manage; Maggie's was Cecelia – she so hated the dullness of Margaret), looked disappointed when they stopped being regular attenders (and in Stan's case, an altar boy) in their late teens, but then found it hard to hide his delight when they'd returned and asked him to marry them. He would doubtless jolly up the wedding reception and probably want to share the karaoke wiith her dad. She smiled when she thought how different he was to the young Very Reverend Rackington, who took school services at Downey and always looked slightly terrified by the mass of young women giggling and passing notes throughout his tedious sermons.

But now, at the very least, she would have to pass on Miranda's message. Well, it would be fine. It wasn't like she was going to see him and turn to jelly, of course she wasn't.

There was a loud banging on the connecting door.

'We will be as late as your naughty little second years, *non*?' shouted Claire from her set of rooms.

Maggie heaved a sigh. Had *everyone* noticed it was her class that had been late?

'Come in!' shouted Maggie.

Claire found her still in front of the mirror. 'I do not want to go to this,' she sighed heavily. She had been embroiled in a secret affair with the Classics master, which had ended after he went back to his wife and left the school. Without even that excitement, Claire found being holed up in Cornwall very tedious indeed.

'Me neither,' said Maggie, with emphasis. Claire looked at her curiously, so Maggie finished up with, 'It's so dull, and Dr Fitzroy doesn't like me.'

The head of Downey Boys had seen Veronica's employment of a comprehensive teacher as a quaint experiment, like attempting to domesticate a monkey.

'He doesn't like women,' said Claire. 'Only the very strange work in schooling that is only for boys, yes?'

'Definitely,' said Maggie, as much to convince herself as anything. 'Definitely.'

Downey Boys, a smart fifteen-minute hike along the cliff path, was much older than the girls' school, dating back to the mid-eighteenth century. This, however, made it seem brighter and more contemporary than the forbidding, high-turreted Victorian gothic of Downey House. The sash windows were elegantly spaced, the rooms and dorms bright and sunny. The setting sun reflected off the clean glass in Dr Robert Fitzroy's large meeting room where teachers from both schools were mingling and discussing the plans for the year ahead. Handsome, gangling sixth-formers, smart in their navy blue uniforms or, for some of them, their Officer Training Corps garb, handed round drinks and canapés.

Veronica stood back on the threshold. Well, there was nothing else for it. She spied Daniel almost straight away, tall and good-natured looking, with a shock of strawberry-blond hair that was not unlike hers until she tamed it straight with some ferocity each morning. She took a deep breath, drew on her inner reserves of fortitude forged in a tough early life, and stepped forward to greet her estranged son.

'Mr Stapleton,' she said, without a hint of the torment raging beneath her neat cashmere twinset. 'How nice to see you again.'

Maggie caught her breath. David was standing next to the window, making Mrs Offili, head of music, and Janie James, the notoriously tough PE teacher, laugh raucously. The light reflected off his almost-black, unwieldy-looking hair, and caught his wide, slightly manic grin. He was as tall, skinny and angular as ever, with a light tan complementing his dark, quick eyes. Maggie probed her heart as one would a loose tooth. What did she feel? Did it hurt?

But she thought it might be just a general pleasure at seeing again someone she liked and respected. Yes, that was all it was. A friend. Definitely.

As she moved slowly into the room, she heard his voice cry, joyfully, 'Maggie!' Almost without thinking, she moved towards him, only to find her route blocked by Dr Fitzroy.

'It's Miss Adair, isn't it? Still with us?'

'Yes, sir,' murmured Maggie.

'Well, well. I thought you'd be pregnant and on the list for a council house by now . . . Oh come on, don't take me seriously, I'm only joking. Will you have a drink?'

He procured her a glass of white wine from a passing tray. 'So what were you thinking of teaching this year?'

Maggie glanced out of the corner of her eye. Sure enough, David was heading towards them. She felt her heart beat faster. In a friendly way.

'I thought First World War poets to my Middle School seconds.'

'Ah, capital idea. Though don't get too politically correct on us, will you?'

'I don't think there was much correct about the First World War,' said Maggie.

'Yes, well, perhaps. Don't forget Kipling, that's all I mean.' He took a deep oratorical breath. *'Have you heard news of my boy Jack?'*

'Not this tide,' joined in David softly, suddenly appearing at her side.

'Ah, hello, David! Yes, capital stuff.'

'Then hold your head up all the more, this tide and every tide . . . sounds like a Coldplay song now, of course,' added David.

'It sounds amazing,' said Maggie. 'I can't believe I've never heard it.'

Robert snorted.

'And don't start on my schooling again, please. Kipling is just unfashionable, that's all.'

'Political correctness gone mad,' sniffed Robert, but he cast her a smile as Maggie and David attempted an extremely clumsy social kiss and nearly clashed noses.

'Hello,' she said, suddenly shy. 'Did you have a good summer?'

'Magnificent,' he said, grinning. 'What about you?'

'Great,' she said firmly.

'Well, that's good.'

There was a pause as David rubbed the back of his neck, then headed for neutral ground.

'Are you going to teach the First World War poets?'

'What's wrong with that?'

'Nothing, I suppose. It makes my boys awfully drippy and they all get terrible crushes.'

'Oh yes. The Brooke effect.'

'They grow their hair floppy and walk about arm in arm.'

'Like public school boys.'

'Well, when you put it like that . . .'

'What are you teaching this year?'

'*The Beano*, I think. And *Loaded* magazine for Media Studies. Apparently we have to look to our grades now.'

'Now, McDonald, that's not what I meant at all and you know it,' said Robert sharply.

David rolled his eyes. 'Well, I wish they'd make up their minds. They can have grades or they can have an education and perhaps they can have both, but not always.'

Robert harrumphed and bore off to see his elegant head-teacher counterpart, who was looking a little distracted this evening.

'So,' said David, after a pause.

'Oh, I ran into Miranda,' Maggie said quickly – too quickly, she wondered? 'It was quite a coincidence. She gave me a lift from the station.'

'Coincidence, eh?' said David, giving her a look.

Maggie thought about it. It hadn't occurred to her that Miranda would look out for her on purpose.

'Oh,' she said. 'Well. Anyway.'

'How is she?'

Maggie looked frankly at him. 'Honestly? Between you and me?'

She thought about soft-soaping what Miranda had said, or subtly twisting it to make her seem unpleasant, but what was the point?

'She wants you back,' said Maggie. 'I think she wants you back really badly.'

David grimaced. It was obvious talking about his private life didn't come easily to him.

'She thinks she does. Then after a month she'll start talking about shoring up our equity options or something again and I won't understand it and she'll get jealous of Stephen

Daedalus and start hankering after the bright lights of Exeter and then it will all start over . . .'

Stephen Daedalus was David's loyal, beloved and somewhat boisterous mongrel.

He let his voice tail off, but his eyes were far away. Maggie sighed. He must still be thinking of her regardless.

'How did she look?'

'Gorgeous,' said Maggie, truthfully. Miranda was so tall and blonde and striking it would be ridiculous to imply anything else. 'She looked gorgeous. Sad, of course.'

'Well, of course,' said David, a shadow of his smile crossing his face.

'Are you going to give her a call?' asked Maggie bravely.

'How's Stan?' asked David, changing the subject. David and Stan had met the previous year and were like two alien species. Stan thought David was fey and peculiar. Maggie suspected that David never thought of Stan at all. She wasn't sure what was worse.

'Great! Great, he's great,' said Maggie. 'Celtic won the league, so . . .'

'That's good, is it?'

'Don't you follow the football?'

David looked embarrassed. 'I know, I know, it makes me less of a man.' He lowered his voice. 'I have a terrible affliction. I . . . don't like football.'

'Oh God,' said Maggie. 'How can you function?'

'With great difficulty,' said David. 'It's really awful, having to run your life when you're only interested in books, films, music, art, dogs, people and beer.'

'That does sound boring and empty.'

'It's very lonely, having to curl up in front of a fire on a wet Saturday afternoon with Stephen Daedalus and a book rather than hauling out with ten thousand other men to a muddy field in the rain to shout loud abuse at people wearing different colours from myself. I'm practically a girl.'

'Do you wear pink fluffy mules when you curl up on the sofa, eating chocolates out of a heart-shaped box?' teased Maggie.

'As long as it doesn't get in the way of my crochet,' he said seriously.

You see, just think of him as a girl, Maggie told herself firmly. A female friend. A friend.

'Hello, Daniel,' said Veronica gently.

Daniel steeled himself. He was nervous enough already about taking on his new job – it was quite a step up from his old role in Kent, and Downey Boys was a famous and established school. Originally a teacher, he had taken an inspector's position when the chance arose to visit Downey House, as he followed the trail of his birth mother. His evident qualities, however, hadn't gone unnoticed, and he'd been surprised and flattered when Dr Fitzroy had offered him a job – and even more surprised when he'd accepted.

He told himself that it had nothing to do with the fact that his birth mother was the headmistress of the girls' school across the way. His adoptive mother and his wife had both been very concerned, but knew better than to try and talk him out of something that loomed so large in his life.

'Hello,' he said. He held out his hand and she took it, gratefully.

'You look well,' she said. 'Did the children have a good summer?'

Daniel nodded. 'Relocating to Cornwall from the home counties . . . it's just been amazing. They're in heaven, they think they're on holiday every day.'

Veronica smiled at the thought. 'Living on the beach?'

'Living on the beach, playing in the sand ... I never thought I'd see Sam eat a prawn, but there you are. It's amazing.'

'I'm so glad,' said Veronica. 'I'm so glad you can be happy.'

She started again. 'I'm sorry about last year . . .'

Daniel's mouth twisted. 'So I suppose you haven't told anyone here yet?'

'I just wanted to wait for the right moment—'

'Which might never come.'

'I mean, it will be a shock—'

Robert came over and clapped Daniel on the back heartily. He wouldn't dare touch Veronica, of course.

'Dr Deveral, you know our new history teacher . . .'

'I do indeed,' said Veronica. 'You're extremely lucky.'

'I hope so. Got to pep up the old leagues.'

Veronica raised her eyebrows. 'Indeed.'

'Who ees zat?' Claire whispered to Maggie, staring in Daniel's direction. David had excused himself; Maggie wondered if it was to make a phone call.

Maggie craned her neck.

'He's one of the inspectors from last year, isn't he? I wonder what he's doing here. And anyway, he's wearing a big shiny gold wedding ring, so stay *well* away.'

'*Pff,*' said Claire. 'This is life, yes? It is nothing without a leetle risk.'

'Yes, a risk to you!' said Maggie firmly. 'Not to some nice guy with a nice wife who wouldn't have a hope if you sashayed over and Frenched him up with your raincoats and stuff.'

Claire frowned. 'Ah do not understand what you zay but I do not theenk it is very complimentary at me. But you, you are perfect, yes? In your life, always perfect.'

36

'*No*,' said Maggie. 'Was just trying to be helpful.'

Claire grimaced. '*D'accord*. Another glass of the pee of goat?'

'I think I'm going to head back,' said Maggie. David had gone to Stephen Daedalus, and she had said her polite Hellos to practically everyone else. 'I have a heavy class to prepare for tomorrow.'

Simone didn't know why she was nervous. She was clued up on the syllabus, she'd done really well last year, she was more than justifying her scholarship. Nonetheless at breakfast on the first morning, when Mrs Rhys provided the huge first-day spread that the girls often complained had to last them the entire year, she found herself mechanically slathering butter and jam thickly on white toast and cramming it into her mouth. Suddenly she caught sight of Zelda, who was picking listlessly at a fruit salad whilst boldly staring at her. Simone smiled, tentatively. She had started to come out of her shell a little, but still found it difficult to start conversations with strangers, especially tall, lanky glamorous strangers.

'What?' she said.

'Oh, nothing,' said Zelda.

'What?'

Zelda looked at Alice and Fliss.

'Well,' she said, 'it's just something we quite often do, like, in American schools? But I don't know if you'd like it here.'

The other girls' ears pricked up immediately.

Zelda genuinely didn't mean it to sound cruel. It just seemed obvious to her and she hated wasting time.

'What?' demanded Simone, getting irritated. She wasn't going to relinquish her hard-found acceptance to some mouthy American who looked like Miley Cyrus.

'A makeover,' announced Zelda, pushing back from her fruit salad.

The other girls gasped in admiration. It was one thing to talk about Simone behind her back, quite another to announce it in public.

Fliss was appalled. How dare this girl push in and decide she knew what was best for everyone? She hoped Alice was going to go for her with a really sharp put-down.

But to her amazement, Simone simply laid down her toast.

'OK,' she said nonchalantly.

Although Simone was trying to act as coolly as she could, inside her heart was beating incredibly fast. A makeover! How long had she dreamed of someone coming up to her and saying, 'You know, inside I bet you're really gorgeous. Let's bring out the real you.' She had a secret fantasy of one day meeting Gok Wan, and him buying her lots of lovely clothes and making her look great and feel fantastic about her body. This big-haired American wasn't quite as good, obviously, but she would have to do.

All the other girls were looking at her and smiling. Pretty, blonde Sylvie Brown was even clapping. They looked so happy and excited, and Simone enjoyed their reaction.

'You're really pretty,' continued Zelda. 'Bit of weight off, get the skin sorted out, a few new clothes . . .'

Simone didn't want to figure out how she could afford new clothes for now, she was too excited and flustered by suddenly being the centre of attention.

'Do you really think so?' All the girls said Of course, and made noises of agreement.

'Uh-oh,' said Alice in a low voice into Fliss's ear. 'We've created a monster.'

Fliss smiled, but she couldn't help feeling put out. Why

was Simone getting all the attention all of a sudden? She was used to her quiet, funny, mousy friend. She wasn't sure she wanted her turning glamorous. Alice was quite enough to cope with as it was. And as for Zelda . . . She had a sudden horrifying vision of the three of them all swanning around, dark hair swinging, wearing trendy clothes and leaving her out. She didn't like it, and slowly pushed her bowl of cereal away, the girl who couldn't even attract a boy from her home town.

Maggie tried to smile when she thought of herself this time last year, terrified of her first encounter with her class. Now she felt . . . Nope, she couldn't deny it. She was still nervous. She glanced at her notes. Just one new girl, that wasn't too bad. Miss Starling was taking the first years this year. She didn't envy them.

Smoothing down her new pale grey tea dress – heavily discounted in the Jesiré sale – she smiled brightly in the mirror. Rose-pink lipstick, a touch of blusher, a hint of her summer tan still there. Not bad. She thought briefly of Stan, who started work at the paper distribution plant at five o'clock in the morning and by the time he got home was often too knackered to notice what she looked like. Well, not to worry about him now. She headed towards her classroom.

Maggie was surprised to see the new girl loitering by the door, as the rest of the class took their seats inside. (She had said hello to Felicity and asked her if she'd had a good holiday. Felicity had tried not to smirk. It had been an uncomfortable moment for both of them.)

Normally new pupils tried to hide themselves inconspic-uously amongst their new classmates. Maggie smiled in what she thought was a reassuring manner, remembering how scared she'd been the year before – and she'd been the teacher.

'Hello,' she said kindly. 'I'm Miss Adair, your form mistress and English teacher. Don't worry, I think you're going to like it here.'

Zelda had had the welcome speech about a million times before.

'Yeah yeah,' she said. 'Do you want me to introduce myself and say where I'm from and all that blah blah blah . . .'

Maggie glanced at the enrolment form.

'Well, Zelda, if you'd like to—'

'Yeah, whatever.'

Zelda squared up to the front of the class, and Maggie had no choice but to stand back and let her get on with it.

'Yeah, hi everyone,' drawled Zelda. 'My name is Zelda Derene Towrnell. I was born in Washington DC.'

She turned to Maggie. 'That's in America.'

'Yes, thank you, Zelda,' said Maggie tightly. She'd never been to America.

'And my dad's a major in the US marines. He's over here teaching your limey soldiers how to help kick butt in whatever place the United States of Ass-kicking gets stupidly involved in next.'

'Watch your mouth please, Zelda,' said Maggie, shocked. The girls were obviously enthralled by the tough-talking, undoubtedly glamorous stranger. They'd probably all have American accents in a week. 'We absolutely don't tolerate that kind of language here.'

'Yes, ma'am,' said Zelda, leisurely. 'Sorry. That was an outburst of independent thought. It won't happen again.'

Maggie gave Zelda her very sternest look, picked up a sheet and put a mark next to her name. The last thing she needed was a girl who probably wouldn't be staying at the school for very long and had no fear of consequences, encouraging the girls in impudent behaviour.

And another voice at the back of her mind said she did believe in free expression, didn't she? She did believe in encouraging the girls to speak their minds, engage in the wider world, however black and white their opinions might be. But there were opinions and there was rudeness, and this was definitely in the latter camp. On the other hand, it could be useful . . .

'Well, let's engage with what Zelda has said, shall we?' she added, indicating the girl to the empty seat next to Alice.

'This term we're going to look at the First World War poets, in conjunction with your History module. An entire generation of men suffered the whole breadth of horror and terror that life could throw at them – could throw at anyone. We can't know how many Beethovens and Einsteins, Picassos and Dickens were lost. But there were some who took that rage, that horror, and turned it into beauty, and its only possible redemption. We have it in their work. The men themselves, whether they lived or died, often could not be saved.'

Maggie noticed the mood of the class, previously perky and anticipatory with the smell of new schoolbooks and pencil sharpenings in the crisp air, had tuned in, become interested. Perhaps David was right, and they were all going to get caught up in the doomy romance of the whole terrible era. Well good, she thought. As long as they engaged.

'Are we allowed to conscientiously object?' drawled a voice. Zelda.

'And you, missy, can keep quiet in my classroom!' The second she'd said it, Maggie was furious with herself for losing her temper. Ten minutes into the start of term as well.

The rest of the class looked shocked and a little wary. Maggie took a deep breath and composed herself.

'Turn to page 356,' she said, brusquely. 'Simone, can you start?'

After a pause, there was a satisfactory rustling in the classroom.

'*What tolling bells*,' started Simone tentatively, '*for those who die as cattle?*'

Engaged.

'Not engaged?' Claire enquired crossly. 'Well, he asked you, so indeed you are engaged. And zat is zat.'

Claire, Maggie and Miranda were in a corner of the local village pub. Miranda had kept her word and rang them for a 'Girlie session', as she termed it. She was certainly very organised. There was only one pub, and teachers were discouraged from 'frittering' (Miss Starling's word) their evenings there. However sometimes needs must, and tonight was one of those evenings, so they sat choking over the unpleasant white wine.

'Yeah,' said Miranda, 'but he said I negated it when I took the ring off, threw it at him and told him it was a cheap piece of shit.'

'You did that?' said Maggie wonderingly.

'Well, I was under a lot of pressure at work at the time.'

'Men love passionate women,' said Claire, huffing into her glass. 'This wine is the piss of the dogs my uncle raised.'

'So what did he say?'

Maggie realised she had a slightly unhealthy interest, but couldn't help leaning forward anyway.

Miranda sighed. 'Well, he was holding his ground. But then I used my secret weapon.'

'*Non!*' said Claire. '*Formidable!*'

'What? What?'

'Men,' Claire went on with a knowing look, 'they cannot resist to see a pretty woman cry.'

'Really?' said Maggie.

'Well, it was just a *few* tears,' said Miranda.

'Did it work?'

Miranda shrugged. 'I think we're still on.'

'But do you still want him?'

By way of an answer, Miranda turned her gaze to a drunken old man sitting in the corner of the pub on his own. Nursing a whisky, his watery gaze was distant and vivid red veins mapped his face.

'It's not like my life is crawling with potentials,' she said, steeling herself and knocking back her glass. 'Anyway, what about you? You're engaged too, if I remember rightly? How are the wedding preparations going?'

Maggie smiled a little tightly. 'Oh, we're getting there. My nephews are very excited. They're going to be page boys and have Skean Dhus.'

'What is zis?' asked Claire.

'It's like a small sword you hide in your sock when you're wearing a kilt. I'm not sure letting my nephews anywhere with small swords is the wisest of plans.'

'Where is it going to be?'

'In a hotel near where we live that does a lot of weddings,' said Maggie, a tad defensively. She'd been to lots of parties and dances there growing up, it was within their budget and it seemed fitting.

She couldn't shake off, however, the idea that she should be more excited. She was, of course, but she felt a little as if she and Stan were married already, and this was just expensive fuss. Or that it wasn't, a very small voice inside her whispered, well, it wasn't her *dream* wedding. She realised thinking like that was stupid and spoiled. She made all right money, Stan got by. It would be completely and utterly stupid to spunk thousands of pounds they couldn't afford or get into debt just to hire a dumb castle or stately home, when all their friends and family would be delighted to be just where they were, all together.

'What about ze dress?'

'I think I need you to help me with that, Claire. Something French and chic. Otherwise I'll look like a big, white, upside-down mushroom.'

'You must get it made for you,' said Claire.

'When I get a jillion pound raise!'

'*Non*, it is a must. You must get it made for you. So it will fit like a glove.'

'Well, in that case I'd better postpone the wedding, give me enough time to slim down so they can get a measuring tape round me.'

'I think you have a gorgeous healthy figure,' said Miranda, politely avoiding gazing at the empty crisp packets by Maggie's glass. 'Don't change a thing.'

If you really thought that, you wouldn't be such a hungry-looking size eight, thought Maggie to herself, then felt mean, dissatisfied and not really a blushing bride.

Maggie rose early, feeling thirsty and worried about having drunk too much wine the night before. A walk, definitely, to clear the cobwebs.

It was fresh and very blowy, but the sun was strong for late September and she could feel her head clear as she hit the cliffs.

The warm tongue licking her hand didn't, as it might once have done, take her totally by surprise.

'Stephen Daedalus!' she cried in delight. The dog was overjoyed to see her again, and leapt up on her jeans.

'Now you *know* that is naughty,' she mock-scolded him, then gave in to the moment and rolled him around on the dewy ground, scratching between his ears in the way she knew he loved, which was how David found her five minutes later. Maggie scrambled up, pink-cheeked and out of breath.

'*Not* the most dignified of positions,' she smiled.

'Oh, I don't know,' said David, smiling back. 'You have a dandelion in your hair.'

'I missed him,' she said.

'He missed you.'

They fell into step, then both picked up a stick for the dog at the same time.

'Let's see whose he goes for,' said David. He hurled his far across the bracken. Maggie, who'd never been sporty, got hers about ten metres. Stephen Daedalus immediately aimed for that one.

'You are a VERY LAZY DOG,' said David, as Stephen charged back to Maggie's feet.

'You can't get over the fact that he likes me more than he likes you.'

'No he doesn't! He tolerates your weak throwing arm and inability to stop giving him treats.'

Maggie smiled. Then she told him about blowing up at the new girl.

'I can't just ignore it. They'll all start ... what's the American word?'

'Sassing you,' said David.

'Exactly.'

'The thing is, she really is quite cool.'

'Well, get her to express it then. Defuse her rebellious status. She won't be cool if the teacher thinks she's great. And get her to talk about her dad. Don't you think it would be good for your girls to hear about someone who really puts their life on the line? Most of their fathers spend their lives jammed to their desks and those blueberry things.' He shivered.

'It doesn't sound like she'd have him come in.'

'That doesn't matter. Get her to share her experiences.'

'Like show and tell?'

'Yes! Exactly. Typical American – if you can't beat 'em, join 'em.'

'Maybe I will. I saw Miranda. She seems cheerful.'

David looked awkward. 'Yes, good. She's good, I think.'

'So it's all back on?'

'Uh ... well, we're thinking of having a trial period.' David pushed his long hands through his unruly black hair. 'Anyway. We'll see ...'

'Sure. Good,' said Maggie. 'I'm glad it's working out. Right. I'm off for breakfast.'

Stephen Daedalus pricked up his ears.

'That dog! You should teach him to say "sausages".'

David caressed his ears. 'Stephen Daedalus is far too intelligent and cultured to bother with sausages. *Foie gras*, maybe.'

'You think?'

'It's not his fault he's the best dog in the world.'

'It's not,' said Maggie, shaking her head as she went back through the wrought-iron gate at the bottom of the grounds. It was amazing, really, the affectionate way David talked about his dog, compared to how he spoke about his so-called fiancée.

Veronica was deep in thought. She had spent a sleepless night looking at her dilemma from every conceivable angle, trying to bring her usually logical problem-solving intelligence to bear on something which made her heartsick.

46

Perhaps . . . She couldn't simply announce to the world that she had a son, without facing so many intrusive questions, so many enquiring glances and curious eyes, so much gloating that the remote, untouchable headmistress had . . . Had given away her own child.

It could ruin her. Ruin the school. She looked around at her elegant office. She couldn't bear it. Everything she had strived for, longed for, wanted. All gone. Where would she go, unemployable at fifty? Nervously she fingered her rope of pearls.

But then again, she owed Daniel. She *owed* him. Her own flesh and blood. She had failed him once, she couldn't do it again. Oh dear. Why was life so difficult?

Miss Starling hardly waited past the knock to walk into Veronica's office, with the same, mildly offended gait she always displayed.

'June,' said Veronica.

'The treasure hunt,' said Miss Starling. 'I disapprove.'

Veronica felt much happier to be back on solid ground. There were a great many things of which June Starling disapproved, and being outside during lesson hours, fraternising with the boys' school and giving the impression of confusing learning with fun was quite high up there. Hence her usual assault on the annual second year's treasure hunt, held in early October when the foliage was at its loveliest.

'They never sleep, they get far too excited and I think it unwise to mix the schools, it makes the girls dreamy and unreliable.'

'They are teenage girls,' said Veronica. 'That could be expected in any case.'

The treasure hunt had been instituted a few years ago by Miss Gifford, the energetic and somewhat masculine young

47

Geography mistress. Essentially it was orienteering over the surrounding area, using fixed points, latitude, longitude and map-reading skills, and was usually highly successful in increasing pupils' understanding, apart from a small incident two years ago when one of the seniors had brought in a GPS and somewhat ruined it for everyone.

The boys' school and the girls worked together, making eight teams each, and it had become as fixed an event on the school calendar as the Christmas concert or the spring fete. Veronica knew that if June had her way she'd cancel both of those events, too, but she was also one of the best, most tireless and dedicated teachers the school had ever had. Veronica didn't like upsetting even someone so easily upset.

'We'll keep a close eye on them,' she said, in a mollifying tone. 'Miss Gifford says it's a really good way to jump-start their GSCE in Geography.'

'And misbehaviour,' said Miss Starling. 'It's a dangerous time.'

'I know,' said Veronica. 'Don't worry, there'll be plenty of supervision.'

It was after supper and the four girls were sitting in their dorm. Zelda was painting her toenails and Simone was watching with great interest.

Zelda was worried, though, although she wouldn't admit it. Normally her bolshy routine sufficiently impressed the other pupils and cowed the teachers so she wouldn't get too much hassle off anyone, but here it hadn't gone quite like that. The English teacher had been sharp – not that she cared, America hadn't even got into that dumb war till it was nearly all over – Miss Beresford the Maths teacher had stuck her at the back of the class on her own and ordered her to catch up, and Chemistry had left her competely bamboozled.

The international schools she had attended were mainly people passing through and having fun and learning a smattering of about six languages. The schools in the US were quite lenient. But here everyone looked really serious and bent their heads to their desks. Simone, Zelda's pet project, had answered almost every question in every lesson. It felt really strange that these girls, who felt so much younger than her in every way and whom she'd been ready to take pity on, were in fact streets ahead of her academically. She knew she wasn't stupid, she'd just never felt the need to work, and no one had ever seemed particularly bothered at home.

She covered up her surprise and nerves by reasserting how much cooler she was than the other girls. First, she'd sat Simone down in front of a special magnifying mirror she'd brought with her.

'Now look,' she said.

Alice and Fliss, fascinated, were hanging around in the background.

'Do I have to?' asked Simone, who was still marvelling that anyone would want to pay this much attention to her. 'Normally I don't.'

'You don't look in the mirror?'

'Well, I check I don't have anything in my teeth,' said Simone, feeling more uncomfortable now. She'd learned early on that the mirror was not her friend. Plus, one day she'd been trying to pose by sucking in her cheeks and Joel had come in and found her at it and laughed his head off, then impersonated her for weeks. Ever since then she'd scuttled past her reflection in shop windows. She found excuses not to be in photographs. It was such a reflex she didn't even consider it any more.

'Well, start,' said Zelda, who looked in the mirror a lot.

She forced Simone's face around.

'See? You have beautiful big dark eyes. But they have bags under them. You have to go to bed earlier and drink more water.'

'Can I go to bed now?' asked Simone nervously.

'But this is, like, for your own good,' said Zelda sincerely.

'You don't have to do it if you don't want to,' cut in Fliss, who was pretending to study at the desk by her bed but couldn't help glancing over.

'Sure you do,' said Zelda. 'It'll be cool.'

Simone glanced at Alice, who shrugged.

'You want to do it?' she said. 'It's totally up to you.'

'I do,' said Simone, a quiver in her voice.

'Cool,' said Zelda. 'Who's got tweezers? It's gonna be a *long* night.'

'Hey,' said Maggie on the phone. 'What are you up to?'

'Not having sex with my wife,' said Stan.

'Number one,' said Maggie, 'I'm not your wife yet. And two, isn't it half time? You're calling me at half time?' She heard the noise of the pub in the background. 'You totally don't miss me.'

'I do! Plus I need to ask you something. Oh yeah, some dry roasted peanuts, please. Three packs, aye.'

'Are you having dry roasted peanuts for supper?'

'*Supper?*' jeered Stan. 'What do you mean, *supper*? Do you mean tea, or do you mean something else altogether?'

Maggie rolled her eyes. OK, so she'd picked up some phrases from being down south. It was hardly a crime, was it?

'It doesn't matter what I mean. Three packets of dry roasted peanuts can't possibly be good for anyone.'

'Yes, miss,' said Stan, taking what sounded like a long

draw from his pint. 'I thought you werenae supposed to start nagging till after we got married.'

'What did you need to ask me?'

'Oh yeah. My ma wants to know what the colour theme for the wedding is. She wants to buy her outfit in the sales.'

'The what?'

'The colours, you know? What colour the bridesmaids will be wearing and what colour your flowers are and all that. I don't know, girl's stuff, isn't it.'

Maggie thought about it. She just hadn't considered it at all.

'Ehm,' she said, 'I don't know. Tell your mum to buy whatever she wants.'

'Well, she's not going to like that, is she? She just wants to know what will fit in.'

'But *I* don't know yet!'

'OK, fine, don't blow your top! I thought girls were meant to be all into this kind of bollocks anyway.'

'It's not bollocks, I just haven't had a chance to think about it, that's all. Just tell her to get something nice that covers her tattoos and we'll take it from there.'

There was silence on the end of the phone. She'd gone too far.

'Oh, Stan, I didn't mean it like that. Don't be daft.'

'Maybe you're too good for us now, down south, is that it?'

'No, of *course* not.'

'Maybe you're just too posh. Maybe you need a horse and carriage and all of that before you'll deign to walk down the aisle, is that it?'

'Of course it's not, Stan! Of course not!'

The background noise got louder and she could tell the match had kicked off again.

'So why haven't you shifted yourself? My mum is going to spend a lot of money and you can't even tell her what kind of dress she can have! And by the way, there's all sorts of letters and crap at the house from the venue about what kind of stuff we want and you didn't even take them with you.'

'I've been busy,' said Maggie weakly.

'Oh yeah, with your seven-week summer holiday,' said Stan. 'I'm getting back.'

'No, don't go . . . Let's sort this out.'

But it was too late. When she called his phone again it was switched off.

Chapter Three

The day of the October treasure hunt dawned mixed and muggy. The rain was holding off, just about, but there were ominous black clouds massing over the far cliffs. Miss Gifford was insistent that they went ahead, however. Second years were formed into dorm teams, headed by a senior pupil who was meant to be testing their leadership skills, told to put on waterproofs and wellingtons just in case and handed an Ordnance Survey map and their first clue per team. They had to find the grid reference point and work from there.

'Please not Hattie for team leader,' said Fliss through gritted teeth as she shrugged her way into her too-big waterproof. Simone squeezed into hers. She felt a little light-headed; she'd only had fruit for breakfast, and hot water with lemon. She'd felt like an idiot filling her cup for the first time the previous week, but Zelda insisted this was what Scarlett Johansson had every day. Sure enough, within three days everyone was doing it.

The two schools met at the head of the cliffs. The boys were revved up and anxious for a challenge, almost straining at the leash. The girls glanced over at them and universally wished they weren't wearing the standard red cagoules. Fliss suddenly noticed Zelda was wearing hers knotted casually around her shoulders over a striped Breton top and wished immediately she'd done that too.

Shanthi, a gorgeous Indian girl from the fifth form, walked up to their group with a smile.

'Are you the Plantagenet seconds? All right, you lot, I've got you. I was hoping old Grassy Gifford wouldn't have changed the clues since we did it, but apparently she has, so I'm going to be no use to you whatsoever. And I'm not running either, it's bad for the skin. I'll be under that tree reading *Vogue*, and I don't want to hear from you lot unless you're actually bleeding from an open wound, OK?'

Slightly intimidated, the girls nodded.

'OK. Fine. Scram.'

'I won't be like that when I have to lead a group,' said Fliss. 'I'll be, like, really cool and stuff.'

'Yeah, I think you lost the coolness when you volunteered to lead the group,' said Alice, and Zelda sniggered. Fliss felt herself colour. It didn't get any better when she suddenly caught sight of Will Hampton standing on the other side of the hill, trying to contain a group of younger looking boys. Her heart leapt.

'Will's here!' she couldn't help squeaking to Alice, praying she wouldn't use the knowledge to tease.

Alice's eyebrows perked up. 'I can't believe you can make him out from this distance,' she said, but gave Fliss a reassuring smile. 'Shall we aim to beat them?'

Fliss smiled gratefully. 'Maybe just follow them.'

Simone glanced at the first envelope she'd been given by Shanthi. Just as she did so, Miss Gifford lined them up in a row. Will's team was some distance away behind them.

'All right, children. Line up. Now, try not to rely on your leader too much.'

'Shouldn't be a problem for us,' said Alice.

'Don't follow one another, the clues are all different.'

'This teacher is a complete obsessive,' David whispered to Maggie. They were hovering by the side with four other second-form teachers who'd been roped in to supervise.

'Well, maybe that's good for them,' said Maggie, looking doubtfully at the rainclouds. 'Teach them that if something is worth doing, it's worth doing . . . blah blah, you know.'

David smiled. 'And as long as something is worth supervising, it's worth supervising for five hours.'

'It takes *five hours*?'

Claire stomped towards them in a Burberry raincoat that, on her, was not in the least chavvy.

'Every year thees is the most boring theeng. I shall hide in ze woods and smoke ceegarettes.' She knelt down towards Stephen Daedalus. 'Dog. I do like you. OK, *d'accord*? But you must not jump on me. Zat would not be good for my jacket, dog, and therefore not good for you. Thank you, *merci*.'

Stephen Daedalus sniffed respectfully.

'*Bonjour, mademoiselle*,' said David. '*Allez-vous bien?*'

'*Oui, mais . . .*'

And they started to chat in French. Maggie tried to look interested and tapped her foot. Finally they stopped.

'Zees man is the only one between here and Boulogne who can speak at all,' said Claire to Maggie.

'Really?' said Maggie, hoping she didn't sound too jealous of their ability to casually slip in and out of another language.

'Yeah, she tells me all her deepest darkest secrets, don't you, Claire?' teased David, as Claire rolled her eyes at him and Maggie turned her attention back to the pupils.

The whistle blew and there was a great fumbling with envelopes.

'For your first grid reference, multiply the number of chimneys on Downey House by the number of crenellations on the west tower,' read Simone.

'I thought this was Geography, not Maths,' grumbled Alice.

'You know, in my old high school,' said Zelda, 'they'd, like, *totally* never make us do this. And we get to drive to school.'

'The drive from the dorms to the school isn't actually that bad,' said Alice, looking around for Fliss to try and make her laugh. But Fliss was staring, trying to make out a figure in a blue anorak who was disappearing with a group of laughing, haring boys, far away over the cliffs.

'It's a hundred and seventy-two,' said Simone. Then she turned round. 'Isn't *anyone* going to take part in this except for me?'

In fact by the time the girls had discovered the tiny red box, impossible to spot unless you knew its exact location, with its code inside hiding global positioning co-ordinates, they were quite excited. Occasionally they would hear the yelps of other teams galloping past them, including the Tudor girls, who had obviously got their sums wrong and were running back and forth asking if anyone had seen a box. The teachers followed behind them at a safe distance, refusing to answer clue questions (they knew better than to try and upset Miss Gifford's carefully constructed plans), but instead granting loo passes and diagnosing stinging nettle bites.

The clouds advanced relentlessly. Maggie glanced around suddenly and realised that it was dark; a huge black nimbostratus (as Miss Gifford had effortlessly identified, though sadly not forecasted) had appeared to crest the hill and now loomed towards them, ominous and heavy.

The girls were down in the small copse at the bottom of the hill that most of the pupils insisted on calling 'the forest'. The map references had led them directly into its heart, and they were on the look-out for something nailed to a tree. Zelda was jumping and nervous, and pointed out that in American forests there were bears, snakes, coyotes and prairie dogs.

'Is everything bigger there too?' said Alice. Fliss knew Alice winding her up was just her way of making friends, but Zelda didn't seem to mind in the slightest.

'Yeah,' she said complacently. 'It's just, like, you know . . . better?'

'What's that?' said Simone. They all stood still. It was very dark inside the forest now, the rainfall only drops away. Fliss, who'd seen *The Blair Witch Project* at a faintly scandalous Halloween party when she was twelve, went rigid.

'Ssh,' she hissed. Another twig cracked on the ground. The girls immediately panicked and started giggling and gathering close together.

'It's a witch,' said Fliss.

'Axe murderer,' said Simone.

'It's probably Mam'selle Crozier sneaking out for a fag,' said Alice with her usual perspicacity.

They huddled in horrified joy when the big fat raindrops first started down on them. Within seconds it was a downpour that bounced off their waterproofs but made a joke of their jeans and ran down the insides of their wellies.

'My *hair*!' shrieked Zelda, as the source of the foot-cracking revealed himself: Will, and a shivering group of boys behind him.

'Hey hey,' said Will, beaming at them. 'Are you the treasure?'

*

Maggie looked around. Apart from David and Stephen Daedalus, there were no other teachers to be seen. They must have taken heed of the rain coming in, but she and David had been talking about Matthew Arnold and she simply hadn't noticed where they were. In fact they were right by the cliff edge, a kilometre and a half away, at least, from either school. None of the pupils were in sight either.

'Oh God,' she started, as the rain began to pour. 'We're going to get absolutely drenched.'

'In the autumn, in England. It's outrageous.'

'Should we go and find the children?'

'I think children are mostly waterproof,' said David. 'And they've probably all dived for the trees and the school anyway.'

Certainly, there wasn't a soul to be seen on the crags. The rain intensified and soaked through Maggie's Primark coat.

'This isn't funny,' she said.

David glanced up at the drenching sky. 'We're not going to be able to stoic this out, are we?'

'I don't think so,' said Maggie, getting rain in her mouth as she opened it to speak.

'OK,' said David. 'Come on!' And he grabbed her hand. 'Follow me! Come on, Stephen Daedalus.'

He set off over the crags, and Maggie let herself go to run at full strength beside him. As she did so, trying to keep up with his long legs, she realised how long it had been since she had run – *really* run, not some half-hearted jogging at the gym or aimless strolling. Her legs and shoulders stretched as she flew through the raindrops and she found she was laughing as well as panting, sodden, but with an effortless, light feeling of freedom pounding through her veins.

'STOP!' hollered David, grabbing her back from the cliff edge. He glanced right and left. 'OK, it's here. Jump!'

And, without letting go of her hand, he threw himself over the edge.

Will advanced. Fliss felt her heart stick in her throat. Then he put on his big movie-star grin.

'Hey,' he said. 'We got lost. I think.'

'You got lost here?' said Alice, hollering above the noise of the rain on the leaves. 'It's about ten minutes from the school.'

'I'm new,' said Will. 'And from Guildford. This is like the rainforest to me.'

He looked around. 'Uh, anyone want to shelter?'

Fliss raised her hand before she realised she was alone.

Then she stuck it down again.

They – Will and his band of sniggering, slightly awkward-looking second-form boys – made a circle with their cagoules and let the girls shelter inside, even though Zelda was far too tall and popped out, getting soaked anyway.

'This is very chivalrous,' said Alice. Fliss was too over-whelmed to say anything at all. Here was Will, his chest exposed, sheltering her! She could feel a huge, nervous lump in her throat. All she wanted to do was . . . she couldn't even admit to herself what she would like to do. It made her feel hot and embarrassed and a little trembly. Nonetheless, she couldn't take her eyes off him.

'Naturally, ma'am,' said Will. 'We're from that posh school up the hill. Oh yeah, so are you.'

How could she do it? wondered Fliss as she heard Alice effortlessly chatting with Will about music, films, all sorts of things she knew about and could have offered an opinion on. Why didn't her friend get nervous like everyone else? It sounded like Alice and Will had known each other for years, when Fliss had been the one watching him for years from afar. She was talking to him like he was a completely normal person. And worse, he seemed to be enjoying it, laughing at Alice's wicked descriptions of the slightly toadish appearance of the Geography mistress.

One of the second-form boys let out a big sigh. Simone, who was standing next to him, glanced up. If she didn't know, she'd say he was much younger than his fifteen years. He was chubby, Asian, with a sweep of black hair plastered by the rain on to his head. He looked absolutely miserable.

'What's up with you, sucko?' said the boy beside him, who had pulled the hood of his cagoule so tightly around him that all that remained visible was a pair of sharp blue eyes. 'Too much of a gay baby for a bit of wet weather?'

If the boy was upset he didn't really let it show. 'Yes,' he said, 'I'm a gay baby. That's right, Stokes.' He turned away, as if he were imploring the sky.

'I just ... I mean, why are we out in this? It's not like it takes more than ten minutes to figure out how longitude and latitude work. I mean, if you read Dava Sobel it's all in there anyway.'

'I *loved* that book,' said Simone instantaneously, without even remembering to be shy. Then she checked herself as the boy turned his dark eyes on her.

'Have you seen the Harrison c-clocks?' he said. He appeared to have a slight stutter. 'They're at—'

'The Greenwich observatory! I know, my dad took me last summer! They're amazing.'

'They are,' said the boy. 'Did you know Philip Pullman used H4 as the inspiration for his alethiometer?'

Simone didn't, and any discussion of one of her favourite writers meant that her normal self-consciousness was completely forgotten.

God, even *Simone* is talking to someone, thought Fliss, drenched, cold and miserable.

Well, this is cruel and unusual punishment, thought Zelda, as the rain trickled down the back of her neck.

'Where the hell?'

Maggie glanced around. She was on a concealed ridge, just under the crags. David had vanished.

'Where are you?'

'You ask a lot of questions,' came a voice from behind her. She turned quickly and, sure enough, just down the ridge a little was a dark cave.

'God,' she said. The rain was, if anything, getting stronger.

'Quick! In here!' came David's voice. 'Unless you're half fish.'

Maggie tentatively stepped inside the cave, giving her eyes time to adjust to the darkness. 'How did *this* get here?'

The tall dark shape of David was standing next to a white rock formation in the ceiling. 'There must have been waves up here once, millions of years ago. Amazing, isn't it?'

The cave went back about thirty feet, and smelled of the salt water so far below. Maggie glanced around and touched the slimy walls.

'Yes,' she said. 'I'm surprised half our sixth year doesn't come down here to drink beer.'

'It's almost impossible to find unless you know where it is,' said David. 'Stephen Daedalus came across it one day. Howled his head off. I thought I'd lost him.'

Maggie looked around. The rain cut off the entrance like a curtain. There was no noise from the outside world at all.

It came out of the blue. She had had no expectations that this would happen. But suddenly it seemed unthinkable that it would not.

'Maggie.' He said her name, but with a deep, questioning tone. Before he'd even finished she had turned towards him.

She had dreamed of this moment for such a long time. But she had never expected the passionate intensity with which he strode towards her, grasping the tops of her arms. His dark eyes burned into hers as he asked her a silent question and her body answered: yes.

His kiss was fierce, as if unleashing something pent up inside of him for a long time. Maggie felt light-headed, as if she was losing the ability to breathe, and she returned it with a fervour that took her by surprise; a passion so strong she found she wanted to be crushed, completely obliterated in him. She kissed him back with equal strength and they found themselves hard against the wall of the cave. Maggie felt as if a dam was breaking inside her and raised her arms, letting David pin them above her head. She could feel his long, hard body pressed against hers and all she could think was *more*. She was panting now as he continued to kiss her deeply and she found herself muttering words: 'Please,' she said. '*Please.*'

David pulled back. His eyes looked wild and his breathing was heavy. She noticed his hands were shaking.

'Oh, Maggie,' he said. 'Oh, Maggie.'

Maggie knew he was right to pull back, she was behaving wantonly, in the wrong place, at the wrong time . . . but the huge feeling of emptiness was nearly overwhelming.

'I know,' she said. 'But . . .'

He looked at her with such longing that it took her breath away.

'You're engaged,' he said shortly. 'We're at work. This is . . . this is *wrong*.'

The simplicity of what he said was so harsh. But so true.

As Maggie scrambled out of the cave, scarcely checking to make sure no pupils had seen her, her mind in turmoil, she could barely see straight.

She tugged down her ruffled clothing, tried to smooth back her hair, but nothing could quell the rapid beating of her heart or stop her head feeling like a washing machine. Partly she felt triumphant. That yes, he had wanted her. Did want her. Just as much as she wanted him. Her insides were gripped with satisfaction.

But the pain. Oh God. How could she be so stupid? The wedding was *booked*. She wasn't on the run from an unhappy relationship, or a cruel man. Stan was her own sweet boy. Not perfect, but nobody was. She wasn't one of her second-formers, with Chace Crawford posters on the wall. She knew what life was like: even if she was with David, she was sure he'd annoy her just as much as Stan sometimes did, have his own foibles and little ways. Everyone did. And a sure guarantee of unhappiness was to jump from man to man, chasing a dream that didn't exist until she was too old and bitter to attract anyone at all.

And it was wrong. It was plain wrong. She had promised herself – her body, her soul – to Stan. For ever. So far, for ever seemed to have lasted less than a year. What kind of person was she? She'd always seen herself as moral, someone who wanted to do the right thing. To be good. Yet here she was, throwing herself into doing the wrong thing, as recklessly as she knew how. If David hadn't stopped them, what would she have done? She shivered to think. Partly from shame; partly from a lust that was to give her many sleepless nights over the weeks to come.

The crazed rain had slowed to a trickle. Suddenly Maggie wasn't sure how long she'd been down there. She climbed ungracefully back to the clifftop.

Sylvie was running towards her, her beautiful hair plastered to her head.

'Miss Adair! All the clues got lost, miss! Or maybe we

couldn't find them. And Alice and Fliss are in the woods with a big bunch of boys!'

As ever, it took her pupils to shake her back to some kind of reality.

'Come on. Let's round everyone up, get them inside and warmed up.'

She looks like Diana, the huntress, thought David wistfully, as he saw her fleet of foot across the meadow grass, her long dark hair spreading out in the wind behind her, before he turned away and whistled for Stephen Daedalus. He hadn't planned anything in showing her the cave; nothing beyond the easy friendship appropriate under the circumstances. But the force of his feelings as she stood in front of him, pink-cheeked, her lips apart as she took in the cave . . .

'Come to me in my dreams, and then
By day I shall be well again.
For then the night will more than pay
The hopeless longing of the day.'

He threw a stick for Stephen Daedalus with far more force than he'd intended, until the dog looked at him warily.

From just over the ridge, Alice, who'd left the boys behind when she'd felt the atmosphere become slightly peculiar – and wanting to get out of the rain – watched them both emerge from the cliffs with some interest. Well, well, she thought. What on earth were those two doing down there? Goody two-shoes Miss Adair and that tasty teacher from the boys' school. That *was* useful to know.

Chapter Four

Maggie woke up with a horrible, hot stone in the bottom of her stomach. She had a foul taste in her mouth. At first she struggled to remember why. Then she sat bolt upright in horror. Oh God. Oh God. What had she *done*? She had ruined *everything*. Her life, everything. How could she have thrown it all away? All for one stupid kiss in a stupid sea-drenched cave. She had lost David's friendship, that was for sure. He was disgusted with her, and so he should be. And Stan . . . Stan. Her heart went out to him. How could she have done this to him? She wasn't fit for marriage. She wasn't fit for teaching: although she'd gone through it in a blur, she'd got a very sharp pulling up from Matron and Miss Starling when half her second-form Plantagenets ended up in the san, because instead of sheltering indoors from the rain storm they'd been cavorting about in the woods with a clutch of boys. She wasn't fit for anything or anyone.

Too upset even to cry, she moved slowly and painfully towards the window. After the grey storm clouds of yesterday it had dawned fresh and bright, the last fading greens of summer – autumn seemed to come late here – bathed in a soft morning light. Finally she choked out a sob. Just as she did so, her phone rang.

Stupidly, cretinously, she wondered for a split second if it might be David. Then she loathed herself all the more for even entertaining the thought. She picked the phone up tentatively, as if it were a poisonous snake.

'Hello?'

'Maggie.' It was Stan.

She closed her eyes. Could he see her guilt from Glasgow? She felt it was radiating off her in waves. Maybe . . . A horrifying thought struck her. Maybe he knew, somehow. Someone had seen them, or David had felt guilty and somehow got in contact, or—

'Maggie, I'm sorry.'

She thought she'd misheard. Shouldn't she be saying this?

'What do you mean?'

'About the other night. I'm sorry.'

Maggie struggled to remember. A row over his mother's outfit. God, it sounded so stupid and felt so long ago now. So innocent, when that was their only worry. She stifled a sob.

'Oh, Maggie, don't cry. OK. I really am sorry, I was just at the pub and, well, you know how it is.'

Now all Maggie wanted to do was bawl.

'I am too,' she stumbled over.

'You know, everyone says it's stressful putting a wedding together,' went on Stan. 'I just want you to enjoy it, OK?'

If anything could have been designed to make her feel worse, it was this.

'OK,' she said, feeling like a hideous fraud.

'When are you coming up?'

Maggie thought about it. It was half term next week – which Stan knew, of course – but she'd been planning on staying behind to catch up on work. Now, though, that seemed like the coward's way out.

'Actually, this weekend,' she said on impulse. 'Definitely.

If I catch the train Friday afternoon I'd be home by eight or so.'

'Do you mean it? That would be brilliant.'

Before the phone call, Maggie had been wondering whether she could, should, tell him. Suddenly she knew she couldn't. All she wanted to do was to be back, safe, in Scotland, where nobody thought she was sluttish, or careless, or borderline negligent. Just to be home.

'I'll check out timetables,' she said.

'Good,' said Stan, sounding extremely relieved. 'Yeah, that'll be great. We'll go to the pub, right? Just kick about, have a laugh. Not get anyone's knickers in a twist about the W word. Look, I won't even say it, OK?'

'Yeah,' said Maggie. 'We'll go to the pub.'

They hung up the phone. And then she really did cry.

'What on *earth* did you think you were doing?' Matron had asked the girls sternly, issuing them with rough clean towels and doling out large spoonfuls of medicine that tasted so unpleasant Fliss wondered if she actually boiled it up herself.

'When the weather comes on you, head for the nearest building. You' – she indicated Simone, who the previous year had got herself very lost on the moors – 'of all people should know that.'

'Sorry, Matron,' they had murmured. How could they say that the attractions of talking to a clutch of male pupils had far outweighed the possibilities of contracting bronchial pneumonia? Miss Gifford had put forward the idea of continuing the treasure hunt today, but had been shouted down by a team of teachers anxious to get their lesson plans back on track. So back to class it was for everyone, and it looked like Miss Starling might get her wish after all.

*

Maggie was desperately hoping her red eyes didn't show. She was also going to have to have a word with the girls who'd run into the woods yesterday, but would leave it for later.

'We're going to look at Rupert Brooke,' she announced to the girls as they looked up at her expectantly.

Fliss gazed at the picture inset in her book. He looked so dreamy and romantic. He looked a bit like Will, if she closed her eyes and squinted hard. She imagined herself in a long dress, something probably a bit like Keira Knightley would wear, waving off Will to war on a steam train. He would clutch her to him and say something like . . . she glanced at the book, '*Oh, never a doubt but, somewhere, I shall wake, And give what's left of love again*.' Then he would go far away to France and probably die, and it would be a terrible tragedy, but she would love him all her life long . . . She was adrift in a happy reverie when she heard her name called, and by the sounds of it, not for the first time.

'Felicity *Prosser*! Thank you for coming back to us.'

Miss Adair sounded exasperated. That rarely ended well.

'Yes, miss?'

'I need to see you after class – all of your team, in fact – so we can have a word about appropriate measures for rain shelter.'

The rest of the class giggled. Fliss didn't care.

'Is that, like, *against the rules*?' Zelda asked. 'Sahry, did I miss something? It's just, in America we don't, like, punish people without telling them what they can and can't do.'

Maggie raised her eyebrows at that.

'No, you're not being punished,' she said, suddenly feeling very tired. 'It's just some things are and aren't appropriate behaviour on field trips, and we should go over what those are.'

It wasn't even possible, she reflected, that any of her girls could have behaved worse than she had.

Simone grabbed two pears from the fruit bowl in the canteen.

'That's not your lunch,' said Fliss.

Simone raised her eyebrows. 'It is. Zelda says I need to eat something light every ninety minutes.'

Their lecture hadn't been too bad in the end. Miss Adair didn't even seem that bothered, she was miles away and just going through the motions of giving them a row. If it had been Miss Starling they'd have been in deep doodoo for months.

'Oh, *Zelda*,' said Fliss crossly. 'Everything *she* says is just *wunnerful*, isn't it?'

'What's that?' said Zelda, emerging from the lunch queue with two pears on her plate. That was the thing about Zelda, she never took offence.

'Nothing,' said Fliss. Alice was following up behind. She had three pears. Fliss looked down at her macaroni cheese.

'Come on, Simone,' she said, turning round. But Simone had gone.

'What's up with you?' said Alice, watching Fliss push her macaroni around with her fork.

'Nothing,' said Fliss. 'It's just, I was kind of looking forward to coming back here this year. But now I'm back and it just seems a bit rubbish.'

Alice raised her eyebrows. 'It's school,' she said. 'This is what it's meant to be like. That's why they call it, you know, "school" and not, "having a really good time".'

'Yeah, I've sure known worse,' commented Zelda, taking

a bite of her pear. 'Well maybe not, like, *much* worse. When do they switch the heating on in this place?'

'November,' said Fliss. 'Dr Deveral says it's bad for our skin.'

'Jeez. I take back that statement. This is, like, the worst place ever.'

Alice looked smug.

'What?' said Fliss. 'What are you looking smug about?'

'Oh, I don't know,' said Alice. 'It's not like I have any secret gossip that could cause a HUGE scandal.'

Both the girls turned round straightaway.

'What is it?'

'I can't tell,' said Alice, delighting in her power. 'No way.'

'Please let it be about Hattie,' said Fliss.

'I can't possibly say,' said Alice. 'But life at school might be about to get a *lot* more interesting.'

'Tell us! Tell us!'

But Alice just looked smug and refused to say a word.

She couldn't help it. She had to know. Carefully, Simone retraced her steps to the little copse where they'd found the second red box, just before the skies opened. It was still there! Carefully she keyed in the three-digit code she'd derived from subtracting the ages of the two schools. The box popped open. Inside was a small piece of rolled-up paper.

'Take the number of letters in the capital of Iran, multiply by the height in metres of Everest (to the nearest 10,000) and subtract from $\bar{L}$ to get the first line of the grid reference . . .'

At one stage it looked like it might rain again, but in the end it didn't and Simone, with one eye on her watch, doggedly marched through the clues in her lunch hour. By ten to two she was homing in, she was sure of it, with the grid reference definitely sending her towards the lighthouse, at the far end of the cliffs. Short on time she ran there, remembering Zelda's imprecations to incorporate exercise into her daily life. Puffing slightly, she ran up towards the steps and looked around, wondering what to do. Presumably these days all lighthouses were computerised, so there wouldn't be anybody—

Just as she was thinking this, the door at the bottom of the lighthouse opened and a bearded man stepped out. He shielded his eyes.

'Are you from the school? I thought we were going to see you chaps yesterday.'

Simone couldn't quite get her breath back, but tried to explain.

'We were . . . the weather . . .'

The man looked confused.

'You let a bit of weather scare you off? I don't know what schools are coming to. Is it just you?'

Simone nodded. Suddenly, however, she heard someone panting behind her. She turned round. Making hard work of getting up the hill towards the outpost was the chubby boy from yesterday. When he saw that it was her, she saw his face drop with disappointment. Not for the first time, she thought ruefully. She did seem to have that effect on boys.

'Why are you here?' he said accusingly, as soon as he could. 'The treasure hunt was called off.'

Simone shrugged. 'I wanted to see where it went. Why are you here?'

The boy shrugged back. 'How can you have got here so fast? It's impossible. Did your teacher help you out with the clues?'

Simone was stung. 'You think it's impossible that a girl might beat you to the clues?'

'I would say it's unlikely,' said the boy.

The lighthouse keeper sighed. 'Uhm, could you two have this conversation another time? I have a Panamax coming up from Finisterre, and I'd like to keep an eye on it.'

Simone and the strange boy immediately lapsed into silence when the adult started talking.

'All right,' he said. 'I have this box here for the team winners, which I suppose must be you two.'

'We're not really on the same team,' said the boy.

'Well, the girl was here first then.'

'It's all right,' said Simone. 'I'm sure we can share it.'

The lighthouse keeper brought out a box and bade them farewell. Although it was well past lunch hour now and they were some distance from school, Simone didn't give in to her customary panic, but instead sat down on the damp grass to open the box. The boy stood hovering around her, giving off irritated vibes.

'What's your name anyway?' she asked.

The boy shrugged. 'Ash.'

He was so rude!

'I'm Simone.'

'Fine. Are you going to open the box?'

Simone did. Inside was a beautiful gold-coloured sextant with *Dorm winner, 2009 Geography Hunt* inscribed on it.

'It's beautiful!' she said, genuinely taken aback.

Ash gave it a look. 'How are we going to share that then?'

'I don't know,' said Simone. She glanced at her watch. 'I have to get back. It's Geography now, weirdly enough.'

Ash was still looking at the sextant. Simone was exasperated.

'Look, do you want it? Do you want me to tell everyone you got here first and you won the treasure hunt?'

For a second Simone thought that was exactly what he

wanted her to tell everyone. But he looked at it for a long time, sighed, then said, 'No. You won it. You take it.'

'Thank you,' Simone said. Then, 'I'm sorry we couldn't share it. Want to borrow it sometime?'

'No, thank you,' he said. 'But I do have the new Garth Nix book.'

Simone's eyes lit up. 'Can I borrow that?'

'If you like,' said Ash. 'See you around.'

And he started off back towards his own school, his face flushed and his hair damp with the exertion. What an odd chap, thought Simone, holding her prize close to her chest.

'Simone Kardashian, is that you?'

Miss Gifford couldn't believe Simone would be late of her own accord, she could hardly say boo to a goose. 'I'm going to have to tell Miss Adair about this.'

'Sorry, miss,' said Simone. What had seemed to her a great adventure last night when she thought of it suddenly seemed terrifying – she was going to get reported! After sheltering with the boys too! Simone never got into trouble, and now she was frantically worried. Would it affect her scholarship? Would she get sent down, or worse? Her hands started to shake.

'Were you off school property in school hours? Are you aware this is not allowed for Year Two pupils?'

Simone could feel a lump start in her throat.

'Um, yes, Miss Gifford.'

The rest of the class – which included the Tudor girls, as this was a mixed session – watched in delighted horror. Simone never ever got into trouble. What on earth could she have been doing? Simone felt her heart quicken. Could she ever manage to speak up for herself? Stand up and talk? She imagined Alice in this situation, or Zelda. They'd just say what was on their minds and be done with it, they wouldn't stand here like big scarlet puddings, struck dumb just because a teacher asked them a perfectly reasonable question.

'Um,' she said again. Then she brought out of her rucksack the golden-coloured sextant. Miss Gifford gasped aloud.

'Where did you get that?'

Simone brought out the pieces of paper. 'I went out at lunchtime to follow the clues ... I wanted to finish the hunt ...'

Miss Gifford took them off her. 'And you did this all by yourself?'

Simone looked modest. 'Well, I'm really sorry, it made me late ...'

Miss Gifford didn't know what to do. On the one hand, lateness and heading off school property was completely unacceptable. On the other, her heart burst with pride that a pupil was so keen to finish her Geography treasure hunt that they would actually break school rules to do it.

She tried to keep her voice neutral, however.

'Very well,' she said. 'I'll have to inform your class mistress. And I would like you to take a detention. But we'll say no more about it, at least you were in the services of Geography.'

Simone stood, unsure of what to do.

'You may sit.'

'But ... what about the sextant?'

Miss Gifford eyed it up. 'Well, I suppose it belongs to the Plantagenet dorms now.'

A great cheer went up from half the class, whilst the Tudor girls looked sulky and muttered things about cheating and not giving everyone a fair chance. Simone's face was still red, but now for a different reason.

'All right everyone, settle down,' said Miss Gifford. 'Back to erosion, please.'

'Well done,' said Alice as Simone sat down. 'Your first detention!'

Simone grimaced. She'd never had a detention in her life before, and had absolutely no desire to start. It would go on her record and everything. Her chest tightened. It wouldn't stop her from going to university, would it? Or get her scholarship into trouble? She'd hardly even worried about the discipline side of things, so sure was she that she'd never do anything to get herself into hot water. And now, here she was, being late for class and roaming out of bounds. Meekly she bent her head to her work, her mind a whirl of confusion.

Miss Starling could hardly control her glee in being proved right, as she led the detention class. Along with a couple of known troublemakers from York House there was Astrid Ulverton, one of the most talented musicians in the school, who was there for forgetting to finish her History prep for three days in a row. Her protestations that she was deep into a new Carl Nielsen concerto had cut no ice with Miss Kellen, the sombre History teacher whose low, slow voice, full of import, was known to have a deadly effect on her students on sunny days just after a heavy lunch.

But Simone Kardashian was definitely the prize.

'Out of school grounds?' she'd said. 'Surely after last year you'd have learned your lesson?' It didn't get much worse than getting told off by Miss Starling. Still, thought Simone, to comfort herself, at least she would have to skip dinner. That would fit in with Zelda's regime.

*

Maggie sleepwalked through the rest of the week leading up to half term. As the girls sighed over Erich Maria Remarque and Siegfried Sassoon, Maggie arranged for a Wednesday evening double showing of *Regeneration* and *Gallipoli* in the film lounge, which sent all four houses into mass hysterics and earned her a stern ticking-off from June Starling about age-appropriate media. All of it just washed over her. She was counting down the hours until Friday, when she could fly home. Would she crumble at the sight of Stan? Would he see it written all over her face? Adulteress? Would he even believe it? He'd shown little but contempt for the gangling, weirdy intellectual ponce from across the crags.

Of course she definitely didn't want David to phone. Definitely not. Which was just as well, because of course he hadn't.

She'd gone through a thousand times in her head what she might say, but every time she looked for a way of explaining it that didn't make her look too bad or reprehensible, she had to see it again for what it was: her cheating on Stan. Throwing herself at a man she fancied. With whom she had a professional relationship. Ten months before her wedding day. Every time she thought of it, she wanted to cry again.

Nope, not an email, not a text message – not, she suspected, that David knew how to text message. He wasn't a text message kind of person. More of a handwritten letter type of person. She hadn't had any of those either, apart from a badly scrawled card from her nephew Dylan, imploring her to COM HOM SOON!!!

'What ees wrong with you?' Claire asked her on Thursday. 'Are you coming out tomorrow night? Miranda and I thought we go into Truro and see if anyone anywhere has heard of what a cocktail might be.'

Maggie tried to smile, but even though the girls were becoming good friends, the idea of seeing Miranda suddenly filled her with dread and self-loathing.

'No, I can't,' she said, grateful to be getting out of it. 'I'm going to Scotland.'

'Ah, a deerty weekend with Stan, *non*? Super!'

'Something like that,' said Maggie.

'You mees him so much . . . ah have noticed you have seem a leetle down, a leetle sad since you come back here.' She looked around. 'I'm not surprised. It like prison.'

'If you hate it so much, Claire, you don't really have to work here,' Maggie surprised herself by saying. 'Go teach French to businessmen in London or something, you'd have scads more fun.'

'What, and leave these girls to your English ways! *Non, non, non*, I could not abandon them.'

Maggie knew Claire was only half joking.

'And, I am a very good teacher.'

That was certainly true. Mam'selle Crozier was feared for her impetuous rages and imaginative scoldings, but admired as glamorous and as having the ability to drag some kind of accent out of the dullest-spoken of girls.

Her words sobered Maggie up a little. If Claire of all people could understand why she was in teaching, and what for, surely Maggie should be able to focus more on what was truly important: her pupils. Mooning around after someone she couldn't have was ridiculous, as was letting impression-able teenage girls cry themselves sick over Mel Gibson in a World War One uniform. She was going to have to focus. Pull herself together. Stay in the real world.

'Thanks, Claire,' said Maggie.

'What for? I do not buy you a cocktail, *non*.'

'No, but you're a tonic,' said Maggie.

'*Bof*, your Breetish humour. Eet is not funny you know. *Monty Python* ees not funny, Ricky Gervais he is not funny, Peter Kay ees not funny.'

'No, he's not funny,' admitted Maggie, 'but—'

'I shall never understand. Never!' said Claire, and she stomped off, rifling in her Hermès bag for her Gitanes.

Chapter Five

Come Friday, half the school disappeared with glee. Many of the girls, however, stayed at Downey House over the half term: those with parents abroad, or who couldn't take time off. Simone was staying, although her parents had insisted on driving down one day to see her. She was planning on writing the best Geography paper Miss Gifford had ever seen. Alice was staying too, and was planning on lying in bed as late in the mornings as was humanly possible.

Maggie's good intentions to devote herself steadfastly to teaching lasted about as far as Bristol. She had set out to get organised and plan for the spring term but, gazing out on the dirty, cold November day, with evening already closing in fast and the train packed and noisy, instead of reading D.H. Lawrence she found herself turning to an old favourite: W.H. Auden.

> 'This is the Night Mail crossing the border,
> Bringing the cheque and the postal order,
> Letters for the rich, letters for the poor,
> The shop at the corner and the girl next door.
> Pulling up Beattock, a steady climb:
> The gradient's against her, but she's on time.'

As always, she found the rhythm of the piece comforting and relaxing. Trying not to knock over the three cans of lager the man in the next seat had lined up on his table, or get too distracted by the incredibly noisy hissing and thumping of the man in front's headphones, she let her eyes close briefly.

'Past cotton-grass and moorland boulder
Shovelling white steam over her shoulder,
Snorting noisily as she passes
Silent miles of wind-bent grasses.'

Before she knew it, Maggie was asleep.

David screwed up his face. He couldn't believe he was doing this, but he was no good on the phone and email was such a horrible method of communication. But he should do the right thing, nip it in the bud properly. It was the gentlemanly way to behave after their . . . slip up; not just running away or fumbling apologies. David prided himself on trying to do the right thing, but this had left him totally flustered, in a way he could never remember feeling before. This would have to be face to face. Just to sort things out, get everything straight in his head. It was only fair.

He suppressed the thought that really it was because he was desperate to see Maggie again. That wasn't the case. He was just doing the right thing, he told himself sternly, as he strode across the hills. God it was a bleak night. He knew she often went to the pub with Claire on a Friday night, so he'd check in there first.

The little village was quiet out of season, whilst it bustled all through the summer with people exploring the beautiful northern coves, yellow beaches and big waves famed in the region. With the night drawn in – Stephen Daedalus was staying very close to his master – the Smugglers' Hole looked cosy and inviting, its old-fashioned lanterns casting a warm pool of light across the little cobbled street, and convivial chatter spilling from inside. David brushed the rain from his mackintosh, braced himself and pushed open the door.

Maggie woke with a start to find the train pulling into Central Station. She hadn't realised just how tired she was, but a week full of sleepless nights and a full teaching schedule had left her drained. There weren't even that many people left in the carriage, just a lingering smell of ketchup and crisps and wet wool and old magazines. She blinked and stretched, taking a long drink of water and marvelling at how dark it was outside.

She felt a hand of fear grip her. She must remember: she did *not* kiss anyone. She was *not* unfaithful. Nothing happened. Nothing worth talking about. It was a moment of madness and she didn't need to poison Stan's mind by telling him about it. He had that slip up himself last year, she reminded herself. Once, after they'd had a fight, she hadn't been able to get hold of him all night and he'd told her later he'd had to fend off a girl. He'd said it hadn't gone anywhere. She thought it had. People do slip up occasionally. But if they truly love each other, it doesn't matter.

She lifted her bag down from the overhead compartment, feeling stiff and a bit spacey. The familiar rough Glaswegian tones welcomed her to Central Station and reminded her to collect all her bags and belongings. She picked up her *Norton Anthology of Poetry* and pen, reflecting sadly on how little work she'd actually managed to complete and, bracing herself, pressed the button to open the door.

*

'Hey,' said Stan. There was no running into one another's arms, of course. They had been together far too long to be doing that. It was for new lovers, thought Maggie. She shouldn't be sad or cross about it. It just showed how secure and comfortable they were, that was all. They didn't have to make public displays.

'How's it going?' he asked, after a clumsy kiss. The air of their last few conversations – stilted, at cross-purposes – still hung in the air.

'Fine,' said Maggie, wondering if he could read the guilt seared all over her face. She pressed it into his coat. 'Fine. Bit tired. Slept most of the way.'

'It'll be all of those nine to four days,' said Stan. Maggie waited for him to pick up her bag, but he didn't.

'Want to go and get a pint then?'

'I'm really hungry,' said Maggie.

'Well, they'll probably have a pie. Or we could get some chips on the way.'

'Let's do that,' agreed Maggie, incredibly relieved that he hadn't seemed to notice any difference in her. But did that mean she was always evasive and a bit grumpy? 'Yup. Great.'

'Are you sure? Was I supposed to have booked us like a posh dinner or that?' Stan looked a little sheepish.

'Why?' she said. 'Do you think I've picked up all these poncey southern ways?'

'Well you have, love,' he said. 'It's just a fact, isn't it?' He looked at her as she hauled her own bag towards the car park.

'I haven't changed,' insisted Maggie.

Stan looked at her, a little sadly. 'You can't even hear it, can you? You even sound different.'

'Well, sometimes I have to speak more slowly so the girls can understand me.'

'Throw the r away,' said Stan, with a touch of bitterness in his voice.

'No,' said Maggie. 'It's stupid, really, Stan. You can't just hate the English all the time. They don't hate you.'

'No, they just think they're better than me.'

Maggie stretched in the car. 'Stan. Can we not . . . I mean, I've come all this way and . . . could we not—'

'Of course,' said Stan. 'Sorry. Come here, darling.'

And as his lips touched hers she briefly, instinctively, drew back before she remembered where she belonged.

David could see Claire tucked into the corner of the snug talking to someone. OK. She was here then. His heart pounding, he approached to ask them what they wanted to drink.

'Hello, David!' said Miranda, holding up an enormous glass of wine next to a nearly empty bottle. 'Why haven't you been returning my calls then?'

David flinched. Why was she calling him? Had Maggie told her? He hadn't realised they were such great friends now. Claire's face was giving nothing away.

Miranda paused for a second, then smiled. 'Are you getting the drinks in or what?'

She couldn't know. She couldn't. David felt a huge wave of relief. Guilt, and relief.

'Of course,' he said. 'White wine?'

Miranda nodded immediately, even though her glass of wine was only half empty. Claire shook her head.

'No more for me, thank you. It is strange, but I have never taken to thees British idea you have of being very sick in doorways.'

'Suit yourself,' said Miranda, as David headed for the bar. When he returned with a fresh bottle and two glasses, she patted the seat next to her. 'Come on, sweetie. Tell us what boring poetry you've been terrorising the fourth-form with today.'

'Where's the other member of your coven?' said David, faux jokily.

'Maggie has gone to Scotland,' said Claire.

Of course. That hadn't occurred to David; that she would just go. To be with her future husband.

Miranda, swigging quickly from her glass, saw an opportunity.

'Yes, she's gone up to do wedding stuff, I think. Wedding, wedding wedding, it's all she's ever on about! I think the name for it is, what, Bridezilla?'

Claire looked a trifle confused, but Miranda was undeterred. If she wanted to get David back, she reckoned this was her best shot – show him that she wasn't like other women.

'I was never like that, was I?' She put her hand over his.

He registered its familiar softness, the beautifully tended nails.

'I do think it's a shame when women are happy to trade their independence for a man,' said Miranda.

David raised his eyebrows. 'I always thought women were meant to be allowed to do whatever they damn pleased.'

'Oh well, of course they are,' said Miranda, filling his glass. 'It's just, you know, a bit sad to get so excited about an outmoded institution. What's he like anyway? Maggie hasn't said much about him.'

'I thought you said she was talking about him non-stop?'

'Uh, yeah, about the wedding . . . The groom could be Ken Barbie for all she mentioned him!' laughed Miranda.

'He ees nice,' said Claire, loyally. 'He has red hair and loves football.'

'Scottish, then,' said Miranda.

'He is nice,' said David, drinking faster than he normally would, angry with himself. He might as well admit it. It was a stupid, dangerous game he'd got involved in, and he'd lost. Served him right.

'"Nice" is always what people say when they mean, "has no distinguishing characteristics whatsoever",' grumbled Miranda. 'At best it means hopelessly average; and at worst it means you hate him and want him killed.'

'It means personable and well-mannered,' said David. 'Which at the moment is more than can be said for you.'

Miranda tossed her long golden hair towards him and gave him a teasing smile.

'Oh, come on,' she said. 'I'm just being honest. You love it really, don't you?'

'I must go,' said Claire.

'Oh, no, Claire, we haven't finished the wine,' complained Miranda.

'Ah theenk you two should stay and feenish it.'

Miranda rolled her eyes as the French mistress stood up and left. 'Subtle, isn't she?'

'Is that better or worse than nice?' said David.

Miranda eyed him thoughtfully. 'You look tired. Have you been missing your Miranda?'

David looked at her pretty face, her enthusiastic smile. He thought of their shared history.

'*Do you remember an inn, Miranda?*' he said.

'Stop! I may be pissed, but I am absolutely not pissed enough for your endless bloody stupid poetry. Just answer the question.'

'OK. Fine. Sure.'

In fact, they ended up having a good night in the pub. Well, Stan did. Of course all his mates were there and pleased to see Maggie, and she did her best to get on with their girl-friends, some of whom seemed alarmingly young. They all worked around Glasgow, and talked about the cool bars they'd been to and the bands they'd seen. It made Maggie feel like a country bumpkin suddenly; she couldn't even remember the last time she'd seen a movie. Most of her evenings were spent quietly with Claire in their joint study, reading and listening to music, or curled up in her sitting room – Claire couldn't bear British telly, so she did that alone. With her long walks along the headland and quiet weekends it could feel like a lonely existence, but it didn't, of course. The presence of three hundred girls easily put a stop to that.

But listening to these girls with their sunbed tans, poker-straight hair and pale pink lipstick talk about the new collections at Cruise or the latest underground nightclub made her feel as if she were getting old before her time. She didn't have much to add that wouldn't make her sound stuck up and pretentious, and nobody seemed terribly inter-ested in asking her about school – and why should they? They weren't long out of school themselves. Probably hated all teachers. They probably thought she was the squarest person there. Maggie sighed and felt sorry for herself and decided she needed to drink some more. And change out of this ridiculous skirt, she was the only person there not in jeans.

'Come on then, mopey. It's a big day!'

Anne had taken a Saturday off from the salon to help Maggie look at wedding dresses, so she wasn't about to let a bit of mumping spoil her day. Maggie had wanted a lie-in – she'd drunk too much last night, they'd moved on to some lurid turquoise shot glass thing and it had made her feel absolutely dreadful. But she'd finally had fun though; ended up trading jeans with Jimmy Mac's girlfriend, what was she called again? Anyway, it had been highly funny, someone had got stuck in a toilet and they'd all burst out at the same time, hysterical. Stan had been delighted with her, kept snogging her behind the snooker table like they were teenagers again, and she hadn't minded a bit – in fact, was delighted to be snogging her fiancé in public, showing everyone how much in love they were, even though they were old fuddie duddies getting married and she was a teacher.

They'd gone back and had drunken fumbly sex just in time before they passed out. Now Maggie was reaping the consequences of having severely cut down on her alcohol intake whilst at work. Her tolerance was minimal, her hangover severe.

'This house smells like a brewery,' said Anne, who, despite the ongoing chaos of Cody and Dylan, managed to keep her little council flat neat as a pin. Whilst Stan had clearly made a cursory attempt at cleaning up, Maggie could see that this meant simply pushing everything under the bed and spraying air freshener about. Given that his mum was back to doing his washing, this wasn't very impressive.

'I know,' said Maggie. 'Well, we were celebrating, of course.'

'Yes, it looks great fun,' said Anne sceptically. 'Come on, get dressed. I don't want to think what Stan thinks passes for coffee in here, let's go out.'

'He's still sleeping anyway,' said Maggie. 'Best not disturb him.'

There was a grunt and a farting noise from the bedroom.

'Ah, married life,' said Anne. 'Bring your make-up bag.'

'Why?'

'Because if you try on wedding dresses looking like that you'll get so depressed you'll probably want to call the whole thing off.'

Maggie groaned.

'Don't cry,' Anne was saying. 'You look beautiful.'

'Many girls cry when they come here,' said the very well-spoken and turned-out lady who ran the wedding dress shop. Or boutique, as she insisted on calling it.

'Yes, but from happiness,' said Anne, in a warning tone.

'I look like two melons in a hammock,' wailed Maggie from behind the curtain.

Anne stalked in. 'You do not.'

Maggie snivelled in response.

'Strapless is very in this year,' said the assistant.

Maggie came out and the assistant made her stand on a chair.

'There. It's beautiful. You look beautiful,' she said robotically.

Maggie took a deep breath and stared at herself in the carefully lit mirrors. The dress was strapless, covered in pink roses on the bodice, and became a large, white skirt with more roses following down the train. It had looked rather romantic on the hanger. Now . . . how could she possibly say "This is hideous"?'

'I don't think strapless is the way to go for me,' she said. Although she wasn't fat, she could see little dimples of flesh bunch over the corseted top of the dress. This was a dress for the bird-boned.

'I don't want to spent the whole day holding out my arms so I don't look like I have bingo wings.'

'Strapless is very popular,' said the lady again. Maggie ignored her.

'Plus, everyone wears them. Then you get the photos back and all the head shots make the bride look totally naked.'

'Well, that's true,' agreed Anne.

'And that's . . . it's just an awful lot of my back on display, don't you think? It's like about a square metre of . . . *skin*.' Maggie peered dubiously behind herself.

'We have lots of others you can try on,' said the woman, looking like Maggie had personally insulted her.

'OK. Do you have something with, uh, sleeves?'

The woman looked momentarily non-plussed. 'Perhaps in our plus-sized section.'

'Oh, let's not start with that, shall we?'

They collapsed at a table in Princes Square, the posh shopping centre. Neither of them spoke for a moment or two, until Anne ordered two large glasses of white wine. When they arrived, she leant forwards.

'OK. What's up?'

Maggie shrugged. 'Nothing.' She took a deep gulp of her wine. Hair of the dog, that might do it.

'We're going shopping for your *wedding dress*. Your *wedding dress*, Maggie. But you look like I'm dragging you to the vets to get neutered.'

'What?'

'Oh, I had to do it to the cat . . . she looked just like you do now.'

Maggie stuck out her bottom lip. 'I'm just tired, that's all.'

'That's not all,' said Anne. 'Don't play the numpty noo with me.'

Maggie took a deep breath. She was tempted to come clean, it would be such a relief to confess everything, get it off her chest, try and make sense of her feelings.

Then she remembered Anne's heartbreak when she found

out her boyfriend, Dylan and Cody's dad, was cheating on her with that slut who worked down the karaoke bar. Her devastation and misery that someone could do that to her. She thought of the endless battles over money; about Cody and Dylan growing up without a father. She thought also about how much Stan was part of the family – he was still going to her mum and dad's for Sunday lunch, he was practically more of a part of the family than she was.

And it was only a kiss, she told herself stubbornly. Just a stupid little kiss like anyone might do in a drunken piece of nonsense. Of course, she hadn't been drunk. But still, the same thing applied.

'Oh, I don't know,' she said finally. 'I'm just feeling a bit stressed with school and everything. The wedding is like the last thing on my mind.'

'I thought you'd be thrilled,' said Anne. 'Everyone else is. Do you not think it's fancy enough for you?'

'That's bullshit,' said Maggie crossly. This was the second time she'd been accused of becoming a snob about it. 'I don't want to hear it.'

'OK,' said Anne. She glanced at the menu. 'I'm going to have the carbonara.'

Maggie sighed. 'I suppose I'll be on the green salads till the wedding.'

'Well, that is a joyful way to think about it.'

'Hmm,' said Maggie.

'Anyway,' said Anne. 'There's something I want to talk to you about. *Real* problems.'

Maggie raised her eyebrows. 'Oh yes, sorry for bothering you with my being exhausted.'

'Well, if that's all it is you shouldn't have done WKD shots till four in the morning, should you?'

'No,' conceded Maggie. 'What is it?'

'It's the school. It's really gone downhill lately. A kid brought a knife into Dylan's class, Maggie.'

Maggie managed not to ask whether or not it had been Dylan. She loved her nephews, but they could be hard work.

'The whole area ... The teachers can't cope, Maggie, they're just getting completely overrun.'

'That's awful, Anne. Can't you take them out and send them somewhere else?'

'The other schools are just the same. And I'm hardly going to send them private, am I? I'm hardly like the mums from your school. Am I?'

Maggie didn't know how to respond to that.

'No,' she said.

'Anyway, you know I've heard they're looking out for new teachers?'

'I'm not a primary school teacher, though, Anne.'

'No, they're looking for a teacher to handle the senior school, too. Look, I cut it out for you.'

Maggie took the ad Anne proffered.

SCHOOL LIAISON OFFICER
Teacher with administrative experience required to liaise between Holy Cross secondary school and the feeder schools of the district in order to facilitate better links between intake expectations and ongoing achievements . . .

'I mean, do you think that's something that could help?'

Through the horrible management-speak, Maggie figured it out. It meant the school was looking for someone to go around collecting the new little shits and trying to stop them being such little shits. It was a completely thankless job that they were looking for some underpaid skivvy to do, and she couldn't think of anything worse.

Anne looked at her hopefully. 'I just thought, someone like you, keeping an eye on the primary schools, sorting them out. I mean, it would be great for the boys – for everyone, really – and you'll be looking for a job up here anyway, and I just thought this would be perfect.'

Maggie didn't know what to say. She would have to come home one day, that much was clear. She didn't think she was going to get Stan down to England without actually knocking him unconscious, and who'd ever heard of two married people living in different countries? That was completely impossible. She'd need to start looking for something at some point.

'Mm,' she said. 'Well, I'm kind of committed to this school year . . .'

'I know it doesn't work like that,' said Anne impatiently. 'Dylan's had three teachers already this year.'

Maggie winced. That really was bad. She hated to think of the boys falling behind.

'OK, well, give it to me and let me think about it, all right?' She finished off the rest of her wine. 'I'll see what . . .'

She let her voice trail off, unable to commit too much.

'Great!' said Anne. 'I'll tell Mum, she'll be so delighted.'

'Don't!' said Maggie. 'Even if I do apply, it's not certain I'll get it.'

Anne pshawed. 'Yeah, like there are a million applicants for these jobs. Dylan was on supply teachers for two months.'

Maggie knew this was true, but didn't want to think about it. There was no doubt that if she applied for the job, she'd probably get it. The interviewers would be very impressed by her time at Downey House, and it would work well with her background . . . And it was, potentially, an interesting job. One where she could make a difference to the hordes of scared, young first years who arrived at big school each year terrified and panicky, who then took refuge in gangs or misbehaviour to bolster up their self-worth. If she could tackle that before they even started . . . well, wouldn't that be worthwhile? Isn't this what she'd always told herself she'd do? So why did she feel so dismayed at the thought? Just how selfish was she?

David leant over the bed to pick up his watch. There, stretched out, her blonde hair fanning the pillow, was Miranda. Even in sleep she looked glamorous, untouchable. He sighed. Was he making a big mistake? Was she? Was this what they wanted?

Miranda stirred and her eyelids fluttered. 'Mm, good morning, handsome,' she murmured. 'You really are getting disgustingly skinny.'

'I've always been like this,' said David, slightly peeved.

'Exactly. You look like a teenager, but you're a grown man. It's not right.'

David rolled his eyes. 'So you want me to do what, exactly? Eat doughnuts for breakfast?'

'Ooh, breakfast,' said Miranda. 'I'm starved. Did you offer? Can I have a latte and could you chop me up some melon? *Please?*'

'I can't work your coffee machine, remember? You told me it was a wilful refusal to engage with the modern world.'

'Oh, I didn't mean it like that!' said Miranda. 'Just bring the pressure gauge up to . . . Oh, never mind, I'll make the coffee.'

'I'll chop the melon,' said David, obediently, following her into her hi-tech and barely used kitchen.

Chapter Six

Post-half term, everyone's attentions turned to the Christmas festivities, much to Simone's horror.

'I'm really very very hungry.' Simone was lying on her bed, groaning instead of doing her prep.

'Yes, you've mentioned that about five times,' said Alice. 'Go eat a big pie or something, nobody's forcing you.'

'No!' said Zelda. 'Stand up!'

Simone reluctantly did so. Fliss pretended to be ignoring everyone and working on her French homework.

Zelda pushed Simone in front of the large and unflattering mirror fixed above the sink in the corner of their dorm.

'Look!' said Zelda. Simone had instinctively cast her eyes downwards. Apart from checking she didn't have anything caught in her teeth, she normally avoided mirrors like the plague. Or rather, if she knew herself to be all alone (which at school was incredibly rare), she would ignore her body and try out her face from different angles, trying to find one where you couldn't see the double chin.

'Look at yourself! Jeez!' said Zelda in quite a scary tone of voice. Simone took a deep breath and stared herself straight in the eye.

'See?' said Zelda. 'You're looking better already. Look, all those spots on your chin are nearly gone.'

It was all Simone could do not to stick her hand up over her chin. Those spots were the bane of her life. However much she scrubbed at them, ignored them, squeezed them or covered them in stuff Fliss lent her, they never went away. They were like a small forest, there to stay.

But now, after a few weeks of eating less – a lot less – and doing as much exercise as she could fit in, they seemed to have . . . Had they . . . they had gone!

Simone gasped. And could it be? It could. Instead of having to contort her face into the normal position where she looked her best, she could see, definitely see, that her double chin had reduced; had almost disappeared. Her cheeks, too, had slimmed down.

Alice came over and stood behind her. 'You really have changed, chipmunk.'

Zelda grabbed Simone's trousers by the hips. 'Look at these! They're far too big for you. Look! Hip bones! You have hip bones!'

'And the dance is coming,' teased Alice.

The Christmas dance was the big social event of the year for the Middle School: a mixer with Downey Boys, with both traditional country dancing and a disco. First-formers were banned, and the Upper School had its own affair with, it was rumoured, *wine*. The girls had talked of little else since half term – who would wear what, who would ask who to dance. The entire year was in a fever of hormonal excitement and the formal dancing lessons were about to start. As PE teacher Janie James wryly observed, it was the only time in the year that sport captured everyone's attention.

Combined with the end of term and Christmas on the way, a vein of excitement ran through the Middle School seconds, and everyone, even Simone, was getting caught up in it.

Fliss had watched the preparations in dismay. Everyone else seemed so sure they were going to have a wonderful time. But she really, really needed to stand out. What could she do?

Simone grabbed the trousers back from Zelda. 'Don't be silly,' she said. But she was growing pink with pride.

'Anyone going to supper?' said Fliss.

'Not me!' said Simone.

'Me neither,' said Fliss. But she left the room anyway.

'What's got into her?' said Zelda, looking at Fliss's departing back.

Alice shrugged. 'Teenage hormones?'

Simone looked after her, torn. Part of her wanted to keep looking at herself in the mirror – maybe even try on some new clothes – and part of her wanted to run after her friend.

'I'm going to see her,' she said.

Alice raised her eyes and got up heavily. 'Well, if it is suppertime.'

'Fruit only!' ordered Zelda. 'No bread.'

Alice rolled her eyes. 'Hey, American,' she said, 'pipe down, OK?'

'I still think we should do our *High School Musical* workout,' said Zelda, unabashed.

'We've got formal dance tomorrow, don't you think that's enough?'

'I *hate* formal dance,' said Simone with feeling. 'We should be doing hockey.'

Alice looked at the rain lashing the windows. 'Inside is *definitely* better,' she said.

'Yeah, but it's just, like, a dance, isn't it?' said Zelda. 'Throwing shapes and shit?'

'Throwing shapes and shit,' mused Alice. 'Uh, not exactly. Does nobody read the syllabus?'

Simone didn't mention that Alice had two elder sisters at the school and a bit of a heads-up on the rest of them when it came to some of Downey House's more arcane rituals.

'So what is it?' said Zelda. 'Some Jane Austen shit?'

'A bit further north,' said Alice, as they left for the dorm.

Zelda tutted. 'Like I know about the geography of this place. Is this country even big enough to *have* geography?'

Miss Gifford happened to be walking ahead of them into the refectory and shot Zelda a very stern look, which Zelda completely missed. Simone instantly went pink, she still couldn't bear to be reminded of her detention.

Fliss was sitting alone at the corner of their usual table, pretending to be engrossed in a magazine and picking listlessly at a tangerine.

'Has she fallen out with us?' said Simone, wonderingly. She hoped it wasn't something she had done. Fliss had been in a mood with her for ages, she couldn't even cheer her up by doing impressions of Miss Adair being cross and Scottish, like she usually did. She didn't realise that Fliss was still jealous of Alice for getting Will's attention; and was now jealous of the attention even she, Simone, was getting for losing weight. Simone was so used to thinking of Fliss as glamorous, popular and blessed, it never even occurred to her that Fliss could feel that way.

Alice snorted. 'What have we done?'

Fliss felt herself colour under the scrutiny of the other girls. She knew they were talking about her. What could she say? What could she do? It sounded so awful; she couldn't shout at Simone and tell her to stop losing weight and getting pretty, it was hard enough that everyone else in the dorm was already prettier and more attractive, which was why Will liked Alice more than her. And they all seemed to find it so easy not to eat, but she found it really difficult. Well. She'd show them. She could eat less and exercise more than any of them. Surely if she was the slimmest and prettiest, Will would notice her after all, especially at the dance?

'What's up with you?' asked Alice. Fliss felt even more annoyed. Why was Alice always so bloody confident all the time? Nothing ever bothered her.

'Nothing,' she shrugged. 'You know. We're *slaves* to our hormones.'

Alice raised her eyebrows. 'Just in a shitty mood?'

Fliss didn't add, 'No thanks to you.' She just sat there, toying with her food.

'You know it's formal dancing tomorrow?' said Simone.

'What?' said Fliss.

'Preparing us for the Christmas ball.'

'You are joking?'

'Dunno,' said Simone. 'Alice knows all about it.'

'It's just stupid poncing about for the boys, isn't it?' said Alice loftily. 'So they can put formal dancing down on our forms like good little ladies.'

'I'm going to refuse to do it,' said Zelda. 'And if they make me, I'm going to sue them.'

But Fliss wasn't listening. Suddenly, her bad mood forgotten, she drifted into a reverie ... Of herself, slim and perfect in a white dress, with a blue sash to match her eyes, spinning gracefully round the dance floor as Will nudged his friends and asked who she was again, he'd hardly noticed her before, but now he could see her in an entirely different light.

'What kind of dancing?' she asked.

Alice rolled her eyes. 'Just like on *Strictly Come Dancing*,' she said. 'You get the costumes and everything.'

'Really?' said Simone. She adored *Strictly Come Dancing*.

She wondered if she'd be thin enough by Christmas to get into something sparkly, with sequins.

'No,' said Fliss. 'Alice is just winding you up.'

'And big feathers in your hair,' Alice went on. 'And a celebrity to dance with.'

'I wish it *was* like *Strictly Come Dancing*,' mused Simone. 'That would be great.'

It was, of course, nothing like *Strictly Come Dancing*. Janey James, the strict but generally fair sports mistress, lined them all up along the walls of the large gymnasium. It was clear she felt this was a total waste of sports time and really thought they should all be outside doing cross-country running.

Simone was particularly nervous. She remembered her first ever school disco. Not quite yet known for her swottiness, she was still fairly optimistic about secondary school. She wasn't the only heavy girl there, and there were lots of nice-looking boys, and she was doing well at Maths; people even spoke to her occasionally in class. Maybe big school wasn't going to be quite as awful as she'd been dreading after all. And her mother, of course, was keen for her to go to the dance; had even made her a special dress for the occasion. Simone remembered every stitch of it. It was red velvet with a white collar, material pulled far too tightly across her emergent bosoms. But it had a swirly skirt that moved when she did, and the colour suited her dark hair and skin. Her mother lent her a slick of lip gloss, and her father dropped her off at the unusually lit-up school with a kiss, telling her she looked beautiful.

That feeling had lasted for precisely five minutes. As she walked into the rec hall, which was covered in flashing disco lights and banners and playing Girls Aloud at high volume, she realised, to her horror, that not a single other girl there was wearing a dress. They were wearing super-tight jeans with little tops, or tracksuit trousers with lots of gold accessories, or miniskirts that slit right up to their bums, with G-strings hanging out over their backs. But not one was wearing a childish, homemade dress. Or anything like it. Everyone looked so *different* out of school uniform . . . Well, she'd had no idea, really. Everyone was looking at her. She could tell. Estelle Grant, the meanest girl in the school, walked slowly up to her. The year group watched to see what Estelle would do. Simone felt her heart pound painfully in her chest.

Estelle stood in front of her in her Kappa top, black string-vest and black miniskirt. She looked like one of the Pussycat Dolls. She certainly did not look like a schoolgirl.

'Nice threads,' she said to Simone. 'What are they, Prada?'

The trio of girls who followed Estelle around regularly all threw back their heads and howled with laughter. Simone tried to walk past her to see her friend Lydia, who was sitting by herself at the edge of the dance floor wearing the white blouse and black skirt she normally wore to waitress in her family restaurant. At least she faded into the background. But Estelle was blocking her way.

'Did nobody tell you you're allowed to wear your *own* clothes?' she said again. 'Not, like, something you stole off a doll?'

Out of the corner of her eye Simone could see Mr Graves, the Biology teacher, approaching the situation rapidly. Simone knew, of course, that letting a teacher deal with the situation would only make matters worse in the long term. She should really say something clever and witty back to Estelle, or even better, just whack her one. That would stop it. But the pounding of her heart and the lump in her throat made any kind of retaliation impossible. All she could do was stand there, feeling her face flush hotter and hotter.

'Everything all right here, girls?' said Mr Graves.

'Oh, yes, sir,' said Estelle. 'I was just telling Simone how nice she looks.'

'She looks less of a dangerous liability than you, that's for sure,' said Mr Graves. Estelle scowled and mouthed 'Paedo' out of his eyeline.

'Is that right, Simone?'

Simone could do nothing but nod. She and Lydia had spent the entire night sitting against the wall drinking fanta, as everyone else danced and laughed and had a fantastic time. Only once, when The Killers came on, their absolute favourite song ever ever ever, did they get up and move, unsteadily and clumsily, from foot to foot with each other in the darkest corner of the dance floor.

'How was it?' her father had asked anxiously. Simone would never know, but he'd kept his car parked outside the entire evening. Just in case.

Simone shrugged. 'It was OK.'

It broke her father's heart to see her unhappy. He loved her so much. What could he do?

'Want to go and get cheeseburgers and milkshakes at McDonalds, huh?'

Simone had looked up at him, sniffing a bit. 'Yes please, Daddy.' And he took her hand in his and gave it a big squeeze.

This is going to be different, Simone was thinking to herself. I am different now. It is different. It's like Zelda said, I am a positive person. I make my own destiny.

'Kardashian! Over there!' came Janie's penetrating voice. Simone glanced up. She was being herded to one side of the room with Zelda, big lanky Astrid Ulverton, poor Bessie from Tudor House, whose parents were always taking her out in the middle of term to send her to fat camp ... Simone's heart sank. She didn't even have to hear JJ say it.

'All right. This wall here. You're going to be the boys.'

'And hop and back and swap your partners to the left, and one two three, and *one* ...'

This was hard work. Especially when you were going to have to remember it all again in reverse, thought Simone dolefully. They were changing partners every turn and she had to remember to step twice up in the circle otherwise she held everyone else up. She was so intent on counting out her steps that she didn't notice Fliss taking her hands.

'Isn't this great?' said Fliss dreamily. She followed the steps perfectly, twirling daintily and spinning away. Simone watched her in awe.

'You're a really good dancer,' she said.

'I'm going to have to be,' said Fliss.

As dance class progressed, though, they did improve – particularly Felicity Prosser, Janie James noticed, who was obviously practising in her own time, though she was looking a little thin and drawn. She'd mention it to her form teacher, Maggie.

Really it was amazing that the girls memorised any of the steps at all. All their time seemed to be taken up with chattering about which boys would be there: Gabriel Marsh, the tall captain of the cricket team with the curly hair who looked like something out of *Hollyoaks*? Mohammed, the liquid-eyed minor prince from the Middle East? Will Hampton, who'd had his own band? And how much make up *could* they wear, please, miss?

*

'I just surely wouldn't want to see my girl going to a school that's biased and against my true ethics, that's all.'

Once upon a time, Maggie remembered, when she'd been teaching at Holy Cross, she'd given Fallon McBride a suspension. Her mother, a terrifying woman with huge tattoos all over the tops of her breasts, had marched up to the school, Fallon in tow, and threatened to give Maggie a 'doing' if she didn't scrap it. 'Ah cannae have her roon the hoose, she does mah head in' had been the reason.

Maggie had rather hoped to avoid this kind of confrontation at Downey House, so had been surprised when she'd answered her office extension to hear a molasses-slow southern voice, of a type she'd usually only heard in films, introduce himself as 'DuBose Towrnell, Zelda's pa', then proceed to ask why she'd been teaching such peacenik garbage in class.

Maggie had been too surprised that anything she'd been teaching Zelda had been making the faintest impression – as well as enjoying the sound of his voice – that she didn't know what to say.

'So you gotta see both sides, yeah? I just don't like all this propaganda.'

At first Maggie had been shocked. Then, on balance, she'd reflected on two things: first, even though she couldn't be further apart in her beliefs from an American soldier on the subject of war, perhaps it was right that the girls knew there were two sides to every story; second, and more importantly, perhaps this might be the thing to stop Zelda handing in the bare minimum of work and spending most of her days in class surreptitiously experimenting with lip gloss. Her excitement at this caused her to overlook the note from Janie James about checking Felicity Prosser; Felicity had always held a sullen air in her class and she hadn't noticed any change in that.

'All right, everyone,' she announced brightly. 'Today we're going to look at the war poets from another angle – from those who believed in and supported the war. Thanks to Zelda's father, by the way, who suggested it.'

Zelda dropped her head to her hands and let out a huge groan. 'Aw, *man*! I *told* him not to say anything!'

'Now, Zelda, I'm sure he was just trying to get involved.'

'Yeah, poke his nose in where it's not wanted – typical bloody US soldier.'

Some of the class nodded approvingly. Maggie sighed.

'Zelda! No more cheek, please! Turn to page ninety-five, you'll see it starts, *There's a breathless hush in the close tonight, Ten to make and the match to win . . .*'

Zelda let out a huge sigh. Maggie looked up.

'One more word out of you and you'll not be going to the Christmas dance.'

At this the whole class let out a groan of dismay. Maggie bit her lip. All she wanted to do was be a good teacher. Why did she keep ending up as the bad guy?

Simone had her hand up.

'Yes, Simone?'

'Uhm, sorry, but isn't this the poem about how only the upper classes know how to behave themselves in war by killing everyone?'

And I've even betrayed my own principles, thought Maggie, reading on: '*Play up! play up! and play the game . . .*'

Veronica hadn't even known why she'd taken the dune path down towards the beach. It had been such a sharp Sunday morning but the sun was in the sky and after another one of the reverend's particularly tiresome sermons, she'd felt the need to get away from everything for a bit; from the school, the other teachers, the day to day niggles of roll calls and applications.

She scrambled slightly down the slope, feeling a small pain in her ankle, but recovered quickly enough.

The winter beach was deserted in both directions. Even in summertime it was too out of the way and windswept to garner much in the way of tourists. The waves crashed grey and ominously on the shore, cold and relentless. Veronica pulled her scarf tighter around herself. The colour of the sea suited her mood.

As she walked along the shingle, keeping a brisk pace against the chill wind, gulls overhead calling shrilly, she realised that in fact she wasn't quite alone; there was a group of figures rushing around about a hundred metres away. They were too small to be school children, and as she grew closer she realised they were toddlers, bundled up in warm jackets and hats till they looked like fat penguins, wobbling up and down with buckets and spades. Veronica smiled to see them. Then, drawing closer, she froze. The children were with Daniel, and a woman with long blonde hair blowing in the breeze who could only be his wife.

They hadn't seen her, or hadn't realised it was her yet. There was still time to turn back. The little family – two boys and a girl, she knew – looked perfect, playing beautifully in the surf, a lovely little family unit . . . She felt her heart wrench. She knew families weren't perfect, she saw the results of that in some of the girls who passed through her doors every year. She knew marriage was difficult, had proven too hard for the majority of her own friends. That raising children meant sacrifice, and that her own life had been built on hard work and making the best of the difficult hand she had been dealt. It didn't stop, though, an almost primal yearning; a desire, a want in the very pit of her stomach. It was all she could do not to shout out loud. It was so unlike her, and she was frozen to the spot.

At that instant Daniel lifted his head from where he'd been attempting to unravel a kite for his eldest boy, and caught sight of her. She immediately clasped her hand to her mouth and backed away, as she saw his face squint in the weak sunlight. He'd recognised her.

Veronica felt like a stalker. Imagine if he thought she'd followed them here to stare at his children, or worse. She continued to back away, but he shook his head. Then he beckoned his wife over and spoke in her ear. His wife checked the children then looked at her husband. Daniel then beckoned Veronica.

Despite the cold, Veronica suddenly felt the heat in her face. What was he going to say? Was he going to order her to stay away from his family? He couldn't, could he? They'd decided to move to Cornwall, after all – that wasn't her fault, was it? Was it?

Slowly, tentatively, she moved towards the group. Daniel moved in her direction. She clasped her coat more tightly around herself.

Finally they were standing face to face. The woman with Daniel was quite exceptionally pretty, with a kind, open face and glorious streaming blonde hair, which the children appeared to have inherited.

'Susie,' said Daniel, gently, turning to his wife. 'Uhm, this is Veronica. My, uh, my birth mother.'

Susie smiled a warm, nervous smile and held out her hand. 'I've heard a lot about you,' she said.

Veronica's heart leapt. Had he spoken about her? Well, that was silly, of course he had. But of course Susie would already have a mother-in-law, and—

'Who's this, Mummy?' A small, freckle-faced boy of about five, with his mother's beautiful hair and his father's shrewd green eyes, raced up, followed by the other two.

Veronica knelt down in the sand. 'Hello,' she said. Frosty as she may appear to adults sometimes, she knew how to talk to children. 'My name is Veronica. I'm a friend of your daddy. What's your name?'

'Rufus,' said the boy. 'I like submarines.'

'Ooh, me too,' said Veronica. 'You know, I've been on one.'

The boy's eyes widened. 'Really?'

'Really,' she said. 'Maybe one day I'll tell you all about it.'

Daniel smiled at her as she got back up. 'He's obsessed.'

Veronica glanced out to sea. She thought she knew a bit about the reasons for that.

'I know it's a freezing day,' said Susie, 'but I just had to get them out of the house! You know what they're like when they're cooped up.'

Veronica smiled like she did know.

'They're lovely children,' she said. Their little girl – their baby – was sitting by the water's edge trying to eat sand. 'Is she all right to be eating so much sand?'

Susie smiled. 'Oh, they've all done it. Didn't kill the other two. I just pretend they're getting lots of roughage.'

Veronica felt her heart tug. She liked this woman. She liked this family. And she was so inextricably connected, but . . . She glanced out to sea. There was one thing she could do. That she owed Daniel.

'Would you like to come to tea one day soon?' she said. 'So we could talk?'

Daniel looked taken aback. He immediately glanced at his wife.

'Um . . .' said Susie.

'I'm sorry,' Veronica cut in at once. 'I didn't mean to spring that on you.'

'No, it's not that,' said Susie. Daniel seemed struck dumb.

'Well,' Veronica started to retreat, 'of course, you know where to find me.'

'We do,' said Susie, taking her husband's hand.

'Anyway, I must go,' said Veronica quickly. 'Goodbye, Rufus!'

Rufus turned from where he was struggling with the kite and gave her a cheery wave. 'I want you to take me on a submarine!'

'Rufus!' said his mum. 'Sorry.'

'Take me on a submarine PLEASE,' came the voice.

'My door is always open,' said Veronica, smiling sadly as she turned back to pick her way against the wind along the beach.

And then, three days later, he had rang. Just like that. Yes, he would like to come for tea. Yes, Tuesday at four would work well.

They were stilted on the telephone, but Veronica still felt a profound joy, mixed with extreme nervousness. She had the fire laid in the grate, and extra scones sent up from the ref. The winter chill had really set in now December was here, and the girls no longer walked the perimeter of the four towers to get to class, as they did in sunnier weather, but raced through the unheated corridors, cheeks pink. It cut down on a lot of tardiness, not heating the corridors. Veronica had thought Miss Starling was being a little cruel suggesting it, but it had turned out to work rather well.

Her office today, though, was warm and cosy, its well-chosen furniture and treasured works of art adding to the room a sense of calm. She looked around, trying to see it through his eyes. She didn't want to make it seem . . . well, too comfortable, almost. As if her life had been good without him.

*

It had not been an easy decision for Daniel to make. He had lain awake, talking to Susie, who longed to help him do the right thing but wasn't entirely sure what that was. In the end, it had come down to one thing: I have to know, Daniel had said. I don't know why, but I have to know all I can. She's my mother.

Susie, close to his adoptive mother, counselled caution. 'You just don't know her,' she'd insisted. 'And everything you have to do with her makes you unhappy. Plus, I don't like this whole thing about keeping you a secret. If it were me I'd want to shout it to the world. And I don't like the idea of you making Ida unhappy.'

'I know,' Daniel had said. 'I know all that, I do. But there's so much about myself I have to learn. And . . .' He'd been surprised to hear himself defending her. 'She's a good woman. She is. She's a legendary headteacher, all her pupils adore her.'

Susie had sniffed a bit at this.

'I mean, she does have her reasons for the secrecy thing.'

'Yes. Bad ones.'

Daniel was silent. Susie leant over in the bed and kissed him.

'Sweetheart. Do whatever you must, OK? But stop worrying about it so much.'

'You know, I think she'd love to meet the children properly.'

'One step at a time, OK?'

The night before their meeting Susie had drifted off peacefully enough. But he had tossed and turned the hours away, endlessly playing out scenarios in his head. The worst, of course, being some nightmare about his real father – rape, or

109

incest, or any one of a million horrible things. He couldn't think like that. He couldn't.

As he entered, Veronica could see straight away how nervous he was; it was mirrored in her own compulsive re-ordering of her desk, lining up the teacups when Evelyn brought them in. She wanted to put him at his ease but didn't have the faintest idea how to go about it.

'Hello, Daniel,' she said. 'Please, sit down. I lit the fire . . .'

'Yes, it's getting perishingly cold . . . feels like it might snow.' He attempted a weak smile. 'Didn't get this in Guildford.'

Veronica smiled nervously back at him. 'So I imagine. Tea?'

Daniel concurred and Veronica poured. Daniel felt the softness of the armchair and the peace and calm of Veronica's room begin to work its magic. It was hard to believe there were three hundred unruly girls somewhere in the building; they could be miles away. And it was hard to believe that he was about to hear things that might upset him – or worse, fail to answer his questions at all.

Veronica put down the milk jug decisively.

'Now, Daniel, I hope you won't mind if I tell you this all at once. Perhaps you could save any questions until I've finished.'

She lowered her head. 'I hope you understand . . . I haven't discussed this with anyone for nearly forty years. It's not very easy for me to think about.'

Daniel nodded to indicate that he did understand. Inside his heart was beating wildly.

'Once upon a time . . .' began Veronica. She smiled. 'I realise that is a silly way to begin. Still, all stories start somewhere. Once upon a time, there was a reasonably daft, certainly under-educated girl who lived in Sheffield. Her name was Vera. She lived with her father, a steelworker, her mother and her three brothers in a terrace in Darnall.

'If I were describing her as one of my girls, I would say she was a dreamer. A bright girl, not really encouraged in her school work – her father didn't believe in education for girls – but a big reader. She liked Jane Austen, Tess, *Wuthering Heights* and all sorts of silly romance stories, and she truly believed that in love one had a great passion for which one would sacrifice just about anything.'

Veronica's voice sounded far away. Daniel heard a northern timbre creep into it.

'One day, Vera's father left his lunch behind, and her mother sent her down to the docks with it, skipping like Little Red Riding Hood. I think that perhaps Vera's mother had forgotten that she was no longer the sweet little girl whom the other workers would pet and give lollipops to. Instead she was growing too quickly into a body she didn't understand, full of curious passions and unexplained yearnings.

'After she'd found her father, she wandered slowly home between the cranes and delivery trucks on the dockside.'

She paused.

'And then, out jumped the wolf . . . or rather, a man, Bert Cromer. An acquaintance of her father whom she'd noticed before, at church with his own family or staggering out of the pub on week nights. He had dirty, sharp teeth and a sniggering way of looking at her that was uncomfortable and unpleasant.

'"Well, well, Miss Vera," he said, stepping out in between two large canisters, in a secluded part of the shipyard. "What have we here?"

'"I'm taking ma da his lunch," Vera said, looking for an easy exit. She couldn't see one.

111

'"Are you indeed?" said the man. "So you just happened to be down here, on your own, flouncing about dockside? There's a name for ladies who do that. Do you know what it is?" He moved closer to her. She could smell him; he smelled of stale beer and bad breath.

'"Do you, little Vera? Is that what you're going to do for a living now? They won't like that down the chapel. Always got your nose in a book, I've seen yer. That won't do yer much good, will it? But maybe it's taught you a few things."

'And he reached out and put a hand on Vera's dress. She jumped back, but couldn't see anywhere else to go. He was blocking the route ahead, and behind were only the empty crates, carrying Sheffield steel and Sheffield cutlery all round the world.

'Vera let out a little sound.

'"New to this, are you? Well, we might make it easy on yer." He was completely facing her now, pushing her backwards to one of the crates.

'"Let me go!" said Vera as strongly as she could manage, suddenly terrified. "Get off me." Her voice sounded pitifully weak and girlish.

'"Walking down the docks, in clear daylight. Brazen as brass," said Bert Cromer.'

Daniel swallowed. He could see the tension in Veronica's face and shoulders, could see her reliving the event as if it were yesterday. He wanted to cry, put his arm on her, apologise for the horrible horrible event, for his foul father. He felt, obscurely, that somehow it was his fault; it worried him to imagine what he himself was capable of, what darkness he might have inherited.

'I said no,' Veronica went on. 'Quite clearly. I said no.'

There was a long pause as they both gazed out on to the

frost-spattered lawn outside Veronica's window, into the darkening sky and the shadowy outlines of the headland.

'Then he was there,' said Veronica simply. 'Right there. I don't even know how he got there, or how he heard us. He must have been working nearby, the ship was nearby.'

'Who?' Daniel hadn't meant to interrupt, but he couldn't help himself. It didn't seem to matter though, Veronica hadn't even noticed. Her eyes had taken on a dreamy expression.

'I didn't even know what he said. It was just a kind of gut-teral, angry stream of sounds. But you could tell what he meant all right. And then he hit Bert on the head for good measure. Then he pulled out a spanner and offered to hit him some more with that, if that's what he wanted.'

She smiled to herself.

'He was very poetic of gesture. Bert was a coward really. All bullies are, of course. As soon as Piotr hit him, he scarpered off like a skelped rabbit. And he stayed well away from me after that.'

She paused, and sipped her tea, tidily.

'It took me about two seconds to fall in love. Piotr Petrovich Ivanov. You had to use his full name, and that was it. I used to think there were so many people in Russia, you needed to use all the names to differentiate. But it's just their patrimony. That doesn't matter, of course. I loved it anyway. I used to roll it round my mouth at night. *Piotr Petrovich Ivanov*. It was so beautiful, so exotic.

'He wasn't even meant to be off his boat. They weren't allowed in those days, do you remember? In case he got infected with evil Capitalist ideas. He'd come off for a look around, because he never let anything like that get in his way. He was puffing on one of the stinking black Russian cigarettes he smoked – they were absolutely filthy things. I

113

adored the smell, I must have reeked of them. I can't believe my parents wouldn't have noticed that before.'

As if coming back to herself, Veronica sat a little straighter in her chair.

'He spoke no English, barely a word. A little more by the time he left, three weeks later. Not much. *Cee-ga-rette. Ve-ron-eeka* – that's what he called me, not Vera. Like a nickname. *Ya tebya ljublju.*

'I adored him. He was strong and brave and good and handsome and I loved everything about him.'

'What happened?' asked Daniel, fascinated.

Veronica looked at the high-cheekboned face, the pale eyes with the dark hair.

'You are so like him to look at. In terms of what you're like . . . well, I suppose I never truly got to know either of you.'

She looked down.

'Of course in those days there wasn't any internet, or mobile phones, or even a reliable mail service to Russia. It was a closed continent, unimaginably vast and mysterious. And I am sure, you know, he had a wife and a family and so on back there. He was a man, I was a girl. In a funny way, too, at that age, I almost . . . there was a part of me that knew. That knew it would be a tragic love affair. I was so full of silly stories and great passions . . . I did not expect, though . . . well, you.'

She smiled apologetically.

'I wrote and I wrote to the address he gave me. Nothing, of course. Was it a false address? Did I write it out wrongly? Did the state intercept his letters? A wife? I have so many questions too, Daniel. And I cried a thousand tears. Oh yes. Well, he never . . . he never came back for me. And then I started to show of course, in the way of it, and that bastard Bert spread it around that I was the shipyard slut . . . I thought my father was going to smack that baby out of me. So my mother sent me away. The gossip, the fuss . . . you wouldn't think it was the seventies. But it was.

'If I had been brave . . . If I had been brave, like Piotr Petrovich Ivanov was brave, then I wouldn't have given you up. Not for a second. And if things had been different . . . I do believe love does not always need language or culture. We could have perhaps . . . well, I will never know, of course. I think as far as the Communist tragedy goes, we were very much amongst the better off.'

Veronica looked to be straightening herself up.

'And after everything I decided that, after all, books were safer; studying life was better than living it. So here we are.'

She said 'So here we are' in the most matter-of-fact way she could muster.

Neither Daniel nor anyone else looking at her would have guessed for a second that, in her mind, she was sitting on the front of a bicycle Piotr Petrovich Ivanov purloined one night, riding round the shipyard at midnight after she'd crept out of the house, both of them screaming with laughter and frozen joy as the black water of the port lapped at the dock's edge.

'So I'm half Russian?' said Daniel, wonderingly.

'You are Daniil Petrovich Ivanov,' said Veronica. 'That is what I wanted to call you. Of course they wouldn't hear of it. Russians are godless, the nuns said. So I called you after the man who slew Goliath, who plucked the thorn from the lion's paw. My own name I changed as soon as I was allowed. I hated Vera anyway. I may have lost him, but I get some comfort from that. In my head, you know, I spell it with a k, and always will.'

Daniel stared into the fire.

'More tea?' said Veronica.

Chapter Seven

'Boys and girls together. I'm telling you, it's a disaster. Always.'

'Yes, Miss Starling.'

Maggie felt mutinously sure that she was the only teacher still new enough to the school to have Miss Starling give her a long lecture on why she didn't believe in the mixed school dance. Especially since she'd done nothing since half term except put her head down and work really really hard. She'd agreed, in the end, to buy the dress she'd tried on. It was in her price range, and when you came down to it, wedding dresses were all the same, weren't they? They'd also put the deposit on the venue. There was either whisky or vodka for everyone on arrival, red or white with dinner and champagne for the toasts. When they got closer to the time they could decide if they wanted chicken or salmon. So, it was all practically organised and everyone could stop bugging her about it. She bit her tongue at that. They weren't bugging her, of course. They loved her. They were excited. So should she be.

And she was doing well, she knew she was. Her second-year group seemed to be doing all right – Simone Kardashian for one was looking much better. She'd lost a lot of podginess and Maggie was really proud of her. She liked to see teenage girls, normally so unaware of their own beauty, look good and make the best of themselves. They should know how beautiful they were – Maggie envied them their long smooth limbs and shiny hair. Felicity Prosser was looking pinched and sullen; Maggie would have to have a word. She sighed. If only she didn't find that little madam quite so difficult, she'd pay her more attention.

Her other classes were doing well, though, and Maggie had even conquered, over long nights of painstaking figuring out, her own distaste for the lyric poets. She had her priorities straight: work, family, a wedding. It was all good. Did she truly envy the tearful hysterics of second formers, wild with excitement of whether a boy would ask her to dance? Well perhaps, if she were honest, hearing their excited chatter, just a little. But everyone had to grow up sometime.

So even the idea of tonight – the school dance – seemed unusual: she had given up going out almost altogether. She didn't want to join in Claire and Miranda's cosy girls' nights. Miranda was obviously very happy at being back with David and she didn't want to rain on that parade, or even risk having a couple of glasses too many and saying the wrong thing at the wrong time. She'd enjoyed her nights alone up in the tower room, a glass of wine and a book of poetry, curled up in front of the fire. Sometimes she worried she might turn into Miss Starling. But not often.

'It always leads to *derring do*,' Miss Starling was continuing. Maggie thought that perhaps she haunted the corridor outside her rooms, waiting for her to emerge so she could continue one of her harangues.

'Derring do?' enquired Maggie. That sounded rather a grand name for what was likely to be a little vomiting in the bushes and some snogging that would be picked over and probably regretted the following day. Maggie smiled briefly as she imagined Miss Starling at one of Holy Cross's Christmas parties, which were famous for their debauchery. The teachers usually behaved just as badly as the pupils, too. They normally had to get professional cleaners in afterwards.

'*Mis-be-haviour*,' said Miss Starling, as usual overemphasising the wrong syllables.

'Ah,' said Maggie. 'Well, you look very nice.'

As usual, Miss Starling was wearing a synthetic blouse with a brooch and a knee-length skirt of no distinguishing characteristics whatsoever. She had a slender figure, but Maggie couldn't imagine she had ever been pretty – had her mouth always been so pursed? Her nose always so thin and pinched-looking?

Maggie was wearing her red dress again. It was the only nice thing she had really, or at least that was suitable for a school dance rather than a holiday in Spain. It set off her dark hair nicely, and after adding some cherry lipstick she was rather pleased with the result. It had made her briefly remember the last time she'd worn it and David had looked at her with those melting brown eyes, and they'd been caught alone under the mistletoe and she'd come so close to . . . She shut her thoughts closed with a snap. That was all in the past now.

'Shall we go down together?' She smiled sweetly at Miss Starling and led her off towards the spiral staircase, just before Claire, running late as usual, came careening out of her room, draped in an exquisitely printed dress and cursing like a navvy as to the whereabouts of her shoes.

The atmosphere in the girls' dorms was absolutely fierce. Boy-starved since the ill-fated Geography field trip, the levels of primping, expectation and nerves were approaching fever pitch, regardless of how many salutary, ardour-dampening chats they'd had from Miss Starling in the preceding weeks.

Skirmishes were breaking out over mirror space: 'One between four. This country is barbaric,' Zelda pointed out, as well as reminding everyone that in America the dorm would be the size of one girl's normal en-suite bathroom. Everyone, as usual, ignored her grumbling comparisons.

Fliss was in a dreamworld of her own. For the last few weeks she'd danced every spare second she could find, practising the steps. Some of the girls did extra dance classes on Saturdays, but up until now Fliss had never been that interested. Now she badgered little Sylvie Brown to show her *ronde de jambes* and arabesques until her muscles ached and Sylvie begged for mercy. She'd scheduled these practise sessions for mealtimes too, so she would have a legitimate reason for skipping supper. Matron, who kept a weather eye on these kinds of things, was about to have a word with Maggie about it. It wasn't right. Fliss's pale face looked more drawn than ever, her blue eyes huge and vulnerable-looking in the peaky face. Her hip bones had started to stick out.

Alice had noticed, but considered it none of her business. Naturally slim, she looked upon any kind of controlled eating as a form of attention-seeking. Fond of her friend, she didn't want to give Fliss that indulgence. Plus, Fliss seemed to be actively avoiding her. Alice couldn't believe it was because she'd talked for five minutes to that Will guy, she'd hardly given him a second glance. It couldn't be. It would blow over.

Simone, on the other hand, was giving Fliss all the reinforcement she didn't need and shouldn't have.

'Ohmygod you're so thin!' she said every day. 'You look like a model or something.'

Alice wanted to say she didn't look like a model, she looked like a warning poster for drugs, but bit her tongue. She sensed that on one level Fliss wanted nothing more than a big argument with her and she didn't want to start it.

Fliss gazed at herself in the mirror. Her blue party dress was falling off her. It was ridiculously big. Fliss hugged herself with delight. Also, it was freezing in here. Why couldn't they heat the place properly? The amount of money her parents paid, it was an absolute disgrace. Up until now she'd been hiding under big jumpers, but tonight her gorgeous new figure could be revealed. She hadn't eaten anything at all today except for an apple at lunchtime, and she'd drank a lot of water. And danced, of course. She was going to take this place by storm, she knew it. She pulled an emerald scarf of Zelda's tightly round her waist. She looked tiny, there was no doubt about it. It would all be worthwhile. And Will would see her . . . But at first, of course, she would ignore him, accept the invitations of other boys who were bound to come her way. She felt a momentary flutter of anxiety about this – the other boys would ask her, wouldn't they? – but dismissed it. She'd be with Alice, who knew half the boys anyway because they were friends of her sister, and Zelda, who'd have so much make up on the boys would ask her out almost by accident. Of course they'd notice her too.

Then, perhaps a few dances in when she was being as thin and graceful as Keira Knightley, Will would not be able to take it any longer and he would make his way across the dance floor – maybe he would separate her from dancing with another boy, that would be good – and ask her to dance and she would look up at him like this – she practised in the mirror – and—

'Jeez, what are you *doing* in there?' screamed Zelda at the top of her voice. 'Not all of us have naturally straight hair, you know! We need a little more time!'

'Coming!' shouted Fliss. She felt a little light-headed for a second, and leant her forehead against the cool of the mirrored glass. Cool, that's all she needed to be. Cool, calm and collected, and she would be fine.

Simone looked at the stiff brown velvet and sighed.

'You are lucky, you know, angel,' her mother had said. 'How many other girls' mothers love them so much they make their own clothes?'

'But can't I at least choose the pattern?'

'I know what suits my beautiful girl best.'

That was entirely debatable, Simone thought, but, as usual, she'd acquiesced for a quiet life.

Still, at least the dress didn't pull around her chest any more. In fact, it was noticeably looser on her. She felt pleased.

Zelda stopped in front of her.

'Simone,' she said, shaking her head. 'Simone Simone Simone.'

'My mum made it,' Simone muttered.

'Why wouldn't you let us take you shopping?'

Simone flushed. How could she say that she didn't have any money for shopping? It didn't compute to Zelda, she thought shopping was just something one did, like reading a book, or breathing, and she couldn't bear the thought of accepting their charity, however kindly meant.

'Is that really all you have?'

Simone shrugged. 'I could go in my pyjamas if you like.'

'This is *not* a time for jokes!' Zelda frowned and went over to her own cupboard (or closet as she called it), filled with beautiful clothes perfectly put away.

'Let me see, let me see.'

Simone didn't want to be a part of this. Zelda may be tall, but she was slender too. Nothing she owned had the faintest chance of getting over Simone's chest, even now she had lost some weight.

'You're no sylph yet, Sims, but I bet we can find something. And you have to let me make you up, you have eyelashes like a cow.'

'Uh, thanks. I suppose.'

'Yeah!' Zelda was firing everyone up. 'We're good to go! Everyone is HOT! SOOO HOT! Yeah! Give us a twirl!'

Simone stifled a giggle. But she couldn't help feeling excited. In the back of her closet, Zelda had found a long draping black dress. It was meant to be baggy, but on Simone looked clinging and curvaceous rather than stretched. Simone never wore black – someone had told her once it was the colour fat people wore, so she'd always avoided it – but it went well with her dark wild curls, finally set free from the frizzy braids she normally wore, and smoothed down with about a pint of Zelda's relaxing serum. Her dark eyes had been made even larger and darker with three coats of mascara, and a cherry red stain on her lips and cheeks had given her a dramatic gypsy look.

'You could get served in a bar,' said Alice, semi-admiringly.

As a final dramatic touch, Zelda took a red scarf and loosely knotted it round her hips.

'Do you think?' said Simone doubtfully.

'All she needs is the rose in her mouth,' said Alice.

Simone sighed. 'Well, it doesn't matter to me anyway. If I'm not allowed to wear my glasses it's not like I can see anything anyway.'

'Hush, you doubters,' said Zelda. 'I am Queen of the Makeovers, and I say, HOT!'

Fliss hadn't really been able to listen to anything, she felt a little spacy and light-headed with excitement. She was sitting on the bed, her right foot twitching.

'Can't we just go?' she burst in. 'What if everyone's already there and they start the dancing without us?'

'No,' said Zelda carefuly. 'We have to make an entrance.'

'Well, no one is going to miss you,' said Alice. Zelda had conformed to the dance guidelines: her dress was below the knee and had straps. However it somewhat contravened the spirit, given that it had a huge split up one leg, was silver, and the straps were made of Swarovski crystals that glittered and reflected the light.

'Do you think the teachers will mind you wearing a dress that costs more than their entire salary?' asked Alice mischievously, glancing at Fliss. But Fliss was still sitting on the bed, twitching and staring into space. Alice fervently hoped that tonight she would pull a boy, learn how to snog and get over this ridiculous phase, it was pulling them all down. She herself looked elegant and appropriate in a pink silk fifties-style dress with a tight belt pulling in her tiny waist.

'Ya think?' answered Zelda, frowning. She always took everything literally. 'I mean, you know, they're always welcome to borrow it.'

Alice laughed. That was Zelda all over – not the sharpest tool in the box, but endlessly generous.

'I think it would suit Miss Gifford,' said Simone. Post-detention, Miss Gifford was the only mistress Simone felt allowed to slag off, so she did so on occasion, feeling terribly daring.

'No, old JJ,' said Alice. 'It'd be good to see her muscles poking through.'

The girls laughed.

'You could put it on Dr Deveral,' reflected Zelda. 'She'd probably make it look sorta classy.'

'Well, that's more than you're doing,' said Alice.

'Come on!!! Let's GOOO!' said Fliss, anxious beyond endurance.

Once again, Harold Carruthers, the caretaker, and his team had done the school proud. The refectory, normally a clashing maelstrom of chatter and banging cutlery, with steam rising from large catering vats, had been completely transformed.

Now the wooden walls were hung with heavy Christmas wreaths, thick with red holly berries. Candles had been posted in the high windows to add flickering shadows to the room. All the tables and long benches had been cleared away and the canteen area itself closed off. Refreshments – orange or apple juice, hot sausage rolls, jacket potatoes, stuffing sandwiches and horseradish crisps all followed by slices of the school's special Christmas cake (that Joan Rhys still sent to old girls around the world every year, it provided a flourishing business on the side) – would be set up on a long buffet table at the back at nine p.m.

The band were a local folk group who could play music in a variety of styles, and there was also a mobile disco to be set up later after the formal section had been completed. There were two hundred and fifty pupils there in total, stiff, nervous and anxious in new shirts and dresses, desperately trying to give off an air of worldly sophistication that, however privileged their upbringings, they couldn't pull off quite yet.

Maggie felt her heart soften as she looked at them all. In the classroom they could be bumptious, aggravating, clownish, but here they were just extremely young women- and men-to-be, filled with the worries and anxieties of every person that age who ever lived. Am I normal? Am I all right? Will they accept me? Will anyone ask me to dance? It seemed like yesterday that she'd been in exactly the same position. When Stan, of course, had asked her to dance.

Having managed to lose Miss Starling, who was demanding to see the DJ's 'song list', as she called it, to make sure he didn't play anything too risqué or suggestive, she and Claire took up an unobtrusive corner overlooking the dance floor. They weren't there to supervise, not really, just to generally fend off any unnecessary behaviour with a light touch.

Slowly, tentatively, the room began to fill up – nobody wanted to be first to arrive. But as all the boys had arrived together in a clump, speed-marched from over the hill (there would be a coach arriving to take them all back at 10.30 p.m. precisely), girls were emerging from everywhere to get a good look at the talent.

Sylvie Brown was wearing a light-green prom dress that made her pale eyes look enormous. Her blonde hair cascaded like a cloud down her back. Maggie and Claire saw the stir she made amongst the boys and smiled at each other. There was nothing quite like a petite blonde. Andrea McCann, the second year's star hockey player, slouched in in a plain black dress, looking like she'd much rather be out in a muddy field, even in the dark, than tarting herself up for some dance. Zazie Saurisse was far too glamorous and chic for the event and looked as if she'd scare the boys rigid.

Some girls walked in confidently, a little older and already aware of their ability to turn heads, to be liked and admired in male company. Long, clean hair swinging, smooth limbs in pretty prom dresses, Maggie would have felt churlish to deny them their confident smiles, the flashes of white teeth, even if she couldn't avoid feeling just a little jealous. Then there were others, not quite so confident, looking around nervously to see what the other girls were wearing, who the boys were looking at.

The boys, in dinner jackets or lounge suits, did look rather dashing, Maggie had to admit. Not like the spotty little scamps with the shaven heads, tracksuits and nascent pot bellies she remembered from her old school. They looked like young Hugh Grants in the making: callow, clean, polite, but unmemorable somehow, although Maggie had no doubt that wasn't how they appeared to the girls. To them, they would be great heroes of teenage romance, carrying expectations they couldn't possibly hope to fulfil.

She caught sight of David, chivvying the boys along. Well, of course. That was hardly unexpected. She ducked her eyes before he could see her. He was wearing the same dated velvet jacket he'd worn last year. It suited him. She would keep out of his way, that was all.

'Shall we spike the punch?' she asked Claire.

Claire nodded vigorously. 'Normally I dislike the English tendency of endless drinking,' she said. 'But tonight, to get through thees, I may have to make exception. Or let them all get pregnant. I have not yet decided.'

Maggie's response, however, was knocked out of her as she registered the little group entering through the refectory's double doors.

Linking arms, the four of them entered the ref. Maggie was not the only one to notice and react accordingly. Most of the girls in their year leapt forward, startled.

'Mon dieu,' said Claire. *'Regarde le papillon.* Simone is your leetle butterfly.'

Indeed she was. Maggie almost couldn't believe that the nervous, near-silent scholarship girl was this curvy, smiling, vibrant-looking beauty. It was a different girl altogether. Incredible.

That hadn't been what had made Maggie gasp, though. It was her own idiocy. How could she have been so caught up in her own obsessions, her own problems, as to ignore what was happening in *her* guidance class, right in front of her very eyes. The very thing she absolutely knew to watch for in teenage girls going on right under her nose, when these young women were meant to be in her pastoral care.

'Oh my God,' she said. 'Look at Felicity Prosser.'

Claire was shaking her head. Fliss's bony shoulders protruded from a dress that could hardly keep itself up. There was almost no difference between the front and back of her. Her eyes looked wide and spacy.

'Dear me,' said Claire. 'Dear me.'

Maggie wanted to rush up to her with a blanket, haul her upstairs, put her to bed and forcefeed her toasted cheese sandwiches till she could stand up again. Her ankles didn't look able to support her body.

Maggie could hear murmurs around the hall. Her Plantagenet girls were certainly being noticed. Zelda looked ridiculous, of course – her hair was about a metre in the air and she looked like a forty-year-old cocktail waitress in Vegas; Alice looked perfect as ever, and Simone looked like someone had just handed her a big pile of gold bananas. But Fliss . . . what was the matter with her? After last year's travails she'd been getting better marks, doing well. She had friends, didn't she? What on earth was going on?

Maggie realised she was making excuses for herself. She should have noticed. She should have seen it.

'Maybe I'll go up and have a word,' she said.

'Not now,' counselled Claire. 'This is her big evening. Don't embarrass her.'

'But everyone's going to be talking about her, whispering . . . it's not right.'

'So you're going to bundle her off to bed, yes? In front of everyone? *Non*, Maggie, thees is not right. Eef there is a problem here, thees will not solve it.'

Maggie reluctantly realised Claire was right.

'I can't . . . I just can't believe I didn't notice.'

Claire patted her kindly on the arm. '*Bof*, all these young girls, they are exactly the same, *non*? One moment they are up and the next they are down and unless we put them on the scales every week of course it is hard. I did not notice either.'

But it wasn't Claire's job to notice, thought Maggie. It was hers.

'You cannot think of it tonight,' said Claire. 'And look at your beautiful Simone.'

Simone couldn't believe it. As soon as she'd entered the room she could feel everyone's eyes on her. At first she thought they were going to point and laugh, that they were staring at her because she looked so terrible and ridiculous and she was going to be the laughing stock of the school.

But then Astrid Ulverton – who would never make a cruel joke, there wasn't a mean streak in her body – came dashing up to her with Sylvie.

'Simone, is that really you? You look incredible!' gasped Sylvie.

Astrid nodded. 'You do. You look really pretty.'

And that was like the cue for all the girls from her class – and some from the other houses, too – to come over and make admiring and somewhat envious remarks. Simone blushed pink and couldn't hide her pleasure. If those girls from St Cats could see her now!

Fliss stared in amazement. When all eyes had swivelled towards her as she entered the ref, head held high, she'd felt pleased, as if it was her due. She'd worked hard, starving herself for this. But now the girls were coming over to congratulate Simone, and their glances slid off her and they looked away, uncomfortable. One or two of them whispered to one another.

Jealous, thought Fliss furiously. They were all just jealous, that was it. They were all sucking up to Simone because she was still comfortably fatter than any of them, so they were just patronising the fat girl, that was it. But they couldn't talk to her, because they knew she was thinner and better than any of them. She felt her fingers tighten.

She didn't feel any better when Hattie, surrounded by her annoyingly twittish bright and breezy hockey chums, bounced over. Fliss had been avoiding her for weeks. Hattie stopped in front of her. For once she wasn't wearing the smug, supercilious look she usually put on around her little sister. She looked actually, genuinely, shocked.

'Felicity! What . . . what the hell is the matter with you?'

'Hell' was very strong swearing for Hattie. In truth, though her sister annoyed her with her attention-seeking ways and pretty, delicate demeanour (Hattie had always been the 'clodhopper' in the family. Her father thought this was funny, contrasting her with the paler, altogether less ruddy-looking Felicity. Hattie hated it. Why couldn't she have been dainty too?), she was genuinely shocked by how skinny her little sister had got. She looked like she was suffering from a disease. She couldn't deny it. She looked anorexic.

Felicity stuck out her chin. 'Nothing. Did you get that dress in the DFS sale?'

Now it was Hattie's turn to flush. Her mother had bought

the dress, a supposedly sophisticated black number, in the January sales. Now she was far too big for it and could feel her shoulders bursting out of the fabric. Why couldn't she stop growing? She felt twice the weight of all the boys there and was sure that Fliss was going to get asked to dance before she was.

'We're not talking about me, we're talking about you. Why have you lost so much weight?'

Fliss shrugged. 'I haven't, not really. Haven't really noticed.'

Hattie bit her lip. 'You look like something from the Irish famine.'

'You don't,' shot back Fliss.

Alice could sense a nasty situation developing. 'Hi, Hattie,' she said, desperately. 'You look nice.'

Hattie glanced at Fliss's smart-mouthed friend. She usually had a hidden agenda. 'Hmm,' she said.

'Where's the juice table? I'm parched.'

'Forget that, where's the MEN table? I'm parched!' said Zelda, blissfully oblivious to the atmosphere. She linked arms with Simone and Fliss and the party moved on.

The band were fantastic. After playing a medley of popular hits to get everyone into the room and relaxing a bit, Dr Deveral stepped up in front of them. Maggie was dying to shout 'Give us a song!' but of course wouldn't dare on pain of death. Nonetheless, there was always something forbidding about her boss that brought out the naughty schoolgirl in her.

Veronica was wearing a beautiful deep-green velvet dress that made her look elegant and somehow timeless. Against the old wooden panelling of the refectory walls, with their heavy boughs of holly and mistletoe, she herself seemed part of the school, something fundamentally rooted there.

As she turned to face the hall – there was no need for a microphone – an instant hush descended.

'Welcome, everyone!' she said. 'Our Downey girls, of course, all of whom are looking very beautiful tonight.'

There was some clapping at this.

'And our brother school, Downey Boys. You are our very welcome guests here.'

This was said lightly, but no one was left in any doubt that they would be expected to behave as very good guests indeed.

'Christmas is a time to celebrate, to bring light out of the dark, as many of us believe the Christ Child led the world out of the dark. It is a time to wassail our neighbours, to laugh and make merry, and throw the cares of the year behind us.'

Veronica glanced briefly to where Daniel was standing with his group of charges. He let a small smile cross his face.

'So please, make merry and have fun. Because, for some of you, next year brings exams . . .'

Veronica smiled as the hall groaned, but then the band struck up the first dance, a Gay Gordons.

Almost instantly, as if repelled by magnetic forces, the boys and girls who had been milling in the middle retreated to opposite sides of the room, the walls lined with chairs.

The agony in the boys' eyes was clear to see. Not much making merry here, Maggie reflected. For all their bourgeois self-confidence, scratch the surface and they were just little boys after all.

Dr Fitzroy, resplendent in a pair of most peculiar tartan trews, soon dispelled the awkward atmosphere. He strode up the boys' line, loudly and furiously imprecating. 'Come on, men! Are you men or mice? You don't want to confirm what they say about boys' schools, now, do you? Come on!

131

Look at those beautiful women over there, knockouts every single one of them. Get yourselves a partner immediately, or I'm taking you all home and putting you on all-night detention.'

Maggie smiled and watched as he made a courtly bow towards Dr Deveral, who acquiesced and lent him her arm. They led off on to the floor, as, tentatively, some of the older boys moved across to chat and tease the older girls they already knew.

Famke Medizian, a pretty but unthreatening fourth-form girl on the debating team – and thus well-known to the boys – was the first to be picked, by a tall boy with a protuding Adam's Apple. She took his arm immediately, which was the cue for the floodgates to open.

Simone was content to bask in the compliments of the other girls. She had no expectations of being noticed by the boys too, and sat down quite happily. Fliss, on the other hand, was hyperactive, nervously glancing up and down the line of boys. Will was at the end and didn't seem to have seen any of them.

'Oh, for goodness' sake, Humph,' grumbled Alice, as she was swept away by one of her older sister's admirers. 'If you stand on my feet you will BLOODY regret it.'

Humph blushed companiably. He had accepted it as his lot in life to always be unsuccessfully in love with at least one Trebizon-Woods sister.

'You wanna get into this?' came an American voice next – it was Forest, a tall black boy whose father was also stationed at the base. He and Zelda had spent some weekends together looking for proper milkshakes and complaining about breakfast cereal. The girls thought he was handsome, but Zelda was helping him as he prepared to come out to his parents.

132

'You are the only person who is going to be worse at this that me,' said Zelda happily. 'And I know the man part, so you can be the girl. Perfect.'

'Shit, girlfriend, I can *move*, you know? Just not to this shiz.'

'Shiz?' said Zelda. 'Forest, you're getting more American on purpose.'

'Well, I am sorry, ma'am,' said Forest with a courtly bow.

That left Simone and Fliss. Fatty and Thinny, thought Fliss bitterly. Simone didn't even care, she was just so pleased to be at a dance without people teasing her. Well, it was early, and Will hadn't even seen her yet, so . . .

The floor was now a thicket of dancers, bouncing, spinning to the sound of the violins and accordions. It looked like fun. Fliss told herself again it didn't matter. This wasn't even her best dance anyway. When Hattie came round in the circle, led by a spotty Chemistry specialist she knew from the lab, Fliss looked away from her like she didn't care.

Simone knew how important this dance was to Fliss, even if she didn't know exactly why. She desperately searched for the right words to say.

'You look lovely,' she said awkwardly. 'The boys probably can't see you, you're looking so slim.'

Fliss didn't even answer. She felt her face flush and the horrible word 'wallflower' bubbled up inside her, as the dancing segued into an eightsome reel and the dancers changed partners or kept to the floor. Nobody was approaching them. She glanced nervously at the other girls sitting around the side of the room. All of them looked the same, pitifully embarrassed and upset.

There was Hilary O'Fielding from Wessex House, whose acne hadn't responded well to the sunbed treatment at all, which meant she now looked spotty *and* bright red; Phyllis

Mason, whose strong, newly found religious beliefs this term prevented her from dancing (Fliss wasn't sure why she was attending), and a large clump of boys hovering round the punch and refusing to dance. They were guffawing loudly about something. Fliss envied them.

A short boy who looked too young to be there started sidling up to them. Fliss glanced at him without much interest. He looked like a midget who'd snuck in from Year One. She didn't want to dance with him, she was about four inches taller than him. She'd be a laughing stock. She decided to turn him down gracefully but quite clearly, so that everyone else could see that she had been asked, she was just being picky.

The boy sidled up uneasily, looking as if he were trying to creep up without being noticed. He had the most peculiar side-slipping gait. Fliss didn't recognise him. One of the weirdos from Downey Boys, she supposed. Just her luck.

'I hate this,' said the boy.

Fliss wasn't expecting that. She glanced up, brow furrowed. But the boy wasn't talking to her at all.

'Why did you come then?' said Simone reasonably.

Ash pouted. 'For the good of the school,' he said crossly. 'And to stop them calling me Pussyballs for about five minutes. And Cassiopeia is coming into our orbit tonight,' he went on. 'That's a constellation.'

'I *know* what it is,' said Simone.

'I'd rather be with my telescope.'

'Well, just sneak off then.'

'You don't look like you're having fun either.'

'Well, that's where you're wrong,' said Simone. 'So there.' Ash was so annoying.

'You look different,' he said after a while.

Fliss let out a huge groan of boredom.

134

'Your tuxedo is too big for you,' commented Simone.

'I know,' said Ash. 'I don't care. It's stupid.'

But he made no move to go. Instead he sat up by Simone. Even though it was only the boys' school weirdo, Simone still felt herself flush. A boy! Sitting beside her!

'I feel like Holden Caulfield,' said Ash. Simone looked at him. Someone further to what her imagination (rather sexily) conjured Holden Caulfield to be, she couldn't imagine.

'They're all phoneys,' she said helpfully.

'Yes!' said Ash, in genuine surprise. 'That's it! That's exactly how I feel!'

'And now,' announced the bandleader, 'it's time for the ladies' choice.'

Fliss felt her back straighten. Ladies' choice? She hadn't known there was going to be a ladies' choice. Instantly all the girls were back on this side of the room, giggling and fluttering like excited birds. Zelda moved over to where Fliss was.

'Come *ahn*, Fliss!' she hollered. 'Are you going to have some fun at this thing or what?'

Alice glanced around the room. Suddenly, she stopped. It was as if she'd never seen him before. She even blinked. But there he was. Fliss's crush. Will Hampton.

He was in front of the punch bowl, telling a joke to some friends. And she couldn't tell if it was in the cheeky crease of his grin around his eyes; the upward pitch of his eyebrows that meant, even when he wasn't, that he always seemed on the point of laughter; his sparkling blue eyes; or the way his beautifully cut dinner jacket fit snugly across his broadening shoulders. He threw back his head to laugh, the flashing lights off the mirrorball catching his finely cut profile, and in that instant Alice saw everything Fliss could see, wanted everything Fliss wanted – and more.

Fliss's hands were twisting uncomfortably in the lap of her dress, the knuckles white. It was now or ... Could she? Dare she? She thought of the prospect of his hands in hers, his shoulders next to hers ... Already girls were sprinting cheekily across the dance floor and grabbing their prizes as the boys learned to accept their place in the pecking order of life. Sylvie Brown had cheekily asked Mr McDonald, the cute English teacher. Right. It was now or never. Trembling with nerves, feeling hot and cold, she set off in Will's direction.

Will had been part of the boys' group laughing by the orange juice. He wasn't really bothered with the formal dancing, he just wanted to watch the girls and then see if anything good would happen at the disco later. Suddenly, on instinct, he turned his head and his breath caught. Alice. That friend of the Prossers, that was her name. He'd thought she looked hot before, but nothing had prepared him for tonight. Her flushed cheeks as she caught him looking, her long, shining hair cascading over her shoulders, the suggestion of the curve of her waist under the pale pink silk. Dumbstruck, they gazed at one another.

Suddenly, he noticed someone standing in front of him.

'Uh, Will?' said the voice. He glanced down, blinking. Was that really Hattie's little sister? She looked absolutely terrible, like she'd been ill or something. All scrawny and twitchy, she looked about ten years old.

'Hey,' he said, trying to glance over her shoulder to see if Alice had moved. Would she come over? She had to, surely.

'Uh, do you want ...'

Will remembered it was ladies' choice. The force of his feelings struggled with his innate good manners, and the manners prevailed.

'To dance?' he said. 'Sure.'

And once this was over, he'd find her.

Alice was shocked by how much she minded when she saw Fliss had got there first. A huge brawny chap who looked like an all-England rugby player caught her eye and grinned hopefully at her. She let him take her arm without thinking. Only one name filled her head. *Will*.

'Would you like to, mm, maybe, mmm, dance?' stuttered Simone. She was surprised at herself. Normally she wouldn't have dreamt of saying anything like that. It must be the dress. She couldn't believe she'd even opened her mouth.

'NO!' said Ash.

The dance was Strip the Willow, which involved one couple forming an arch for the others to dance through. It reminded Fliss of a wedding. Every time they had to hold hands to dance through the arch, Fliss looked up at Will hopefully. He didn't return her gaze – in fact he seemed very distracted. Fliss decided to concentrate on showing him how daintily and prettily she could twirl and skip. She wanted to enjoy the music, the candles twinkling, the rustle of skirts, scent of perfume and clashing of polished shoes on the ancient wooden floor. Here she was finally, lighter than air, hand in hand with the boy of her dreams. She *would* be happy. She would. Alice twirled in front of her with some tall rugby boy, and Fliss gave her a little wave, to show her that it had all worked out, she was with the boy of her dreams, her love.

Alice ignored this, however, and as soon as the dance was over made her way to where they both stood. Will brightened immediately as she approached.

'Hey, it's the Dashing White Sergeant next,' he said, with an enthusiasm that would have surprised his dance teacher. 'Shall we?' And he offered an arm to Alice, and one to Fliss.

The Dashing White Sergeant was a complicated dance, involving two groups of three – two boys and a girl and two girls and a boy – forming a circle, then breaking into lines. The boy or girl in the middle of the three then had to dance with each of his or her partners before the line went on around the room to form another circle. It was fast, tricky, fun and romantic. Fliss would have preferred to have been the one girl between two boys, but didn't want to complain – it was Will asking her for a second dance!

'MAGGIE!'

Miranda's educated tones rang out across the noisy room. Dragging David in her wake she crossed the width of the dance floor. She was wearing a slightly unlikely tartan dress with a huge bow on the shoulder.

'Where on *earth* have you been?' Miranda kissed her forcefully on both cheeks. 'I know you've got the wedding of the century to arrange, but it is just *no fun* drinking wine and complaining about men without you.'

Maggie instantly felt a little ashamed. Miranda just wanted to be friends, and she had indeed been avoiding her. But she couldn't sit and listen to her crowing over how David had come crawling back to her, full of apologies for breaking it off, determined to make a go of it . . . From the way Miranda had talked about it, he had turned into a cross between George Clooney and Santa Claus to win her affections, even though she still mocked his efforts. Well, they were a couple. David had probably always loved her. It was right they were back together. She still found it painful though.

'Hello,' she said. 'You look good. Hello, David.' Maggie didn't meet his eye.

'Come dance with us,' said Miranda. 'It's that mad one where they need threes.'

'Oh, I'm not sure I really know how to—'

'Come on! It's a bloody jocks' dance! You've got to, I'm completely hopeless. Come on, otherwise those bloody cow-eyed teenagers will start pestering David again and I'll be forced to cop off with one of those hot sixth-formers.'

There was no getting away from Miranda's emphatic charm. Smiling apologetically at David, who had gone slightly pink around the ears, Maggie stepped with them on to the dance floor.

'And . . . eight to the left and eight to the right and form a circle . . . Now your partner on the right, now the left, swing round, swing round, swing round, swing round . . .'

The caller talked them through the steps as Maggie stood nervously in their circle. Opposite them Claire was looking queenly in between Dr Fitzroy and the young History teacher.

'Why are we doing thees when we could be sitting down talking Philosophy and eating a good deener?' enquired Claire loudly.

'*Pour encourager les autres!*' boomed Dr Fitzroy, as the music started up and David took Maggie's hand.

Maggie felt it there: strong, with long graceful fingers, warm and dry. Apart from the day he'd grabbed her in the rain, it was the first time he had ever taken her hand, but somehow it didn't seem that way. It felt like it had always belonged there. He didn't squeeze it, although she had thought that he might.

It was very loud. Although it was some time since Maggie

had been to a ceilidh, she'd certainly attended plenty in her time and the rhythm of the music pounded hard through her DNA as they started to circle.

Miranda had not being lying about being bad at dancing. She had absolutely no idea what she was doing. As David stepped to the side and then tried to spin her round, she careered wildly into Dr Fitzroy and let out a loud, snorting laugh.

Then it was Maggie and David's turn to face one another. She was still unable to meet his eye. In fact, it turned out, she didn't have to. Somehow their arms linked instinctively, their feet moving in perfect harmony. As he spun her round, the red dress streaming behind her, she felt as if she were floating, or spinning on ice. She landed right in the heart of the beat, her arm outstretched, his hand automatically where it needed to be to take hers, to carry on the dance.

Fliss danced her *pas de bas* as neatly as she could. But, she began to notice with a growing sense of dread, it didn't matter. Whichever way she twirled, however daintily she proffered her arm for the spin, Will's eyes were always elsewhere, flickering, following Alice's dark hair bouncing and shining in the light of a hundred candles. When Will had to spin her, he did so politely (in fact, though she didn't know it, he was terrified of breaking her). When it came Alice's turn, he whizzed her round as fast as he could, even picking her up by the waist and pushing her around, both of them laughing and teasing one another. When they had to put up their arms to move around the room, he pretended to tickle her armpits. He playfully bumped hips with her on their way round. There was no doubt, truly, who he was dancing with. As the music seemed to grow louder and faster, as the whole room became a mass of swirling colours and whirling bodies, Fliss felt a black gloom fill her up like oil, piling up and choking her till she could barely move.

The music seemed to be even louder and faster now. Miranda had dropped any pretence of trying to keep up and was now swearing manfully and throwing herself around on purpose. Maggie and David, on the other hand, couldn't put a foot wrong. Everywhere she turned, there he was; they did not need a count, or a beat, but each found the other wherever in the dance they needed to be. Maggie felt she had entered an altered state where time had turned liquid, where they were swimming through the dance. She was only aware of his turning back, his outstretched arm, his effortless movements exactly mirroring her own.

Only at one point was their equilibrium disturbed. Miranda, red-faced and cross at her inability to pick up the steps, spun out of control and bumped fiercely into Maggie, who found herself thrown into David's arms. He clutched at her elbows, then, in consternation, they both lurched backwards. Maggie found suddenly she was breathless.

The dance ended, finally. Flushed and giggling, Will turned to Alice, pulled her close and spontaneously planted a huge kiss on her forehead.

'That was great!' he said.

Normally Alice would have shrugged backwards and stepped away from such contact with a boy. But in Will's strong arms, the faint, sweet smell of young sweat from his shirt, his smiling face and his eyes locked on to hers . . . she found herself standing, unmoving, in his arms, looking up at him.

*

As the music ended, David turned to bow to both of his partners. Miranda was clearly pissed off, her face was puce and her dress was tugged off at one shoulder. He couldn't look at Maggie, although he could still feel her small hand in his, the lightness of her movements. Dancing with her had been like . . . Well, he had felt like he could have danced for ever. He hadn't wanted it to end.

He turned to her, as was customary. Maggie was pink-cheeked and biting her lip, and David bowed to her deeply. She curtseyed too, and, rising up, met his eyes. Their gaze held just a touch longer than necessary, but they still had not spoken.

Suddenly, a scream rang out.

All the teachers charged across to that side of the room. Crumpled on the floor, like a tiny doll, was Felicity Prosser. It was Alice who had screamed.

Maggie knelt down and put a hand to her forehead. The girl had obviously fainted and was already beginning to stir. 'Get Matron!' she heard somebody shout. Maggie gratefully took David's outstretched jacket and covered Fliss's painfully thin limbs, then as Fliss opened her eyes and stared up uncomprehendingly at the crowd surrounding her, allowed him to lift her and carry her to the san.

'One of these years we're going to have a Christmas event without you rendering yourself unconscious,' Maggie heard him joke. The previous year, Fliss had fallen off the stage protesting against school rules.

Once in the calm of the san, deathly quiet after the noisy ballroom, Matron came bustling forwards.

'Have you been drinking, child? Taking anything? Just tell me, you shan't get a row.'

Maggie raised her eyebrows at that. Fliss shook her head in mute misery.

Matron looked her over with a sniff. 'I said it already: this child is not eating enough. Dr Deveral didn't think it would be a problem in this school, but it obviously is.' Matron lifted a lifeless arm. 'Look at her arms, they're like pins!'

'Uh, I'd better get back,' said David, looking uncomfortable. Maggie glanced up at him and they exchanged apologetic smiles.

Maggie crouched down next to Fliss's bed. They'd never been the best of friends, but under the circumstances she'd have to do.

'What's up, Felicity?' she said, in the gentlest voice she could muster. 'Is something making you unhappy?'

Alice, hotly pursued by Will, stuck her head round the door.

'Are you all right? Fliss, Fliss, are you all right?'

'Alice Trebizon-Woods! No boys in here, you know the rules!' barked Matron. But it was too late.

Seeing them together, Fliss felt her eyes glaze over with tears, and let her head sink back on the bed.

Maggie cottoned on immediately. 'Out, you two,' she said. 'Go back to the dance. It's just the heat and the excitement. She'll be fine.'

Alice looked hurt, and guilty.

'Come on,' Will said.

'I'd better go on my own, thanks,' said Alice, grudgingly.

Maggie didn't need to ask any more, and Fliss was disinclined to tell her, but she felt comforted by Miss Adair just sitting there holding her hand and for once not peppering her with questions about how she was doing, where she was in the class and the usual things she heard from her mother and father once a week.

Of course Miss Adair, being totally ancient and, like, nearly married and everything, couldn't possibly imagine what it was like being in love with someone who was in love with someone else. Nobody could. Nobody could understand. Everyone else was having a huge laugh – she could hear the disco starting up downstairs. See? Nobody cared about her.

Drenched in self-pity, Fliss took a great heaving breath and let out a shuddering, choking sob. Maggie squeezed her hand tightly.

'I know,' she said. 'I know.'

'You can't!' said Fliss melodramatically. 'You couldn't possibly.'

'What, you think I've never been fourteen?' said Maggie. 'Not only have I been fourteen, but when you get to my age you won't even think it was that long ago.'

Fliss sniffed sceptically. 'It's all . . .' She wondered whether she could try a swear word out in front of a teacher. 'It's all so shit.'

'I know it feels that way at the moment,' said Maggie. 'But it will get better. I promise.'

'I don't see how,' said Fliss pitifully.

Matron entered the san carrying two plates of sandwiches and some tea. She gave one to Maggie, who was surprised to find herself tearingly hungry. Fliss, however, looked at hers with an expression close to terror.

'I don't want them,' she said. 'I ate before.'

'That's right,' said Matron. 'Skinny people who've just had a good meal often faint on the dance floor. Unless you want me to call the doctor, Miss Prosser, as well as your parents, you'll eat that plate right now.'

'Don't call my parents!' said Fliss, her eyes wide.

Maggie patted her on the hand. 'Fliss, you know . . . you know you've lost too much weight, don't you? That you look frightening?'

'I don't look frightening,' said Fliss. 'I look like girls in

144

magazines. I look like a model.' She sniffed. 'And Will still didn't like me. Maybe he thinks I'm fat.'

Maggie and Matron exchanged glances.

'I'm not happy about this,' said Matron. 'Not happy at all.' She sat down beside Fliss on the chair. 'Now listen, madam,' she said. 'How you look is no concern of mine. You could grow a horn in the middle of your forehead for all I care. But your health is my concern.' She leant over. 'When was your last period?'

Fliss squirmed awkwardly. 'I don't really keep track.'

'Was it recently?'

Fliss shrugged. 'Not really.'

'And have you been having dizzy spells?'

Fliss shrugged again.

Matron wrote something on a piece of paper. 'All right,' she said, 'sit up.'

Matron leant in and smelled her breath. 'Just as I thought,' she said. 'Halitosis.'

'I don't have halitosis!' said Fliss, horrified.

'Oh, of course you do,' said Matron. 'It's really horrible. Your breath really stinks. All people who get funny about their food get gum disorders. Have you got blood on your toothbrush?'

Fliss flushed and went silent.

Matron shook her head. 'What people will do to themselves,' she wondered. 'I suppose you don't really care yet whether you might want babies one day. But, you know, this could make it very hard for you to conceive. Speaking of which' – she turned her attention to Maggie – 'you want to get a move on.'

'Ehm, one, I'm getting married; two, I'm only twenty-six; three, you're treating someone else and four, it's none of your business!' said Maggie. 'Doreen, honestly!'

'I'm just saying,' muttered Matron.

Maggie shot Fliss a quick conspiratorial smile and was gratified to see that her lips almost twitched. Then the seriousness of her situation reasserted herself and her face was drawn back into gloom.

'Have you started to get really hairy yet?' asked Matron.

'What do you mean, hairy?' asked Fliss, looking alarmed.

'Oh yes, when you get too thin your body produces fur to keep you warm. Have you been feeling the cold?'

Terrified now, Fliss nodded. She was freezing, all the time.

'Yes, people with eating problems get covered in fuzz, like monkeys. It's quite funny really. Not that there'll be anyone around to point and laugh, so don't worry. It's not like you'll be here.'

'What do you mean?' said Fliss.

Matron looked sad. 'I'm sorry, Felicity. I don't think you're well. I don't think you're well at all. You may have to leave us for a little while.'

Now Felicity was white with horror. 'You're not going to send me to an asylum?!'

Maggie leant in, worrying that Matron was being very hard on her. 'Doreen, don't be terrifying. Fliss, you'll need to be checked out by a doctor. If they agree you're having trouble eating, we may have to send you home for a little while to get well, that's all.'

'But I'm *fine!*'

Fliss was shaking now. Didn't they understand that she *had* to be thin?

Alice glanced again nervously in the direction of the san.

'Will, it's not really . . . My friend really likes you.'

'Well, I can't help that, can I?' said Will reasonably. 'Anyway, I've known her since she was a kid. It would be,

146

like, paedy or something even if I did fancy her. Which I don't.' He gave her a piercing look. 'I fancy you.'

'It doesn't matter,' said Alice, who was having, so far, the most dramatic night of her life and was enjoying it all immensely, even the bad bits. 'We just can't.'

Will glanced at her with regret. But he could wait.

'OK,' he said. 'But you can come dance with me. Come on. Just a dance.'

Alice glanced towards the san again. 'Just a dance,' she said. 'As friends.'

'As friends.'

As he pulled her into his strong arms she reflected on her noble self-sacrifice.

After ascertaining that Fliss wouldn't be requiring a wheelchair to get back to her dorm, Maggie took her arm and walked her down the quiet back passageways. The disco was in full swing, but the heavy walls of the old school blocked out most of the noise. They walked in silence, Maggie wanting to wait until Fliss felt ready to talk. She knew under normal circumstances that she would be one of the last people Fliss would choose to confide in, but these were very far from normal circumstances.

'They're not . . . I'm not really going to have to go to hospital, am I?' she said, with a tone of bravado she didn't feel.

Maggie looked at her. 'I don't know,' she replied, 'I'm not a doctor.' *But you should have called one in*, a voice inside was telling her. *You should have noticed.*

Fliss fell silent again.

Maggie reflected on the views of eating disorders at her old school, Holy Cross. Skinnyness was definitely not an epidemic there; quite the opposite in fact. Being too slim was seen as being a 'snobs' disease, something only spoiled rich girls could get. Ridiculous, of course, and very cruel. Still, she wondered if there might not be something in it. No, of course not.

Maggie suddenly remembered the little alcove, a bench set underneath the circular staircase. It was a good place to be private in an environment where privacy was a rare commodity, and she had used it to comfort Simone the previous year. She steered Felicity there now.

'What happened?' she asked.

Fliss swallowed hard. She wondered if maybe it might be better, might feel a bit better if she did tell someone. She couldn't tell her so-called friends – who knew what Alice was doing *right now*. And she wasn't going to tell her evil bloody sister or her parents, that was for sure. Her mother never ate anyway, she'd probably approve.

'It's nothing,' she said.

'Is this to do with Simone?'

Fliss shrugged. 'Well, Zelda put her on this big special makeover programme and it was like everyone was like, Hey, you guys, look at Simone, she's so gorgeous and let's make a big fuss.' Fliss knew she was sounding childish.

'What about Alice?' asked Maggie gently. She knew how delicate and passionate the ties of girls' friendships could be.

Fliss shrugged. 'Oh, I think she's getting like some kind of new boyfriend. Some boy from my village. I don't care though, anyway.'

'Ah, the boy with Alice.'

This time, Fliss's bravado couldn't hold. She tried to speak but her sentence faded away in a blur of a large sob.

Maggie paused. Oh well, here was the nub of it. Alice and that boy. She hadn't liked Matron's harsh approach too much, but maybe it might help. And maybe the Christmas holidays would be enough time away from the other girls to help Fliss get over a little bit of heartbreak.

She wanted to take Fliss in her arms, tell her it didn't matter, that there would be so many other boys, nice ones, ones who would like her. So many fun times she could have with her friends, too. But she couldn't have any of them locked up in her room, starving herself.

'There, there,' she said.

Fliss let out long, loud sobs now. 'I thought . . . I thought if I were really thin he'd like me . . . think *I* was the glamorous one.'

'Well, I'm not surprised, that's what every stupid magazine in the world tells you,' said Maggie, patting her shoulder.

Fliss sobbed on. 'Does everyone think I'm some kind of scrawny nut job?'

'*Noo*,' said Maggie. 'Oh, Felicity. I wish . . . I wish I could tell you that things will get better in a way that you could believe. But they will. There'll be other boys, much nicer. Who'll see you for what you are, not how tiny your waist is. I promise. I promise.'

'What's going to happen?'

Maggie sat her up. She couldn't lie. 'Your parents will have to fetch you. We'll explain the situation, and hopefully they'll find you a doctor. You won't be suspended, Felicity, we'll send your work on, but you won't be able to return until you're fit and well.'

Felicity broke down into huge sobs.

'Come on,' said Maggie, trying to lighten the mood, 'I thought you hated it here anyway.' Felicity just sobbed harder, and Maggie held her tight.

'I'm so sorry,' she whispered. 'I should have noticed earlier. I'm so, so sorry.'

Fliss was still snivelling. Then she paused.

'I just want to fall in love with someone nice one day and get married and get to be happy. Like you, miss.'

'Do you see?' said Ash.

They were lying on their backs in the copse, staring at the clear, starry night sky. It was freezing, but they had heavy coats on top of them and were huddling together to keep warm.

'There she is. It would be about a million times better with a telescope,' he added grumpily.

Simone squinted her eyes upwards. She did see. A tiny, circular sweep of yellow gaseous cloud in the far corner of the night sky.

'Cassiopeia,' she said. 'It's a beautiful name.'

'After the Queen of Ethiopia,' said Ash. 'Well, according to the Greeks.'

'Yeah, all right,' said Simone. 'Do you always have to know everything?'

There was a silence. Simone sensed him feeling tense.

'I don't . . . I don't know what it's like to kiss a girl,' he said finally. His voice went a little high and squeaky.

Simone felt her chest tighten. But . . . Ash? She hadn't even considered it, had really thought that it would be interesting to see the stars, seeing as she wasn't going to be doing any dancing. Her heart began to pound fiercely.

'Uh . . . no?' she said.

'Hmm,' said Ash uncomfortably.

They lay in silence for a few minutes more, both of their faces turned up towards the cold bright sky. Finally, Simone decided.

'You can kiss me if you like,' she said.

'Really? You wouldn't mind?'

'Well, I won't know till you try,' she said, trying to turn her awkwardness into a joke.

'I've read about it,' he said. 'Apparently I should put my hand on your face, like this.'

His hand was cold and a little damp. Simone pressed her own hand on top of it.

'Don't do it like the book says,' she said. 'Just do it how you think you would like to.'

And she closed her eyes as they moved closer, the steam from their breath mingling in the dark air. He smelled of mint tea and shampoo and something else she couldn't identify. And suddenly, the night was not so cold any more.

Chapter Eight

I sent away for the application form for you in case you forgot was written on the bright yellow Post-it enclosed with Anne's letter.

Maggie shook out the paperwork from the envelope. The application form for the school liaison officer in Govan was about ten pages long. She glanced at it. There was room for three essay questions. *Describe one situation in your professional life when you made a positive contribution to equal opportunities,* it said. Maggie groaned and decided to deal with it later. She had to talk to Felicity's dorm this morning, and wasn't looking forward to it. She was going to do it before class, just to get it out of the way. Felicity's parents had arrived, looking harried and confused, early that morning, and driven a wan-looking Fliss away. Joan Rhys had said she'd managed a couple of pieces of toast before she left, which Maggie was taking as a hopeful sign.

Zelda knocked quietly on her door. Miss Adair had asked to see her, when all she'd done was try and gussy up fat old Simone. She was feeling victimised. Maggie was quasi-ambivalent herself, given that the effects on Simone – her shiny hair, new figure and newfound confidence – were so obviously good. But it had to stop.

'Good morning, Zelda,' she said, welcoming her into the cosy office-stroke-study she shared with Claire.

'Morning,' said Zelda. 'Can I have a cup of coffee?'

'No. Only fourth-formers can have coffee.'

'Oh, cool. More rules. Excellent.'

'Don't be cheeky, please.' Maggie stopped herself. This wasn't how she wanted things to go. It wasn't a disciplinary matter.

Zelda plonked herself down in a chair without being asked. 'What have I done now?'

Maggie looked at her grades with some despair. It wasn't that Zelda was stupid, she simply took no effort with her work at all. None.

'Are you happy here, Zelda?' she asked.

Zelda shrugged. 'Been to better, been to worse.'

Maggie leant forward. 'We want to be better, Zelda. There's a terrific education on offer here, if you just make the tiniest bit of effort to grasp it.'

'For what,' said Zelda, 'so I can just get moved on again? Who cares?'

'But you've got so much promise,' said Maggie. 'If you poured half as much energy and creativity into your work as you did to Simone's makeover, you'd be doing really well.'

Zelda looked uncomfortable. 'I thought that was what this was about.'

Instead, Maggie told her about what had happened. 'We're worried about Felicity.'

'She wants you to be,' said Zelda, uncharacteristically sharply, then stopped herself. 'I mean, she's fine. Everything's fine.'

'I know fine, well everything's not fine,' said Maggie. 'And Zelda, I'm asking you. Please take the pressure off the dorm. What you've done for Simone is great. What it's doing to Felicity Prosser is not.'

Zelda sighed.

'And I can trust you not to repeat this conversation?'

In fact, Maggie fully expected her to repeat it word for word. It wouldn't do either Alice or Simone any harm to hear what was approved of and what was not.

'Yeah, whatever,' said Zelda.

Maggie watched her beautifully styled hair leave the room. If she could get just a tiny amount of that attention to detail she put into her appearance into her work, who knew what she could do?

I am going to engage that child, she said to herself. I don't care what it takes.

Another week brought end of term and the school was full of jabber.

Zelda listened to the other girls without joining in. It wouldn't be Christmas for her – four thousand men on a huge army base, sharing catering turkey. She thought wistfully of DC in the snow, the lights glistening on Potterfield drive, their white colonial house festooned with lights, everyone wearing their reindeer jumpers. Here outside it was just grey and horribly cold and miserable.

Simone was just worrying about whether her mother would try and get her to eat too many chocolates. Every so often she would remember back to the night with Ash. It felt like a dream, something that had happened to somebody else. She touched the slight rawness he'd left on her chin wonderingly. Proof that it really happened.

Alice was feeling alternately cross and guilty. It wasn't her fault Will had fallen for her, was it? She hadn't asked for it. On the other hand, she knew in her heart of hearts that she'd considered Fliss's behaviour attention-seeking and hadn't offered to help. She'd ignored it. It gave her an uncomfortable nagging feeling.

Nobody was in the mood for double English.

'Now, I'm not going to make you work today,' said Maggie.

There was a ragged cheer.

'But there is something,' she said. 'I just wanted to send you off on holiday with this. It's a poem I like a lot. It's not a set text, you may just like to think about it. Unfortunately,' she continued, 'if I read it with my accent it will sound totally ridiculous and you will all laugh. Fortunately we have a country woman of the poet here – you have a bit of a southern accent, don't you, Zelda?'

'Ah sure do, ma'am,' drawled Zelda, who'd spent enough time on bases in Georgia and Tennessee to do it well. Maggie was pleased at the response; Zelda couldn't hold a grudge if she tried.

'It's from a great, great countrywoman of yours. Could you come and read it out for us, please?'

Zelda looked as embarrassed as she could, which wasn't very, but the rest of the class cheered happily. This was something different.

Zelda stepped up. 'You could have warned me.'

Maggie shrugged. 'Ah, you'll be great. Do you recognise it?'

Zelda glanced at the book.

'Of course,' she said scornfully, making Maggie more determined than ever to get her marks up.

'Great,' said Maggie. 'Girls, I present . . . Maya Angelou. Also known as Zelda Towrnell.'

Zelda smiled half-heartedly and began.

'Pretty women wonder where my secret lies.
I'm not cute or built to suit a fashion model's size
But when I start to tell them,
They think I'm telling lies.

155

I say,
It's in the reach of my arms
The span of my hips,
The stride of my step,
The curl of my lips.
I'm a woman
Phenomenally.
Phenomenal woman,
That's me.'

Zelda's slightly husky tones picked up the verse perfectly. Maggie had been right; it could have sounded risible in her Scottish accent, but with Zelda speaking it made perfect sense. At the end of the verse, a few of the girls even clapped and cheered. Alice sat back, thinking, Yeah, well, chubby women always pretend this is true.

'I walk into a room
Just as cool as you please,
And to a man,
The fellows stand or
Fall down on their knees.
Then they swarm around me,
A hive of honey bees.
I say,
It's the fire in my eyes,
And the flash of my teeth,
The swing in my waist,
And the joy in my feet.
I'm a woman
Phenomenally.
Phenomenal woman,
That's me.'

That's me, thought Simone. Then she flared her eyes wide, amazed she could have even entertained that idea about herself.

'Men themselves have wondered
What they see in me.
They try so much
But they can't touch
My inner mystery.
When I try to show them
They say they still can't see.
I say,
It's in the arch of my back,
The sun of my smile,
The ride of my breasts,
The grace of my style.
I'm a woman

Phenomenally.
Phenomenal woman,
That's me.'

That's not me, thought Fliss sadly, reading it at home two days later, between the nutrition sheets her nice cheerful lady doctor had left her. She was nothing like a woman. She had no hips, no breasts to speak of. None of the lovely bouncing confidence the poet had. She wondered what it must be like to be like that.

'Now you understand
Just why my head's not bowed.
I don't shout or jump about
Or have to talk real loud.

157

When you see me passing
It ought to make you proud.
I say,
It's in the click of my heels,
The bend of my hair,
the palm of my hand,
The need of my care,
'Cause I'm a woman
Phenomenally.
Phenomenal woman,
That's me.'

The class erupted in applause.

'And that's the message I want you to take away with you this year,' said Maggie. 'Happy Christmas, everyone.'

Chapter Nine

Maggie sat round the table with the rest of her family, Stan and Stan's dad, of course. He was drunk and mumbling incoherently about Celtic football team, but that didn't make Christmas any different from usual. They just ignored him.

And they tried to ignore the screams of Cody and Dylan, who'd insisted on having the *Doctor Who* Christmas special on very loudly all through lunch and were waving their new Daleks and screaming along in time. And Anne and her mother, who were loudly discussing floral arrangements and whether purple heather and red roses would go together.

Stan had given her a blue jumper for Christmas. Not a very nice jumper either. It was a lot like something his mother (who was at her new boyfriend's for Christmas) would wear.

'Sorry,' he said, seeing her face. 'I thought you liked those kinds of clothes now.'

Maggie didn't want to take in the whole world of 'those kinds of clothes' he might mean.

'And I thought we should be saving for the wedding,' he added.

'It's lovely,' she said, feeling unexpectedly disappointed. It was only a silly Christmas present after all, who cared? She'd bought him the best of *Top Gear*, the brand new Celtic Away strip, which cost a fortune, a fifteen-year-old bottle of Talisker, a bottle of Hugo Boss and a new watch. She knew it was guilt that was making her spend so much money. He'd looked more and more worried as the wrapping paper had built up.

'These . . . these must have cost a fortune,' he said unhappily as he opened every new gift.

'Don't you like them?'

'Well, yeah, but we've still got a lot of catering to pay for . . . I mean your mum and dad are really helping, but they don't have that much, and . . .'

'It's OK, Stan,' said Maggie. 'You know, I'm making quite a bit more money now, and . . .'

Well, that hadn't been the right thing to say either. Now they avoided eye contact over the sprouts in the small, over-heated room. The dining table normally sat against the wall, they only used it at Christmas.

Stan was taking in the plates to the kitchen with bad grace. Maggie was filling in the form with worse.

'You might even get an interview before you have to go back,' said Anne. 'Those ridiculous holidays public school kids get. I suppose they all have to go skiing and things.'

'They have to go skiing and piss on peasants, yes,' said Maggie, sighing. *Describe a situation in which you implemented cultural change management.* What the *hell* kind of questions are these?

'Oh, stick anything,' said Anne. 'As soon as they see your name against that posh school, you'll be a shoe-in.'

'You think?' said Maggie. 'Hmm. Maybe I could write about the time I had to tell Zazie Saurisse that just because she's considered a princess in her home country it doesn't mean she's exempt from wearing plimsolls.'

'I'm doing just fine in here on my own, thanks,' hollered Stan from the kitchen.

'Yeah, that green squeezy stuff?' shouted Anne. 'You put that on dirty dishes to make them clean.'

'Hah ahah,' said Stan.

'What's got into him today?' said Anne.

'Oh, apparently I bought him too nice Christmas presents,' said Maggie grumpily.

She looked out of the window. Kids were on the street, throwing stones at a lamp post. That felt seasonal. Cody and Dylan had already broken their big *Transformers* lorry and were bickering crossly about whose fault it was. All the oldies were asleep on the sofa in front of the blaring telly.

It felt ridiculous, of course, given that she was surrounded by the people she loved most in the world; the people who loved her too. So how could she feel so lonely? She wished there was someone she could ring . . . She thought fleetingly of David. He would be having a wonderful time somewhere, she knew. And schoolgirl fantasies were for schoolgirls.

'Well, it's not jewellery then,' said Miranda, trying to smile but looking a bit tight around the face as she picked up the book-shaped parcel.

'Uh, no.'

David was already regretting agreeing to visit Miranda's parents for Christmas. His mother had died years before, his big brother Murdo was on manouevres in Iraq and his father, who didn't really see the point of Christmas without his wife or his manly elder son, was taking a lecture cruise in the Hellenics.

Miranda's parents, Roy and Pat, were perfectly nice. Their home in Southampton was terrifyingly clean and pastel. Pictures of Miranda, their only child, were everywhere; her

Junior Gymkhana rosettes still covered an entire wall in the sitting room.

Miranda opened the gift. It was a signed first edition of *Follyfoot Farm*. David knew Miranda had loved the books growing up and had tracked it down on a visit to Hay.

'Oh,' she said. 'I think I have this one. But thank you!'

He opened his gifts. There was a trendy Ted Baker shirt, a slim-fitting pink jumper – pink? – and a midnight-blue silk tie.

'Do I wear all these together?' he asked, puzzled.

'No, of *course* not, darling,' she said. 'I'm going to take you sales shopping too! We have to replace those dreadful striped pyjamas. And, you know, nobody wears boxer shorts any more.'

David smiled carefully. He remembered back to when they had first met. Her energy, her enthusiasm, it hadn't seemed like raw ambition then – it had felt fresh and natural, after all the dreamy, bookish girls he'd met at university.

And she'd been impressed then with his love of books, his goal of being an inspiring teacher, had thought it something impressive rather than pitiful. How had they changed so much that they couldn't even choose each other Christmas presents?

Pat and Roy demanded full silence for the Queen's speech, and Roy actually stood up to salute the national anthem.

'She's a wonderful woman,' he imparted to David gravely.

David nodded. Were they actually going to watch television all day? Miranda's parents' house backed on to a golf course and the white frost was crackling invitingly on the ground. Plus Stephen Daedalus wasn't allowed in the house, as Pat didn't like hairs everywhere.

'I have to take my dog for a walk,' he said. 'Anyone coming?'

Roy shot him a sharp look. 'Not during Our Majesty, please, if you don't mind.'

After the speech, Pat passed around shop-bought chocolate biscuits and tea. 'I never cook,' she said proudly. 'I have two personal chefs – Marks and Spencer!' Then she chuckled delightedly like she'd just said something naughty. David had rather a soft spot for Pat, even if he found her heating-up indigestible.

'Now you two,' she said, as the *EastEnders* theme tune lugubriously started up. She turned towards them and clapped her hands. 'It's nearly the New Year! So we must, you know, set the date! When's the date?'

David glanced at Miranda, appalled, but she was sitting there quite comfortably. They'd only been back together a couple of months . . . they'd broken off their engagement, hadn't they? He'd thought this was quite casual, and certainly had no idea her parents thought they were still getting married. But as he looked at Pat's beaming face and Miranda's complacent smile, he realised how naive he'd been.

'Well, you know . . .' he said desperately. 'I really must walk the dog. Miranda, are you coming?'

'Outside, where it's freezing?' she said. 'You must be joking! Anyway, it's the *EastEnders* Christmas special.'

David set out on his own. The contrast between the alarmingly overheated house and the crisp air was extreme, and he stuck his hands in his pockets. In one of them was his seldom-used mobile phone, bought only because housemasters needed to be contactable in emergencies. He pulled it out, ruefully, as he headed for the golf course. There was only one person he could even think that he'd like to call, but she wouldn't want to hear from him. He imagined her surrounded by her loving, laughing family, drinking whisky, singing, dancing, Stan by her side. He snapped the phone closed and, regretfully, put it away.

'Hoy!' shouted a man in a vividly patterned jumper. 'You can't walk your dog here! This is a private members' golf club! Bloody signs everywhere!'

David heaved a sigh and turned back.

Veronica felt her heart pound as she walked up to the house. It was lovely, an old white-washed farmhouse with a bright red door, a holly wreath perched on it jauntily. She took a deep breath and knocked.

Immediately came the tumultuous sound of three young children and their dog, throwing themselves down the stairs to see who it was. Veronica experienced a moment of panic – maybe she shouldn't have come. Maybe this was all a terrible mistake.

Then the door swung open and, standing there, looking just as nervous as she did, were Daniel, Susie, Daniel's parents Ida and John, and three very excited children, all completely oblivious to the atmosphere.

'Look!' shouted Rufus. 'I got a new submarine!'

'Well, that is just fantastic,' said Veronica, kneeling down. 'You must have been a good boy for Santa.'

'VERY good,' said Rufus.

Veronica stood up.

Ida, instinctively kind-hearted, put out her hand. 'It's nice to finally meet you.'

Veronica stared at this woman, who'd had everything she'd always dreamt of. Sometimes she'd hated her, consumed by terrible jealousy for what this woman had got to experience, the things that had been taken away from her.

But at other times, like now, looking at this happy, prosperous, loving family, all she could feel was overwhelming gratitude.

'It's very nice to meet you,' she stuttered. 'I suppose I owe you a vote of thanks . . .'

Ida looked a little wrong-footed. Then she smiled.

'No, you don't,' she said. 'I need to thank you.' She cast a meaningful glance at Daniel. 'It was a pleasure.'

The two women looked at each other, the weight of their lives passing between them.

'Come in, come in!' bustled Susie. 'We'll all catch our deaths!'

Fliss was comfortably wrapped up in a blanket in the sitting room in front of the fire. Hattie humphed past her. She had her mock GCSEs when they went back to school in the New Year and had absolutely loads of studying to do. Fliss, on the other hand, seemed to be watching *Harry Potter* movies back to back and working her way through a selection box.

'Your breath smells,' Hattie said helpfully as she crossed the thick carpet.

Fliss shot her a lazy look. 'Yes, but after I've eaten all this chocolate it won't smell any more. Whereas you'll always have BO.'

'SHUT UP! Mum! Mum!'

Fliss's mother looked at their father. 'I thought they'd grow out of this when they got past five,' she said. 'I feel a migraine coming on.'

Their dad grimaced. 'Is it too early to start on the sherry?'

'And to think,' said their mum, 'that considered not sending them to boarding school.'

They both burst out laughing, then sobered up.

'Do you think she'll be all right?' said Mrs Prosser.

Her husband shrugged uncomfortably.

She controlled her own food intake with an iron fist. Well, you had to these days, didn't you? Keep looking good, keep your man interested. She did wonder if she'd passed her habits on to the girls . . . although Hattie was just such a *lump* at the moment. But yes, she'd need to feed Fliss up, if only to get her back to school. Secretly she thought she looked rather chic.

'She'll be fine,' said Tony. 'A few trips to McDonalds.'

Fortunately Dr Horridge, whom they'd called in at great expense, had slightly better advice than this to give and was to spend a lot of time with Fliss over the coming weeks and months, gently encouraging her to break the link between controlling her food and controlling her life. Fliss's genuine desire to return to school would also be a great motivator, but for now a cosy fire, her dog snuggled up to her, the telly on, her family around and a box of chocolates within easy reach didn't seem like bad medicine.

Veronica had worked very hard on getting it right, and it turned out she had. Her little wooden gifts – a working light-house for Rufus to guide his submarines home; a caterpillar and a pull-along dog for the littlies – had been a huge hit without being showy or extravagant, and the carefully chosen books for the adults well-received.

After a wonderful dinner – Susie and Ida had cooked well in harmony, Veronica had noticed – they sat back around the table, the children playing or asleep, and Daniel impressed on Veronica to tell the story once again. Through his eyes, she saw, it wasn't tragic or horrific or shameful, but rather slightly romantic. He was proud of it.

Ida, Susie and John listened with interest. At the end of it Ida clasped her arm and patted it.

'You know,' said John, 'he's probably still out there some-where.'

'*John*,' said Ida crossly. 'Behave yourself.'

'I expect not,' said Veronica. 'Life expectancy for Russian men is very low, and I wouldn't like to disrupt his family, I've already disrupted yours . . .'

There was a chorus of disagreement at this. Veronica felt a little pink in the cheeks and reminded herself not to drink any more wine.

'And anyway, I never heard from him again, although he had my address,' said Veronica. 'So.'

'So,' piped up Daniel's dad again, 'are you going to let the school know then? Stop keeping our boy a secret?'

'JOHN!' shouted Daniel and Ida in unison. Veronica sat back, shocked.

Susie, thoughtful as always, clapped her hands and sug-gested a game of Scrabble. On her way to get the board, she squeezed Veronica on the shoulder. Veronica normally dis-liked over-familiarity. But under the circumstances, she was extremely grateful.

Chapter Ten

A new year!

Lent term began on 9th January. As usual, Veronica had an in-service day for teachers from both schools the day before term started to get them up to date on joint activities for the coming months.

David couldn't help it, he was so looking forward to seeing Maggie. It had been ages. And even though he was sick to death of Christmas and parties and everything to do with it, Miranda wanted him to come to her spring awards bash in February. He had suggested cooling off their relationship a little, but she had looked at him with her huge guileless blue eyes and put on a little girl's voice and it looked like she'd been about to cry, so he'd changed the subject very quickly. It wasn't, he reflected, as if there was much else out there – she was a beautiful girl, and not everyone would be willing to take on a near-penniless English teacher on the wrong side of thirty, whose career prospects would be a lot better if he didn't keep turning down every promotion that would stick him in an office doing paperwork all day instead of doing what he loved: teaching.

Claire was sitting at the back of the ref reading *Paris Match*, dressed in an utterly beautiful new purple coat and looking affronted, as if three weeks in Paris simply hadn't been enough.

'*Salut mon brave*,' said David, slipping in next to her.

'Daveed! Seet with me, we can chat through very boring meeting. Still.' She looked around. 'At least there are none of those *oreeble* pupils.'

'No,' said David. 'Uh, where's Maggie?'

Claire took a quick glance around. 'It ees secret,' she said.

'Excellent,' said David. 'I love secrets.' But something cold clutched at him.

'OK,' said Claire. 'I am very unreliable.'

David raised an eyebrow, then put on his glasses and pretended to be reading the agenda.

'She has an interview,' whispered Claire. 'For a job.'

David bit his lip to make himself look unconcerned. 'Oh really?' he said. 'Whereabouts?'

'But Glasgow of course!' said Claire. 'You know, she gets married, she gets a job at home . . .'

'She always did say she had to go back,' said David. 'I just . . . I didn't expect it to be so soon.'

Claire gave him a shrewd look. 'You will miss her, *non*?'

David found himself caught between a sudden desire to confess everything to Claire, just for a sympathetic ear, but remembered in time that she had said herself she was 'unreliable'. Anything he told her would get back to Maggie. And that would be impossible, wrong. She had chosen her path, and to do anything would be dog-in-the-manger . . .

'Oh, well, you know. There's not so many of us undersixties around that we can afford to lose some.'

'That ees true,' said Claire, mollified.

David picked up the agenda again. But it scarcely mattered; he couldn't read a word of it.

*

Maggie couldn't work out what it was. Was it some kind of dress-down day? Why were the interview panel wearing elasticated trousers and baggy, stained tops?

Then she realised they were just dressed for work. She bit her tongue and smoothed down her smart Marimekko shirt; she was turning into a snob.

'So you've been working in the private sector?' said a woman with a layered haircut so short, precise and unflattering she could only be making some kind of point. 'What made you go there exactly?'

'Well, it seemed a good opportunity to expand my, uh, skill set,' said Maggie, grasping for the right bureaucracy-heavy terminology.

'Don't you feel the private sector is a parasite, sucking away the good marrow from our schools and fostering class war, discontent and inequality?'

Maggie recognised herself from a couple of years ago. Maybe some world views were never challenged.

'I believe every child deserves the best, and none deserves censure for their parent's decisions,' she said.

'But what about a culture that fosters entitlement?' spluttered a very fat woman from the end of the table. She spat a little as she spoke.

'Why shouldn't they feel entitled?' said Maggie, feeling her familiar temper rise – but this time from the opposite side. 'I wish every child could feel as entitled and privileged as the students I've taught at Downey House. I wish every child could feel that the world is there for them, and that they have the potential to succeed in it. That's why I'm here.'

The panel glanced at each other.

'So you think you'd want to bring some of that *boarding school* ethos to your work here as a liaison?' said the woman with the short hair. She was smirking. 'Jolly hockey-sticks? Midnight feasts for everyone?'

The others on the panel laughed.

'I don't see why I can't bring some of the methods used in public schooling to this environment, no,' said Maggie, feeling her voice grow small, even as she tried to keep a lid on her temper. Who were these know-it-alls who were so sure their way was right? If everything they did was so fantastic, they wouldn't need to be hiring someone to encourage kids to attend school in the first place. And she was going to be working with them.

'Things are a bit different up here,' said the fat woman.

'I've worked up here,' said Maggie crossly. 'And I've worked down there. And as far as I'm concerned, kids are just kids.'

Simone was utterly shocked when she learned Fliss wasn't coming back straight away. She'd been under the impression everyone thought Fliss looked as amazing as she did. As far as Simone had always been aware, the thinner the better. But apparently not. So she had a plan for when they were back. Her mother, banned from sending treats to the school under the new regime, and worried that her daughter was looking peaky and thin (never mind the many compliments she'd received, the girl had to *eat*), was only too happy to oblige. Which was why Simone turned up in the old beige Merc with an extra large box for the start of the new term.

'What's that then?' asked Zelda. Their dorm was utterly freezing, and both the girls had jumped into bed in the middle of the afternoon. Simone had noticed that half of the other Plantagenet girls arriving back had their hair styled exactly like Zelda. They looked like they were all about to enter a Miss Young Texas pageant.

And Zelda's mother had actually got out of the car and paraded around the school in a fur coat and cowboy hat! It didn't get much more glamorously exotic than that, as far as Simone was concerned.

'Hon*ey*!' she had said to Zelda. 'How can you *stand* the cold? DuBose, can't you do something?' But DuBose – although an evil soldier, of course, was still so tall and handsome in his uniform that the girls were hanging out of their windows to look at him, until Miss Starling shooed them back inside – had merely grunted and suggested Zelda stopped getting everything her own way all the time.

'And I want to see your grades up,' he'd added.

'But, Pops!' Zelda had imprecated, holding on to his arm in a way he'd always found hard to resist. 'How can I when it's so *cold*?'

And sure enough, a fur coat turned up in the post a week later. Zelda hastily changed it for a fake fur one, after she came across Sylvie Brown crying about all the 'dead polar bears'. There were just so many strange British sensibilities she would never understand.

Back in the dorm, Simone said, 'Aha! The box is for you, actually. Well, all of us. My mum's made us a midnight feast to celebrate when Fliss comes back! I don't *think* that's in bad taste, do you?'

'Truly?' said Zelda, who didn't care about taste one way or the other. 'Fantastic! Will it keep? I hope it's lots of fruit for you.'

'No,' said Simone, proud to be standing up to her. 'You have to eat junk food at midnight feasts. If you eat it at midnight it doesn't count. It'll keep till Fliss gets back.'

Zelda frowned. 'I'll have to get a new toothbrush.' Zelda brushed her teeth for about an hour a night.

'I think you're worrying too much about it,' said Simone.

Suddenly Zelda remembered something.

'I have contraband too!'

'What?'

'I smuggled it in from the base. They've got it all there. Oh God, to show you I'll have to get out of bed. Man, this place is inhuman.'

Steeling herself, Zelda leapt to the cupboard and burrowed around under her suitcase, returning triumphantly with a bottle of Jack Daniels.

Simone looked at it in shock.

'Zelda! No! If we get caught with that, it's just instant expulsion! Straight away, no questions asked!'

That was very much the impression Veronica, Miss Starling and the team attempted to convey to the school. It usually worked quite well on the younger years.

'Simone, we're nearly fifteen. For goodness' sake, live a little! Half the girls our age in this country are pregnant by now!'

Simone still looked at the bottle like it was a poisonous snake. 'I think I'll stick to cake,' she said.

'Suit yourself,' said Zelda, squirreling away the bottle at the bottom of her wardrobe.

Alice, however, thought a midnight feast was a great idea.

'Three weeks and Fliss'll be back – if she can gain three kilos,' she said. In fact, she'd heard it from Hattie. Fliss hadn't wanted to speak to her over Christmas, and Alice hadn't pushed it. Hattie had also said Fliss was loving therapy because she got to talk about herself all day, but Alice had put it down to sour grapes.

What she didn't know was that Fliss had also managed to say hello to Will at the carol service. He had very kindly enquired after her health and said how glad he was she was better and that she looked well and how was her friend? Fliss was more determined than ever to get back to school.

For once, Maggie's heart failed to be lifted as, on her own this time, she saw the four towers of Downey House glistening in the frosty January sunshine as she crested the hill in the cab she'd caught from the station.

She felt guilty and disloyal, going for an interview for another job. She didn't want the job and she didn't want to leave, but what was she going to do? Hide down here for ever as her whole life fell apart? And it wasn't as if she was doing a sterling job. To have one of her pupils suffering nearanorexia on her watch – that was an appalling failure in her duty of care. And she'd not worked the girls nearly as hard as she should have done – too much mooning about her romantic situation. That was another reason to get the hell out of Cornwall. Otherwise, what was next? She'd be at David and Miranda's wedding, smiling and trying to look pleased for them, when all she would feel would be jealousy. Why was it so hard to live in the real world?

But somehow, even with all that, she would still be so sad to leave, she knew she would. She felt so torn.

Well, she could work on doing her best. To pay close attention to the girls, work them hard this term. Be a good teacher. Then a good wife.

So, the following morning, Maggie was pleased to see her class looking relatively bright-eyed and bushy tailed – although there was obvious disquiet at Fliss's empty seat. Maggie had decided the best thing to do was to tell everyone the whole story (apart from the Will parts, of course), then hope they brought any concerns or worries to her afterwards.

'Is she going to die?' asked Sylvie Brown, her big eyes wide.

'No,' said Maggie. 'But recovery can be difficult and we'll all have to support her.'

'Did they force-feed her?' asked Zazie. They were all fascinated.

'Certainly not, she wasn't that ill,' said Maggie. 'It's just important to catch these things early.' She looked round the class slowly. 'So just be aware . . . I'm watching you all, and not just for spelling.'

The class groaned, good-naturedly.

'Now,' said Maggie, 'it's Shakespeare this term. We're going to look at *Romeo and Juliet*. And I think you're really going to enjoy it. It's a love story about people your age.'

Alice's ears pricked up. She was feeling she hadn't quite been getting the credit she deserved for not even mentioning Will since she got back. It was only cruel forces holding them apart.

Simone thought nervously about Ash. She'd only had one email from him since she got home, which hadn't stopped her driving Joel crazy by hogging the computer and keeping him from *World of Warcraft*. She'd memorised every line. It said: *We don't have stupid Christmas. Christmas is culturally stupid, but no Christmas at all is actually worse. Festivals of lights are not the same. And Cambridge and my dad have both said they don't care what my marks are, I can't go till I'm eighteen and have, quote, 'grown up a bit'. . The world is full of idiots and they're all against me. Yours Sincerely, Ashley Mehta (Downey Boys).*

OK, so it hadn't been a love letter as such. But he'd been thinking about her, and that was definitely something.

'Has anyone seen the Leonardo DiCaprio version?' Maggie asked. A couple of the girls nodded. When Maggie was growing up, Leo had been the biggest thing in the world, bar no one. In fact, Leo and Claire Danes were what really turned Maggie on to English literature in the first place. She never told anyone that, of course, pretending it was her love of reading alone that had done it.

'Well, if you all study extremely hard, we'll watch it one day. And if you behave yourself, they're also putting *Romeo and Juliet* on at the Minotaur Theatre in June, so there'll be a joint Downey Boys outing to that – I'll send a consent form to your parents.'

'What are we, six?' whispered Zelda to Alice. But Alice was reading the back of her book with an unusually dreamy expression on her face . . . Two young lovers, held apart by social constraints, even though their love was strong enough to endure . . . It was definitely Will and her!

'We don't know very much about Shakespeare's life,' Maggie continued. 'We don't know where he spent his youth, or much about his love life, apart from the fact that in his will he bequeathed to his wife Anne Hathaway his "second best bed" – which implies at the very least that he had interests elsewhere. But his ability to capture the feeling of young love – and Romeo and Juliet are believed to be very young, your age; Romeo is about fourteen, Juliet too – has resonated down the ages, with almost no one catching it quite so well. So, Simone, can you turn to page eleven and begin reading, please, till we get our heads into the rhythm.'

'*Two households, both alike in dignity,*' read Simone obediently, '*In fair Verona, where we lay our scene.*'

Zelda yawned ostentatiously. Maggie shot her a look. She'd hoped that looking at an American poet might have piqued Zelda's interest last term, but obviously it hadn't. She just wished she could engage the girl in something more than her hair and nails.

*

Veronica sat in her office, grimacing at the form. Evelyn hovered nearby, ready to offer non-intrusive assistance.

'I do *hate* this affair,' said Veronica.

Evelyn nodded sympathetically. The official public school Expo took place in March every year, in Birmingham. Every school had a stall to attract parents looking for the right place to send their children. Veronica understood the anxiety of a parent desperate to do the right thing for their child, but did find it a little wearying answering repeated questions about how they would handle India's wheat allergy and what their programme was for 'gifted' children. She understood this was a selling job, and that her school was also a business. But she found the mercantile aspect a little distasteful, particularly in this tougher economic climate with many families having to tighten their belts. Selling payment-spreading schemes and discussing sibling discounts were not things she liked to get involved in, but her head of finance, Archie Liston, was even more publicity-shy than she was and refused to come to these events. He was an excellent accountant, though, so Veronica didn't feel able to coerce him. Fleur Parsley, the drama teacher, always went down very well at these events – particularly with the fathers – and enjoyed them too, so she would accompany them, as well as Janie James, whose no-nonsense manner was generally a hit. Veronica excused Miss Starling, on the grounds that whilst parents might theoretically approve of strict teaching for their offspring, they occasionally found meeting an austere teacher from their youth a little off-putting.

Dr Fitzroy, of course, would be in his element. Effusive and personable, he also enjoyed the socialising element with other headmasters, swapping war stories and enjoying good brandy. At least he would be nearby, and could often be relied upon to intervene cheerily whenever Veronica's smile looked like it might be about to seize up.

Veronica ticked the boxes on the form for where their stand would be, which conference hotel she would take, how much publicity they would require. She felt tired just thinking about it. Ah well, a necessary evil.

She passed on the paperwork and picked up the form Matron had filled in following Felicity Prosser's unfortunate incident at the Christmas dance. Maggie, however, seemed to have it under control now and there seemed to have been no further cases – eating disorders could often prove infectious. It had been something of a gamble employing her, but she'd proved herself as dedicated to the girls and the school as Veronica could have wished. She was pleased. Although Maggie was showing signs of strain that Veronica didn't think had anything to do with Felicity Prosser. Veronica knew she was getting married – to the quite brash-looking young man who'd visited the previous year – and hoped it wasn't stress from the wedding. She supposed she'd lose her back to Scotland eventually . . . Well, that was another problem she'd deal with as it arose.

'More tea?' said Evelyn.

Veronica glanced up. 'When did they put mind reader on your job description?' she said wonderingly.

Chapter Eleven

In fact the primroses were budded by the time Fliss felt well enough to return to school, four weeks after the start of term. She'd kept up with her work whilst she was away, but still felt a little nervous about heading back into the hurly-burly.

'Just remember, I'm always on the phone,' Dr Horridge had reminded her. 'Just stick to our plan. They'll also arrange for you to see someone local once a week, and Matron will be keeping an eye on you.'

'About four hundred people will be keeping an eye on me,' grumbled Fliss as she went to pack her bag. But staying at home was so boring, and although Simone was keeping her up with the intrigue – she was sad to have missed Zelda's great coat scandal – it wasn't the same as being there.

It felt strange to be dropped off, all alone, but as she rounded the gravel drive and saw Matron, Miss Adair and her dorm-mates all lined up to welcome her, it was all she could do to keep the tears from her eyes.

After a quick pep talk from Maggie, the girls were allowed to take her upstairs. It had been so quiet at home, it was hard to get used to the bustle.

'Tonight!' Zelda was saying. 'At midnight!'

'Well, yes, that would seem to be the point of midnight feasts,' said Alice.

'We're doing what?' asked Fliss.

'I don't want to drink,' said Simone.

'Who's drinking?' said Alice.

'Zelda has booze,' said Simone miserably. 'It'll spoil our feast.'

'Well, that rather depends on the booze,' said sophisticated Alice. 'If it's a sweet white wine, we've no hope.'

'It's Jack Daniels.'

Fliss perked up. 'Ooh! I've heard you can mix that with Coke so it doesn't taste so revolting.'

'We are NOT taking drugs,' said Simone.

'*Cola*. Cola, Simone, don't bust a gut.'

Simone didn't look mollified, but the other girls were excited.

'I'll set my alarm,' said Zelda.

'I don't think I'll sleep anyway,' said Fliss. 'God, it's good to be back.'

'Aren't you worried about getting into trouble?' asked Zelda.

The other girls scoffed.

'Midnight feasts aren't *trouble*,' said Alice. 'At this school they're practically on the syllabus!'

'Stop moaning,' said Miranda sharply.

'I'm not moaning,' said David. 'I was politely wondering what's wrong with my cufflinks.'

'They have dogs on them.'

'Not real dogs.'

'*David*.'

Miranda took out a box from her dressing table. 'Here. I bought you these.'

David opened it. They were plain steel, with *Ralph Lauren* engraved across them.

'My name's not Ralph Lauren,' grumbled David.

'Stop moaning! And zip me up.'

Miranda did look very glamorous for her office night out. She was wearing a very short, tight kingfisher-blue satin dress that would have been unforgiving on anyone in less good shape. David found it a bit obvious for his taste, but on the other hand she did look good, he knew.

'They're having an awards ceremony!' said Miranda. 'I think I'm going to win Senior Sales Rep of the Year.'

'That's great,' said David.

'You need to help me write my speech. I'll have to do it when we get there.'

'You need a speech? Can't you just say thank you?'

'Well, you know. It's a big award.'

'But I don't know anything about sales repping!'

Miranda gave him a look. 'I know how much you care about my job, David.'

David saw his mistake. 'I'm sorry. I will write something for you. Of course. In the car on the way.'

'You know,' said Miranda, 'all the top salesmen in the region will be there. There are definitely openings at entry level . . . it wouldn't pay well at first but, with bonuses, within two years you could be en route to making a proper amount of money, and then we could think about getting married. Of course we'd have to move to Southampton, but you know Mummy and Daddy are so excited about doing that and I'm sure they'd help us with a deposit anyway. I'd love to be nice and close to them, that would be wonderful.'

I have to tell her, thought David. I just have to. She's a nice girl, and I was weak, and I gave in, but now I want out. But it's all my fault for leading her on. So how can I?

The hotel, the Princess Royal in Truro, had obviously seen better days. Once a properly grand venue, generations of well-heeled holidaymakers travelling abroad had seen it tip into a slighty dusty, florally decorated neglect, held afloat by weddings and corporate functions, having not yet been targeted for a fawn and beige boutique makeover. As David and Miranda entered, a board with plastic lettering, one 'e' missing, directed them to the Prime Assurance awards.

'The credit crunch really is starting to bite,' sniffed Miranda, but David rather liked the Victorian wrought-iron staircase and the winter garden, with its suggestion of glamour past.

'Oh, come on, it's romantic,' he said.

'It's smelly,' said Miranda. 'And the food is going to be terrible.'

'Let's not go then,' said David. 'Let's have a drink, listen to the pianist then go somewhere else.'

'Could you *be* less supportive?' stormed Miranda crossly. 'This is my *career*. I know you don't care about having a career, but that doesn't mean we're all stuck in the same—'

A row was narrowly averted as a large group of shouting men, already looking pink in the cheeks from bonhomie and beer, entered the foyer. Miranda immediately arranged her features into that of a woman not engaged in a row with her boyfriend.

'Ken! Jim! Declan! Great to see you,' she called, beaming.

'Look at you,' said the beefiest, who had sweat beading on his forehead despite the frosty night outside. 'Corr!'

'Yeah, who crammed you into that dress?' said another. 'Lucky bugger.'

'Uh, that would be me,' said David, trying to make it up to Miranda and gamely sticking out his hand.

'Oh aye,' said the man, as all three of them eyed David up and down. His bought, not rented, tuxedo; his long, thin frame – things that marked him out as not one of them, and both David and Miranda were painfully aware of it.

'What line are you in?' said another of the men, quite aggressively.

'I'm a teacher. Up at the boys' school.'

This was, apparently, hilarious.

'What, little boys and that?'

'What do you teach? Do you like to give them encouraging pats now and then? Just on the bum and that?'

David stared at them. There were bullies in every year, in every walk of life, he'd met them all before and they certainly weren't going to phase him now.

'Do you want a drink?' he said to Miranda, and before she had time to answer he headed for the bar.

'He's a rude bugger, innee?' said the beefy man, Ken, obviously unbothered or unaware that he'd just accused another man of being a paedophile. 'Never mind, sweetheart, you look good enough to eat.'

'You certainly do,' said Declan, who had a reputation amongst the other reps as being a bit of a smoothie with the women. 'Hope you're on my table.'

Miranda was cross with David. Why was he so bloody sensitive all the time? Anyway, he chose the bloody job. He had to know he was a complete embarrassment, surely?

'I do too,' she said, her eyes round.

'Well, come on then,' said Declan. 'Let's go have a look at the table plan.'

David returned from the bar with two gin and tonics in slightly smeary glasses, to find himself alone. He decided the best thing to do was to drink them both.

Stan was nervous. He wished that he'd taken the train so he could at least have had a couple of lagers to calm him, but that would be stupid. He'd finished his early morning shift at nine and jumped straight in the car.

It had been Anne's idea. Be spontaneous, she'd said. She'd even found a hotel on the internet for him to book – a proper posh one, too. Stan didn't feel very comfortable in places like that, but Anne had assured him that Maggie would like it a lot if he turned up, she sniffed, 'looking respectable', which Stan took to mean that his football shirt probably wouldn't do. The hotel had a dinner, bed and breakfast package which seemed expensive, but Anne had really pushed for it.

In truth, Anne was worried. Maggie just seemed a little down about things – not the way a bride should be at all. She liked Stan a lot and wanted to give them a little shove, to remember what they liked about each other, before five hundred miles of countryside got in the way.

Maggie grabbed her mail from her pigeon hole. She liked Friday evenings. No marking to do, she'd sometimes go out with a couple of the other teachers for a quiet drink, or stay in by herself with a magazine, some Maltesers and some television, happy that the responsibilities of the school were, for one night at least, off her hands. Perhaps Claire would fancy splitting a bottle of wine, if she wasn't going out or haring off to try and catch the Eurostar. She was going to put on her cosiest pyjama bottoms, her largest pair of socks, and have a nice, quiet relaxed evening. Let's face it, thought Maggie, she didn't know how many more of these she was going to get.

Humming to herself as she opened her door she was surprised to notice it wasn't locked. But not half as surprised as she was, on opening it, to see Stan, looking embarrassed in a slightly shiny silver grey shirt, in the middle of the room.

'What . . .?' Maggie was careful to keep an accusatory tone out of her voice. 'What are you doing here?'

Then she stepped forward and gave him a hug. 'You gave me the shock of my life. I thought I was being burgled. Not that you look like a burglar,' she added quickly. 'You look great. I like your shirt.'

Stan grinned. 'Thought I'd come and surprise you, aye?'

'Well, you did,' said Maggie.

'Yon headmistress let me up. She's all right that yin. For a teacher, like.'

Maggie reflected that it was just as well Stan had come across Dr Deveral and not Miss Starling.

'So . . . why?' she asked eventually.

Stan grinned. 'Well, maybe – *maybe* – I've booked us into a luxury hotel in town along with a posh slap-up dinner and all that and maybe you have to get your glad rags on because maybe your fiancé is a bit of an old romantic after all.'

He fished in his bag and withdrew a slightly battered, but nonetheless unprecedented bunch of flowers.

Maggie smiled in delight and shook her head. 'You are a dark horse, Stanley Cameron,' she said.

He moved in and kissed her.

'Well, get dressed then, wife to be,' he said, smacking her sharply on the bum. 'Haven't got all night to mess about. And I've got to drive back tomorrow.'

Maggie stopped. 'You drove? You've got to drive all the way back tomorrow?'

'Got the early shift on Sunday, haven't I?'

Maggie blinked. She wouldn't have thought he was capable of such a gesture, or that she would ever receive one. She was incredibly touched and pleased.

'I was going to wear those big fluffy pyjamas you love so much,' she laughed.

'No chance,' said Stan. 'My fiancée looks sexy – or else!'

Giggling, Maggie disappeared into the bedroom.

The Grand Banqueting Hall was filled with tables. Miranda worked mostly with men, and although some of them had brought bored-looking wives and girlfriends along, many had not, seeing the evening more as a chance to get drunk for free, bond with the boys and try their luck with the waitresses. Miranda was certainly the most striking looking woman there, with the fishtail of her blue dress flashing dangerously in the lights. Eyes, already blurry with the free wine, followed her across the room as she found her table, while the other women gossiped. There was to be a dinner (chicken a la King or salmon roulade) followed by the awards presentation, followed by a disco. David checked his heavy watch surreptitiously as the men on the table – including the broad-shouldered Declan – discussed Saturday's match whilst keeping an eye on Miranda's bosoms in the blue dress.

Miranda drank one gin and tonic too quickly to settle her nerves, then another one because it was there. By the time the waitress came round pouring 'Red or white?' she had decided tonight she was going to let her hair down and enjoy herself, particularly if her boyfriend was going to sit there with a face like a bloody wet weekend. You know, he wasn't the best she could do. Not by a long shot. Every man in this room – almost all of whom took home more money than he did and at least had a bloody home to call their own rather than a glorified bloody dormitory – liked the look of her, she could tell. She'd show him what he was taking for granted. She picked up her glass and found it empty again.

'Don't worry about that,' said Declan, magicking up a

bottle from somewhere and filling her glass to the brim. 'You just have fun.'

'I can't wait till midnight,' Fliss said. 'Dr Horridge said I should eat whenever I feel like it.'

'Oh yes?' came Alice's voice in the darkness. 'Can that be now?'

'I could eat,' added Simone. In fact, it was more nerves that made her say that. She was already worried enough that someone would discover the alcohol.

'Yeah, darn it,' said Zelda. 'We can have a nine o'clock feast. Your ma's packed enough that we'll still be eating at midnight anyway.'

There was a general muttering of agreement.

'OK,' said Zelda, directing operations. 'Simone, to the food.'

Mrs Kardashian had indeed done Simone proud. Inside the hamper was every type of chocolate bar imaginable, as well as crisps and nuts. There was even a carefully wrapped and preserved piece of Christmas cake which was just about still edible. The girls, a month into term, were already tired of the general austerity of the Downey House catering service, and squealed delightedly. Alice brought out a two-litre bottle of Coke and four plastic glasses from under her bed.

'Maybe we should have invited the whole form,' said Simone.

'Maybe we *shouldn't* have,' said Fliss, already filling her mouth with chocolate. 'This is amazing, Simone! Your mother is a marvel.'

Simone wouldn't go quite that far, but she did have her moments. She licked honey off her fingers like a bear.

'OK,' said Zelda, passing out cups. 'We don't have any ice, but it will have to do.'

'I'm not having any,' said Simone.

The other girls all groaned.

'No! I'm not! And I don't care if you think I'm square.'

Alice leant off her bed to grab her arm in shock. 'Simone! Are you SQUARE?!'

And the entire room exploded in giggles.

Maggie smiled at Stan while they stood in reception. He looked like he was checking them in as Mr and Mrs Smith. The Princess Royal was the smartest hotel in Truro, she supposed, although it looked a little dated to her and not really like pictures of hotels she saw in magazines. Still, she felt very lucky. She was wearing a pretty green dress she'd found in the January sales and had bought extravagantly without knowing when she would get a chance to wear it. At the back of her mind, she supposed she could justify it as a going-away dress for her wedding, although that was so far away of course. It had a wide boat-neck that framed her face, and a tight waist that drew attention away from her bum. It fell below her knees – and it swished. Maggie had never entirely grown out of the appeal of a dress that swished.

'Do you like it?' she'd asked Stan.

He'd looked at her critically.

'What?'

'No, aye I do, aye. You look good.'

'But . . .'

'But what?'

'Well, it sounded like you were about to say "but".'

Stan shrugged. 'You're a good-looking lassie, Maggie. You should show it off a bit more.'

'What do you mean, "it"?'

'Well, dress a bit more sexy, like. Cause I think you're sexy.'

'Well, good,' said Maggie. 'But I'm not sure I could handle miniskirts and stilettos.'

'Well, maybe you never know until you try.'

Maggie conceded this was indeed the case, but she was still pleased with the green dress.

'We have to hurry if we want dinner,' said Stan, looking worried. 'They're about to close the kitchen and they've got a big function on.'

'Well, nice of them to welcome us,' said Maggie, who'd rather thought they should probably have nookie first – if Stan had too much to drink at dinner, it would be pretty rubbish later on. Best to get it out of the way.

A fifteen-year-old waitress in a nylon shirt and waistcoat led them into a lounge where a fire was crackling.

'Our grand dining room is out of commission,' she said nervously in an Eastern European accent. 'Tonight, we are welcoming guests to our nook.'

Maggie and Stan caught each other's eyes and began to laugh. This could be fun.

'A large vodka and Coke and a large Bacardi and Coke,' he said.

Maggie was about to say that she didn't drink Bacardi any more and would rather have wine, but stopped herself. Tonight, at least, she could drink Bacardi.

Simone could see the difference in them. The laughing was growing more hysterical; the food a little messier.

Alice was talking about the Egyptian waiter who'd fallen in love with her last year and tried to swap six camels for her.

'He just kind of lurked about all day in front of my dad, it was totally embarrassing,' she said.

'How did you get rid of him?' asked Simone.

'Oh, I didn't get rid of him, I snogged him mental up the back of the souk. Have you ever seen Egyptian men? They're *gorgeous*!'

The room collapsed again as Zelda passed around the bottle.

'Simone . . .' she said enquiringly. Simone primly put her hand over her cup.

'*Come* on, Simone,' said Fliss, slurring slightly. 'It's called growing up. Nothing can happen, it's just here, we'll look after you.'

'Si-mone! Si-mone! Si-mone!' Zelda started chanting, and the others joined in. Pink at being singled out like this, Simone finally uncovered her hand from the top of her cup. She was nearly fifteen after all, hardly a child.

'Not too much!' she said warningly, as Zelda sloshed a measure in her glass.

'Of course not!' said Zelda.

Miranda hadn't eaten any of her supper. David kept trying to get her to drink some water, and she called him a boring bastard and batted him away like a fly. He'd sat there like a bloody useless pillock, even when the boys took pity on him and asked him what car he drove. And why shouldn't they take the piss? It was ridiculous to drive an ancient navy-blue Saab at his age. He hadn't even tried to laugh and join in the joshing, just given them a tight smile and not said anything. It was pathetic.

Anyway, it didn't matter now because the awards were starting. A comic that she'd seen on telly was standing up and telling jokes about the Managing Director having sex with a goat; he was hilarious. She shouted out a few 'Yo!'s and tried to give him a standing ovation, but the others pulled her down for some reason.

That didn't matter, it was her category now. And the award for Southwest Sales Rep of the year goes to . . .

Someone was holding her hand in excitement. She glanced down and noticed it was Declan. Oh, that was nice, he wanted her to win too. She took another slug of her wine for courage . . .

'Miranda Carlton!'

The room erupted in applause. Miranda jumped up out of her seat, screaming in excitement. The other men at the table took it in turns to hug her. Then she went for the podium. Her shoes wobbled and she thought she was going to fall, but nobody would notice, would they? There was a great gale of laughter from the crowd, but they were just pleased, weren't they? She turned round and gave them a cheery wave.

The comedian off the telly gave her a kiss and said, 'Well done, darlin'.' He must fancy her too. She took the metal pointy thing off him and waved it in the air, then leant forward to the microphone.

'Thank you . . . Thank you so much, everyone . . . There are some people I would like to thank, of course . . . and you know, I have seen the MD having sex with a goat and you know it didn't look as bad as everyone thinks . . . the goat seemed to be enjoying it.'

The entire room howled with laughter and stamped their feet. David bit his lip.

'So I want to thank Ken, Jim, all the *gorgeous* men who've supported me through this!'

There was a large roar at this too. Miranda couldn't believe she was going down so well.

'There'll be a little treat for you later . . .'

'Get 'em off!'

David got to his feet. This was going way too far, and

Miranda obviously had no idea what she was doing. He headed towards the stage, grim-faced. Miranda saw him.

'And my miserable boyfriend, I'd like to apologise for him . . .'

The audience went quiet. David reached the lectern and jumped up.

'Come on, sweetie,' he said. 'That was a great speech, but I think you can go now.'

'No!' she yelled. The comedian tried to help David get her off the stage.

'Leave 'er alone!' shouted one voice from the audience. David glanced around at a sea of red, howling, drunken faces.

'Miranda,' he said desperately. 'I really think we should go.'

'Spoilsport!' howled Miranda into the microphone. 'Someone get me another drink!'

A great cheer went up as David and the comic finally helped her down from the lectern.

'God, they're noisy next door,' said Stan for the fourth time.

'Mmm,' said Maggie. They'd ordered off the set menu and their food was terrible; a congealed-looking steak and kidney pie, preceded by melon and parma ham, which Maggie thought had gone off menus in the dark ages.

Conversation between them had been stilted, after discussing – yet again – Stan's miraculous journey. The conference next door was certainly very noisy.

Maggie glanced around the room. There were about six other couples dotted about, mostly in their fifties and sixties, the women in pastel suits, the men in brightly coloured golfing sweaters. They had red cheeks, and hair coming out of their ears, and tufted eyebrows, and white hair on the backs of their hands. The women wore glasses and looked anxious; their eyes darting to the waitresses, their mouths a moue of worry. None of the couples were talking to one another except to pass comment on the bread, or the wine, or the whereabouts of the waitress.

Maggie felt a thin line of panic rising in her breast. Would this be them then, one day? Completely lost for conversation, nothing left to say to one another, except to comment on the food and stare with a glazed expression into the fire? She searched in her head for something, anything, to say. Stan was drinking quite heavily, she noticed. It was a sign he was nervous too. She tried to give him a happy smile.

'So, have you heard about that job yet?' he blurted out.

Maggie froze. So that's what this was about. Maybe he thought he was going to cart her off the next morning.

'Have you come to *fetch* me?' she asked.

'No!' said Stan, genuinely wounded. 'I know you'd have to give notice and all that.'

'Well, no, I haven't heard about the job yet, and *if* I got it and *if* I decided to take it' – Stan flinched at that – 'then I wouldn't even *think* about starting until the next academic year. I'd never leave Downey House in the lurch. So don't think you're here to bloody carry me off.'

'I didn't think that!' said Stan, hurt. 'I thought we could just have a nice evening, without you getting so bloody defensive all the time.'

'I'm *not* being defensive,' said Maggie, conscious that they were beginning to attract glances from the older couples at the other tables. 'I'm just sick of this big Scottish conspiracy to kidnap me from this "evil" place, as if I don't know what I'm doing!'

Stan stared at her. 'Well, maybe you know *exactly* what you're doing.'

'And what do you mean by that?'

Stan shrugged. 'Well you've got it all how you want down here, haven't you? Cushy number, nice place on your own, fiancé nicely tidied away up north, everything perfectly arranged so you can be as selfish as you like and do whatever you like.'

'That is totally unfair,' said Maggie, getting angry, even as she realised there was definitely something in what he was saying. She had got used to a compartmentalised life, for sure.

'No messy schools or families or arrangements to deal with. You're living like a bloody schoolgirl yourself. And it's bloody selfish. '

This hit home.

'Shut up!' said Maggie, no longer caring who was looking. 'Just *shut up!*' She stood up. 'I'm going to the bathroom.' The young waitress leapt forward to take her half-full plate.

'That's right,' said Stan. 'Whenever there's a problem, Maggie just leaves. That's your answer to everything. Where next, the Channel Islands?'

'SHUT UP!' said Maggie again, her eyes half-blinded with tears as she ran out of the room.

Simone was feeling woozy and giggly. Oh my goodness, her friends were so funny! They were being totally outrageous, and Zelda was talking about how she'd nearly gone all the way in the summer with a young officer, until he'd found out who her dad was and run for his life. The others were laughing too, except for Alice who was complaining that they didn't have any cigarettes. Fliss said don't be stupid, that would get them thrown out for sure, so Alice had sighed and suggested why don't they play this silly drinking game where if you didn't say the right words you had to play truth or forfeit.

194

In fact, so excited was Simone that she couldn't even join in the silly game – something about counting in threes – and missed her turn.

'Simone! Simone!' the others screamed.

'No, no, be quiet!' she hissed, as they giggled and tried to make themselves quieter.

'OK, you have to answer a truth question or take a shot,' said Alice under her breath.

'I'll answer the question,' said Simone nervously.

'All right, but if we don't think you're telling the truth you have to take the shot anyway,' commanded Zelda, whose hair had become very dishevelled.

'Those are American rules!' said Fliss, who was lying full-length on the floor. 'No American rules.'

'America rules!' sang Zelda, punching her fist in the air and collapsing in giggles.

'SSSH!' said Simone.

'Come on, we need a question for Simone,' said Alice. She rolled over langorously on the bed, on to her tummy. 'Simone?'

'Yes?' said Simone, feeling a little uncomfortable. The girls at her old school were always asking her stupid questions they knew she couldn't answer, just so they could laugh at her.

'Have you ever . . . kissed a boy!'

Simone flushed instantly. At last! She hadn't wanted to discuss it before, not with the bad atmosphere in the dorm, but now she could reveal it.

'Well . . .' she began.

'She has! She has!'

Fliss sat upright. 'Who?'

Simone flushed even pinker. She felt she was being initiated into a proper grown-up world, where she could talk about boys and drink booze and be a proper member of the gang, without ever having to feel like left-out, bullied, friendless Simone ever again.

'Well, you know at the Christmas party . . .'

Fliss stared in disbelief. 'Not that little midget.'

There was a sudden silence in the room. Alice looked at Fliss crossly. Fliss polished off the last of her drink.

'I didn't mean it like that!' said Fliss, seeing the other's faces. 'I didn't!'

'Yes, you did,' said Simone dully. 'It's all right.'

'What's he like?' said Zelda encouragingly. But it was too late. The moment was gone.

'Well, he's pretty short,' said Simone. She sipped her drink for want of something to do. It didn't taste as repulsive as it had before.

'It always has to be about you, doesn't it?' said Alice to Fliss.

'What?' said Fliss. 'I'm sorry, I just blurted it out. It was a mistake.'

'It's always Fliss's problems, or Fliss's boyfriend, or Fliss's take on Simone.'

'That's not fair,' said Fliss, stung. 'You're the one that's been mooning around like some sad bloody heifer, as if I'm deliberately keeping you apart from some great love affair, instead of some cheap shag – whilst I've been ill, actually—'

'What did you call me?' yelled Alice, mishearing.

'I mean, if you're so desperate to shag him, just shag him. Don't mind me.'

Alice jumped up. 'How *dare* you! At least I didn't try to starve myself to get attention . . . like that's attractive.'

'No, because you just love yourself so much all you have to do is show off all day about how *sophisticated* you are.'

'Well, maybe compared to Guildford, I am.'

196

'Or maybe you're just a bit looser.'

'Looser than what? The dress you were wearing at the Christmas party that you would have been quite happy to take off for him?'

The girls were nearly nose to nose, breathing heavily. Simone hated conflict of any kind, and was staring at them, not knowing what to do about it, feeling terrified. Zelda was watching with curiosity, still eating a Snickers bar.

'Don't you dare talk to me like that!'

'Well, don't you dare talk to me about what Will and I have. Because it's none of your business, and besides, you're too immature to understand.'

Fliss saw red and without thinking, grabbed the closest thing to hand – one of Alice's shoes – and threw it across the room. The lightbulb above the sink immediately shattered, and Alice went for her, pushing her over on to the bed. In a trice they were in a tangle on the eiderdown, pushing and trying to get at each other's hair.

'Stop it!' Simone was shouting in an anguished whisper. '*Stop it!* They'll hear us!'

But Fliss and Alice were too far gone to hear here, and the footsteps were already audible coming down the hall.

Miranda had shaken off David and now he couldn't find her. He assumed – hoped – she was in the Ladies. The awards had gone on but the high point of the evening was obviously over, and the comedian who'd been helpful before was now making lots of unkind jokes about her. David could feel everyone's eyes on him; some of the women's were pitying (and eyeing up his tall dark frame in the shabby tuxedo); the men's scornful that he couldn't control a sexy creature like Miranda. He tried to ignore everyone and ordered a whisky from the waitress, even though he knew it would make him feel maudlin. What a terrible night.

At first, as Maggie staggered into the small ante-room looking for the loos, which seemed to be signposted six miles away, she couldn't quite tell what she was seeing. Her eyes were blurry with tears and she felt an overwhelming sense of frustration and anger. She so wanted to shout at Stan, tell him it was all his fault. But it wasn't, was it? It was her who'd moved away, who'd torn up her roots. He'd never changed. She had. But she couldn't set her life on fire, surely?

Looking for somewhere to have a quiet cry, she didn't notice the couple at first. They seemed to be in a frenzy, tearing at each other's clothes, trying to devour one another. It looked less like kissing and more like almost-violence. As soon as she noticed them, she tried to back away, but it was too late. The woman raised her head. It was Miranda.

David set his glass down with a bang. They were clearing the tables for the dancing. She'd been away for twenty minutes, this was getting ridiculous. He was going to find her and tell her he was leaving, with or without her. He stood up.

Miranda gasped and pushed Declan away. Her head was spinning.

'M . . . Maggie,' she stuttered.

Maggie stared at her in disbelief. 'Uh, hello,' she said, not knowing what else to say.

'Uh, uhm.'

Suddenly Miranda thought she was going to be sick. Declan was still holding on to her elbow.

'Come on, love,' he said. 'Let's go somewhere a bit more private.'

Miranda reached a beseeching hand out towards Maggie. 'Please,' she said. 'Don't tell David.'

'Don't tell David what?' came the voice, a tall figure silhouetted in the doorway.

Miranda's face changed suddenly. It grew harder and she jutted out her jaw defiantly. 'I don't need you to tell me what to do,' she hissed.

'Evidently not,' said David, stepping forwards. He took in the whole scene and, although he couldn't possibly have said anything so cruel, he couldn't deny that amid his obvious shock was a distinct feeling of relief. And sadness. Miranda had so much beauty, brains and charm. He wished she could find a man to make her happy. It hadn't been him, and he didn't hold out much hope for the pudding-headed man clasping her by the elbow.

'Come on, love,' whispered Declan again. 'Let's get out of here. I've got the bridal suite.'

Miranda, wobbling in her shoes, walked up to David. 'So, I guess this time I'm dumping you,' she said.

David put up his hands. 'I guess so,' he said. He rubbed the back of his neck with his hand. He hated scenes. Miranda didn't seem to mind them.

'Goodbye, David,' she said. This would have come off as more dignified if she hadn't fallen off one of her shoes. Declan caught her just in time.

Maggie and David stared at the couple disappearing up the stairs.

'Oh God,' said Maggie. 'Oh my God! Are you OK?'

David sat down heavily. 'Yes,' he said. 'Yes, I am. Sorry, what are you doing here?'

Maggie shrugged. 'Uh, just for dinner.' She was conscious of not saying Stan's name out loud. David wasn't listening anyway.

'I just wish it hadn't been so *messy*,' he was saying. 'I should never have got back together with her.'

'She's made a huge mistake,' said Maggie loyally. 'She'll realise in the morning.'

'Well, I think that's immaterial now she has Lumphead Loggins up there,' said David.

'Are you really not that fussed?'

David could feel the whisky in his veins and suddenly felt immensely tired. 'Would you come and sit on the arm of this chair and tell me comforting things?'

Maggie did so.

'It had to end,' said David, staring out of the window into the darkness beyond. 'I just wish . . . I just wish she could be happier.'

'What about you?' asked Maggie softly.

'I, of course, get to drown in whisky and self-pity. It's all rather fun really,' said David. They sat there in silence.

'Oh, Maggie,' he said. 'Oh, Maggie, Maggie, Maggie.'

'What?' she whispered.

Agonisingly slowly, his fingers crept towards hers. She watched, hypnotised, as, like it had a mind of its own, her own hand – her left hand, the one with the small-stoned ring – opened and clasped his.

But Maggie didn't get to hear the end of the thought, and David didn't get to formulate it, for, rampaging in, his red hair sticking up in a fury, his cheeks pink with firelight and beer and self-righteous anger, was Stan.

Stan shook his head in disbelief at the sight of the two of them.

'I can't . . . I can't . . . that poofy English professor from over the hill? All this time? And I thought . . . Christ, Maggie. Every time I see you he's there. Every time I hear about the school it's David this, and David that. And I thought, Oh, that's nice, Maggie's taken pity on the weirdo, she's found a friend to talk to . . . not *once*, not *once* did I ever think you'd be interested in a lanky weirdo like—'

'It's not like that!' said Maggie. 'David's just split up from his girlfriend. We're not doing anything!'

David put a hand over his eyes.

'So you stormed out on me to come and comfort him,' said Stan. There were tears in his eyes, Maggie saw, with a sudden lurch of tenderness. She stood up. She hadn't denied it.

'How could you, Maggie? I trusted you.'

'And I trusted you!' said Maggie.

Stan looked guilty. 'But nothing . . .'

'You know it did,' said Maggie miserably. Stan's silence confirmed her worst fears.

'It was *one time*,' he said eventually. 'So what – you're getting your revenge with spiderlegs here?'

'It's not like that,' repeated Maggie.

'No, it's not,' said David, getting up between them. 'Maggie loves you, Stan.'

Maggie swallowed hard.

David, standing up, revealed the difference between his height and Stan's, but it didn't stop the shorter man. Stan pulled back his fist and punched David hard in the face.

David staggered back. He couldn't believe how much it had hurt. He clutched his hand to his jaw. Maggie's mouth opened in shock. What was Stan *doing*? She suddenly felt herself rooted to the spot, unable to move towards either man.

'I probably deserved that,' David said.

'Yeah, you bloody did,' said Stan, rubbing his knuckles. 'Now what are you going to do, Maggie?' His voice was shaking.

Maggie looked from one man to the other, feeling completely and utterly torn. Stan was holding out his hand.

David was not.

David couldn't do this to another man, especially not one he had always thought of as a decent sort. Look, even Miranda couldn't be with him for five minutes without wanting to pull someone else, and Maggie had been positively avoiding him all year. Stan and Maggie had real love, a history; one day they would have a family. Maggie and he had a stolen kiss on a hillside, and a lot of fantasies built from reading far too much poetry. It was absurd to promise Maggie a dream he couldn't deliver. Tonight had shown him the kind of man he was. Completely inadequate in every way.

His hand wasn't there. Maggie raised her eyes slowly. All the worrying, all the silliness – it had all been for nothing – completely imaginary on her part, just as she'd always thought. She was such an idiot. She felt her face burning.

Suddenly, her phone rang.

'For Christ's sake,' said Stan. 'Who's that, George Clooney?'

The phone stopped, then started again, sounding even more insistent than before.

Maggie picked it up.

'Miss Adair?' It was Miss Starling's voice. She sounded coolly, controlledly, furious. 'We appear to have a situation with your form.'

*

Maggie drove – she'd hardly touched her wine at dinner, and the adrenalin punching through her veins would have cleared the alcohol in any case. Stan stayed behind; David went to catch a cab home before Stan hit him again.

Felicity Prosser, Simone Kardashian, Alice Trebizon-Woods and Zelda Townell had been apprehended, completely drunk and having a screaming fight with one another. The room was smeared in chocolate and food products, a light-bulb had smashed and one of the curtains was torn.

Miss Starling was standing in Dr Deveral's office in a long grey flannel nightdress and dressing gown, white with rage. Dr Deveral had managed to get dressed.

The four girls were standing in a line in front of the desk. Simone was sobbing violently, Felicity Prosser more quietly. Zelda looked defiant, Alice uninterested.

'I'm sorry,' said Maggie, rushing in. 'Prior engagement.'

Miss Starling sniffed.

'We understand,' said Dr Deveral, glancing at Miss Starling. 'It is Friday night, after all.'

Maggie looked at the four girls. Why did it always have to be her form causing a commotion, as everyone else cheerfully settled down to prep? She quickly calculated their respective emotional states. No point in asking Simone anything, and Fliss seemed to have tightly drawn into herself.

'Alice. What happened?' she barked sharply.

Alice glanced around tentatively. 'Well, we, uh, found some Jack Daniels.'

'You *found* it?'

'Yes. In the woods. One of the older pupils must have hidden it.'

'You *drank* something you found in the *woods*? Sorry, Alice, please don't treat other people like idiots – and don't think I'm going to believe that.'

Alice didn't look even mildly contrite. Zelda heaved a sigh. This was going to get sticky, she could tell.

'I brought it in, ma'am,' she said quietly.

Maggie turned to her. 'Well. A bit of honesty. At least that I can respect.'

Alice resented that. Protecting your friends wasn't lying, it was the right thing to do. Everyone knew that.

'Simone didn't want to have any,' she said, to show Miss Adair that she could be just as honest as anyone else. 'We made her.'

'Is that true?' Miss Starling shot at Simone, who nodded miserably, her face sodden. 'You girls *forced* alcohol on another?'

'It wasn't like that,' snivelled Simone, but it was too late. Miss Starling was looking at her watch.

'I think we'll have to phone the parents.'

All the girls set up a howling but Miss Starling stilled them with a glance.

Maggie turned to Dr Deveral. 'Can we speak just as teachers for a moment?'

Dr Deveral nodded, and the girls were sent outside.

'And not a *word* from any of you in the hallway,' warned Maggie as they left the room, Fliss and Alice in particular exchanging filthy looks.

'OK, what happened exactly?' said Maggie when the girls were safely outside. She felt unbearably, overwhelmingly tired.

'Well, you'd have known if you were here to supervise,' shot Miss Starling.

'But I arranged to have tonight off,' said Maggie patiently. Miss Starling was being blatantly unfair; she'd had permission for her night off the premises. It wasn't worth getting upset over though. 'But you're right, if I'd been here that would have been better.'

Dr Deveral was impressed with Maggie's cool head under the circumstances. A year ago she'd have blown up at June Starling for the unfair accusation. The fact remained, though, that Maggie's girls did seem to attract way more than their fair share of trouble.

'So is there real damage to the room?' asked Maggie, who'd seen a lot of alcohol abuse in her old school. She glanced at Dr Deveral, who shook her head. 'It's not an automatic expulsion, is it?'

Veronica shrugged. 'It's difficult. Two of the girls are nearly fifteen, which is a slight mitigation, I suppose. And you have to weigh the severity of the punishment against the crime ... an expulsion from Downey House could hover over their whole next six or seven years; affect their university applications.'

'I'm very keen that doesn't happen to Simone,' said Maggie.

'So am I,' agreed Dr Deveral.

'It's clearly in the rules of the school,' said Miss Starling. 'We can't condone underage girls drinking in the dorms! It's against the law!'

'No one is doing that, June,' said Veronica, taking off her glasses and rubbing her eyes tiredly.

'I suppose this is all all right where you come from, isn't it?' said Miss Starling to Maggie.

Maggie turned round, shocked. 'Ex*cuse* me?'

'Well, it's obvious you have lower standards of discipline where you come from. Obviously the girls are picking up on these habits.'

Maggie felt like she'd been slapped. 'I can assure you, that could not be further from the truth—'

'I mean, you've been out at a bar yourself, it's obvious.'

'June, that is *enough*,' cut in Dr Deveral. The tone of her voice was several degrees below frosty. 'I think Maggie and I can handle this now.'

Miss Starling bristled. 'With respect, headmistress.'

'You are not showing my staff respect, Miss Starling,' said Veronica. 'Perhaps we can have a word in the morning.'

Miss Starling left, but not without shooting Maggie a venomous look.

'Dr Deveral, I promise, I have absolutely *never* encouraged this kind of behaviour in the girls.'

'No,' said Dr Deveral, looking suddenly weary. There was a pause. 'But you must admit, Maggie, yours does seem to be a particularly troublesome group.'

Maggie swallowed hard and bit her tongue. She felt a flare of anger at the injustice – as well as a little voice inside asking, Well, had she perhaps been neglecting her form? With her head full of her love life and her own future?

'Now, what do you suggest we do?'

Maggie did her best to pull herself together and act professionally.

'We need to separate Felicity Prosser and Alice Trebizon-Woods,' she said first. 'Together, those two are nothing but mischief.'

'I agree . . . Goodness, if we even tried to rusticate them, I doubt I could get a Trebizon-Woods to come and pick Alice up. I think they're in Bhutan.'

'I suppose Zelda brought the booze from the base,' said Maggie. 'She just . . . she just doesn't want to fit in here.'

Dr Deveral looked sad. 'I'd hope every girl would be enriched by being at Downey House.'

Maggie didn't say anything. The last thing in the world she wanted to do was let Dr Deveral down.

'I'll try harder,' said Maggie.

Veronica gave her a look. 'Thank you,' she said. Nothing more needed to pass between them.

'All right. What about I speak to all the parents in the morning,' said Maggie. 'Plus detention till Easter, and suspension of privileges till the end of the year.'

Dr Deveral looked up, a sudden glint in her eye. 'Harold Carruthers needs help with his spring planting. He was asking me if he could get a man in. We could put the girls on early morning hard labour.'

Maggie raised her eyebrows. 'That could be just the thing. Make them too tired to get into any trouble. And I'm changing that dorm,' she added. 'I'll take Alice out, she'll cope well elsewhere. Whereas I still need to keep an eye on Felicity.'

Dr Deveral nodded.

'And we'll make it very very clear to them how lucky they are to be avoiding anything worse.'

Maggie wondered if she could say the same for herself.

It was four very sorry schoolgirls who trailed back to bed at midnight. Fliss and Alice had been forced to apologise to one another in front of the teachers, but it hadn't done the trick – they were still refusing to talk. Alice's mouth was set in a stern line. She had a half-day's grace in the morning to move her things, and the prospect of endless hard labour and extra prep stretched well out into the distance, with looming headaches for all of them. Fliss would have some very tough explaining to do to her therapist. Simone wanted to be sick every time she thought of what her dad was going to think when he heard, and how disappointed he would be. Zelda couldn't believe the school was so tight-assed. But there was one thing they all agreed on.

'I'm never drinking again,' said Simone. The others nodded their heads.

Maggie stood in the quiet hallway. The moon shone through the long-leaded window. She knew what she had to do.

She let herself in. Her heart was in her mouth. The figure was dark and prone under the bed covers. Gently, she called his name.

'Hmm?' The figure shifted.

Maggie moved towards the bed. 'Can I come in?' she asked, tentatively.

Stan sat up.

'I just . . .' he said. 'One thing I have to know.'

This was it. Maggie swallowed hard. The thing that had been gnawing at her, tearing her apart.

'Did you . . . did you sleep with him?'

'No,' she said.

'Did you kiss him?'

Her pause told him everything.

'Yes,' she said finally. 'Just once.'

There was a silence. Stan lay down once more on his side of the bed. In horror, Maggie gradually realised that he was crying.

She lay down next to him. 'Are we still . . . can we . . .?'

'Do you want to?'

'Oh yes, Stan. Oh yes. I can't tell you how sorry I am.' She was crying too now.

'But if you ever—'

'I won't . . . never! I promise.'

Slowly their bodies moved closer together, and they held on to one another in a damp salty embrace until, exhausted, they finally fell asleep.

*

At breakfast, which they took late, and quietly, but this time Maggie was thankful for it rather than concerned, she felt in the pocket of her jacket and pulled out the white envelope she'd plucked from her pigeon hole.

'What's that?' asked Stan.

'I don't know, just mail. Oh,' said Maggie, opening it.

'What?'

'I am sorry to say that your application has been unsuccessful on this occasion ... Bugger! Those horrible old witches at GDE haven't given me the liaison job!'

Stan glanced up from his full English. 'Why not?'

'It doesn't say.' Maggie scanned the rest of the letter, which was standard stuff. 'Ugh, it says that if I want, I can call them up to discuss it.'

'Well, do that then.'

'No thanks,' said Maggie. She put the letter down, feeling depressed. 'I know why anyway. They thought I was a toffee-nosed snob for working down here.'

'They're not the only ones,' muttered Stan.

'Yes, I know that, thank you, Mr Working Class Hero. Oh God, how annoying. I didn't even *want* the stupid job.'

'Well, maybe that came across,' said Stan perceptively. 'They could probably tell.'

'I didn't do it on purpose,' said Maggie. 'I'll apply for another job.'

'Course,' said Stan, 'I know. But maybe they could tell you were, you know, a bit reluctant.'

'Well, I'm not reluctant now,' said Maggie. She thought of the horrible looks Miss Starling had given her the night before; her unruly Middle School seconds that she didn't seem to have a hope of controlling. 'I'll finish my year out here and find something new in the summer. I'm sure Dr Deveral expects me to leave anyway.'

'That's the spirit,' agreed Stan. 'Aye, that'll do.'

'Oh God, I have four sets of angry parents to wake up this morning, some of whom aren't even in the same hemisphere,' said Maggie.

'And I have five hundred miles to drive and a nightshift,' said Stan. 'Best get on it, eh?'

Maggie gave a tentative smile. 'Thanks so much for coming down, Stan. I'm . . . I know it was awful, but I feel I got much more sorted in my head.'

Stan nodded. 'You daft lassie. All that bloody mooning around.'

Then he leant over. 'Maggie, if you do it again . . . if you ever do it again, it'll kill me, I swear to God. It'll kill me.'

Maggie swallowed. 'I know. I won't.'

'I don't want you to see him, do you understand?'

Maggie nodded.

'I mean, I've given him a warning he won't forget, but Maggie . . . if it wasn't for me being such an idiot last year, I'd have just called it off, you know?'

'Uh-huh.'

He asked her the same question he'd asked her last night before they'd fallen asleep. 'Just tell me . . . swear on Dylan's life. You never slept with him.'

'I swear, Stan. It was one kiss. You have to believe me.'

'I do,' said Stan. 'I have to believe you.'

And he kissed her and was gone.

Chapter Twelve

Saturday was a blowy and bright February morning, and Maggie wanted it to sweep the cobwebs, and the past, away. She hung up the phone after her calls with some bemusement. With the exception of Simone's parents, who had peppered her with questions, none had seemed that troubled by the girls' misdemeanours. The Prossers just wanted to know if Felicity was eating and said it was fine, Fliss had been drinking wine and water with dinner since she was twelve years old. Zelda's mother had drawled that this was a definite step up from the drugs, but please could they not expel her as she didn't have time to track down yet another school. She'd left a message at the Trebizon-Woods' with a maid that didn't seem to speak much English. And she'd have been even more surprised if she'd seen Simone's mum and dad hang up the phone then hug one another.

'She didn't get sick! She was fine! And she didn't want to drink! But all her friends persuaded her! She was invited to the party!' They were practically bouncing with glee.

Out at 6 a.m. the following Saturday morning, though, following the tracks of Harold the caretaker with small crocus bulbs, the girls weren't in the least bit pleased. Alice and

Fliss were still ignoring each other completely, with Fliss now conversing through Simone, and Alice through Zelda.

'This is *ruining* my nails,' said Zelda. 'I can't believe they didn't let me off – these cost a packet.'

Simone shivered in her thin jacket. 'Does this burn calories, Zelda?' she shouted.

'Sure does, Slim-one!' yelled Zelda back cheerily. 'So, Fliss, don't work too hard.'

Fliss had no intention of working too hard, not like Alice, who was setting out bulbs with a will, if in a slightly strange shape.

'What are you doing, Alice?' asked Simone.

'Why, getting my revenge, of course,' said Alice. 'On that Miss Adair. I always do. You know this was probably her idea.'

'Well, yes, but what?'

'You'll see,' said Alice. 'You know that little secret I mentioned?'

Simone nodded eagerly but, infuriatingly, once again Alice refused to breathe another word.

Veronica fought her way through the Birmingham traffic. Industrial towns reminded her too much of her upbringing; she had a great inclination to dislike them. And after thirty years by the sea, she found it hard to understand why anyone would want to live in a city, even if she had managed to track down tickets to the symphony orchestra for tomorrow evening. It was Tchaikovsky, her favourite. She wondered if Daniel would like to come. She'd offered him a lift to the Expo, but he was popping over to see his mother in Guildford then taking the train from London. She could run him back home, though.

The huge exhibition hall was taken up with hundreds of

stands and tables, all promoting the solid educational advantages of their own schools: those specialising in art, or sport, or helping 'those with varied requirements' (a euphemism for 'who've been expelled from everywhere else'). She saw many faces she'd met over the years at headteachers' conferences, and whilst on good terms with many, she tended to avoid forming close friendships with rivals. She was viewed with respect, but not intimacy, which was exactly what she liked. Spring term, after the Middle School seconds' midnight-feast debacle, seemed to be progressing well, and things were definitely calmer. The mock exams had come off well, too, and they looked set to make a good showing in the league tables, which was a huge relief.

Dr Fitzroy was thankfully at the stand next door, exuding loud bonhomie. He could take the strain. He'd brought along Daniel, and David McDonald, that slightly eccentric English teacher. It was good to include the younger teachers, let parents see that their little ones would be in a modern environment. But of course you needed a touch of gravitas too; Mr Graystock, the Classics teacher, exuded this in spades.

Veronica said good morning politely to all of them, as well as Fleur Parsley and Janie James, who she'd brought from her own school. Always good to emphasise the artistic and sporting benefits of Downey House – the things state schools simply didn't have the resources for.

David seemed a little gloomy, she noticed. Normally he was jumping off the stand and talking nineteen to a dozen, alarming just about as many parents as he enthralled. She wondered why. Dr Fitzroy was bullish, talking about how they were really going to have to fight now, as the credit crunch took its toll; and how school fees, although usually the last thing parents wanted to cut back on, eventually fell victim too.

'Tradition! Honour! Excellence!' he boomed. 'That's what people want!'

As the hall started to fill with anxious-looking parents and their bored offspring, everyone sprung into action. Evelyn handed out beautifully printed leaflets with pictures of the school glinting in sunshine reflected off the sea. It looked like something out of a fairytale, and few of the mothers could pass by without exclaiming at it.

Veronica spent the morning discussing whether an asthmatic child would be able to take the summer saltwater swims (she privately thought the child in question, who had purple shadows under his eyes and a rather large bottom, would benefit at Downey House the second she put her Nintendo DS down); as well as a mother who was very loudly enquiring about stabling her daughter's horse. Veronica wasn't sure if this was for her benefit or that of the other parents passing by, but she did the best she could. Far more questions came about spreading payments and costs; discounts for siblings and potential scholarships. Veronica felt bad telling nicely-dressed, but obviously feeling-the-pinch parents that Jessica, good as she was at writing stories, was very unlikely to win a scholarship if up against the sixteen-hours-a-day-in-the-library, pulling-themselves-up motivation of a Simone Kardashian – these nice girls from nice schools just didn't have quite the same desire to escape, and scholarships had to be kept for those in genuine need.

By the end of the morning she was quite exhausted, and had been delighted when Daniel had suggested lunch somewhere nearby that he'd read about online. She hated to push the advantage, squeeze herself into his life. Their obvious proximity meant she was constantly terrified of becoming a nuisance to him and his family.

On Daniel's part, he was finding it, though extraordinary,

a very rewarding experience getting to know his clever, prickly birth mother, so different from warm, uncomplicated Ida. Somewhere in the back of his mind he even had a plan forming, a stray thought, about perhaps even just looking into the possibility of just finding out – just to see – if his father was still alive. One day. But he didn't want to scare her with that yet. He enjoyed her company and, if he were honest with himself, was flattered by her obviously over-whelming interest in his life and family, however much she tried to hide it. Just like their two other sets of doting grand-parents, no detail of Rufus, Josh or Holly's dealings were too small for Veronica's ears. A generous man, Daniel saw a sur-feit of love and affection for his children as nothing but a good thing. And he felt, with some awe, pleased that he so enjoyed the company, as an adult, of his mother.

'Sneaking off again, you two, are you?' boomed Dr Fitzroy as they left at the same time. 'People are starting to talk.'

Veronica winced with exquisite distaste. Daniel didn't look too happy about it either. But the subject of telling the world hadn't come up again, and that suited Veronica fine.

'Look at them go, eh, David?' said Dr Fitzroy, nudging his colleague. But David could do nothing more than shrug weakly. The sparkle had gone right out of him. Was he sick?

Choosing a high-profile restaurant near the Expo centre in the middle of a headteachers' conference was obviously a terrible idea in retrospect, and both Daniel and Veronica felt it. It seemed every headteacher from the west of England managed to be passing, and of course wanted to drop by Veronica's table for a quick word. Veronica could almost hear them as they left – headteachers, alas, being no less susceptible to gossip than any other sector of society. 'Isn't he dishy?' 'Who'd have thought it?' 'Well, *I* always thought she was a . . .'

'Sorry about this,' she grimaced to Daniel, waylaid for the sixth time. Daniel shrugged; it was impossible to have a conversation anyway, with the sense of being constantly eavesdropped. They finished hurriedly, both refusing pudding or coffee, and Veronica understood immediately when Daniel said he had some errands to run and did she mind terribly if he didn't accompany her back to the exhibition hall?

After a long afternoon standing and smiling, Veronica had made up her mind. That night was the headteachers' dinner. She was scheduled to sit next to Daniel already, they'd arranged it. Something would have to be done.

Later, after a long bath which had done nothing to quell her nerves, Veronica put the final touches on her make up. A grey fine cashmere twinset and a soft red skirt and boots looked elegant and discreet; her hair was the same refined pale blonde she'd kept it since she started to go grey. Fastening a Links necklace round her neck, she checked her reflection one last time. She didn't *look* nervous. Which, given what she was about to do, was half the battle.

The headmasters' dinner was a hearty annual affair, full of gossip about who was moving where, which famous off-spring were misbehaving, why so and so had had nine expulsions in one year, who had poached the King's Choir Chorus Master . . . Normally, Veronica quite enjoyed them. The keynote speeches, usually by retired teachers of esteemed colleges, were amusing and erudite, and the tone light. It was a good break from the harsh financial realities that the trade fair showed up.

Tonight, however, she was shaking. She'd had a few words with the toastmaster and, although he looked a trifle confused, had a healthy respect for Dr Deveral and her school, so acquiesced accordingly.

As soon as she took her place next to Daniel, she could feel the room buzzing and muttering – who *was* this young teacher Veronica insisted on touting about everywhere? The idea of being the topic of vulgar speculation was completely abhorrent to Veronica – she'd undergone enough of it in her life – and she felt progressively more uncomfortable. Daniel sensed it and tried to make things easier on her by spending a lot of time talking to the woman on his right, a lady vicar from a high church school in rural Wales, which didn't exactly make his evening go with a bang either.

Finally, as the pudding plates were being cleared away and coffee circulating, the toastmaster rose and tinked his glass. The hubbub gradually died away.

'Now,' he said, 'before I welcome you most respected ladies and gentlemen with a few of the choicer selections of Britain's youngest and brightest this year, we have in our midst a lady who wants to say a few words: Dr Veronica Deveral.'

There was a rustle of whispering. Veronica, no stranger to public speaking, suddenly felt a hole in the pit of her stomach. Was this a truly ridiculous idea? Was it going to end her career? Turn her into a laughing stock? Ruin everything?

But what alternative did she have?

Rising, she gripped her napkin slightly for support. Only Daniel noticed; he didn't know what she was doing, thought she'd perhaps been scheduled to speak anyway.

'Hello,' said Veronica, her voice a little quiet. 'It's good to see you all here again – I think I know most of you.'

There were some mutters of agreement at this.

'For those I don't know, you must excuse me.'

Veronica took a long pause and a sip of water.

'You know,' she continued, 'I always say to my girls, "Tell the truth, spit it out, it's all for the best."'

Now she had the entire room's attention.

'But of course, when it comes to oneself, it's quite different, I'm afraid . . . It has come to my attention that there has been some speculation as to the nature of the relationship between myself and Daniel Stapleton here, History master at Downey Boys.' She swallowed. 'To stop idle gossip and exaggeration, I will tell you myself. Nearly forty years ago, as a teenager, I, along with many others, had to give a child up for adoption. Now, all this time later, I have been extraordinarily blessed to have the opportunity to meet him again.'

Daniel's mouth was hanging open.

'Good Lord!' Dr Fitzroy was heard to say.

'By coincidence also a teacher, I'm lucky enough that he works nearby, and I'm so proud of the exceptional man he has become, thanks to his wonderful adoptive parents. I'm so lucky to get the chance to get to know him. And that's all. I'm sorry for interrupting your evening. Thank you.'

Veronica sat down, to a stunned and silent room.

Daniel took her hand just once and squeezed it.

'Thank you,' he said, with tears in his eyes.

'I should have done it before,' said Veronica. 'It was ridiculous that I would treat your kindness with secrecy.'

'What's going to happen now?' said Daniel.

'I have absolutely no idea,' said Veronica. 'You know, I can't bear drinking, but do you think you could ask the waiter to get me a brandy?'

To her surprise, the waiter was back in two seconds with a large balloon of Cognac. 'On the house, ma'am.'

'What?' said Veronica.

The waiter looked at her, his large dark eyes glistening, then spoke in rich Brummie tones. 'I'm adopted, ma'am. I tried to find my birth mother, loike, but she just didn't want anything to do with me. So, you know. He's lucky, right. And my mum and dad are great too.'

'Oh,' said Veronica. She glanced up. Ernie Fisher, a very smart grammar school boss from East Anglia, was standing in front of her, twisting his fingers.

'Veronica,' he said.

'Ernie.'

'I know we don't know each other well, but I wanted to tell you that both our children, Mae and Angus . . . you know, we couldn't have our own. If someone like you . . . Well, we'd never have known . . .'

He, too, seemed about to break down. Veronica found herself clasping his hand too.

The toastmaster tried to continue with the speeches, but there was a steady stream, it seemed, of people in the room who'd had their lives positively touched by adoption, or who merely wanted to sympathise with how things were back then, or to tell her she was brave, or to say how happy they were for her. Veronica felt completely taken aback by the amount of human interest and warmth; the number of similar families out there that, because of her own desire for secrecy, she'd never met, because she'd carried herself around like a locked box for so many years.

Daniel was quite pink, and pleased, too, as people came to look at him standing next to his mother.

'You know,' he said to Veronica quietly, 'I really think this is going to work out all right.'

Chapter Thirteen

Why was it, Simone wondered, that the first term of the year seemed to take so long, then the rest just whizzed by? Spring term – made dreary by Fliss's absence and punctuated by hard labour – had gone in a blur, and now the Easter holidays were coming. She'd only realised how the seasons were changing when Miss Adair sidled into class one morning, looking slightly embarrassed.

'It's such a lovely day,' Maggie had announced, 'that we'll put *Romeo and Juliet* to one side just for a moment.'

This didn't please Alice, who was revelling in the doomed romance of it all.

'And celebrate this glorious morning.' She handed out photocopied sheets. 'This is one of the oldest songs or poems that we have in English. Does anyone recognise it?'

Astrid Ulverton, the class's most talented musician, raised her hand at once.

'It's a round, miss.'

'It is indeed a round, yes,' said Maggie.

It was such a beautiful morning, and Maggie was desperate for the Easter holidays. Knowing they weren't far off, she'd felt entirely jolly waking up.

Painstakingly she took them through the Middle English words – they particularly liked 'bucke uerteþ', 'the stag farts' – and, once she was sure they understood it, started up the song.

'So, I'm not much of a singer, but, Astrid, if you can help me, I'm going to split the class into three groups and we're going to go for it.'

The class perked up as they always did when they were doing something different.

'OK, you lot, follow me.'

And Maggie's wobbly but sweet alto started on the ancient words:

'Sumer is icumen in,
Lhude sing cuccu!
Groweþ sed and bloweþ med
And springþ þe wde nu
Sing cuccu!'

After a few times around, the class managed to get the three different parts and joined the voices together. Across the school, windows were opened at the sweet sound, and all the classes enjoyed a little more of the beautiful morning. In her office, Veronica threw open the French windows and sighed. She would miss that Scottish teacher, if she really did go.

'And oh,' Maggie added, as her smiling class was leaving, 'I've had some good news. We've had our outing to the theatre approved. If you lot work extra hard over the Easter holidays, you can actually go and *see Romeo and Juliet*.'

There was a good-natured cheer.

Easter in Scotland was chilly, both outside and in. Maggie and Stan dutifully visited the hotel where they would be getting married, and approved wedding invites. They were polite to one another; affectionate, even, in company. Only sometimes at night would Maggie lie, looking at his so-familiar outline in the sheets, and wonder if it was possible to be getting married and to feel lonely. Then he would turn to her and embrace her, and she would banish those thoughts to the back of her mind. There were the girls to think about: exam term was coming up. If she was going to leave Downey House, she wanted to do it with her head held high; show Miss Starling and everyone that she was perfectly capable of taking on a smart school and doing well with it. She wasn't going to scuttle back to Scotland with her tail between her legs. So why did it feel like that?

'I have now answered every essay question on *Romeo and Juliet* – ON EARTH,' said Fliss with horror, banging her text-book closed. Still at least detention was over now they were back for summer term; no more back-breaking gardening and the detentions had gone on for so long now that practically everyone had forgotten what they were for. Although Zelda hadn't smuggled in any more contraband, so presumably it had worked, to a point.

And, the only exception being Simone, whose marks were always excellent, all of the girls had seen an improvement in academic performance – Fliss in particular, who had some ground to make up from the term before. So the rhythm of the school indicated that their work-load was about to ease up a little, just as some breathtakingly good weather arrived – soft, spring breezes pushing puffy white clouds above the sky; the sea looking warm enough to swim in (although, as Janie James had sternly warned everyone, it was most certainly *not*). The older girls moaned as they poured over revision texts for their exams, but for most of the Middle School seconds, it was a time for lounging in the

222

grounds, attempting to cultivate early tans and not complaining too much about Janie James' term of hockey.

There were two flies in the ointment, as far as Simone could see. One was that Alice and Fliss were still not speaking. Astrid Ulverton had moved into their dorm in place of Alice, and they all missed her spiky asides. Astrid was nice, but all she cared about really was playing the clarinet and practising. And, though Alice could be bitchy, she was so funny too.

Fliss tried to pretend she didn't care, but it was obvious she did. Alice looked like she really didn't care, and probably didn't, but as far as Simone knew, she wasn't seeing Will.

Simone had been co-opted into taking Fliss's side, against her will – she thought if Alice and Will fancied each other, it wasn't fair to keep them apart just because Fliss used to like him. Whenever she'd tried to explain this to Alice, however, Alice had brushed her off as if she couldn't be bothered to discuss it with a kid like Simone, and that hurt. Why couldn't they just all be friends again?

The second thing was that, after sending a friendly email to Ash, she'd never heard from him again. It was keeping her awake at night. Was it because of her weight (which seemed to have stabilised and made her a pleasantly curvy, if not stick-insect, size for her height – Matron and Miss Adair kept going out of their way to tell her how good she looked now, and instructing her to eat white bread)? Something she'd said? Was she not smart enough for him?

She'd avoided going to the lecture society or the inter-school debating league in case she ran into him. It was horrible to think that he'd just wanted to take advantage of her with a casual snog, but had absolutely no interest in ever seeing her again. That hurt so much to think about that she had to quickly pick up a book or a cake if the thought ever crossed her mind. She wished she had someone to confide in, but Fliss had just been mean and no one else took her seriously. So she'd used the detention time to catch up on some pretty serious prep, and was already quite well-advanced into her GCSE work for the following year. *Romeo and Juliet*, however, made her cry. Imagine, a boy who loved you so much he would do anything for you; risk death, climb balconies, cross countries and deserts. Simone felt absolutely convinced in her fourteen-year-old head that there would never ever be a boy who would feel that way about her.

Maggie read the words again. The euphoria she'd felt as term ended seemed to have dribbled away up north. The weather, glorious in Cornwall, had been dank and miserable up in Scotland, although she and Stan were carrying on as best they could.

She was scandalising both families, but Stan had only snorted when she'd suggested adding part of the old English prayer book to their wedding ceremony. The priest had been resigned, indicating that most people wanted it these days; they just liked it. The Catholic service was ecclesiastical and restrained, but Maggie felt she wouldn't really be married until she said the more famous words: *With all my wordly goods I thee endow/With my body I thee worship*. A binding promise. That was what they would have. *To have and to hold, for richer, for poorer, for better, for worse.* Her and Stan. Just as it had always been.

She picked up her corrections. Felicity Prosser was much improved. Simone was of a high standard, as always. Zelda's work was still dashed off with only the barest care for spelling or punctuation.

She felt it scarcely mattered any more. Miss Starling had

still treated her like dirt, ever since that awful night the dorm had been caught with booze. She couldn't make it any clearer that she didn't feel Maggie belonged at Downey House. However many corrections Maggie did, however much she had thrown herself this term into teaching and imparting knowledge – there had been no more DVD fests – she couldn't help feeling the same way sometimes. That it would be best for everyone – absolutely everyone – if she was no longer there. That she belonged somewhere else.

What God has joined together, let no man put asunder.

She closed her eyes, remembering when Stan had kissed her off on the train.

'For the last time,' he'd said.

'Yes,' said Maggie, feeling a weight in her heart. 'For the last time.'

'See you soon, wife.'

Chapter Fourteen

The morning of the play outing dawned perfectly; a beautiful June day. Maggie wondered if her wedding, now only two months away, would be so lovely. Everyone was relieved – going to an outdoor theatre was one thing, having to sit there through a howling gale was quite another.

The Minotaur was an entirely outdoor theatre, hewn from Cornish rock, that sat at the very tip of England. On a beautiful day like today it made a wonderful setting for a play, and the Roman columns that made up the amphitheatre suited the Italian tone of the traditionally staged version.

Maggie had woken absolutely determined not to be phased by seeing David. That part of her life was over, and it had done nothing but cause everyone misery. So when the Downey boys dismounted from the bus for their pre-show tour of the theatre, she was able to nod to him politely.

'Hello,' he said, equally politely. She gave Stephen Daedalus a scratch. 'I thought he'd be wearing a ruff,' she said.

'Ha, very good,' said David. 'Uhm, how are you?'

'Good!' said Maggie. 'I meant to say . . . sorry about everything last term . . .'

David waved his hands. 'Not at all, don't even mention it. I did deserve it, after all, and it's in the past . . . Can we be friends though?'

'Of course,' said Maggie, more heartily than she felt.

Alice Trebizon-Woods watched their exchange with interest. Alice hated her new dorm. Her new roommates were a bunch of ninnies. She missed her friends and felt she'd been unfairly singled out. OK, so she went for Fliss, but it had been Zelda's Jack Daniels. She'd still show that snotty Miss Adair.

'Great. Great,' said David. 'Right, I'd better round up my shower.'

'Course,' said Maggie, watching as David turned round.

'All right, everyone,' he said loudly. 'By the way, I've heard it said that those who think *Romeo and Juliet* is too soppy are always the ones who end up crying the most.'

There were snorts at this.

'And I hate to conform to gender stereotypes, but the stage director has offered to give you a masterclass in stage fighting if any of you would be the least bit interested in that . . .'

He was drowned out by the hearty cheer that went up and raised an eyebrow at Maggie as he carted the boys inside.

'Yes, us too,' said Maggie, before the girls could ask the inevitable. 'Line up, please.'

The girls paired off, Fliss and Simone at one end of the line; Alice and Zelda at the other. Although Maggie thought it was a good thing that they were no longer influencing each other, she was also sad. Girls' friendships were such fragile things, after all. She would have thought that with every successive post-feminist generation things would get easier, and their self-esteem would improve, but it didn't seem to be going that way at all. It reminded her, too, to call her sister. Anne had thought the same as Stan; that she'd messed up the interview on purpose, but in fact she was going to ask if she would clip some more jobs out of the paper for her. It was time to go.

'What's this?' Zelda was asking. It wasn't like her to be curious about something academically related.

'It's hair and make up,' said the friendly tour guide who was showing them round. 'Do you want to take a look?'

'*Do* I?!' said Zelda, and dived in.

The tiny make up room, with three stools crammed in next to each other, looked like a treasure trove to Zelda. It was stuffed full of every conceivable type of cosmetics, boxes upon boxes of different shades, false noses, wigs and hair pieces of every colour and type. There was putty to build different face shapes, hair to make moustaches and beards, even warts that could be stuck on.

'Oh. My. *Gawd*,' said Zelda. '*Look* at this stuff. Do they use it all?'

'Lots of it, yeah. If you like, you can have a word with our make-up supervisor later.'

'I sure would like that, ma'am,' said Zelda, still looking around as if she'd been let into Santa's workshop. Alice looked at it and yawned. She wanted to meet some actors and see the boys.

On the round stage, the stage fighting demonstration was going extremely well, as Will Hampton volunteered, to the catcalls of the other boys, to take on a plywood broadsword.

'Now, you want to lunge straight at me – but miss, please,' said the instructor. 'See my arm under here? That's what you're after.'

Will slowly, but deftly, parried and made a good show of attacking the instructor, who immediately faked his own death to a mixture of cheers and groans from the watching pupils. Fliss caught Alice's eye watching with rapt interest and flicked her eyes away.

Alice didn't care, as Will turned towards her and, in one smooth movement, plucked a handkerchief out of his top blazer pocket.

'Will you hold my colours, milady?' he said, bowing towards her. All the girls thought this was the most romantic thing they'd ever seen. All the boys wanted to be sick, though many of them envied Will his confidence.

'Is this clean?' said Alice.

'Come *on!*' hollered the instructor, hauling his pike above Will's head. 'You'd be dead by now!'

Fliss turned away, but not before she'd noticed Alice carefully tucking the handkerchief into the top pocket of her blouse.

'Are you the form teacher?' asked a friendly looking woman of around forty with bleached blonde hair. 'Only, you all look so young these days it's hard to be sure.'

'That,' said Maggie, 'is about the nicest thing anyone's said to me in months.'

'Oh dear,' said the woman. Maggie liked her immediately. 'I'm Ailie, the make-up artist. Trish told me you had one of your girls interested.'

Suddenly Maggie had an idea.

'Ailie,' she said. 'Can I ask you an absolutely huge favour?'

'Really?' said Zelda. 'You're kidding me, right?'

'No,' said Maggie, Ailie standing beside her, both their faces absolutely guileless. 'Ailie usually has an assistant.'

'There are a lot of assistants in state-funded theatre,' said Ailie, coughing.

'And she's sick. And we were chatting and she asked if I knew of anyone who was good at putting on make up . . .'

The longing in Zelda's face was so strong, Maggie wished she could take a picture. Ailie had loved the idea, saying if it went well, she might make it a permanent feature for student tours; she could certainly help with the dull bits like mascara, and washing the sponges. When Maggie had explained that Zelda had trouble getting interested academically, kind-hearted Ailie was only more keen to help.

'That's exactly what I was like,' she'd said. 'I wished someone had taken the trouble to give me a leg up. Would have saved me a lot of time. I suppose that's what you schools can do, isn't it? When you've got tiny classes and time to think about your students, and lots of good teachers, and trips like this . . .' She sounded a bit wistful. 'OK, send her up.'

The performance was played out against the backdrop of the setting sun over Crean bay, the setting of the sun matching perfectly the darkening mood of the piece. Maggie watched with some satisfaction her brood get increasingly engrossed; it helped that the main parts were played by very young-looking actors. This wasn't always the case, but it definitely helped. The very thorough work she'd thrown herself into in the term leading up to Easter had obviously paid off; every single face was engrossed, even Zelda's, who was eyeing up the well-mascara-ed dancers with an eye she fancied was now becoming professional.

But there was something more. The sunset, the words, the music and the astonishing setting somehow conspired to place a magic on the stage and wreathe an enchantment around the audience; in the warm, sweet-scented night air, everyone could feel and sense it, as insubstantial as fairy dust, but somehow rendering the drama being played out on the stage as all-important, as the niggles of everyday life retreated into dreams.

Fliss's mouth was wide open. This was all her romantic sensibilities thrown to life. As Romeo declaimed, *My lips, two blushing pilgrims, ready stand / to smooth your rough touch with a tender kiss*, she shivered. This was what she had dreamt of. This is what she had wanted with Will, two people so mad, so crazy for each other, even though the rest of the world wanted to tear them apart.

She looked at Alice, who was looking at Will, who was looking back at her, and felt a sudden stab of shame. Did they feel like that? It wasn't right to keep someone from someone else just because you liked them first. Will was never going to like her. And now she was being just as bad as the Montagues and the Capulets. Under a pink sky, where the stars were just beginning to pop out, Fliss hung her head. How could she have been so mean? No wonder she was so unhappy. She wanted Alice back as her friend, she thought. Very much. She would fix it. She would.

Maggie had started off watching the girls but, as it went on, found herself increasingly drawn into the familiar tragedy. She didn't see David watching her either, or see his lips move, almost unconsciously, to the crushing line, *Oh, I am fortune's fool.*

Simone and Ash were seated almost directly across from one another. Every time she noticed him, he seemed to be glaring at her. She tried to stop looking, but she couldn't help it.

At the interval, people were reluctant to move, still caught in the spell, but Simone wasted no time.

'What *is* it?'

Ash pouted and looked at the ground.

'You didn't email me.'

'Of course I did!'

'You never emailed me back again,' she said.

'Well, that's because your email was so silly.'

In fact, Simone's missive had been very carefully thought through, and she had tried extremely hard to find the right balance between joviality and letting him know she was thinking about him.

'Fine,' said Simone. 'That's what I thought. Fine. Goodbye.'

She stormed off and plonked herself next to Fliss, who of course, as usual, was far too wrapped up in herself to pay her the least bit of attention. In fact, after two minutes, Fliss stood up and wandered off. Fine. Simone pretended to look through the programme.

Ash came after her with two cups of hot chocolate.

'D'you want a hot chocolate?'

Simone shrugged. 'Not p'ticularly.'

'I bought you one.'

'I didn't ask you to.'

'Fine.'

They sat in silence for a while.

'I didn't mean your email was silly,' said Ash finally.

'Then why did you say those exact words?' said Simone.

'Because . . . I meant, well, I thought you would have said something. About the Christmas party. I thought you were just ignoring it, like.'

'Well, I wasn't going to . . . go into lots of detail or anything, was I?'

'I dunno,' said Ash. 'I thought girls did.'

There was another pause.

'I don't know much about girls,' said Ash.

It was the first humble statement Simone had ever heard

him make. She looked at him. Then she smiled, a little. And he smiled back. And then they both burst out laughing.

'Well, I don't know much about boys,' said Simone, choking back the giggles.

'Boys are easy,' said Ash. 'We eat a lot and then we kill ourselves over a bird. Oh, sorry, did you not want to know the end?'

'I know the end,' said Simone, rolling her eyes.

'Can I come back on your bus?' asked Ash.

'Dunno,' said Simone, slightly shocked. She wondered if Janie James would allow it.

'OK,' said Ash. 'Do you want that hot chocolate?'

Simone started laughing again. 'Why, are you going to give it to some other girl if I don't take it?'

Ash grinned. 'Maybe.'

'Well, all right then,' said Simone, glancing quickly around for Zelda just in case. 'But next time, I want apple juice.'

Fliss ran over to where Will and Alice were standing apart, separated by large groups of boys and girls but still with eyes only for each other. Fliss didn't quite know what to do.

'Alice,' she said.

Alice gave her a snotty look. 'Yes?' she said, as if Fliss were some distant relative she barely remembered, rather than her once best friend.

'Err . . . can I have a word?'

Alice shrugged, and they walked over to the stone wall overlooking the ocean.

'Alice, look. I'm really sorry. About Will.'

Alice nodded as if she didn't really care either way, but inside she was glad this had happened. She missed Fliss, but couldn't let herself step down in an argument; she'd have forfeited Will for ever if necessary.

'What do you mean?'

'I mean, I really . . . I mean I had a big crush on him. But that was nothing to do with you and I shouldn't have asked you not to see him. I'm sorry.'

This was very gracious on Fliss's part, and Alice acknowledged it.

'I'm so glad we can be friends again,' she said, taking Fliss's hand. 'I hated you not talking to me.'

'You weren't talking to me either!' said Fliss.

'Never mind that now,' said Alice, her pleasure only slightly marred by the sense that her delightful martyrdom was going to have to come to an end. 'You really don't mind?'

Fliss shook her head. 'I'll get over it,' she said.

Maggie managed to keep up light and easy banter with the other teachers during the interval, so that was good. And Zelda came up to her with stars dancing in her eyes.

'They need me back down there, miss! And she said there might be some room for me if I wanted to help out in the summer, that I'm really good.'

'Zelda, I could not be more delighted,' said Maggie, honestly.

'There's one thing though,' said Zelda, looking unusually modest.

'What's that?'

'You know the suspension of privileges?'

'Mmm?'

'Well . . . I was *rilly rilly* hoping that I might be able to go and tell my parents . . . and it is Friday night and, well, the bus goes right past the base on the way home . . .'

Zelda looked so contrite and pleading that Maggie smiled.

'All right, all right.'

'Yeah!' said Zelda. 'Can you sign my slip?'

Maggie did so.

'And this one.'

'What's this one?'

'Felicity Prosser's. They invited her over for the weekend too.'

'They did?' said Maggie. 'Don't push me, Zelda.'

'I can't, Miss Adair, I have *work* to do!'

And Zelda pirouetted off towards the stage door.

'You are *meeracle* worker,' said Claire gloomily. 'I have more chance of being eaten by giant bat that ever getting that American girl to conjugate *être*.'

Maggie didn't know what it was. The heady scent of the wildflowers that grew out of the towering rocks; the fading warmth of the sunlight; even, merely, a chance to sit down after the exhausting events of the last few months.

But somehow, the play moved her as it had never moved her before. The plight of the lovers – that could sometimes feel a little plotted in less deft hands – suddenly, on this starry night, so beautiful and young amid the columns of the stage, pushed her beyond measure. By the time Romeo bought his poison from the reluctant apothecary, she was choking back great, weeping sobs; the final moment of catharsis, when Juliet wakes to find what she thinks is her love sleeping beside her, made her so uncharacteristically tear-sodden she had to hide her face in her handbag in case any of the girls saw her. It was unprofessional.

The only person who seemed to notice was Claire, sitting beside her, who squeezed her arm with some concern, but still Maggie couldn't stop crying; through the final scenes, through the applause and the standing ovation and the

235

repeated curtain calls for the actors; through the bustle of standing up and getting the girls out in time, a steady beat of tears fell from Maggie's eyes. Only when she briefly escaped to the toilets could she make the least attempt at pulling herself together. But then she would think again of this beautiful Cornwall night; how this was the last time she would come here and sit under the stars; how love, lost, could never be found; about all the youth and promise around her, and her own, nearly over, and she would start all over again.

After ten minutes, Claire came to find her.

'Everyone ees on the bus,' she said. 'What ees the matter with you? Janie James, that horse of a woman, she has let a few of the boys on. I theenk she is a boy herself.'

'It doesn't matter,' said Maggie.

'What *ees* it?'

Well, it doesn't matter now, thought Maggie.

'Oh,' she said. 'Well. It's just, after I'm married, I'm going to have to leave the school to go home. And . . . well, I kind of had a bit of a thing for David McDonald. And I was just a bit sad, that's all.'

'Beeg long Daveed with the dog?' exclaimed Claire. 'Ah, but he ees *perfect* for you!' She caught herself quickly. 'I mean, well, he likes some things you like . . . No, of course not. I am so sorry, I had no idea. You know, it was the same for me last year.'

The previous year, Claire had had an unhappy love affair with Mr Graystock, the Classics teacher at Downey Boys.

'I know,' said Maggie. 'Please, please, *please* don't tell anyone.'

'Of course not. I know how sad thees ees. But you are pleased to be leaving, yes? To be married and to be in Scotland? I theenk David will be sad.'

'Of course I'm happy to go,' said Maggie stoically. 'It doesn't mean I can't be sad to say goodbye.'

'No,' said Claire. 'I understand. And now, I am sorry. You must come, before they turn into a crowd of storming beasts.'

'I know,' said Maggie, glancing in the mirror and turning on the tap to wash her face. 'Teacher face on.'

The bus wound its way slowly along the curves of Cornwall's landscape. Zelda and Fliss were sitting together. Janie James' relaxed attitude to the doings of boys and girls at the end of term (she believed, having grown up on a farm, that these instincts had to come out one way or another) meant that Simone and Ash, and Alice and Will, were entwined in very separate and private worlds of their own towards the back of the bus.

'I'd have waited for you,' whispered Will.

'What, and not drunk the poison?' joked Alice.

Will shook his head. With infinite slowness, he bowed his forehead down towards hers until they were touching. Then, gently, he brought his hand up to her face.

Fliss stared hard out of the window two seats in front, willing herself not to turn around or look back. A tear wandered slowly down her cheek.

'OK,' said Zelda beside her. 'Are you ready?'

'Ready for what?' she said without enthusiasm.

Zelda reached into her suspiciously large school bag and held up the release form.

'You're coming to spend the weekend with me!'

'What do you mean?'

'I got two passes off Miss Adair. Picked her at a weak moment. It's the base dance tomorrow night.'

'Are you kidding?' said Fliss, excitement mounting.

'Nope! Can you lindy hop?'

'Is it dancing? Then, yes!'

'They are going to *love* you, little miss English peaches and cream.'

'But I don't have anything to wear.'

'*Darling*,' said Zelda, shaking her huge bag. 'Have you learned nothing from your Zelda?'

DuBose and Mary Jo were waiting by the side of the road, next to the Hummer. As Zelda jumped off the bus and started hammering away nineteen to the dozen, DuBose shook his head. He came up to Maggie, who was checking their names off on the list.

'I dunno what you done with my daughter,' he said, putting out his enormous hand, 'but ah sure do wanna thank you.'

Chapter Fifteen

After the wonderful play, Maggie felt more confident than ever that her girls were going to do well in their exams, and, as they had now all been converted by Zelda to ardent pacifists, she'd kept her hopes up for the World War One poets too.

Simone had fretted right up until the last minute of course, but her papers were uniformly excellent – her scholarship certainly wasn't in danger. Alice had done just well enough to avoid attention; Maggie wondered what she could do if she ever pulled her finger out, but blinking into the night over textbooks wasn't Alice's style. And Fliss had slipped a little, but there was evidence in the slightly stained jotters that she was trying extremely hard. Maggie was taking this as a good sign.

Overall they'd done, as a year group, very well, which was almost, but not quite, enough to silence Miss Starling on their disciplinary misdemeanours.

Now bags were packed, trunks ready to be conveyed to the railway station. The next morning was end of term, and everything was ready to go. The dorms were a positive havoc of exchanging of emails and promises of eternal friendships; plans to meet up in Tuscany or Rock, and full scale hubbub as to the whereabouts of hairbrushes and riding boots.

Maggie had gone to bed in good time, she had a very early train to catch. She'd been surprised, a couple of days ago, to get a phone call out of the blue from Miranda, who wanted to chat all about her new beau. Apparently he had a flat in a new development in Portsmouth, and she was taking the train up to London to furnish it! He'd given her his Gold Card and everything. She sounded nervous, but excited and excitable. On telling her she, too, was heading for the train station, Miranda had insisted on giving her a lift; she was changing at Exeter, so they could catch the same train.

Maggie looked around one last time at the neat and comfortable two rooms she'd learned to call home. She'd wanted to go and talk to Dr Deveral, but she couldn't exactly leave yet – she didn't have a job to go to, for a start. It felt horribly cowardly, like running away, but she'd have to see what came up over the summer. Get the wedding over with first, then maybe take a look. Spend some time with the family too. It would be good.

Waking over-early, just at dawn the following morning, Maggie crept out of the school, not even saying goodbye to Claire. Rushing out, she checked her pigeon hole one more time. Just one envelope, internal, with her name on it. Shaped like a book. Probably a suggested text from Miss Starling for next year, that woman *never* let up. Rushing, she thrust it in her bag.

Had she turned back, just for a second, she would have seen the full extent of Alice's revenge. But she did not; instead, she moved smartly towards Miranda's waiting car.

The spring flowers had been very late that year, and only finally, clearly unfurled, much to Harold's disgust, on the very last day of term. It was those clodhopping girls he'd had helping him, he was sure, who'd planted the bulbs far too deep.

By breakfast time it was the talk of an already overexcited school, even faster to spread than the amazing news that Dr Deveral was that Downey Boys teacher's mum! And by ten a.m., one of the victims, on the pretence of giving Stephen Daedalus a particularly long walk that day, had ambled over to see what all the fuss was about.

Dr Deveral had seen it and shaken her head. She'd meant to have a word with Maggie anyway before she left, congratulate her. Her English class had taken the highest test scores in the entire school. Their written Shakespeare and war poets work did her extraordinary credit. She even had a creditable essay from the American girl on the use of disguise on the Shakespearean stage. So a silly little bit of schoolgirl pranking meant very little to her.

David, however, stood stock still and looked at it. In a way it was beautiful. Irises and late primroses formed the shape of a heart, in which, clear as anything, was inscribed: DM + MA.

It was a daft – if quite forward-sighted – prank, he knew, some ridiculous attempt to stir up trouble by the girls. He wondered who knew? All of them? Surely not.

With a sudden grip of panic, David thought of the stupid thing he'd left for her in her pigeon hole. It suddenly struck him as the height of cowardice and meanness. But it was after the theatre; he'd seen her crying. Those weren't the tears of a happy bride, looking hopefully towards the future. He'd thought about it and thought about it and decided that he was going to try, just once more. Just once, before she left, probably, he knew from Claire, for ever.

When he thought of her face that night in the hotel, when

she had looked for his hand and it wasn't there, he wanted to cringe. And now he looked at the flowers: simple, glorious, and, it seemed, screaming a very straightforward message right in his face. He was an idiot. A stupid, bookbeaten coward.

'Good morning, sir. You like the message, *oui ou non*?'

David stared at Claire uncomprehendingly.

'Oh. Hello. Uh, yes, silly, isn't it? But still, I'd hate to destroy flowers . . . Stephen Daedalus could probably eat a few though . . .'

Claire let out a big sigh. 'You know, if I was in France just now I would not have to spell everything out to men who have got the emotional feelings of a *dead snake*. Are you *crazy*?'

'OK, steady on,' said David. 'What are you talking about?'

Claire gave him her hardest stare.

'Maggie, you *eedyot.*'

'Yes, yes, I mean, what has she said to you?'

'That she must go and do what is right for her family and not disappoint everyone because you are not 'ers.'

'I am not *what*?'

Claire sighed and threw up her hands in despair.

'*Elle t'adore! Vous êtes sa sole raison d'être. Chaque jour, chaque instant, elle pense à vous, vous êtes dans sa coeur et dans ses rêves.*'

David stared at her as he desperately tried to work it out in his head. Hope and disbelief were fighting a battle on his face.

'Da-*veed*! *C'est* the language of love.'

David took a quick glance at his watch, blinking rapidly. 'Has she gone to get the train?'

Claire rolled her eyes.

'*Vite! Vite!* You need a new car.'

*

Maggie and Miranda found seats easily. Miranda's idle chatter – she had lost weight and seemed a little nervy – was useful as a distraction. After all, after the train reached Exeter, Maggie could put her head down on the table and cry all she wished.

In some years, she told herself, 'in some years, when I have Stan's beautiful babbies on my lap and I'm jiggling them up and down, and am surrounded by cheeky boys at school and loud, lairy girls full of bravado, and I'm going up Sauchiehall Street with my old friends and we're living in a gorgeous house in the West End or Newton Mearns and my life is all sorted, and Cody and Dylan are doing really well, then I'll look back on this and laugh. I'll tell everyone about the funny couple of years I spent in a weird English boarding school that was like something out of an old book, and how odd everyone was and . . .'

She couldn't imagine telling them about David. She couldn't imagine turning that – turning him – into a funny anecdote. But it would fade. It would fade.

Miranda uploaded a pile of glossy homes magazines.

'Right, you help me pick a bathroom!'

They had touched briefly on David in the car. Miranda had emphasised how fantastically successful Declan was and how pleased she was not to be going out with that loser any more. Then she'd asked, slightly contradictorily, how he was doing, and Maggie had answered, heartwrenchingly, that, truthfully, she had absolutely no idea.

Maggie looked at the magazines without interest, then remembered the parcel in her bag. She lifted it out. Her name on the envelope was typed, but inside was a note, written in a hand she knew very well. Miranda would know it too.

'What's that? That looks boring,' said Miranda.

'Uh, just school stuff,' said Maggie, her heart beating madly all of a sudden. She shielded the book from view.

Miranda sniffed. 'You teachers, you're all alike.'

The note was very stark and very simple. It just said, 'Poem.'

Maggie picked up the book – poems by Houseman – and carefully turned to the marked page.

Shake hands, we shall never be friends, all's over . . .

Maggie stared at it and gasped. So this is what he meant to say – leave me alone, I don't want to be friends with you. Why couldn't he say that face to face? She was only trying to be friendly at the bloody theatre. Bloody hell. Staring out of the window, she felt cross, empty and miserable.

I only vex you the more I try, read the next line. Well, bloody right. Couldn't he even have spoken to her about it? It was so cowardly to give her a book; so not like him. Her eyes glazed over and she couldn't read any more. She wanted to throw the book out the window.

The train hadn't started moving yet. Suddenly, there seemed to be some kind of a commotion outside. Her eyes half blinded with tears, Maggie glanced upwards through the window. Then she blinked again. It couldn't be. It *couldn't* be. But there, vaulting the barrier with his ridiculously long legs and charging up the train . . . It couldn't be. It was. It was David. Hotly pursued by Stephen Daedalus. And about six guards.

'OH MY GOD!' screamed Miranda. 'Look! It's David!'

She stood up dramatically. 'Oh my god. He's looking for me!'

'What?' said Maggie.

'I knew it! He wants me back! I *knew* it!'

David was jumping up and peering in every window as he passed by, but was still a good four carriages away.

'Sod these bloody magazines. Declan's a complete bloody arsehole. I made the biggest mistake of my life!'

Suddenly, they both felt the train lurch.

'Oh my God,' said Miranda. 'What do I do?'

The old lady opposite looked up from her knitting.

'On the wrong train, dears?' she asked worriedly.

Maggie stared at her. 'Yes . . . no . . . maybe. I don't know.'

Maggie swallowed hard. The train had started to move, slowly. David was still way back.

Miranda ran towards the connecting carriage. It was an old stock train, and still had windows you could open. She pulled it down and stuck her head out, ignoring the warning signs not to.

'DAVID!' she shrieked, just as the whistle shrieked. 'DAVID!'

But Maggie thought. How did David know Miranda was on the train today? But he certainly knew it was the last day of term, and that there was only one service to Glasgow. Oh, sod it. She stuck her head out of the window too.

'David!'

David's double take would have been comical, had he not been pursuing a moving train.

'MAGGIE!' he shouted.

'DAVID!' shouted Maggie.

'WHAT?!' shouted Miranda, turning to stare at Maggie.

David looked at them both. He didn't even know what he wanted to say. He hadn't planned anything more than finding out where the Glasgow train was and driving like a maniac to the station. But now he could see her, words, for the first time in a life filled with words, failed him.

'You *are* joking,' said Miranda, finally taking in the situation. 'We're meant to be friends!'

Maggie didn't hear her. The train was moving away, but

she was staring at David desperately, as if that alone would bring him closer. As she was nearly out of reach, he realised what it was he wanted to say. The only thing.

'I love you.'

But his voice was carried away.

'WHAT?' she shouted.

But she was getting too far away, and he couldn't yell any more. Everyone was staring at him. The noise of the train had built up too much, the momentum pulling them apart.

David suddenly felt overcome with foolishness. Stephen Daedalus had panted to a halt at his side; the guards were keeping a respectful distance for the moment, in case he turned out to be a violent nutter.

Maybe it is Miranda, thought Maggie to herself, not daring to believe, then seeing him stop. He sent me that bloody horrible poem. Oh God. Oh *God* how embarrassing.

Closing her eyes, she withdrew her head, then just at the last minute, she waved, feeling foolish and sad.

He waved back.

'I loved you,' she suddenly, stupidly, found she wanted to say. But she couldn't, of course. Instead she swallowed hard, closed up the window as the train entered a tunnel, and slowly, miserably, turned to go back to her seat and work out what on earth she was going to say to Miranda.

Which is when she saw the emergency cord.

I couldn't, she thought.

It's not me.

I'd selfishly ruin the day of every single other person on this train, and the next, probably.

I'd get arrested.

I'm getting married.

I'm a *teacher*!

*

Veronica walked through the classrooms as she always did; she liked to be the last one here, carefully closing up and double-checking everything before she left for the summer. She liked the traces of girls just gone; the faint whisper of their footsteps on the stone steps. And she liked to take time to remember her sixth-form girls, leaving to spread their time here out in the wide world; many to university, some abroad. Araminta Kelly was off to spend her gap year teaching amongst the tribes on the Amazon. Veronica privately thought that what Araminta Kelly could teach Amazonian tribes that wasn't about nail polish and *The X Factor* wasn't going to be that impressive. On the plus side, Shanisa Wallace was off to pre-med at Columbia; Carmen Figue to the University at Heidelberg and Heidi Forrest had finally bowed to the inevitable and was following her father and three brothers to Sandhurst.

Veronica hoped, as always, that she'd done enough. That they'd learned enough, not just from examinations and textbooks, but from the team-playing ethos of the school to stand up for themselves without being overbearing; to be confident without being insufferable. Well, perhaps a *little* insufferable – they were still teenagers, after all.

Veronica picked up a discarded sparkly eraser, and considered keeping it for little Holly. She smiled. Her offer of babysitting services had been readily accepted by Susie. It looked like Daniel's littlies might get to see quite a bit of their Granny V.

But somehow, this brought her a fresh sadness. It was ridiculous, of course. But when she was all alone in the world, defiantly making her own way, she didn't mind so much. There was no one who would dare comment on her private life – or lack of one; no one to wonder what she was doing. Now, being drawn into the orbit of a normal, happy family life, she was coming to realise just how lonely she had been. She hadn't even known before. And she was a little uncomfortable with this side of herself showing. It was a vulnerability. Veronica disliked showing vulnerability; it had not saved her.

Then she thought of Rufus's face two Saturdays ago when she'd taken him to the local library and let him pick out his own book about submarines. It was worth it.

She gently turned the key in the lock of the final classroom, watching the spring sunshine highlight the motes of dust drifting gently in the empty air; a faint dusty echoing of all the girls gone by; girls linked to the school, and to their families, often through generations; their pasts and their futures tumbling past just as she, now, too was linked – broken from her past, perhaps, but with a clear way into a future.

Maggie's poems

My Boy Jack

'Have you news of my boy Jack?'
Not this tide.
'When d'you think that he'll come back?'
Not with this wind blowing, and this tide.

'Has any one else had word of him?'
Not this tide.
For what is sunk will hardly swim,
Not with this wind blowing, and this tide.

'Oh, dear, what comfort can I find?'
None this tide,
Nor any tide,
Except he did not shame his kind—
Not even with that wind blowing, and that tide.

Then hold your head up all the more,
This tide,
And every tide;
Because he was the son you bore,
And gave to that wind blowing and that tide!

Rudyard Kipling, 1915

Dulce et Decorum Est

Bent double, like old beggars under sacks,
Knock-kneed, coughing like hags, we cursed through sludge,
Till on the haunting flares we turned our backs
And towards our distant rest began to trudge.
Men marched asleep. Many had lost their boots
But limped on, blood-shod. All went lame; all blind;
Drunk with fatigue; deaf even to the hoots
Of tired, outstripped Five-Nines that dropped behind.

Gas! Gas! Quick, boys!— An ecstasy of fumbling,
Fitting the clumsy helmets just in time;
But someone still was yelling out and stumbling,
And flound'ring like a man in fire or lime . . .
Dim, through the misty panes and thick green light,
As under a green sea, I saw him drowning.
In all my dreams, before my helpless sight,
He plunges at me, guttering, choking, drowning.

If in some smothering dreams you too could pace
Behind the wagon that we flung him in,
And watch the white eyes writhing in his face,
His hanging face, like a devil's sick of sin;
If you could hear, at every jolt, the blood
Come gargling from the froth-corrupted lungs,
Obscene as cancer, bitter as the cud
Of vile, incurable sores on innocent tongues,
My friend, you would not tell with such high zest
To children ardent for some desperate glory,
The old Lie; *Dulce et Decorum est*
Pro patria mori.

Wilfred Owen, 1918

Longing

Come to me in my dreams, and then
By day I shall be well again!
For so the night will more than pay
The hopeless longing of the day.

Come, as thou cam'st a thousand times,
A messenger from radiant climes,
And smile on thy new world, and be
As kind to others as to me!

Or, as thou never cam'st in sooth,
Come now, and let me dream it truth,
And part my hair, and kiss my brow,
And say, My love why sufferest thou?

Come to me in my dreams, and then
By day I shall be well again!
For so the night will more than pay
The hopeless longing of the day.

Matthew Arnold, 1864

Vitae Lampada

There's a breathless hush in the Close to-night
Ten to make and the match to win
A bumping pitch and a blinding light,
An hour to play, and the last man in.
And it's not for the sake of a ribboned coat,
Or the selfish hope of a season's fame,
But his Captain's hand on his shoulder smote
'Play up! play up! and play the game!'

The sand of the desert is sodden red,
Red with the wreck of a square that broke;
The Gatling's jammed and the Colonel dead,
And the regiment blind with dust and smoke.
The river of death has brimmed his banks,
And England's far, and Honour a name,
But the voice of a schoolboy rallies the ranks –
'Play up! play up! and play the game!'

This is the word that year by year,
While in her place the School is set,
Every one of her sons must hear,
And none that hears it dare forget.
This they all with a joyful mind
Bear through life like a torch in flame,
And falling fling to the host behind—
'Play up! play up! and play the game!'

Henry Newbolt, 1897

Summer is Icumen In

Sumer is icumen in,
Lhude sing cuccu!
Groweþ sed and bloweþ med
And springþ þe wde nu,
Sing cuccu!
Awe bleteþ after lomb,
Lhouþ after calue cu.
Bulluc sterteþ, bucke uerteþ,
Murie sing cuccu!
Cuccu, cuccu, wel singes þu cuccu;
Ne swik þu nauer nu.
Pes:
Sing cuccu nu. Sing cuccu.
Sing cuccu. Sing cuccu nu!

Anonymous, c1260

Phenomenal Woman

Pretty women wonder where my secret lies.
I'm not cute or built to suit a fashion model's size
But when I start to tell them,
They think I'm telling lies.
I say,
It's in the reach of my arms
The span of my hips,
The stride of my step,
The curl of my lips.
I'm a woman
Phenomenally.
Phenomenal woman,
That's me.

I walk into a room
Just as cool as you please,
And to a man,
The fellows stand or
Fall down on their knees.
Then they swarm around me,
A hive of honey bees.
I say,
It's the fire in my eyes,
And the flash of my teeth,
The swing in my waist,
And the joy in my feet.
I'm a woman
Phenomenally.
Phenomenal woman,
That's me.

Men themselves have wondered
What they see in me.
They try so much
But they can't touch
My inner mystery.
When I try to show them
They say they still can't see.
I say,
It's in the arch of my back,
The sun of my smile,
The ride of my breasts,
The grace of my style.
I'm a woman

Phenomenally.
Phenomenal woman,
That's me.

Now you understand
Just why my head's not bowed.
I don't shout or jump about
Or have to talk real loud.
When you see me passing
It ought to make you proud.
I say,
It's in the click of my heels,
The bend of my hair,
the palm of my hand,
The need of my care,
'Cause I'm a woman
Phenomenally.
Phenomenal woman,
That's me.

Maya Angelou, 1978

The Night Mail

This is the Night Mail crossing the border,
Bringing the cheque and the postal order,
Letters for the rich, letters for the poor,
The shop at the corner and the girl next door.
Pulling up Beattock, a steady climb:
The gradient's against her, but she's on time.
Past cotton-grass and moorland boulder
Shovelling white steam over her shoulder,
Snorting noisily as she passes
Silent miles of wind-bent grasses.

Birds turn their heads as she approaches,
Stare from the bushes at her blank-faced coaches.
Sheep-dogs cannot turn her course;
They slumber on with paws across.
In the farm she passes no one wakes,
But a jug in the bedroom gently shakes.

Dawn freshens, the climb is done.
Down towards Glasgow she descends
Towards the steam tugs yelping down the glade of cranes,
Towards the fields of apparatus, the furnaces
Set on the dark plain like gigantic chessmen.
All Scotland waits for her:
In the dark glens, beside the pale-green sea lochs
Men long for news.

Letters of thanks, letters from banks,
Letters of joy from the girl and the boy,
Receipted bills and invitations
To inspect new stock or visit relations,

And applications for situations
And timid lovers' declarations
And gossip, gossip from all the nations,
News circumstantial, news financial,
Letters with holiday snaps to enlarge in,
Letters with faces scrawled in the margin,
Letters from uncles, cousins, and aunts,
Letters to Scotland from the South of France,
Letters of condolence to Highlands and Lowlands
Notes from overseas to Hebrides
Written on paper of every hue,
The pink, the violet, the white and the blue,
The chatty, the catty, the boring, adoring,
The cold and official and the heart's outpouring,
Clever, stupid, short and long,
The typed and the printed and the spelt all wrong.

Thousands are still asleep
Dreaming of terrifying monsters,
Or of friendly tea beside the band at Cranston's or
    Crawford's:
Asleep in working Glasgow, asleep in well-set Edinburgh,
Asleep in granite Aberdeen,
They continue their dreams,
And shall wake soon and long for letters,
And none will hear the postman's knock
Without a quickening of the heart,
For who can bear to feel himself forgotten?

W. H. Auden, 1935

David's poem for Maggie

Shake Hands

Shake hands, we shall never be friends, all's over;
*   I only vex you the more I try.*
All's wrong that ever I've done or said,
And nought to help it in this dull head:
*   Shake hands, here's luck, good-bye.*

But if you come to a road where danger
*   Or guilt or anguish or shame's to share,*
Be good to the lad that loves you true
And the soul that was born to die for you,
*   And whistle and I'll be there.*

A. E. Housman, 1910

Dance Instructions

The Dashing White Sergeant

Tune: Original.

Time: 4/4

This is a circle reel-time dance. Dancers stand in a circle round the room in threes. A man between two ladies faces a lady between two men. The man between two ladies moves clockwise, and the other three counter-clockwise.

Bars description

    1–8: All six dancers make a circle and dance eight slip-steps round to the left and eight back again.

9–16: The centre dancer turns to right-hand partner. They set to each other and turn with two hands, four *pas de basque*. Centre dancer turns and does the same with left-hand partner, and finishes facing right-hand partner again.

17–24: They dance the reel of three, centre dancer beginning the reel by giving left shoulder to right-hand partner. Eight skip change of step. They finish facing their opposite three.

25–32: All advance and retire, then pass on to meet the next three coming towards them. They pass right shoulders with the person opposite to them. The dance is repeated as many times as you will.

Strip the Willow

Tune: Any good jig

This is a long-way figure dance in which a new top couple begin on every repetition.

Bars description

1–4: First couple give right hands, turning each other one-and-a-half times with twelve running steps. They finish with first lady facing second man, and first man standing behind her.

5–6: Advance again and dance back-to-back, passing right shoulder. First lady turns second man with left hands joined, with six running steps. First man runs six steps on the spot as he waits for her.

7–8: First couple giving right hands turn each other in the middle, then six running steps. First lady repeats these last four bars until she has turned all the men, and at the last turn of her partner. They finish with first man facing bottom lady, and first lady behind him. First man turns each lady with his left hand, and his partner with his right, until he has turned the last lady. Then he turns his own partner with the right and they finish with first lady facing second man, and first man facing second lady.

First man turns second lady with his left hand, while first lady turns second man, with six running steps. They turn each other in the middle with right hands, with six running steps.

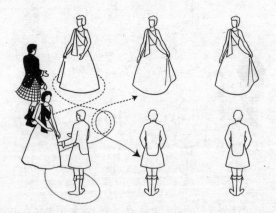

They repeat these two turnings till they have turned everybody in the set, and then turn each other with right hands eleven times, with twelve running steps, to finish on their own sides of the dance at the bottom of the set.

The next couple begins to turn each other at the same time as the first couple are doing their last turning.

Eightsome Reel

Tune: A variety of good reels

This is a round reel for four couples. It is better to treat it when dancing as a square dance, and always stand in the square formation when not dancing. A good plan is to change the tune each time a new dancer goes into the middle.

Bars description

1–8: All four couples make a circle and dance eight slip-steps round to the left and eight back again.

9–12: The four ladies, keeping hands joined with partner, give right hands across to make a wheel and dance four skip change of step round.

13–16: Advance again and dance back-to-back, passing right shoulder. First lady turns second man with left hands joined, with six running steps. Ladies, drop hands, and men, still holding partners' hands, swing them out and give their left hands across in the wheel. They dance round for four skip change of step and finish in own places, facing partners.

17–24: First couple, giving right hands, turn each other in the middle six, running. All set to partner twice, join both hands and turn once round four *pas de basque*. Finish a little way apart, facing partner.

25–40: First lady repeats these last four bars until she has turned all the men, and at the last turn of her partner. They finish with first man facing, each hand-giving.

41–48: First lady goes into the middle and dances eight *pas de basque*, or any reel-setting step, while the seven other dancers make a circle and dance eight slip steps round to the left and eight back.

49–56: First lady sets to and turns her partner with both hands, then sets to and turns the opposite man (third man). Eight *pas de basque*.

57–64: First lady dances reel of three with these two men. She begins the reel by giving left shoulder to her own partner.

Repeat bars 41–64: First lady dancing this time with second and fourth men.

Repeat bars 41–64 until all the ladies and all the men have had their turn in the middle. The dance is finished by a repeat of the first forty bars.

Note from the Author

When I was growing up, attending my normal, extremely bog-standard Catholic school, I was obsessed with boarding school books. All of them. *Malory Towers*, *St Clare's*, *Frost in May*, *Jane Eyre*, *The Four Marys*, *What Katy Did at School*, the *Chalet School* books.

It's not difficult to understand why: the idea of a bunch of girls all having fun together, working, playing and staying up late for midnight feasts, as opposed to the tribal, aggressive atmosphere of my own school, exerted a powerful pull on a swottish, awkward child. None of these books, for example, had playground meetings that decided which girls were going to be 'in' or 'out' that week, cruel nicknames, long hours of Catholic instruction (OK, apart from Antonia White), or compulsory tiny mini-skirts for gym for the boys to line up and jeer at.

So I lost myself in pranks played on French mistresses; school plays (unheard of at my lackadaisical comp); lacrosse (whatever that was) and the absurd fantasy that you could speak English, French and German on alternate days. Incidentally, has there ever been a school on earth that makes you do that?

When the Harry Potter books came out, obviously its wizard lore and storytelling were a huge draw – but part of me still wondered how much of its success was down to the idealised boarding school life of Hogwarts, filled with delicious meals and having great fun with your wonderfully loyal friends, *sans* fear of parental intervention. The fact that boarding school applications rose sharply with each book published seemed to indicate that I might be right.

Of course in my adult life I've met plenty of people who did go to boarding school, every single one of whom has assured me it was absolutely nothing like the books at all – they know this because, oddly, my dormitory-bound friends seem to have read just as much boarding school fiction as the rest of us.

Perhaps it's the certainties of these schools – their rock-solid concepts of nobility, self-sacrifice, 'the good of the school' – as opposed to the reality of the lives of most adolescents and pre-adolescents: shifting sands of loyalties; siblings cramping your style; and the gradual, creeping realisation that your parents are just feeling their way and don't really have all the answers. Whereas boarding schools, of course, always have strict yet kindly pastoral figures – like Dumbledore, Miss Grayling, or Jo at the Chalet – who always know what to do and are liberal with their second chances. The repetitive rhythm of the terms provides solid ground, endlessly comforting to children in an ever-changing world.

As a voracious adult reader, I realised a couple of years ago that I still missed those books. The prose of Enid Blyton jars a little these days (and they do horribly gang up on and bully Gwendoline, for the sole sin of crying when her parents drop her off), although Curtis Sittenfeld's marvellous book *Prep* is a terrific contemporary account.

To Serve Them All My Days by R F Delderfield, though inevitably dated (which adds a wonderfully bittersweet twist to his stories, knowing how many of his boys were unwittingly bound for the battlefields of WW2), appeals to the adult reader, but as for my beloved girls' stories, there were none to be found.

So I decided to go about writing one myself. My previous book *Class* was the first in a projected series of six books about Downey House (of course! There must always be six. Well, unless you're at the Chalet school, in which case there can be about seventy-five). This one, *Rules*, is the second.

Although I'm writing this series for myself, when I've chatted about it I've been amazed by the amount of people (all right – women) who've said, 'I've been waiting for a book like this for such a long time.' I hope I don't disappoint them – and us, the secret legions of boarding school book fans.

Jane Beaton